JOSEPH'S MANSIONS

Frankie Houlihan quit the priesthood for love, only to face heartbreak. Trying to rebuild his life, Frankie accepts a job with the security team which investigates criminal activity in the world of horse-racing. When Grand National favourite Angel Gabriel is kidnapped from the Cassidys' yard the effect on the family is devastating and the consequences far-reaching. In trying to help the Cassidy family, Frankie Houlihan finds himself travelling down just the road he didn't want to take – back into the tragedy at the heart of his own life...

JOSEPH'S MANSIONS

JOSEPH'S MANSIONS

by

Richard Pitman with Joe McNally

Magna Large Print Books
Long Preston, North Yorkshire,
BD23 4ND, England.

British Library Cataloguing in Publication Data.

Pitman, Richard with McNally, Joe
    Joseph's mansions.

    A catalogue record of this book is
    available from the British Library

    ISBN   0-7505-1891-X

First published in Great Britain in 2001 by HarperCollins Publishers

Copyright © Richard Pitman and Joe McNally 2001

Cover illustration © G.B. Print

The author asserts the moral right to be identified as the author of this work.

Published in Large Print 2002 by arrangement with HarperCollins Publishers

Magna Large Print is an imprint of Library Magna Books Ltd.

Printed and bound in Great Britain by
T.J. (International) Ltd., Cornwall, PL28 8RW

For Tilly, with love

1

Seven years and two days after entering Maynooth Seminary on his seventeenth birthday,
Frankie Houlihan was ordained a Roman Catholic priest. He carried out his ministry faithfully
and industriously for eight years, and despite the
occasional misgiving about his own worthiness,
there was never a doubt in the young priest's
mind that he would die with his dog collar on.
The only 'vice' Frankie would admit to was his
monthly outing to the races.

Since his boyhood in Dublin when his father
had taken him to The Curragh and Leopardstown to see some of the great racehorses, Frankie
had loved racing. His father had been a fanatic,
always armed with 'dead certs', horses who'd
need 'a bloody Act of Parliament' to stop them
winning. Frankie had adored his father's fervour
for it; no matter how many of his dead certs lost,
his passion never faded. As a child Frankie was
never happier than when watching his father
roaring his horse on, howling like a madman at
the TV set or in the racecourse stand. An added
bonus for Frankie was that this rowdy joy was in
defiance of his mother, 'stricter than a nun during Lent' as his father always said.

So Frankie's only real indulgence on a meagre
salary was going racing, steeplechasing preferably. He didn't bet often. His enjoyment came

11

from tramping out to the far side of the race-course, well away from the crowds and the noise of the commentary, to stand beside one of the fences. He loved to hear the growing rumble of hooves as the field approached, feel the tension as they met the fence, listen to the slap of the whips, the jingle of clashing stirrups and the curses of the jockeys.

It was at the third-last fence at England's top jumps track that he met his fate. What happened there on a crisp November afternoon was to change thirty-two-year-old Frankie Houlihan's life beyond imagination.

Kathy Spencer was the adopted daughter of a Lincolnshire couple. Kathy had been a high-flyer since her days at Sheffield University where she'd pursued her honours degree in Media Studies with the enthusiasm and dedication she brought to everything she cared about. After graduation, the drudgery of life as a junior reporter on some local newspaper wasn't for Kathy. While the destinations for the CVs of most newly qualified journalists were the offices of TV companies, Kathy, typically, went her own way. She had always believed there was a gap in the market for what she called 'What was it like?' stories. Tall and athletic with long dark hair and olive skin, Kathy was well aware of how her sex appeal added to the marketability of what she wanted to do. So she set herself up as a one-woman adventurer, learning how to skydive, white-water canoe, fly a plane, rock-climb. She wrote vividly of her experiences on each project, did much of her own photography and syndicated the articles around the world where hundreds of thousands of people, especially young women, experienced through Kathy's eyes what it was like to conquer fears and acquire skills most had thought were beyond them.

Cheltenham racecourse was the venue for her next challenge. Internationally famous in racing circles for the quality of its annual three-day festival in mid-March, Cheltenham sets the stiffest of tests for horse and rider. The third-last fence is notorious in racing for catching horses out. It's on a downhill slope; as the pace quickens and the runners come under pressure, an over-bold leap leaves them too stretched to handle the terrain as it falls away. A horse getting too close at take-off tends not to get its undercarriage down quickly enough on the landing side.

As Kathy swung her leg over a horse called Zuiderzie, nervously pushing her feet into the narrow stirrups as the chestnut jogged beneath her, that living-on-the-edge feeling arrived in its old familiar way, rising from the pit of her stomach. It was a thrill of fear, an instinctive acknowledgement by her survival system of imminent danger. And she relished the sensation, the pinnacle of heightened senses as the adrenaline stopcocks opened.

She had no need to do this. Kathy had already earned enough money never to have to worry again, but it meant little to her. She'd have lived this life for nothing, this life on the brink.

As the horses were led from the paddock by their lads, a glint of pleasure and anticipation lit her dark eyes. A TV camera was mounted on a platform at the paddock exit, the lens at the same height as her head. She noticed it turn smoothly towards her. As she reached it she smiled and winked and saw just the mouth of the cameraman as he grinned in return.

As with all her projects, Kathy had worked and trained hard for this moment. She knew how tough it was for some amateurs to get rides anywhere, let alone at Cheltenham. There were only a few hundred races each year that amateurs could ride in, so to have her first ride at the best National Hunt track in the world was an experience she'd never forget, no matter how it turned out.

Although Kathy delighted in the danger aspect, she took every precaution to ensure she escaped injury. Nevertheless, as Zuiderzie stretched out below her to canter to the start, she knew what the statistics were in this business; a jockey could expect a fall every ten rides. Most tumbles resulted in little more than bruising, a few brought broken bones or severe concussion – but there were some from which the rider never got up.

She was twenty-eight, a well-known face among her many fans. She was happy. After the race she was to write, 'Some people say I have a dream life. At the dreaded downhill fence at Cheltenham, I thought I was going to end up with no life at all.'

She describes the moments before the fall happened:

My arms had been tiring gradually since we'd jumped the fifth-last and my legs, God, my legs! My thighs felt like my stretch marks had been laced with acid. I'd been training for six months for this, riding a saddle-less bike up hills, doing innumerable boring squats in the gym, running across sand dunes with a heavy backpack, and now my legs were getting their own back on me. The ache spread to my knees and ankles. I'd been perched in these stirrups for around seven minutes wrestling with this big chestnut thorough-bred and I realized as we came to the fence that Zuiderzie was winning the bout.

My weakening fingers let the reins slip through and he stretched his head further to take advantage. The hill increased his momentum. They tell me we were travelling at about thirty miles an hour. It felt like seventy. No windscreen here to dull the screaming gale, no brakes or steering wheel. Just half a ton of hard-trained muscle, flaring nostrils sucking air, veins raised, head bobbing, mane flying, doing what he loved, what every gene in him had been bred to do over thousands of years. And twenty strides from the big black birch fence, so stiff and broad I could have walked along the top of it, I accepted that I'd lost control.

Everything I'd been taught about trying to 'see a stride' (pick your point of take-off) and getting him organized for it was useless to me. My exhausted muscles couldn't deliver. I was aware now of those around me, hard-faced, half-starved jockeys who risked their lives regularly. Victory at Cheltenham was very sweet to most of these guys

15

and they seemed to crowd me now, surround me in this flashing mass of colour and sound, breaking what remained of my concentration.

Then we hit.

Zuiderzie took off far too late and slammed into the fence. I felt for an instant as though I'd been frozen in time. Then the momentum caught up with me and I felt myself catapulted skywards. It seemed a long time before I crashed. My brain desperately recalled the lessons of the past six months. Don't land on your head. Tuck it in as you approach the ground. Try to land on rounded shoulder-blades and start rolling immediately into a ball. There'll be other horses jumping just behind you, make yourself as small a target for their hooves as possible...

It had all seemed so practical and achievable sitting sipping coffee at the kitchen table. Come the day, I simply didn't know which way up I was until my back thumped into the life-savingly lush turf, pounding the air from my lungs and slamming my helmeted head so hard on the ground that I lost consciousness.

When I opened my eyes a priest was leaning over me. Last Rites were my first thought and I thanked God I had no children or husband to grieve and rage at my selfishness. Then, in the sweetest Irish accent I've ever heard, the priest said, 'Are you all right?'

I nodded.

''Twas a purler of a fall,' he said.

I smiled. 'I haven't heard that word for ages,' I said.

He looked vaguely puzzled. 'Purler?'

'Purler.' I mimicked his accent. I saw from his face, framed against the sky, that neither of us was sure that I wasn't in the first stages of delirium. He blushed. I said, 'Do you like swaddling?'

'It's OK. Haven't done it for ages myself.'

'The word, I mean! It's one of my favourite parts of Christmas, you get to hear the word "swaddling".'

He nodded. 'I think you'll be needing some treatment, Miss.'

'I think you may be right,' I said.

When the first-aiders scooped her up in a stretcher she asked Frankie to come with her in the ambulance.

'I'm fine, thanks,' he said. 'I'll walk back for the fresh air.'

Kathy turned her head, which now housed a jackhammer ache. 'I want to say thank you properly.'

Frankie hesitated.

'In a vertical position...' Frankie smiled now.

'...without a funny hat on.'

He shook his head slowly. The stretcher-bearers stood at the open door of the ambulance looking at Kathy, then at Frankie. She said to him, 'You're keeping these guys waiting.' Still smiling, he moved forward and followed them into the ambulance.

2

It was a week before she saw him again. She had come to the church to listen to him say morning mass at his parish in Warwickshire, St Briavel's. When everyone had left the church she sat silently in her pale blue dress, willing him to come back out of the door which led to the sacristy. And he did, he came out singing softly, a song she didn't recognize. He didn't look her way but genuflected and went up to clear the altar in readiness for evening mass.

Coming back down the red-carpeted steps of the altar he saw her and stopped. And smiled. She felt she should get up and walk up the centre aisle to him but she was suddenly uncertain, nervous, her confidence slipping away. Afterwards they'd laugh about the noise his shoes made as he'd walked towards her. He'd changed into old crepe-soled comfortable shoes immediately after mass and they peeled themselves pore by pore from each polished rubber tile, the sound echoing in the vastness.

She was close to the end of the pew. He stopped. 'Hello again.'

'Hello to you, Father Francis.'

They looked at each other, Kathy's instinct that she wanted this man to love her growing stronger, Frankie aware only that, as with the first time, he was completely comfortable with her. Although this feeling was new to him he had no reason to suspect that it was one he should worry about. His height, his athlete's frame, dark hair and fine features had made him the target of many girls as a teenager but he had never felt strongly for any female.

Kathy said, 'You're looking down at me again. You're always doing that.'

Frankie smiled. 'How's your head?'

'Fine. They kept me in overnight for observation and–'

'And you were out next morning after a hearty breakfast at Cheltenham General.'

'You saw it in the papers?'

'I did. I recognized the smile, which was about all I could see of you last week under that hard hat.'

'Saved my life, that hat did.'

'Ahh, I think that oul' head of yours might have survived without it.'

'This "oul' head" as you put it has only been on my shoulders for twenty-eight years, I'll have you know.'

Frankie feigned surprise. 'And where did ye keep it before then?'

'You're very forward, Father Francis, considering we've only met twice.'

'Now, I've never been accused of that before!'

The banter continued between them over tea in the chapel house with Frankie too naïve, maybe, to think that Kathy's surprise arrival meant anything more than she said it did; to say a proper thank you to him. He walked her to her car that day assuming that when he closed the

19

door he would never see her again. Only as her BMW disappeared through the gates did the slight twinge of regret at her going give any warning of what was to come.

Kathy's mind was turbulent as she drove away from the church that day. She had considered herself an emotionally experienced woman from everything she had put herself through but she had never felt what she was feeling now, and it was scaring her.

She always said she'd been in love three times but she was wondering now if she ever really had been. None of the affairs had lasted more than a year. Each had been pretty hard work, especially at the start, although she hadn't minded that. Till now, she didn't believe love at first sight existed and was convinced that if it did she wanted no part of it. When love came, for her it wouldn't be the schoolgirl hearts-and-flowers stuff, it would be properly built on strong foundations, as everything that was worthwhile needed to be.

Friends called her the classic free spirit and Kathy didn't object to that. But she'd learned early in life that you needed to work hard, harder than anyone else to get what you really wanted. She'd always known this since her days in the orphanage, which was where she'd learned to excel. Her first triumph was the morning she walked down the steps clutching the hands of her new mum and dad, knowing, as they crunched through the snow, that her sixth Christmas was going to be her best ever.

And for that Christmas she was given a present of a book about Amy Johnson, the pioneer who set out to prove that women could be as good as men in the male-dominated world of flying. Johnson's life-story inspired her and her first target was to get into the same university, Sheffield, where the flyer had studied in 1923 for a BA. This was what she worked for all her school life, never being deflected.

And she did it. By the time she was nineteen Kathy had qualified as a pilot. More hard work, lots of planning and attention to detail. People said she was naturally confident, but Kathy knew such a quality could never be natural for her. When she'd been put into care as a three-year-old, her mother had left, taking all the supplies of natural confidence with her. No, any self-assurance Kathy had come from knowing she had prepared to the nth degree for everything that really mattered to her.

As she sped down the motorway that Sunday to her home in the Cotswolds, something that she already knew was going to matter to her more than anything else was happening to her, and she hadn't had to do a minute of preparation or an ounce of work. All that had been required was to fall off a horse. She laughed, deeply, spontaneously and joyously at the ridiculous beauty of it all.

She dreamt of him that night, and found herself at three o'clock sitting upright in bed, her arms out to hold him, the dream had been so vivid. She realized she was awake. Slowly, she lay back down, smiling sadly. Sleep stayed away and she began to wonder if this whole thing was a dream. It made no sense. She had no reason to love this man. She didn't know anything about him other than his occupation.

Vocation, she meant. And how was that to be handled? What could be done to get past that barrier? Kathy realized what she was doing and stopped herself. Frankie Houlihan wasn't another project in her life, another achievement to be notched up. She'd never let him be that. She would stop this now, this planning. She would trust whatever it was that had thrown them together in the first place. She believed in God and she believed in fate. There was no telling which of them had made Frankie go to that particular fence for that one race out of six, no knowing why Zuiderzie had failed to take off at the third-last having jumped all the others perfectly, no clue as to why she felt when she saw him that a part of her she hadn't even known was missing had suddenly turned up.

So whoever had organized all these things, let him have a free hand. She would drift with the current.

Immediately she had decided this, Kathy felt calmer. Deep inside she knew the reason; for them to have any sort of happiness together, she must do absolutely nothing to make him leave his calling. Any decision on that had to be his and his alone.

3

After she'd gone that Sunday, Frankie found it difficult to stop thinking of her. Warm coat on, he had walked in the garden saying his breviary, or trying to. Concentration was difficult. He went inside to eat the roast dinner Mrs Norris made for him every Sunday afternoon. The rest of the week he was alone in the chapel house, cooking and cleaning for himself. He missed Dublin and his family. Three years ago, Archbishop Mahoney had asked Frankie to help out an old friend in England by accepting a temporary posting to the parish of Henley-in-Arden. ''Twill be a short posting, Frankie,' he'd said, 'there's a new man earmarked within six months.'

But the new man had ended up in Kent after the sudden death of a priest there and Frankie didn't know if he'd ever get back to Ireland. Frankie would smile when he thought of the archbishop; he was a great man for the favours and his colleagues knew it well and played on it. The locals used to say that if you saw a priest leaving Mahoney's house you could bet he was on his way to the station. Frankie had been involved in two of his favours before this. One had meant a year in Belfast as chaplain to the RUC. When he'd left the seminary as a priest, Frankie had never expected his 'career' to involve training in self-defence and studying the qualities of body armour.

At least the people of the north had been as sociable, if not more so, as his own countrymen. He found the English difficult on that front, much more reserved. He had no real friends in England. Maybe that was why he caught himself thinking of the girl as he walked again in the garden that Sunday listening to the wind in the bare trees at dusk. She seemed the type who would make a good friend – just for the occasional chat. They got on very well, that was for sure. She had a sharp brain, a quick wit. He liked that. He'd need to buy one of these magazines she wrote for. He was sure her stories would be good.

It was early December. Kathy had been preparing for her main winter project, a dive for treasure in a Portuguese galleon, the *Flor de la Mar*, sunk in 1511 in the Malacca Strait. She'd never been to Indonesia and the onset of the British winter had made her look forward to it for more than just the adventure. But she'd been a bit dejected these past few days. It was over a fortnight since she'd seen Frankie at the church and not contacting him had been one of the hardest things she'd ever faced. She didn't think she could hold out much longer.

Something she'd enjoyed in her early days of 'fame' as a writer had been opening fan mail, most of which came via the various magazines which published her. The pleasure faded as her readership increased and these days she'd put off opening the letters as long as possible. With her

Indonesian trip just a few weeks away, she stared that evening at the growing pile on the dining-room table, made herself a big mug of coffee and sat down with a resigned sigh to plough through. At least there weren't so many from cranks these days. When they'd first started publishing her picture alongside the articles, she got some proposals that she told friends would make a bestseller on their own, X-rated.

Slitting the envelopes with the bone opener given her by an aborigine, she knew before reading how the stuff would break down. Around eighty per cent would be from young girls asking how they could become writers, adventurers, pilots, or whatever the most recent article had concentrated on. Ten per cent would be from men asking her to marry them, join them on a desert island/Antarctic/Himalayan/desert adventure; three or four per cent would be from old people thanking her for bringing back certain memories from their own travels in their youth; one or two per cent criticized her facts, her style, her womanhood etc.; and the others were a mish-mash. She had standard replies for most and needed only to read the first paragraph and the name at the bottom to address them and stuff them in an envelope. By the twelfth letter, she promised herself once again to hire a secretary to do it. When she opened the thirteenth, she was glad she hadn't. It was from Frankie.

Dear Miss Spencer,

I hope you don't mind me writing to you and I hope you remember me. I'm the priest you woke up to at Cheltenham a couple of weeks ago. I enjoyed talking to you when you came to see me in church and I thought I'd go out and buy one of your magazines. So I did and the article I read was the one about you riding in that race. I was so surprised to see my name mentioned!

I wanted you to know that I have been a big racing fan ever since I was a child and I think that your piece is one of the best I've ever read. I've never ridden a racehorse myself, but you made me feel that I knew what it was like not just to sit on the back of one but to actually ride in a race. It's a tough thing to do, to get such a feeling across with all that energy and passion. You're a fine writer, Miss Spencer.

If you are ever passing this way again, you would be welcome to drop in for a cup of tea. If you wanted, that is. Or if you are ever going racing, maybe we'll bump into each other again.

Very best wishes,
Father Francis Houlihan

PS I hope you didn't mind me writing to your magazine but I didn't have your address.

She lost count of the number of times she read it and she took it to bed and put it under her pillow, feeling, for the first time in her adult life, like a child again. She drifted off to sleep with the words 'You're a fine writer, Miss Spencer' in her mind's eye.

4

After Christmas Kathy returned from Indonesia, treasureless but with another good article, and she began to see Frankie once a week. Kathy was always careful to ensure that it was Frankie who said, 'See you next week, then?' She came to know his garden better than the starlings who searched all corners of the dark, wet, winter earth and would joke with him that she had walked more miles in it than when she'd trekked in the Sahara for six months. They never talked of their emotions or thoughts about each other, yet still managed to fill most of their time together with conversation they enjoyed. The silences, as they ambled along, told them more than their words did about their feelings for they were companionable silences. They were content just to walk side by side.

On about her eighth visit, towards the end of February, she sensed a change in him as they walked the half-acre on paths she was now so familiar with. He seemed nervous. The silences were much more frequent and prolonged than they usually were and she began to feel a queasiness in the pit of her stomach. He was either going to ask her not to come again or he was ready to tell her how he felt about her.

He kept her waiting until she was at the door of her car. She watched him, saw his troubled eyes, tried to fix a smile on her own face despite the sick feeling rising. This was the time he always said, 'See you next week'. She waited. He swallowed drily then said quietly, 'Kathy ... would you mind if we met somewhere else next week? Somewhere more ... more private?'

The sudden relief seemed to drain her. She leant back and let the car take her weight. 'I don't mind at all.' Her voice too was quiet. They both knew that they had moved to the next level.

Frankie spent most of that evening praying in the dark church. In self-punishment he knelt on the hard tiles till the pain in his knees was so great it was consuming his mind, interfering with his prayers. He had spent weeks trying to convince himself that seeing Kathy away from the garden would simply be for a change of scenery. Today he finally admitted that the real reason was his fear that his parishioners would start talking. He'd given it no thought for the first few visits, secure in his conviction that they were simply friends and had nothing to hide. But true as this may have been then, he knew it no longer was.

Their weekly walks had come to mean more to him than anything else in his life. In his mind her face awaited him on waking, was with him through the day and smiled at him as he closed his eyes. His dreams were storms of guilt and fear. The strength he prayed for to forget her, to stop seeing her was never delivered. He prayed harder for it, lay in a bath of cold water in penance, rose at four-thirty to pray, begged the Holy Spirit aloud to come down and help him.

And now, he had asked her to meet him in Birmingham, at the Art Gallery.

He stayed all night in the freezing church praying for the power to call Kathy and tell her he wouldn't be there, he wouldn't be seeing her again.

Come spring, they were seeing each other twice most weeks, always away from the church. He hadn't yet been to her home. Neither had said anything at all about their feelings. Kathy was happier than she had ever hoped to be simply being with him. Although she wanted him to tell her how he felt, she recognized that it wasn't necessary. She knew he shared the love they had. She had thought it would become harder, that she'd need to have some declaration from him but it hadn't turned out that way. She'd been certain she'd be burning to tell her friends about him but that desire had quickly faded. She was much more at peace in her mind, knowing with certainty that things would take their natural course.

That autumn, on a glorious October day by the banks of the South Oxford Canal, without breaking his stride or turning to look at her, Frankie said, 'I'm thinking of leaving the priesthood.'

They walked another ten paces before she replied, quietly, 'It's a big step, Frankie.'

It had been almost a year they'd been friends. Still they'd said nothing more intimate to each other than 'I enjoy your company' and 'You make me laugh'.

Frankie said, ''Tis. It's been in my mind for a while now.'

She knew the tortures he must have gone through and the thought of his pain had hurt her. She longed to hold him and sympathize but she simply could not break their unspoken agreement. Whatever weight of argument Frankie had built to justify leaving or not leaving, she could not risk adding a single gram to it. The decision had to be totally his.

She prepared herself for what she knew he'd say next. They were still walking, hadn't broken stride. In the same even voice he said, 'I want to spend the next month praying every day for God's guidance.'

'That's OK. I have my winter project to prepare for.' She worried that it had come out a little too pat, too hurried.

'I won't be able to see you,' he said.

She thought she detected a slight tremor in his voice. She said, 'I understand. I'll pray for you too.'

'Thanks.'

After the longest month of their lives, Frankie wrote to her to say he was going to Ireland to speak to Archbishop Mahoney and to see his family. He asked if she would mind not calling him. Kathy wrote that she wouldn't call and that she'd continue to pray for him.

5

The days running up to 5 November, when Frankie had arranged to meet the archbishop, were full of fear and guilt for him, but to Kathy they brought hope and a lightness of being she'd never felt before. It seemed like years since she'd seen him and she had pined for him, felt like a limb was missing. She'd prayed too. Raised a Protestant, she had long since stopped regular attendance at church. Sometimes, if she was spending the weekend with her parents in Lincoln, she'd go. Her prayers were truly for Frankie. She kept her own wishes out of it and prayed for him to make the decision that would give him the peace of mind he needed. Happiness was too much to pray for on his behalf, she knew whatever he decided there would be a residue of guilt that would take years to fade.

She thought 5 November an ironically appropriate date for Frankie's meeting. One way or the other he'd be lighting his own bonfire, and the effigy he cast on to it would either be her as she was or himself as a priest.

Frankie made his way through Dublin's streets on foot, his black suit and dog collar giving him a status here among the people that was withheld in most parts of England. Even some of the children respectfully silenced their shouts of

31

'Penny for the guy!' as he strode past. He'd arrived by air an hour before, deliberately timing it so that he'd meet none of his family until he'd seen the archbishop.

The great man's house, a square mansion of granite, was in the grounds of the Holy Cross College. In the final half-mile as he closed on the meeting place, Frankie kept up the rhythm of his step and had to consciously stop himself swinging his arms like a sergeant-major. This was his way of steeling himself, of keeping his mood confident. He needed to speak to Archbishop Mahoney secure in the belief he'd now formed; it was vital, in his mind, to accomplish what he'd come for. There was no room in him for nerves, for self-doubt. He'd been all the way along that tortuous path, spent dark nights in his own Gethsemane.

Frankie turned off Clonliffe Road to go through the shiny black metal gate beyond which the entry door to the house lay. Frankie fixed his eyes on it and as he went through it and along the rich brown block paving, the door opened and Archbishop Mahoney himself stood in the doorway dressed the same as Frankie, smiling and slowly raising both hands straight in front of him, tilting his small, almost bald head slightly to the right, his eyes twinkling with genuine warmth and affection. He put his arms around the young priest he'd ordained eight years previously and said, 'Francis, Francis, welcome home!' and Frankie rested his chin briefly on the old man's left shoulder, smelling the soap on his skin. The Garden of Gethsemane came to his mind once more. His image of himself this time was as Judas.

The archbishop led him along varnished floors of old knotted boards, past paintings of the saints hanging below ceilings of varying heights, in rooms whose difference in size would have been plain to a blind man listening to the acoustic effects on the voices of the two men as they moved through the house. The room they sat down in had walls the colour of the reeds carried on Palm Sunday. The big pale green chairs that held them faced each other across a wide hearth backed by a tall marble mantelpiece above which hung a life-size painting of Pope Pius XII.

There were two arched windows whose deep sills held fat pink vases filled with armfuls of fresh flowers emitting scents which perfumed the room. Dusk was falling. Six sets of candle-shaped lights burned around the walls, casting a glow which Frankie thought made the old man look even more serene. The archbishop sat with his hands together in his lap, legs crossed at the ankles. His black shoes shone but Frankie noticed a tiny tear in the right one, just on the fold of the instep. He looked up slowly. All the small talk had been disposed of on the journey to this room. It was time to say the words he had rehearsed so often that he imagined the letters in them to be worn at the edges from the millions of times they had tumbled around inside his head.

He sat forward, elbows on knees, hands clasped loosely and said, 'Archbishop, I have news for you that you would not be expecting to hear. I have decided to give up my vocation. I have

33

decided to leave the formal ministry.'

The old man's smile never changed. He nodded slowly. 'You used the word "decided" twice, Francis. You are a man who's very definite about what he's going to do.'

'There is no need for me to explain to Your Grace how much thought and prayer I have given to this in the past months. Your Grace will know me well enough to be aware of that.'

'How many months, Francis?'

Frankie steepled his fingers then flattened them to join his hands. 'Almost nine, Archbishop.'

They sat looking at each other. The temptation came to Frankie, as he'd known it would, to fill the silence with heartfelt explanations and pleas for understanding and forgiveness, but saying nothing, maintaining the dignity, was what he had prepared so hard for. Any gushings now of the pain of all this, of his sorrow and deep sadness, would only serve his own selfishness further. What he'd said was true, the archbishop would know everything Frankie had been through. Not so much because he had heard the same story more often than he would like from the mouths of others like Frankie, but because he had known him since Frankie was at Maynooth. He'd been eighteen when he'd first met the old man who sat across from him, the benevolent smile slightly faded now but still there. The archbishop knew him better, probably, than his own father had.

'What's her name?'

Frankie resisted dropping his head and held his gaze. 'Kathy Spencer, Your Grace.'

'And the relationship has not yet begun with Miss Spencer?'

That lifted Frankie's heart. 'No, Your Grace.'

There was another long silence. Still Frankie kept the eye contact, watched the smile of the old man who, at last, nodded. 'She must be some woman to take Francis Houlihan from God the Father.'

Frankie had prepared for this too. After so many months of silence, of not being able to tell a soul of his love, let alone Kathy herself, the temptation to open the floodgates and let the thundering cascade loose, not only to say how much he loved her but to justify what he was doing at the same time, was almost irresistible. But he held fast. 'I think Your Grace knows that there is no need for me to answer that.'

'So you'll tell no one how you feel about her until you have told the woman herself?'

'Partly that, Your Grace, but also, I know the immensity of what I'm doing. I've no wish to begin trying to justify it, not even to God himself, for there is no justification in it. I took my vows before you eight years ago and I come back here to tell you I am breaking those vows. There is no justification, only selfishness.'

''Tis a sin, selfishness.'

Frankie nodded.

'That means it can be forgiven.'

'Only if I repent.'

Archbishop Mahoney looked at him, the smile gone from his mouth but the kindness still in his grey eyes. Quietly he said, 'Take some counselling, Francis, please.'

Frankie shook his head. 'I'm sorry, Your Grace. I've sought counsel through God for months. I have made my decision.'

Pushing himself forward in two moves, the old man got up and walked over to sit on the arm of Frankie's chair. Putting his hand on Frankie's left shoulder he said, 'The life of a young priest can be very, very stressful, Francis, and stress can change a man's character until he does not understand what he is doing.'

Frankie turned to look at him, determined to let him see the sincerity on his face. 'No stress, Archbishop, no nervous breakdowns, alcoholism, loneliness or anything else except selfishness.'

'And a love for something you can see at last, eh? Something that responds each time to your love and your prayers to her. Two-way love, Francis, where faith in something you cannot see isn't the binding that holds the whole thing together?'

Frankie conceded this. 'Maybe.'

The old man gripped his shoulder. 'Human love changes, Frankie, as people get older. It can fade. God's love is constant.'

'I know, Your Grace,' Frankie said quietly.

He sighed. 'You know, but you won't change your mind?'

'No, Your Grace.'

The archbishop stood up and walked to the mantelpiece to look down at Frankie. 'You'll give them some time to find a replacement, Frankie?'

'Of course, Archbishop.'

'Three months?'

'Three months will be fine, Your Grace.'

There was silence. For the first time Frankie looked away from the face of the older man. There was no relief in him, only sadness. The flower scents hung heavy. It was almost dark beyond the arched windows. The bare fireplace seemed as cold and empty as his heart. He felt a light touch on his forehead and looked up. The old man smiled and ruffled his hair. Frankie wept.

He made his way down O'Connell Street through the light rain, bypassing the taxi ranks. The walk to his mother's house in Infirmary Road was a long one but Frankie needed the time it would take to try and marshal his thoughts. He went into a hardware shop and bought a black umbrella with a shiny wooden handle.

Turning south on Drumcondra Road he tried to get back into the marching rhythm he'd adopted as he'd gone to the cathedral but his legs wouldn't obey. The dread in his heart at the prospect of telling his mother weighed heavy, making him almost drag his steps.

His mother, who had raised him since he drew his first breath to be a priest. His mother who, as she clutched the hands of midwives and pushed him out into the world, had had the priest standing by to bless not just him but the hospital cot that was to be his first bed. His mother who had insisted that the blood and placenta remnants be washed from his howling body with nothing but holy water. His mother whose life had been stained by bitterness and bigotry. The only thing she had to boast about, the single source of pride in her existence was her son, Father Francis Houlihan. Involuntarily, he drew a huge breath and the sigh that carried it back out made the woman approaching him raise her head to look.

She was pulling a battered metal shopping trolley with squeaking wheels, on which was balanced a suitcase. She looked up at Frankie as they passed each other and he saw tears on her cheeks and pain in her eyes. He stopped, forgetting his own troubles for a moment and looked at her as she went away from him. 'Are you all right, missus?' he called, surprising himself with the richness of his own accent.

She didn't turn round and he watched as she reached the junction and turned to go down O'Connell Street. Frankie flushed the rain from his umbrella, put it above his head once more and continued the journey to his mother's house.

6

Bridget Gleeson, the tearful woman with the suitcase, had heard the priest call her but she had no faith in the Catholic Church any more and little faith in anything else. It had been knocked out of her physically and emotionally and she was doing now what she had long promised she would. Bridget was the mother of twelve-year-old Sean and the husband of alcoholic Brendan. She

38

had held on as long as she could but a woman could take only so much when she was thirty-seven, her life withering further from every drunken beating and the happiness she'd always wished for looking all but beyond hope.

Leaving Brendan after fifteen years caused her no sadness. He'd been a good man before the gambling, then the drink, had swallowed him up and he was a good man still when he was sober. Good and repentant and full of tears and promises ... as they all were. As she'd been warned of so often by her neighbours, their hard, bitter faces bearing witness to voices of experience. Well, Bridget did not want to end up with a face like that. She wanted fun and good times. And she'd had her fair share of them until Brendan had started gambling. His years of losing money to bookmakers and casinos had condemned them to a life of virtual poverty. And she had trudged on, living with it, because there was always some love there for him and she hadn't wanted Sean to suffer from a break-up.

But a year previously Brendan'd started drinking heavily too and taking everything out on her. She'd always sworn she'd stand for most things but not for being battered. She'd warned him. Now he'd wake up from his stupor on the floor by the gas fire (many times she'd been tempted to leave the gas on and unlit for she knew the first thing he did when coming round was light a cigarette) and he'd see she'd finally done it, and he'd be a sorry man.

She'd miss her son. Some day she'd come back for him or bring him to her. She'd miss Sean all right but she had no doubts about his ability to get along without her. If survival of the fittest was important, these past few years in St Joseph's Mansions had given Sean the best possible upbringing. She knew he was intelligent but life as a child on these streets had added vital skills to that; hardness and wisdom and cunning. They had lived in St Joseph's Mansions all their married life and she recalled many good times there. Sean had loved it, the enclosed playground, the hordes of playmates. And she'd been happy there too in what had been a close and supportive community.

Then the drug-dealers had moved in, making junkies of the teenagers, then corpses of the junkies. It had spread like cancer throughout the Mansions, eating away the extremities first but moving with grim inevitability through the body until the heart of the community was barely beating. The Gleesons were one of only three families remaining and now, Bridget thought, there'd be one Gleeson less. St Joseph's Mansions was a ghetto now, and living in a ghetto had never been in Bridget Gleeson's life-plan.

Sean wiped the cold, wet windowpane with the corner of his bedsheet, the image of his mother slinking away in the November rain still strong in his mind. What made him saddest was the sight of those old canvas moccasins she wore lest the click-clack of her street shoes woke his father. The puddles had sucked at the shabby slippers, as though trying to hold her there; she'd hurried on, not looking back, pulling that stupid trolley he'd found in the canal. Sean stared silently; through the trickling condensation he saw the swirling reflections of the orange street lights in the puddle-water settle back slowly till just the pattering rain disturbed them.

She had begged him to go with her. 'I can't, Ma. I can't leave the ponies.' Sean was one of the many boys in Dublin who raced ponies. Most of them did it for the laugh, for the crack, but Sean did it because he wanted to make a career of it, wanted to become a proper jockey.

She'd half-frowned, half-smiled in that way that says you're not living in the real world but she'd done that before to him and so had his father. She said, 'Sean, in a couple of years' time you'll forget the ponies ever existed. It'll be girls and a job that'll be on yer mind and ye'll get the best of both of those in England. Come with me, please.'

'Ma, you know Mr Cosgrave's looking for a new boy. They're all sayin' it and my name's been mentioned.'

She looked frustrated. 'Mr Cosgrave's a proper trainer, he's not interested in street races and kids like you. I'm sorry, Sean, I don't mean to hurt ye and I know how good a rider ye are but Mr Cosgrave lives in a different world.'

'Well that's the world for me, Ma. It's not this one in Joseph's Mansions. I'll not be here for ever. And it's not away over in England where they wouldn't let me near a horse or a pony, so they wouldn't, for I'm only thirteen. When I go over to England 'twill be as a proper jockey to ride in the Cheltenham Gold Cup.'

He'd watched her pretty face crease in sorrow. He sensed that she wanted to reach and cuddle him. But he was too old for that now and it had been her choice anyway. She could have stayed until his father was off the drink, although Sean hated to see her getting a hammering.

She'd said, 'How are you going to cope, living with your father?'

And he'd shrugged softly and said, 'Ahh, he just needs to give up the drink and he'll be fine. I'll get him sorted out before ye know it and ye can come back home. Don't be worryin'.'

Bridget Gleeson looked at her only child. 'Will you come and see me in England?' she asked.

Sean tried a smile; only half of it worked. 'Sure I will, Ma.'

'Your Aunt Phoebe will know where I am.'

'I'll go and visit her every Sunday and take a letter for her to send to you.'

Her tears rose again. Sean said, 'Don't cry, Ma. We'll all be back together before you know it and me da'll be fine. I've a good strong feelin' it'll all work out.'

She pulled him to her, squashing his face into the dark hair on her neck and Sean awkwardly put his hands on her shoulders to help him keep his balance. The determination to stay quite stiff and upright was all that held back his own tears. And even as she bubbled and heaved quietly as she clung to him he felt a surge of optimism that some day everything would be all right again.

The Gleesons' second-storey flat was one of two hundred and eighty-six that made up St Joseph's

Mansions. They were laid out like linked tenements in a brown rectangle which was broken only by the arched entry, the one that Dublin Corporation had to modify shortly after the block was built as they hadn't allowed room for a fire engine to enter.

St Joseph's Mansions had been the first flats of their kind ever built in Dublin, a four-storey, 1920s design that housed many happy families despite the lack of a single bathroom in the whole block. The central quadrangle where so many children had played over the years was now a semi-flooded dumping ground patrolled by shabby pigeons waiting vainly for the return of Mrs Halliday, who'd fed them every day until she'd been driven out. The children's swings had been torn down; only a rusting basketball stand remained, the ring twisted, the net long since gone.

The activities of the drug-dealers and their customers had turned the block into a warren of squalor; a disease-ridden, graffiti-strewn monolith whose stairwells and flaking corridors stank of urine and faeces. Boarded-up doors and windows, Corporation-erected signs warning people of the risks of entering the Mansions, broken fittings, odd-shaped stains ingrained in floors and walls, all mapped the rapid decline of the place and the desertion of its law-abiding inhabitants.

Apart from the Gleesons, only two families remained, both determined not to give in to the criminals who still used the place for their night-time dealings.

The Gleesons refused to move partly because Sean had so many happy memories of growing up there and wanted to stay but mostly because Brendan, Sean's father, had always plied his 'trade' in this area. For five years he had worked for Dublin's richest and most successful criminal, Kelly Corell. Part of Gleeson's work was occasional drug-dealing and this was where his market was. While his neighbours had fought hard to keep the dealers out, Brendan Gleeson had joined the enemy.

Corell would give him other jobs to do too; collecting protection money from businesses, recruiting girls for prostitution, and, Gleeson's favourite task, chauffeuring his boss to the races. He loved betting on horses, had an addiction for gambling that had cost him hundreds of thousands of pounds. But the hope of the big win one day was always there, the win that would wipe out all the failures, all the bad memories.

Sometimes Corell gave him tips and they were usually pretty good. The boss owned a few horses himself, and anyway Gleeson supposed that nobody would give the man duff tips. Not if they wanted to keep their skin unpunctured and bones unbroken.

One evening, while driving Corell home from Leopardstown races, Gleeson was given a task that was completely new to him. Unusually, Corell had taken the front passenger seat of the Mercedes making Gleeson a touch nervy with his driving. Corell said, 'You're a man for the horses, Brendan, aren't ye?'

'I am, Mr Corell. Especially the ones that know

whereabouts to stick their head in front of the others.'

'Good man. Well listen, I've a fella working on somethin' for me in England, over near Lambourn, the big racing place.'

'I've heard of it. Famous place, so it is,' said Gleeson.

'How d'ye fancy a trip over there to do bit of sortin' out of the final details for me?'

'That'd be good, Mr Corell. When would it be?'

'Soon enough. And it's not a thing ye'd be wantin to ask too many questions about, Brendan. That's important. And it's a hundred times more important not to be sayin' anythin' to anybody about it. 'Tis a very expensive investment I have there and a lot depends on nobody knowin' I'll be beatin' them to the punch.'

'Ye know me, Mr Corell. I'd as soon shove a red hot poker up my own arse as mention a word or even a letter about any of your business.'

Corell smiled slowly. 'Now that's a thing I've never tried with anybody, Brendan. Don't be givin' me ideas, man!'

Corell knew that Gleeson's skills were limited but he did what he was told and the job Corell wanted doing wasn't difficult. The main thing was that if something went wrong, Gleeson wouldn't be missed. He was the most expendable of Corell's men.

7

This was Frankie's third trip home since being sent to England. He'd been here just after Christmas in each of the past two years. Stopping outside, he looked over the shoulder-high hedge at the four-bedroom semi he and his five siblings had grown up in. Lights burned in the upstairs bathroom and Theresa's room as well as the living-room, and he could hear in his head the voice of his father; 'If ye's paid for the electricity yerselves, ye'd be a damn sight more careful about leavin' lights on!' His father, five years dead. Frankie shook his head slowly.

Knowing he would never again stand here, he was painfully aware that when he opened the gate, walked down the path, wiped his feet and entered the only proper home he'd ever known, it would be for the last time. His mother would disown him. He looked up and down the dark wet street then turned to gaze at the trees swaying in the park across the road where he'd played football in summer and sledged in winter. He would miss this place.

He faced the house again. The rain beat a steady rhythm on his umbrella. The curtain in the living-room was pulled aside and he watched his mother trying to shield out the light behind her so she could see into the darkness. Frankie felt sick at the hurt he was about to cause her. He drew a deep breath, thought of Kathy, prayed for God's help and slipped the gate latch.

Opening the door quietly, he wiped his feet and leant the furled umbrella in the corner to drip on the blue and cream diamond-shaped tiles. There was the smell. That house smell he'd known since a child but only noticed the first time he'd returned home from the seminary for a summer holiday. He walked quietly along the hall and knocked lightly on the living-room door, then went in.

The room seemed almost blindingly bright. The TV was showing a programme about an oil tanker disaster. His mother was still at the window. She turned as he entered. 'Francis. I didn't hear you come in. I was watching for you.' She smiled with her eyes but very little with the rest of her face. Mrs Houlihan had never been one for big welcomes and, like the last twice he'd been here, he felt she greeted him almost as though he'd just returned from a hurling match or a trip to the shops. She picked up the remote control and switched off the TV.

He smiled warmly and went to her, knowing that afraid as she'd always been of any show of affection, she would raise her joined hands and ask for a blessing. For once he felt like ignoring her plea and hugging her, holding her for as long as he could, knowing he would probably never see her again. But the years of indoctrination about behaving like a proper man kicked in, and placing his hand on her head, noticing the sheen on her closed eyelids, the fine wrinkles on her still handsome face, he blessed her.

She opened her eyes and went to the door. 'Theresa, Father Francis is here!' He heard quick footsteps on the stairs and a whoop of delight and he smiled as his mother said wearily, 'I'll put the kettle on.' Frankie knew she didn't want to witness them hugging. At twenty-two, Theresa was the youngest, the only one still living at home and everybody's favourite. She had never lost her wide-eyed wonder at life and often seemed to behave like a child. Frankie remembered the terrible arguments his parents used to have when his mother insisted on sending Theresa for tests to see if she was 'backward', as his mother would put it. His father's stand against that was the toughest one Frankie could ever recall him taking on anything, but as with the others, he had lost that one too and Theresa visited a string of specialists. No one found anything wrong with her.

She came running along the hall to cries from the kitchen – 'Theresa! Walk!' She whooped again as she leapt into the arms of her big brother and kissed his face, hugging his neck till she almost made him topple forward. 'Frankie! ... Frankie! Frankie! Frankie, I've missed you.'

'I missed you too, Theresa. It's good to see you.'

She stepped away and held his hands, looking him up and down. 'You look fantastic. You're wet. Didn't you get a taxi?' Her eyes shone, as to Frankie they had always seemed to.

'I just walked.'

Her face changed as she watched him; she looked concerned. 'Are you OK, Frankie?'

He nodded, smiling. 'I'm fine. How are you?

What've you been doin' with yourself?'

'Are you worried about something, Frankie?' she asked.

He squeezed her hands. 'Everything will be fine.'

She looked at him silently, a tinge of sadness in her eyes now and he knew she could see something was badly wrong, could sense it. That was the way Theresa was. She moved forward again and put her arms around his waist, her cheek on his chest and hugged him tightly. He stroked her hair. 'You've got your pyjamas on,' he said quietly. 'It's only just gone eight.' She nodded and clung to him.

Their mother came in with a tray of tea and biscuits. 'Come on, now, let Father Francis have his tea! Enough of your nonsense!'

Theresa eased herself away reluctantly leaving a single long auburn hair which glinted like a river threading its way down his black lapel. 'Sit down, Francis,' his mother said.

He sat on his father's chair by the gas fire. He looked at Theresa in her shiny yellow pyjamas. 'Will you have some tea, Theresa?' he asked, concerned now by her bowed head, her sad look which her hair curtained from her mother.

'She will not,' his mother said. 'She has plenty to do to get that room of hers tidied up. Off you go now and give me half an hour's peace with Father Francis.' Theresa turned and wandered out of the room.

'See you later!' Frankie called.

'See you later,' she replied, almost absent-mindedly.

He watched his mother take the tea cosy Mrs Costello had brought her from Lourdes off the blue teapot. As she poured he noticed there were only two cups. She had never intended to include Theresa. Frankie felt a sudden wish to be able to take his sister with him when he left. He was sure Kathy would love her.

Stirring the tea she said, 'So have you good news for me then after your visit to the arch-bishop? I was talking to the women at the institute yesterday and telling them I thought you might be getting a move back home. Mebbe even Dublin itself, I said, and Mrs Kennedy said now wouldn't that be grand. And I said you were due some reward, so you were, for the favours you've done the archbishop himself in going to Belfast and England. What would he have done without you, I said, and they all said exactly the same, that not every Irish priest by any manner of means would have faced the troubles up there or gone to England for three years with no family or friends close by... So what did Archbishop Mahoney have to say to you, then?'

Frankie took the tea and sipped quickly to moisten his drying mouth and to hide the nervous lump he was about to swallow. 'It was me who asked the archbishop for the meeting.'

He could see that the tone of his voice and the look on his face had suddenly sharpened her concentration. She lowered her teacup slowly till it rested in the saucer on her lap. But she didn't have Theresa's sensitivity. She looked puzzled rather than apprehensive. She said, 'To ask for a transfer yourself? Well that's not the done thing,

50

Francis. You must sit and wait until you're called. Sit and wait. It wouldn't be–'

He interrupted her. 'I didn't ask for a transfer, Ma. It was a much more serious matter.' The puzzlement had just a line or two of worry in it now and she sat very still. Frankie said, 'You need to prepare yourself for some bad news, Ma. Nobody's going to die but you need to prepare for a shock.' Her complexion began to pale. Frankie sipped tea again. 'Ma, I'm leaving the ministry, giving up my vocation.'

She sat like a statue, staring at him, unblinking, appearing to Frankie not even to be breathing. The sound of his cup meeting the saucer seemed to fill the room. The silence lasted a long time. Frankie said, 'Did you hear me, Ma?'

She moved, re-settled herself in the chair and raised her cup to drink. She said, 'I thought you might like to have a hot bath before you went to bed and tomorrow we could go into town together, do some shopping after mass.'

'Did you hear what I said to you, Ma? I'm leaving the priesthood. I'm sorry.'

She was still and silent again for a while, then said, 'Tell me I am dreaming this.'

He shook his head. 'I'm sorry, Ma.'

She shut her eyes and shouted so loudly she made Frankie jump. 'Theresa! Theresa!'

The footsteps were on the stairs again, then in the hall and Theresa came in and looked at her mother whose eyes were closed tight now; her head was up, as though sniffing something in the air. 'Ma?' Theresa said.

'Tell me if Father Francis is sittin' there,

51

opposite me.'

Theresa looked at her, then at Frankie, and seemingly unperturbed by the question said, 'He is, Ma.'

'Take him out to the kitchen and ask him to tell you what he told me then come back and tell me what it is.'

Theresa held out her hand, seeming to think this was some game. 'Come on, Frankie!'

Frankie said, 'Ma, listen to me! I know what a shock this is and–'

'No! I'm dreaming it. I'll wake up soon!'

He went to her, rested on one knee, took the tea off her lap and put it on the tiled hearth. He took her hand. She tried to snatch it away. He held on. 'Open your eyes, Ma,' he said quietly, sympathetically.

She shook her head vigorously and pursed her lips.

'Ma, I've prayed to God for many months for the strength to stay. I never ever wanted to do anything else but be a priest. I never wanted anything different from what you wanted. I've dedicated my life to it in the way you have.' Her eyes remained tightly shut. 'A year ago, God saw fit to allow me to meet someone, a girl called Kathy Spencer.' He felt her wince and saw the pain on her face. 'My prayers for guidance and strength have left no doubt in my mind, Ma, that I'm doing the right thing. God is–'

She started praying aloud, 'Hail Mary, full of grace, the Lord is with thee...' she finished the prayer then started again immediately, then once more, pausing halfway through to say anxiously,

52

'Pray with me, Francis!'

'Ma, please!'

'Pray with me!' She squeezed his hand hard and shook it as though it were a handkerchief she was trying to wring with despair. 'Pray with me!' She was almost screaming.

Frankie said the Hail Mary, turning to beckon Theresa to him. She came and knelt beside him, looking confused and sad. Their mother started the prayer again. After ten minutes of constant praying, she still had not opened her eyes.

Frankie said quietly to Theresa, 'Stay praying with her. I'm going to get our Margaret.'

8

A week after chauffeuring Kelly Corell home from Leopardstown races, a nervous Brendan Gleeson was with his boss in south-west England. Corell was in the rear seat of a hired Mercedes and his temper was getting shorter. Gleeson couldn't find the house he was supposed to be taking Corell to and he was sweating, close to panic. Corell was a great guy to be with when he was in a good mood but Gleeson knew how quickly his moods changed. He'd seen Corell's appetite for violence at first hand, having witnessed the man spreadeagling one of his criminal rivals on a snooker table and hammering six-inch nails through his screaming enemy's hands till they split the polished wood of the surround.

Gleeson had pulled into the side of the road near the top of a hill. He had lost count of the times he'd unfolded the fax. It was grubby and dog-eared and the interior light in the hire car wasn't bright. Gleeson screwed his eyes up as he tilted the paper under the weak, pinkish beam. *'About a mile and a half outside Lambourn on the B4001, near the top of the hill. Turn left along a road which goes through tall trees and drive to the big gates at the end then ring the bell.'*

Corell watched him. 'Does it say anything different from the last ten times you looked at it, Brendan?'

Turning to face his solemn passenger Gleeson said, 'Mr Corell, this is the bloody B4001. I've been up and down it for the past half-hour and there's no road! Look!' He tried to give the sheet to Corell who kept his hands on his thighs.

'His number's on it,' Corell said. 'Call him and tell him you're sorry to drag him out on such a cold night but you're such a shite driver that you can't get me there without help.'

Gleeson looked at him and decided not to argue.

Fifteen minutes later, he was driving behind Hewitt's black Audi Quattro. He felt calmer. Hewitt had been decent to him, told him the turn-off was almost impossible to find in the dark. He said quite a few missed it in daylight too. Gleeson said he wouldn't mind having his maximum bet that the turn-off wasn't on this road at all. Hewitt had smiled and said, 'Follow me.' Corell left the Mercedes and travelled with Hewitt.

Hewitt drove fast but skilfully. Corell said, 'I don't suppose you're looking for a chauffeur's job?'

Hewitt chuckled. 'You shouldn't be too hard on your man, Mr Corell. You'll see when we get there, it isn't the easiest of roads to find. I should have remembered you might be travelling in the dark when I faxed the instructions.'

'You coulda rolled out a ball of string from here to Dublin and he still wouldn't've been able to follow it back.'

'That bad?'

Corell smiled, remembering that he needed Hewitt to have some trust in Gleeson's ability to set him up with a decent supplier. 'Nah, he's a good man, really. He's no genius is Brendan but he's smart enough and you can count on him to do what he's told. He'd walk off a cliff if I asked him to, so he would.'

'You must treat him well, if he shows that sort of respect.'

Corell resisted making a clever remark. He realized Hewitt believed that he was simply a businessman, as he'd told him on the telephone. Most people in Corell's world could translate the euphemism well enough but he was conscious that Hewitt came from a completely different background. This was the first time they'd met and Corell was beginning to understand Hewitt's perception of things. Corell seldom set up deals personally, there was too much risk involved. But when he'd first approached Hewitt to work on this project, Hewitt's natural expectations, 'When can we meet to discuss it?', had seemed

55

almost like an ultimatum – deal with me personally or not at all. He realized now he'd misread Hewitt's natural assumption that this was a straightforward business arrangement.

'I'd like to think I have the respect of all the people who work for me,' he said as Hewitt slowed smoothly to turn sharp right.

'I'm sure that I too will find our association a pleasure,' Hewitt replied.

'And a profitable pleasure, too. That's what we all want,' Corell said as they approached the high black gates.

When they got through the entrance and parked, an animated Gleeson came quickly from his car and hurried forward. When Corell opened his door, Gleeson leaned forward, almost blocking his way, and said, 'Road! That was never a road! Jeez, they talk about Ireland being a backward country! That was a pig-track, Mr Corell!' He looked across at Hewitt. 'No offence to your directions there, Mr Hewitt, but Christopher bloody Columbus couldn't have found that turning!'

Hewitt smiled kindly at him. 'He only found America by mistake so you're probably right.' Gleeson went round the car to cement the alliance and stayed close to Hewitt as they walked across the gravel, almost jostling him as he sought vindication, leaning over and looking up into the taller man's face. 'Ye couldn't blame anybody for missing that now, could ye? I mean, what chance'v'ye got when the directions says a road and it's no more a road than ... well, it's like sayin' look out for a racehorse and what ye find's a bloody donkey, eh?'

Hewitt smiled and nodded and made consoling noises as they approached the door of the house and the security lamp flooded the area with a clean blue-tinged light that had an almost chemical quality.

As Hewitt used his thumb to key a four-figure code into a control panel to the right of the dark green double door, Gleeson was uncrumpling the old fax once more; moving beside his boss again and pointing to the words he said, 'Look, road, road! Road my arse!'

Corell said, menacingly quietly. 'Give it a rest.'

Inside, seated in what seemed to Gleeson like a library, he declined the offer of a drink. He was dying for a large whisky and lemonade and a glass of Guinness to chase it. He always felt more like a drink when he was a bit excited about things. But he knew he had a drink problem and he didn't want Corell to get a sniff of that. If the man found out, he'd stop Brendan chauffeuring him and if he lost that part of the job he'd probably lose the rest and be on the streets. 'Ahh, a glass of lemonade would be fine,' he said, trying to look enthusiastic about it.

'There might be some in the kitchen,' Hewitt said. 'Bear with me.'

When he left the room, Corell turned to Gleeson with a quiet but definite command. 'Drink the friggin' lemonade then tell him you've got to go to the car and make a few calls. Wait there till I come out.'

Gleeson left as he was told to. Out in the cold, he watched through the window as Hewitt

57

poured a big measure of whisky from a decanter and handed the glass to Corell. Gleeson sighed with longing and wandered towards the car.

Hewitt seemed all right, really, Gleeson thought. He spoke a bit posh and had skin like a woman but he'd been good enough not to slag him off for being late. He wondered what Hewitt was doing for Corell. He seemed quite young to be doing anything important; twenty-five, twenty-seven maybe, but he had that sort of confident air about him that some people have no matter what age they are, Gleeson thought. Sure he must be smart enough or Mr Kelly Corell would not be employing him, that was for certain.

Corell turned and held up the cut-glass tumbler, facets glinting softly in the pale overhead light. 'Aahh, now that's grand!' he said.

Hewitt smiled. 'A touch of soda, or something?'

''Tis fine as it is, thanks.'

Hewitt settled in the chair opposite and toasted Corell. 'To success.'

'Success.' Corell saluted with his glass and said, 'Would you bring me up to date, now, on how things are?'

'Sure.' Hewitt outlined the scope of the project with great enthusiasm and Corell grew steadily more confident that he had the right man. The young scientist didn't bullshit; he told Corell the timescales were completely unpredictable and that long-term resources would be necessary. 'No problem,' Corell told him. 'Now what about the raw materials?' He smiled.

'As I mentioned on the phone, I need to establish a regular supply of racehorses. I'd want each for twenty-four hours maximum. They don't have to be racing currently and there'd be no necessity for them to be completely sound, certainly not for this stage of the project.'

Corell nodded. 'I was thinking of setting up a deal with a fella in an abattoir. He brings you horses that he'd picked up for slaughter. You do what you need to then he collects them. We pay him two hundred and fifty pounds a time. How does that sound to you?'

'Would you be prepared to pay more if the horse has some talent?'

'If it helps you along with the project, no problem.' Corell smiled. 'Mr Gleeson will sort everything out for you within the next forty-eight hours.'

'Good. And you brought the cash?'

'It's in the car. A bloody big bag of it.'

'Sterling?'

''Tis.'

'Good.'

Corell drank what remained in his glass. Hewitt, looking serious, leant forward, elbows on knees and said, 'Just to be clear – Mr Gleeson's not aware of the actual project we're working on here?'

Corell shook his head. 'He knows what he needs to. He won't ask questions.'

Hewitt nodded, looking like he was trying mentally to tick things off. He said, 'And you don't mind if I call you direct if I have a problem? I know you must be a busy man.'

Corell got to his feet. 'I don't mind at all. This is probably the most important project I've ever launched. I'll give you whatever help I can.'

Hewitt smiled warmly and reached to shake his hand. 'I'm sure we'll make a good team.'

9

Frankie returned to his parish and began making preparations for his final three months. Although he longed to see her, to hear her voice, it didn't seem right to call Kathy on the first day back in England. He waited three days before ringing.

They met on a mellow mid-November afternoon in a park in Cheltenham. The sun was low in the sky, its weak, watery light just enough to cast shadows on the paths which were sticky with wet leaves. He watched her come towards him, the first time they'd met for more than six weeks. She wore a long dark coat, buttoned, with the collar turned up. A white cashmere scarf filled the V at the top, accentuating the rich shades of her olive skin. Frankie drew an involuntary breath; he'd forgotten how beautiful she was.

She smiled as she stopped in front of him and the temptation to throw his arms around her and hold her was the strongest impulse by far he had ever experienced. But he resisted. 'Hello Kathy,' he said and held out his hand awkwardly.

'Hello Frankie.' She shook his hand, careful not to hold on a second longer than might seem proper. 'It's good to see you.'

'Good to see you too.' A smile found its way through the frown that had seemed almost constant these past weeks. 'Do you want to walk or would you like to go and have a drink somewhere?'

'Let's walk,' she said and they ambled off, settling deeper into that comfortable companionship with each stride. A lone mallard glided on a leaf-strewn pond.

'My last day in the formal ministry is January thirty-first.'

She nodded slowly. They walked ten paces before she spoke. 'Does that mean it's your last day as a priest?

'Once a priest, always a priest. That's what we were taught. There's no renouncing of the vows, only the breaking of them. But I suppose that is what it means, my last day as a priest.'

They walked on for a while in silence, then Kathy said, 'Are you OK?'

'I'll be fine. There are some practical things to sort out and I might need to ask your advice on some of the stuff I need to plan for, sort of post-ministry, if you know what I mean.'

'Sure. I'll help in any way I can. How did your mother take the news?'

He sighed. 'As though she'd just found out there was no God after all. 'Twas like the end of the world, Judgement Day and she was stood there waiting for the Lord to appear and tell all the good people that the day of the reward was here only to have the Devil himself come out on stage and say, "Surprise, surprise."'

Kathy smiled gently and watched her suede-booted feet step in time with Frankie's black brogues. Frankie said, 'I thought we were going to have to call the doctor out to sedate her.'

'Is she all right, though?'

'She's well enough to write me letters cursing me to eternity. There are holes in the pages of them where her rage has forced the nib through. And she's well enough to have warned the family under pain of death to have nothing at all to do with me. If I were to die tomorrow, which she says she hopes I will for I've shamed her so that she can never again show her face in the streets of Dublin, she's forbidden every one of them from attending my funeral.'

'Maybe you shouldn't open any more of her letters.'

'I think you're right. I'll see.'

'Don't do it as a penance, Frankie.'

He realized, once again, how well she knew him. 'I won't.'

They walked on in silence for a while, then Kathy said, 'What about the archbishop? How was he when you told him?'

Frankie smiled sadly. 'Ahh, he was grand so he was. He's a proper man. He wouldn't know how to hold something against you, so he wouldn't.'

'Did he try and make you stay?'

'He did. Sure, that's his job. But he was easy and respectful with it like the gentleman he is.'

'Will they find a replacement for you by the end of January?'

'I believe they will.'

They were quiet again for a while. The shadows

lengthened. An overweight jogger huffed past, his trainers slapping the wet tarmac. Kathy said, 'So you start your new life on February the first?'

Frankie nodded, hands in pockets now, looking down. 'I'd like to see you on that day, if I could. I'd like to come and see you at your house for the first time if that's all right.'

'I'd like that too.'

'And between now and then we can still see each other for walks and a chat just like we've been doing, if you want to.'

'Walks 'n' talks,' Kathy said.

They both smiled.

She said, 'That would be nice.'

He walked her to her car parked on the boulevard that fronted the white Regency buildings and neat flowerless gardens. 'See you next week?' he said.

'Can we talk on the phone each day?'

'If you don't mind calling me. I wouldn't feel right using the phone at the chapel house now.'

She smiled. 'Of course I'll call.'

'I'll pay part of your bill,' he said, although he wasn't sure how as he'd soon have no job and nowhere to live.

'You can wash the dishes on February the first to pay your share.'

'It's a deal.'

She got in the car and looked up at him. 'Where are you parked?'

He pointed. 'Just round the corner.'

'You go, then. I just want to make a couple of calls.'

'OK. Will you ring tomorrow?'

'I will.'

'Morning, afternoon or evening?'

'Yes.'

'Pardon?'

'All three,' she said.

He blushed and said, 'See you, Kathy.'

'See you, Frankie.'

She watched him walk away, hands in pockets again, a slight jauntiness in his stride she'd never seen before. At the end of the road he turned and waved. She waved back. He disappeared from her view. She pressed the button to recline her seat sixty degrees, then leant back and let a huge sigh escape her as the tears flowed in silent relief and happiness.

10

During the next ten weeks Kathy persuaded Frankie to become her agent, arguing him out of the contention that he knew nothing about 'agenting'. She promised to teach him all he needed to know. She told him there were four spare bedrooms and a study in her house and he was welcome to stay there and use them until he found a place of his own.

Frankie's successor, Father Boyle, was sixty-eight and walked with a stick. He was partially deaf and partially oblivious too, Frankie thought sadly, to life in general. The man had been carrying out his duties, it seemed, for years with the efficiency of a worn-out old engine barely cranking enough power to keep the parts moving. He made it clear that he was waiting only for his seventieth birthday as the church had moved the retirement goalposts. If he'd retired at sixty-five, he would not have been entitled to a place in which to live out his remaining years. In Father Boyle, Frankie was seeing the result of the shortage of new vocations and the actions of selfish priests like himself. The gaps had to be plugged somehow. Somebody had to pay the price.

His final day was a Tuesday. Bitterly cold morning winds carried the smell of snow and Frankie worried about Father Boyle slipping on the ice which was thick as armour in places. He'd had breakfast with the old priest then went to pick up the single suitcase he'd packed the night before. Returning to the warm kitchen he said goodbye to Father Boyle but got no response. The old man was asleep.

Frankie went through the sacristy door for the last time and into the freezing church. His breath drifted like a cloud of incense. He walked to the altar and knelt. He bowed his head and tried to think of an appropriate prayer. It was too late to say sorry and he was certain that God didn't want an apology anyway. He whispered, 'Thy will be done,' then got up and walked down the centre aisle to leave by the main door, which he pulled shut behind him without turning round. The echo boomed in the cold, thin, empty air.

Frankie had sold his car when first faced with the

prospect of unemployment, so Kathy had offered to pick him up but he'd said he'd rather walk to her door from the station. In the last hundred yards along a secluded tree-lined drive, Frankie marvelled at how grand her house was. He arrived at the door rosy-cheeked and rang the bell.

It was almost a minute before he heard a sound and he was beginning to worry. Then the door opened and she stood there in tight black ski pants and a yellow T-shirt. This was the first time he had seen her casually dressed. He liked the fact that she'd chosen this day. He noticed she had a tea towel in her right hand. She smiled. 'Sorry, I was doing the dishes. Come in.' She stepped back, opening the door wide. He went in and stood in the big bright hall, looking up at the ceiling, which seemed very high. A triple-shaded light hung on a brass chain.

He realized she'd closed the door and he turned slowly, taking in the newness, the dried flowers in large pots on the black and white tiled floor, the polished table with Queen Anne legs, the almost see-through cream drapes. She watched him, his fine-featured face seeming childlike as he took in his surroundings. He was wearing a heavy overcoat he'd bought from a charity shop which made him look older; it was a middle-aged man's coat. She had seen the brown corduroy trousers before too, and the soft tan shoes. The suitcase, ancient as it was, was new to her. 'You can put your suitcase down here, if you want,' she said.

He nodded and bent at the knees, straight-backed to lower it to the floor so slowly it made no sound. 'Got nitro-glycerine in there?' Kathy asked.

Frankie shrugged. 'I didn't want to scratch your floor. The house is amazing.' He was looking through the door into a big room where a log fire burned in an inglenook fireplace.

'Come in and have a proper look. I'll take your coat. Do you want some tea or a drink? Beer or whisky or something soft?'

He followed her into the room. 'A whisky would be nice. Warm me up. It's cold out there. Nice but cold.' He smiled nervously at her.

'Sit by the fire. Get warm. I'll fix you a drink.' She went into the kitchen. He couldn't see her as she called, 'Want anything in your whisky?'

'Some ice, if you have it.'

He heard the clink and she came back, a glass in each hand. They stood on the thick Indian rug in front of the fire. She raised her glass. 'Welcome.'

He raised his. 'It's nice to be here. I like your house. I never pictured you living alone in such a big place.'

'Probably psychological compensation for having nothing but a bed and a locker when I was a kid.'

'In the orphanage?'

She nodded. They sipped their drinks. 'You've done well for yourself,' he said.

'It doesn't really mean much to me, not any more.'

He shifted awkwardly and drank again. She said, 'My priorities changed around fifteen months ago. Every minute that I've spent with

67

you since then has meant more to me than any of this, anything money can buy.' He reddened and looked down at the rug. 'Don't look away from me now Frankie Houlihan. We've spent almost a year and a quarter in small talk and I promised myself every night before I went to sleep that I wouldn't waste a single minute more...' She eased the drink from his fingers and put it alongside her own on the high dark stone mantelpiece. She took his hands in hers, held them softly and said, 'I love you.'

Letting her hands go he opened his arms slowly, evenly, a gesture he had performed before only at the consecration of the blessed sacrament. She stepped forward and he gathered her in till her head rested on his left shoulder and her arms were around him. They stayed that way for a long time before Kathy spoke softly; 'If you knew how much I've longed for this.'

'Me too,' he said. 'I love you, Kathy.'

She held him tighter and the tears flowed silently down her cheeks in celebration. After a minute she wiped them and made space between her and Frankie so she could kiss him.

'God, this is the part I've been dreading!' he said, looking genuinely worried.

'Well, thanks a million!' she smiled, cheeks still wet.

'You know what I mean. I've haven't done this since I was at school.'

'It's not rocket science, Frankie, just pucker up those lips.' She laughed.

Shutting his eyes, he tried to do what she said, making her laugh more. 'I was only kidding! You don't need to pucker up! Just relax.'

'Can I keep my eyes closed?'

'If you like.'

He did. She kissed him gently and primly for a few seconds then pulled away. 'Here endeth lesson one. You can open your eyes, sonny.'

He opened them and they laughed together.

11

The morning after taking Corell to Hewitt's, Brendan Gleeson woke in his bedroom in the Chequers Hotel in Newbury with a hangover. He'd had to drive Corell to the airport before returning to the hotel and he'd been determined to make up for lost drinking time. Checking his watch he saw he was already ten minutes late for his meeting with the slaughterman. 'Shit!' he said and reached for his jacket, which lay on the floor. If he messed this up Corell would go crazy. From his jacket pocket he pulled the fax with Hewitt's directions on it. He'd written the slaughterman's mobile number at the bottom. He dialled it, hands shaking from the effects of the alcohol. Monroe answered on the first ring and told Gleeson he was waiting for him downstairs. 'Gimme five minutes,' Gleeson said and went to the bathroom to throw water on his face.

The slaughterman was waiting in the corner with two untouched half-pints of orange juice on the table. That was the sign they'd agreed on the phone so Gleeson would recognize him. It had been the slaughterman's idea; Gleeson was impressed but couldn't wait for a drink. Raising a thumb to the man and smiling, he motioned to the bar and went to get himself a drink. He carried a pint of Guinness and a large whisky and lemonade to the table. 'Mr Monroe?' he said.

'Mr Gleeson.'

'That's right.' He put his drinks down and they shook hands. Gleeson sat across from him on a narrow rectangular stool and rested an elbow on the table, forcing it on to its one short leg and spilling Guinness. He cursed and grabbed the glass. He drank half of the contents then nodded to the orange juice. 'Want a proper drink?'

'No thanks.'

Gleeson drank again, watching Monroe. 'You look worried, Mr Monroe.'

'Should I be?'

'Not so far as I'm concerned. I just wanted to put a little business proposal to ye so ye can make yerself a few quid.'

'Doing what?'

'Before we talk about that, you need to understand the importance of keeping this quiet. Whether you decide to do it or not, you can't talk about it. Not now, next week, next year, whenever. It's important for your own, eh, what do they say these days, quality of life?'

'You already said all this on the phone. I told you, I don't have a problem with keeping my mouth shut.'

Gleeson smiled and drank some more. He liked

the fact that this guy was so easily wound up. He much preferred dealing with people he could boss around. Guys like Hewitt that had some sort of special brief from Corell and acted almost like his boss, he found hard to cope with. But with the Monroes of the world he could act superior. He said, 'The people who gave me this project are very serious about confidentialism.'

Monroe knitted his brows in puzzlement at the word. Gleeson continued, 'They are men that secrecy and loyalty mean a lot to.' Gleeson loved to hint about IRA connections; his accent was a bonus for this sort of stuff.

'Is that a threat?' Monroe asked.

'Not at all. I just want to make sure you know what the, eh, whole package is.'

'Well, I told you, I don't have a problem with it!' His voice was raised.

Gleeson looked around. They were alone in the bar. 'Keep the head, son, and I'll buy ye a hat.'

Monroe's ice-blue eyes glinted with anger and he lifted a glass and drank some orange juice, put it back down and folded his arms.

Gleeson lit a cigarette and drank some whisky. 'Now,' he said, 'this is the deal. You know the racehorses you get to take for slaughter?'

'Uh-uh.'

'Well I want you to take a little detour on the way to the slaughterhouse and let a friend of mine borrow them for a day.'

'Borrow?'

'Before you shoot them.'

'You're kidding!'

'Now why would I be flyin' from Dublin, payin'

71

all that money in air fares to sit here kiddin' with you?'

Arms still folded, Monroe shook his head slowly. 'Where does your friend live?' he asked.

'Near Lambourn.'

'Whereabouts?'

'Are you interested?'

'What's the money like?'

'Two hundred and fifty pounds a horse, minimum.'

Monroe sat forward. 'How many horses?'

'As many as you can get – but they need to be racehorses and if you can get a good one the money goes up.'

'What does he want to do with them?'

Gleeson slugged from the whisky glass then smiled. 'He's gonna tie his washing between two of them and make them run round the garden till it's dry.'

Monroe stared sullenly at him.

Gleeson said, 'It doesn't matter to you what he does with them, does it? You drop them off, then pick them up a few hours later, collect your money then go and do your job.'

Monroe stared at him for a while then said, 'OK. I'll do a couple, see how it goes. Who pays me?'

'My friend does.'

'Where do I take them to?'

'We'll drive up there and I'll show you. It's a hard place to find.'

'When do I start?'

'Yesterday.'

'We'd better move then.' He got up. Gleeson

finished both drinks. Monroe jangled his car keys as he watched Gleeson drain the glasses. 'I think I'll drive, eh?'

Gleeson smiled at his sarcasm. 'Sure. So long as you can bring me back.'

Monroe was walking by now. They got outside and he said to Gleeson, 'If something happens and your scam goes tits up, I'll deny I had anything to do with it.'

'Listen, son, if anything happens you will keep your mouth completely shut. I don't exist. Neither does the guy I'm taking you to meet. Understand?' Monroe scowled and turned away towards the car.

Passing through Lambourn village Monroe said, 'Where did you get my name and number?'

'A friend of mine in Ireland. Said he thought you might be up for it.'

'What's his name?'

'It doesn't matter. You're here now so he was right, wasn't he?'

As they turned along the track leading to the house on the hill, Monroe said, 'I know this place. A guy called Kennedy used to train here. Went bust and did a moonlight about three years ago.'

'Is that so?' Gleeson asked in an uninterested voice as he looked out of the window at the thick woods bordering the narrow track on both sides.

Monroe said, 'How long's your man been here?'

'The less you know, the better for you, son. I just want you to meet Hewitt so you know where you're going and who's paying you.'

73

They trundled towards the big gates in silence, Monroe's jaw set hard and his eyes glinting with anger. He didn't like the way Gleeson spoke to him. As he braked to a halt, he noticed the closed-circuit camera mounted high on the black gatepost turn towards the car. 'Is that attached to a recorder?' he asked.

Gleeson didn't know but wouldn't admit that. 'I told you, the less you know the better. If you want to ask questions, take your nice looks and go and get a job on a quiz show.'

Monroe pulled the handbrake up and turned to Gleeson. 'Listen, mate, two hundred and fifty pounds a horse isn't a lot of money and you want me to risk my job for it. I'm not bringing a horsebox up here every couple of days for it to be caught on tape when I don't know what's happening at this place or where the tape's going.'

Gleeson smiled at him patronizingly. 'Stop worrying, son. If you don't want the job just tell me now before I ring the bell. You can head back to the slaughterhouse and keep shooting cows for two hundred and fifty pounds a week if you want. Four horses a week for here makes a grand.'

Monroe looked away and revved the engine hard. Gleeson said, 'Is that a yes or a no?'

'I told you in the hotel, I'll try a couple. If I don't like it after that I won't do anymore.'

'Stop whingeing, then. Let's go in and see Mr Hewitt.'

As he drove Gleeson back to his hotel after meeting Hewitt, Monroe wondered what the guy was doing up there, why he wanted the horses.

He wasn't a horseman, Monroe would bet on that. His hands were too soft. Monroe noticed it when he shook hands. Hewitt had had a pen and little notepad in his top shirt pocket and there had been a white garment lying across the arm of the chair in that room they'd been in. He'd thought it was a dressing-gown at first but it had been more like a hospital gown or a lab coat. Still, he seemed much more civilized than Gleeson, had better manners. Monroe glanced at him as he pulled up outside the Chequers and decided that a chimp had better manners than the Irishman so he probably wasn't paying Hewitt any compliments.

Gleeson got out then stooped and looked into the car at Monroe. 'Thanks. I'll say farewell. There'll not be any need for us to meet again unless you decide you're going to be a naughty boy.'

'Yeah, if I do you'll be the first to know, Mr Gleeson.'

'You're right. I will be,' he said, trying to look stern and dangerous. Monroe smiled dismissively, shook his head and drove away as the Irishman slammed the door.

Gerry Monroe was one of those rare people with a natural affinity for horses, especially thoroughbreds. Horses did things willingly for Monroe that they'd only do for others under duress. Horses would even run their hearts out for him and that facet alone would have made him a great jockey, which was what he'd wanted to be. But his personal tragedy was that he was too

75

heavy to ride on the flat and he'd found out very quickly in his brief career as a jump jockey that he didn't have the nerve for it. As much as he trusted his own ability, however much his mount would give in effort, Monroe was terrified at the prospect of attacking those big black fences on half a ton of galloping muscle and bone surrounded by others, all travelling at thirty miles an hour, being squeezed up, jostled, forced into errors that might see him crashing to the ground.

During the twenty-seven races he rode in before retiring, Monroe could picture nothing but severed spinal cords, caved-in skulls, hospital beds, wheelchairs and coffins.

He quit at the age of twenty-three, staging a very soft-looking fall in muddy ground at Hereford on a gloomy November afternoon. He claimed the fall had damaged his back so badly that he'd never be able to ride again. For more than two years he'd taken his regular payment from the Injured Jockeys Fund, knowing it wasn't merited, knowing he was stealing it. Then they'd stopped paying him after a specialist could find nothing physically wrong. Embittered, Monroe had found a job.

He still worked with horses. Used his special affinity now in other ways to calm them, make them trust him, even as he placed the muzzle on their heads and squeezed the trigger.

He parked the red Passat outside his council house on the western edge of the village and went inside. He was thinking about Hewitt and Gleeson. There was a lot of money involved in what these guys were doing. Had to be to take

76

that big place on the hill, install cameras, bring dickheads like Gleeson from Ireland and pay him two hundred and fifty pounds a time to get their hands on a racehorse for a few hours.

Monroe filled the kettle in the small kitchen, went to the bookcase by his chair and pulled out a thick softback with a picture of the Kray twins on the front. He liked to read about crime and criminals, had fancied himself to have the brain for it and he'd dabbled in a few dodgy deals. He'd set fire to a stable once to help the trainer collect a big insurance payout, so he supposed he was a criminal really, but anything he'd done had been like what he was doing this time, working for somebody. As the kettle boiled he stared through the steamed-up window; the thought that idiots like Gleeson could be pretty high up in whatever organization he was involved with bolstered his confidence that he himself could, one day, make some very serious money.

12

While his father had been in England for a few days, Sean Gleeson had tried to clean the flat. He'd bribed his mates to help him but had to throw them out after an hour because of their carry-on and messing around with the washing-up liquid and the mop and pail. Now the floor was soaked. They'd been slagging him off too when they'd found his da's dirty underpants and the bits of mouldy food and empty bottles and cans. And Barry McDonald had held his nose and said 'Dis place feckin' stinks!' and the others had laughed at what he'd said and the way he sounded and they'd all started saying it and holding their noses.

Sean looked around him. The place did stink. It had stunk even when his mother was here to clean it. The whole block stank, he thought. The living-room light was the only bulb that still worked. He supposed he'd need to buy some for the other rooms for his father wouldn't spend his money on anything for the flat. Sean knew he hadn't exactly been brilliant himself at keeping the place clean. He'd made the best of the fact that his ma hadn't been here to nag him about tidying his room and putting lids back on bottles and clearing up after him.

But it was getting beyond a joke now, and his da was getting mad because the place was like this and she wasn't here to clean it. When he was drunk he kept saying he'd go and find her and drag her back by the hair. Sean had seen her dragged by the hair before and he knew it was best to try and keep him from going to look for her.

Sean found a bin bag and started shovelling the rubbish into it. His mates had piled it up against the wall just inside the main door. He finished this then looked at the mound of dirty underwear and socks. The washing machine was broken and there was no way he was going to do these by hand or risk the shame of taking them down the laundrette. Hooking each with the corner of the shovel he dropped them into the bin bag.

It was dark outside. He checked the time. His father was definitely due home today but he knew he had a few hours yet for the pubs weren't shut. He dragged his bin bag to the kitchen, switched off the light in the living-room and climbed on a chair to clutch the bulb in the sleeve of his sweatshirt and transfer it to the kitchen.

Close to midnight Sean finally finished. He stood in the centre of the living-room, then moved to make a final adjustment to the one easy chair they had, its cotton covering now shiny with grime so it looked more like old canvas. Sean smiled and shook his head, held his nose and said aloud, 'It might look better but it still feckin' stinks!' and he went into his bedroom and reached under the bed to pull out the last wads of hay from the bale he'd been given by the coalman for helping drive the horse and cart.

As he made his way downstairs, he heard his father coming up, recognized the tuneless singing and the way he burped after each hiccup. Sean raced back up and climbed a flight beyond their door. He knew that if he was there when his da got in he'd just force him to make spaghetti on toast for him and then he'd slop half of it on the carpet. If he left him to his own devices he'd fall asleep in the chair in five minutes. When his father was safely inside he crept back downstairs with the hay.

In the square of tarmac in the centre of St Joseph's Mansions that had once been a play-ground, was Sean's iron-grey pony, Pegasus (the name suited Sean's sense of romance and destiny; the ponies belonging to his mates had names like Corky and Charlie, Kim and Prince). He pricked his ears at the sound and smell of his owner and whinnied lightly as Sean approached saying, 'Hey, no noise after eleven! That's the rule. Ye'll get us thrown out of this fine accommodation so ye will.' Pegasus was tethered to the rusty railings. On his back was a rug that deserved the name as it was made out of an old carpet and tied round his middle with four tatty elastic snake belts linked together.

The pony butted him, trying to get at the hay. He pulled a handful from the wad. 'Hey, where's yer table manners?'

He stood close to Pegasus, comforted by his munching and warmed by his body on this cold February night. Scratching the grey neck lightly he said, 'Big race on Saturday, Peg, chance to make a proper name for ourselves.' He stared at the clear starry sky then put his hands under the pony's chewing jaw and tried to force its head up. 'Look Peg, stars, that's where we're heading.' The pony butted him again, pulling free from his grip. Stepping back he put his hands on his hips and said sternly, 'Pegasus, you have no bleedin' sense of ambition whatsoever.'

Back upstairs, he went inside quietly but could hear the snores as soon as he opened the door. He tiptoed into the living-room and found his father in his usual position half-sprawled in the chair, mouth open, dead to the world. As ever his jacket lay on the floor and his trousers were open at the waist. Sean scooped up the jacket and rifled the pockets. It was the only way to get any money out of him. He reached in, felt some paper and, as he pulled it out, he heard his father grunt and move. Shoving the paper in his pocket he dropped the jacket and ran to his bedroom. He locked the door. When he felt for the paper he'd just stolen he realized it wasn't a banknote. He looked at it – some directions and a telephone number. He looked towards the room his father was in and said, 'You old bollix!' and threw the paper on top of the battered chest of drawers.

Before getting into bed, he opened his school notebook and wrote a letter to his mother. It was hard to keep up his promise of writing every week, especially when you weren't really able to tell the truth about how things were. It was hard too, to remember to call at Auntie Phoebe's regularly to get the letters his mother had sent. But it was good to read that she was doing fine and working in a big hotel in London, though she'd been careful not to write down the name of it in case his father found the letter or battered the information out of him.

He paused and chewed his pen, trying to think of nice things to say and wondered if his ma did the same, wondered if she was really happy. He only managed a page. He folded it and raised his eyes to the ceiling as he pictured Auntie Phoebe saying what she always said: 'That's about four hundred envelopes you owe me, Sean Gleeson, and about a hundred pounds' worth of stamps!' The piece of paper he'd taken from his father's pocket lay beside him. He noticed the word Fax on the top of it and he wished he had a fax machine so he wouldn't have to go to Auntie Phoebe's and borrow envelopes and stamps any more.

13

After three months living together at her house, Frankie and Kathy were married at Cheltenham racecourse. The reception for a hundred guests was held on the top floor of the grandstand, in the glass-fronted restaurant where they could see in the distance the spot where they'd first met. Frankie's wedding gift to his wife was a miniature replica of the third-last fence made with black birch cut from the fence itself and mounted in a deep frame of oak. She gave him a framed gift, too; the shoes they'd worn on their walks in the months after they'd met. His old, crepe-soled brown ones and her tan shoes with the leather laces which had now been tied to Frankie's laces and mounted in a wood and glass case with the gold-plated inscription, 'Frankie and Kathy, 100 miles of walks 'n' talks'. She gave him a new pair of shoes too, in the softest nubuck leather. She'd had them made for him in Italy.

Her secret present to them both was a thatched cottage in Winterfold Woods in Surrey. They'd happened on the cottage when out driving one day and Frankie had taken a wrong turn. They'd both thought it beautiful and Kathy had noted the number on the For Sale board. She'd made arrangements with friends to move all their stuff while she and Frankie were away. Although he wouldn't know it till she took the 'wrong' route on their way back from the airport after the honeymoon, this was where they were going to start their marriage.

The wedding guests were all Kathy's friends. Frankie's sister Theresa had written saying that their mother had warned the whole family that anyone attending the wedding would be disowned by her, left out of her will and damned to hell for eternity. Then Theresa said she didn't care and would do everything she could to be there. But on the day she didn't make it and Frankie sat at the raised table staring at a gathering of strangers. He'd met maybe a dozen or so in the preceding months, and of those he could recall only three or four names. His ordination, the only other major ceremony he'd been involved in, came to his mind; he couldn't think of a face in the front rows of the cathedral that he hadn't known. But it was a brief sadness on a day that made his heart glad.

They'd had a wonderful three months really getting to know each other and now they were back where they'd first met and when they left the racecourse this time it would be hand-in-hand, never to be parted again. They'd head into the future relishing the promises it held. Apart from the joy of being together every day, Frankie felt he had a real contribution to make to the partnership.

He was now officially employed as Kathy's

agent and had established a good relationship with a number of the editors she worked for. He'd also negotiated sponsors for her travels in the shape of a major airline and an international hotel chain. At the start, Frankie had lacked confidence in himself and was almost afraid of calling up these experienced business people to try to arrange deals. But he'd found most of them behaved like perfectly ordinary, friendly people and not at all like the hard-edged tyrants he'd imagined they might be. Kathy's name, of course, opened many doors.

Their honeymoon was to last three months. During the first year they'd known each other, when Frankie had been battling his own demons and Kathy had been simply waiting in hope and getting on with her life, she had promised herself that if they ever were to marry, she'd take Frankie to all the wonderful places she'd been to. She dreamed of a honeymoon moving from place to place, at their leisure, seeing and doing everything together. For Frankie it would be a first; for Kathy, a chance to do it as a tourist, to relax rather than train and practise and write every night.

During the final three months of Frankie's priesthood she had spent many hours entering routes, flight times, possible hotel bookings, car and equipment hire details and other planning factors into her laptop computer. Not knowing at that point when they'd be married, she'd input data for the whole of that year. The menu of possibilities became so complicated that she bought special project-planning software to handle all the permutations.

The investment paid off and they wandered the globe for twelve weeks, climbing in the foothills of the Himalayas, parascending in Jamaica, rounding up cattle in Montana, diving in the Seychelles, sailing a yacht round the Western Isles of Scotland, travelling in a camel train in the Kalahari desert, white-water rafting on the Amazon, driving a husky team in Alaska, abseiling in the Grand Canyon...

They spent the final week of their honeymoon trekking in a wilderness area of Yosemite National Park, camping out at night, tying their food in specially made bags and suspending them in trees well away from their camp to deter wild bears, bathing naked in the rivers in the morning sun, cooking bacon and eggs for breakfast that seemed to taste better than any food either of them had ever eaten. During that week they saw no other human being and they became creatures of the earth, inseparable in their own minds from the birds and the animals, the trees and flowers, the rivers and mountains they were living with. Their lovemaking, naked in the open on sweet grass, warm sandy riverbanks, the soft moss of the forest floor where the sun through the trees dappled their moving bodies, strengthened this union they felt with nature. Since meeting, each had felt they had found a part of themselves that had been missing. They knew they were incomplete without each other. They fitted neatly together to make the whole being that was them, and their lovemaking sealed the bond, fused them with its power and intensity.

On the final night, they went again to the riverbank a hundred metres from their camp and lay on their backs in the sand, holding hands and marvelling at the stars gleaming like new in the vastness of the blue-black dome. They breathed slowly, in the same rhythm. Frankie squeezed Kathy's hand and said, 'You know, it's been easier to understand the glory of God here than in a thousand consecrations standing at an altar.' She squeezed his hand in reply and he knew that meant she agreed with him.

Raising himself on his elbow he gently stroked a strand of hair away from her eye. He said, 'I've learned more about myself and my feelings ... who I am, you know, in these past few months than I have in my whole life.' He felt awkward then with what he'd said. 'Does that sound all sort of hippyish and half-baked?'

Shaking her head, she looked at him with that candid intensity he loved. 'No, it doesn't. I'm glad you can tell me how you feel. I'm glad you feel it.'

'I am too.' He gazed at her. The natural tan her skin always carried had deepened, contrasting startlingly with the whites of her eyes, which sparkled with wellbeing. 'You're very beautiful,' he said. 'I love you.'

On the flight home, they discussed future projects. Frankie made a list of the things Kathy had already done and written about, pencilling tiny doodles against each as they both suggested new ideas. Frankie seemed enthusiastic and Kathy played along. She thought it best not to mention that she didn't want to go on with her career too much longer. She wanted to have a baby. The growing urge over the past few weeks to get pregnant had surprised her with its force. The unspoken plan had been to wait a couple of years but Kathy was now thinking that one year would be long enough. But she knew how much Frankie was enjoying his role in the partnership; she needed to wait for the best opportunity to start discussing her retirement with him. Here, halfway across the Atlantic, his mind obviously spinning with ideas and hopes, wasn't the best time.

She looked at his list. He said, 'What do you think?'

'Know what I'd really like to do? I'd like to ride in a race again.'

'Would you?'

'Win a race. I'd like to win one. Although I'd settle for completing the course this time.'

Frankie thought for a while then said, 'D'ye think we'd sell the idea again? You've already done it once.'

Playfully, she nudged his elbow. 'We could do it for fun this time.'

He smiled. 'You really want to?'

'I do.'

He closed his notepad with an air of decisiveness. 'Let's do it!'

14

Sean Gleeson loved that Saturday morning feeling of not knowing what the day held, what adventure was laid out on that highway from dawn till dusk. Although today he knew exactly what the afternoon held, something he loved even more than Saturdays; pony racing.

Sean had raced Pegasus against other kids and their ponies whenever he got the chance. Sometimes they'd race along dual carriageways just after dawn on Saturdays or Sundays. Occasionally they'd stage races in the streets of the city's deprived areas. Wild-eyed kids, some as young as nine, riding and roaring like Cossacks on the backs of piebalds and skewbalds, bays and greys, galloping along past cars and bus stops, shops and houses, the click-clacking of the hooves bouncing echoes among the blocks of flats, drawing the dwellers to their windows to scream abuse or encouragement, to see some ponies slip and slide and fall, rolling their tiny jockeys along the road to collect high-speed cuts and grazes and the occasional broken bone.

People began betting on the outcome of these unofficial races. With money at stake, it was inevitable that one man would try to get an advantage over his fellows and some began helping with the training of the ponies. Boys were watched closely to see who had the gifts of balance and good hands, rhythm, calmness and a spark of fearlessness – boys who'd have the making of a proper jockey. And of the hundreds riding their street ponies, Sean Gleeson was recognized by the shrewd punters as being among the top handful. He wanted, some time far in the future, to be champion jockey – of Ireland and of England, although he'd decided he'd settle for one or the other.

And today he was to ride in his biggest race so far; down on the beach at Laytown. Mr Patrick Cosgrave, no less, a fine trainer of ponies, had booked him to come and have his first ride in this class of event, way above anything he'd ridden in before. Cosgrave had said he'd have proper breeches and boots and colours for Sean, and the thought of it all made the world sparkle brighter than it ever had on any Saturday morning of the six hundred and ninety Saturdays Sean reckoned he'd been alive. Sean made his way on to Summerhill Parade to wait for Cosgrave's car.

In loose silks of lemon and cerise, Sean sat on the back of a little bay pony called Shelley's Shebeen and circled quietly with the other runners for the third race at Laytown, where the only grass in sight grew in a few tufts on the dunes. Laytown races took place on the beach and the most crucial aspect of organizing the meeting was ensuring the times coincided with the ebb tide.

Official, proper horseracing at Laytown was a summer sport. The trainer who'd booked Sean, Cosgrave, had arranged this special racemeeting for ponies only. He'd paid for vets and a doctor to be in attendance and had marketed the day much better than horseracing officials sold their days. Thousands turned up. For many it was their first-ever racemeeting and some regretted not dressing warmly enough as they shivered in the cold wind coming off the sea and swarmed into the packed beer tents for shelter and hot Jameson's whiskeys.

Sean felt the wind on his face and tasted the salt spray. The ponies tasted it too, champing away, bridles clinking over searching tongues.

He wished his father was there to see him and be proud of him. His da loved the horses but Sean had been too nervous to tell him about today. Besides, he hadn't been properly sober for weeks so Sean doubted he'd have remembered to come anyway, even if he'd told him.

He looked around at the seven other runners, became aware of the cries of the bookies and listened for the price of his own horse; she was third favourite at four to one. He'd heard talk that Cosgrave had backed her to win quite a lot of money, but the trainer had said nothing about it, and Sean thought it was good of him not to put pressure on.

Sean watched the starter as he mounted the steps. He forgot his nerves now as he pulled the pony into line with the others at the tape. The starter raised his red flag. Sean realized too late that he'd forgotten to pull down his goggles. The flying sand would blind him but if he let go the reins now to try to do it he might miss the break and get the pony beaten at the start.

As the flag dropped and the crowd roared, he

decided there was only one thing for it and kicked the little pony straight into the lead. That was the opposite of what the trainer had told him to do and Sean knew Mr Cosgrave would be going off his head watching this; but he needed to keep from getting sand kicked in his eyes and this was the only way.

The race was over six furlongs and he drove the filly along at a steady gallop at a speed he judged she could just stay in front, then perhaps she could quicken by ten per cent or so in the last furlong to hold them off. Sean concentrated on pumping rhythmically with hands and heels and he couldn't stop himself smiling. On the outside edges of his conscious mind he was vaguely aware of the commentary over the PA and of the blur of changing colours as he raced past the crowds on the dunes, but he felt completely at one with this speeding pony and it was the best feeling he'd ever known. He felt invincible and something told him not to wait for the last furlong but to crank up the pony's speed gradually till she reached her limit. The filly seemed to sense the very thought in him and she quickened slightly, then ten strides later she did it again, then again and yet once more. And it was doing what Sean knew it would to the others. He'd stolen a march at the start and his rivals thought he'd ease her a bit in the middle and then try to wind her up again. And that's where they thought they'd catch him. But they never got the chance, for Sean's tactic of quickening just a little bit but often meant they could never really get their ponies back on the bridle. They were unable to let their mounts draw a good breath under them to prepare for the finish.

Sean and Shelley's Shebeen won their first-ever race together. Cosgrave threw his hat in the air, almost hitting a big herring gull. The crowds were glad, for the filly had been well-enough backed. And Sean, laughing with nerves and delight and wonderment at this feeling of triumph that he'd never known rode the filly at a walk into the little makeshift winners' enclosure and everyone clapped and cheered. Clapped and cheered Sean Gleeson, making the first step on the ladder of his dreams feel like the top step.

15

On that Saturday afternoon, at around the same time as Sean was steering Shelley's Shebeen across the winning line, Kathy Houlihan, aboard the big bay gelding, Sauceboat, was being led by her lad around the paddock at Stratford in the English Midlands. Frankie walked quickly alongside. The horse was jogging, zig-zagging on the strip of tarmac, ducking his head then raising it quickly, almost jerking the reins from the lad's hand.

'God, he's on his toes!' Kathy said, adjusting her stirrup leathers. 'I think my nerves are getting to him.'

'Mine too,' Frankie said, having to break into a jog himself at times to stay at the horse's side.

'He's like a boxer before a fight, isn't he? He's bobbing and weaving like Tyson!'

Kathy smiled at that and said, 'Hey, who's the writer here, me or you?' Sauceboat bucked, throwing her forward, making her shout, 'Whoa!' After falling off Zuiderzie at Cheltenham, she didn't want to suffer the indignity of landing on the ground before they'd even left the paddock. Sauceboat's trainer, Miles Henry, hurried across to take the rein on the opposite side from the lad who smiled at him in relief.

The trainer said, 'Not on his best behaviour, I'm afraid. It's not like the old bugger. He usually wanders round half-asleep.'

'He does, doesn't he?' Kathy said as she settled back in the saddle, conscious that the racegoers surrounding the paddock were watching, waiting for the only woman rider to be dumped on her bottom. She took a tighter hold on the rubber-clad reins, resisting the urge to clutch at Sauceboat's mane, too. She had hoped to ride Zuiderzie again but the horse had been moved from Miles to another trainer. Miles had recommended Sauceboat as 'the ideal horse for you to ride over hurdles'. She knew he was just too kind to speak the truth; 'he's a quiet old plodder who won't exhaust you and make you fall off as Zuiderzie did'.

And he'd felt safe and comfortable these past couple of months or so when she'd ridden him out at least three times a week. This was by far the most active she'd seen him and she began to think that he might just have a better chance than his trainer and the bookies thought. Sauceboat

93

had been placed four times but had never won. He was an outsider at 16/1 but as Miles led her out on to the track and released the reins, she felt raw power as Sauceboat stretched his neck and launched into a gallop towards the start. Frankie's cry of 'Good luck!' sounded faint as she accelerated away. From behind, he and Miles watched her shoulders and arms swing from side to side as she wrestled the straining animal for control.

Frankie, worried, glanced across at Miles. They'd come to know each other well in the run-up to this race. The trainer smiled and reached to put an arm around his shoulder. 'She'll be fine, Frankie. The fizz will go out of him before he gets to the start. Let's go and watch.'

They went into the stand and raised their binoculars.

Sauceboat was still on his toes at the start as he circled with the other fifteen runners. Miles had told Kathy the horse would settle himself naturally towards the rear of the field once the race started. 'Try and make progress as you come out of the back straight for the last time. You'll have to give him a smack or two and he some-times responds if you can lean close to his ear and shout something.' Kathy had said the only thing she'd be likely to shout was 'Help!'

Sauceboat pricked his ears as he heard the starter climbing the rostrum and he pulled hard to get to the lowered tape.

'Line up, jockeys!' commanded the starter. The horses were seasoned handicappers and they came slowly but readily into line. 'Right!' shouted

94

the starter and pressed the lever to raise the tape. Within twenty strides, Kathy found herself in the lead. Hauling at the reins, she tried to settle Sauceboat as they approached the first but he was ignoring her. Head down, neck outstretched, he skipped lightly over the hurdle and resumed his relentless gallop. Kathy glanced behind. They were already ten lengths clear of the others and she knew she was going far too fast. No way could Sauceboat keep up this pace. But there was no way, either, that she could hold him. She decided quickly to stop sawing at his mouth with the reins. It was best, she thought, to try to relax, try to look as stylish as possible for as long as he was in the lead – which, she was confident, wouldn't be for much longer.

But a circuit later he was still well clear. With just two to jump, nobody was making any headway. In the stands, Frankie and Miles looked at each other in puzzled, happy wonderment. As they approached the last hurdle, Sauceboat was twenty lengths ahead and seemed, if anything, to be accelerating again. Frankie started shouting and jumping up and down and when the pair cleared the last safely he threw his arms around the trainer and they both started bouncing on their toes.

Sauceboat galloped past the winning post carrying a bemused Kathy, whose dazed smile began to fade quickly as she realized the sweat and foam-streaked bay still wasn't stopping. Standing in her stirrups and leaning back she pulled as hard as she could but it didn't slow him. She pictured herself, in what should have been a moment of glory, being carted around for another couple of circuits until this brute finally became tired of galloping. Approaching the top bend, she transferred her left hand to the right rein, hauling on it with both hands to try and turn him towards the white plastic rail in the hope it would act as a barrier.

Sauceboat turned towards the rail but didn't slow. He crashed through it, sending white shards like bullets into the grass. There was another rail. He went through that too, still galloping head-long. Kathy found herself laughing nervously, hands still on the right rein, still hoping he would turn, slow down. Her thighs and forearms were burning, shoulders aching, fingers weakening quickly. There were some trees ahead. That would stop him, surely. He seemed to be heading for them, a row of elms, autumn leaves drifting from the branches in languorous slow motion that seemed to mock Kathy's predicament on this mellow afternoon. She thought of baling out, taking her chances in a certain tumble at thirty miles an hour before he reached the trees. But the experience she'd gained in all the dangerous things she'd done kept her cool, persuaded her to play the percentages. She knew that only a blind animal would run into a treetrunk. He'd change direction or stop – had to. Her view between his pricked ears showed the thick tree on the extreme right of the row rising like a long gunsight. He was going straight at it. In the final few strides before impact she closed her eyes and Sauceboat wheeled violently right to pass the trunk. Kathy was thrown, her body whipping almost horizontally through the air the way it used to as a child when her father would swing her by the feet in the garden. The side of her head was the only part of her to hit the trunk. The sound of her helmet cracking coincided with the clean snapping sound as her vertebrae parted, breaking her neck, killing her outright.

16

The numbness held Frankie together till after the funeral. If he had any feeling at all it was that this was not happening to him. He was witnessing it from afar. He was an automation making arrangements for the burial of a young woman. A few small things were to stir him: seeing their wedding guests return in mourning clothes; picking up his sister Theresa's tearful message on his mobile saying that their mother had locked her in her room to stop her coming to him; finding unused wedding gifts stored in the cupboard under the stairs; and the grief of Kathy's adoptive parents when they'd come to see him on a dark day in Winterfold Cottage.

But there were no tears from him during those days. Anaesthetized by whatever self-protecting chemical his brain was producing, the only time he felt any strong emotion was when he opened the card from his mother, the message causing him to throw it across the room. He'd received over a hundred cards. The words of sadness and sympathy had begun rolling into one another until he came to his mother's. It said, *'I hope she's burning in hell.'*

The Stratford stewards had called an enquiry into the race that resulted in the death of Kathy Houlihan. The initial thoughts of the panel were that Mrs Houlihan's inexperience as a jockey had been a major factor in the 'tragic accident' although they decided to postpone any public announcement on this out of respect for the relatives of the deceased. Still, when the appropriate time had passed, the panel intended to recommend a review of Jockey Club rules in relation to riding permissions for such amateur or 'celebrity' jockeys.

Sauceboat had been caught by a stable lad and the horse had been dope-tested before being loaded into his horsebox for the journey home. Miles Henry, the trainer, had been so affected by Kathy's death that he had been unable to drive home. He was helped into the horsebox cab by his head lad and he travelled back in a stunned silence.

When the horsebox-driver pulled into the yard at Lambourn, he helped the trainer down and took him into the house before returning to unload the horses. When he lowered the ramp, the first thing he saw was the big brown face of Sauceboat. The horse was lathered in sweat and shaking, almost vibrating as though leaning against a pneumatic drill.

Hurrying up the ramp he saw that the horse was sweating so heavily he could see steady drips from the gelding's belly. He ran down the ramp and across the yard to the office. The vet's number was pinned on the wall above the phone.

By the time the vet, Peter Culling, reached the yard Sauceboat was in his stable, still sweat-soaked but heavily rugged to try and calm the shivers.

Culling shook his head and hurried into the box. Sauceboat's lad peeled the rugs off. Miles Henry had been alerted and stood anxiously inside the stable door. 'What is it, Peter?'

'God knows.' Culling opened his bag. He was a powerfully built man standing five-ten. His receding sandy hair looked even thinner under the single strip light.

When the trainer saw Culling's face he said, 'Peter, you look terrible, are you feeling all right?'

The vet looked away from him. 'It's been a long week, Miles. Late nights, early calls, you know the way it gets sometimes.' He bent to remove a thermometer from his bag.

Miles Henry said quietly, 'You know what happened with this horse at Stratford today?'

The vet nodded. 'I was there. Terrible. Worst thing I've ever seen on a racecourse.' His voice was shaky as he eased the thermometer into the horse's rectum.

The trainer sighed and said, 'Me too. When the shock wears off I'm dreading the guilt. Kathy had been training here for months. She'd only been married back in May...'

Miles Henry was waiting for Culling to make some consoling noises but as he raised his stethoscope he said, still not meeting the trainer's gaze, 'Can we drop the subject? I need to concentrate on trying to save this horse.' He spent almost ten minutes examining Sauceboat before turning to the anxious trainer. 'It's got to be something in his gut. He's in a lot of pain. I want to get him back to my place and put him out, have a proper look.'

'OK. OK, do that. I'll ring the owner. Don't do anything too expensive till I've rung the owner.'

'Well make it quick, Miles.' He turned to the lad. 'Can you help me get him back in the horsebox?' The dark-haired boy nodded, seriously worried about 'his' horse now.

Peter Culling had converted part of his barn into an equine operating theatre. Sauceboat's lad and the box-driver led the shivering horse into the white-walled semi-padded room as Culling came through an internal door leading from his office. 'I've called my assistants, they'll be here soon. Thanks for your help. I'll ring and let you know as soon as there's some news.'

Sauceboat's lad, no more than nineteen, stroked the horse's matted neck. 'I'd like to stay, sir, if you don't mind. I'll help.'

'I'm sorry, that won't be possible. It's outside the guidelines; I'm afraid. You'd be best back at the yard. I promise I'll call you very soon.' Culling looked exhausted. The boy handed him the headcollar lead and turned slowly away. The box-driver, a man in his sixties, put an arm around the lad's shoulders as they went out the door.

When Culling heard the horsebox pull away, he opened his bag again. Taking out a syringe and a small bottle of liquid he turned and injected

100

Sauceboat just under his windpipe. Within a minute the violent shivering eased. Soon it stopped completely. Culling led the horse out of the theatre and into a box in the adjoining part of the barn.

Stooped and almost dragging his feet he went back to his office and called Miles Henry. The line was engaged. Minutes later the trainer rang him. 'The owner says do whatever you have to and bugger the cost.'

'I'll try, Miles, but we might not save him whatever we do.'

'Mr Graham knows that. He'll stand the bill, don't worry.'

'OK, I'll get to it now. I'll ring as soon as I come out of theatre.'

Culling put the phone down. A drinks cabinet in the corner of his office held a decanter of cognac. The vet poured a small measure and sipped gently as he stared at the wall, his thoughts elsewhere. Returning to his desk he leafed through a notebook, then punched another number into the phone. It rang for some time before it was answered. Culling said, 'Gerry, I've got another one for you. Can you pick him up tomorrow?... Good.'

He hung up and left the office. Back in the silent house he went to the conservatory and sat staring desolately at the darkness outside. For almost two hours he barely moved; then he checked his watch and got to his feet as though the weight of Sauceboat himself lay on his shoulders. He made his way to the horse's box. Sauceboat was calm and still and his coat was drying. His eyes looked bright and when Culling swung a full haynet inside the box the horse began eating immediately. Culling filled his water bucket before returning to his office.

He dialled Miles Henry's number. Mrs Henry answered and Culling had to wait almost a minute before the trainer came to the phone.

Culling said gravely, 'Miles, I'm so sorry, we lost him on the operating table.'

17

At noon on Sunday Gerry Monroe stopped the horsebox outside the vet's place, jumped from the high cab and strode purposefully towards the barn door. Peter Culling had warned him that he wouldn't be at home but there was a combination lock on the barn door and Culling had given Monroe the numbers. He dialled them in and sprang the lock. A few minutes later he was leading Sauceboat out to the horsebox. The horse was perky and looked reasonably well considering what he'd been through. His coat was dry though the heavy sweating of yesterday meant it would take some energetic grooming to tidy him up.

Monroe loaded him without trouble, then went back and locked the barn door. The box he drove was an old wooden-sided one that rolled along the lanes of Lambourn swaying gently and labouring as it climbed out of the valley up the

B4001. Just before reaching the crest of the hill, Monroe wrestled the steering wheel round to turn the box along a track which ran parallel with the ridge a hundred yards or so above it.

Particular caution was needed here as potholes were scattered like craters on a shelled road and the springs and wooden slats of the box groaned and squealed each time a wheel dipped.

Approaching the end of the track Monroe saw that the big black gates to Hewitt's place had been opened as promised. As he came off the last easy curve through the gates Hewitt stood waiting. Monroe stopped and jumped out, giving his usual small wave as Hewitt raised his hand to acknowledge him. He led Sauceboat round the back of the big three-storey house aware that Hewitt was watching the horse walk, studying his action, looking at his conformation. This was the tenth horse Monroe had brought since Gleeson, the Irishman, had approached him. The first time he'd met Hewitt, Monroe had been convinced that he wasn't a horseman but he seemed to have been coping well whatever it was he was doing with these horses.

Monroe put Sauceboat in the end box and turned to see Hewitt walking slowly towards him, smiling, counting out banknotes. Monroe folded the wad and shoved it into the pocket of his jerkin knowing he didn't need to check it.

'Thanks. Six o'clock OK to call back?'

'That will be fine. And you haven't forgotten my requirement, Mr Monroe?'

Monroe was sick of hearing this line but tried not to show it. 'No, Mr Hewitt, I haven't. It's always at the front of my mind.'

'Do what you can.'

'Count on it.'

'Good. Come back around six. Just do your usual. You know where he'll be.'

'Fine, Mr Hewitt, no problem.'

He returned just after six cursing the driving, swirling rain that swept down the valley from the ridge, drenching him as he hurried to the back of the big house. Sauceboat was in the end box and followed him meekly when he tugged at the headcollar, dragging his hooves slightly as they all did when he came back for them.

The bay gelding was more lethargic than most of the others had been and Monroe took some time to get him up the ramp. When he unloaded him at the other end, at his place of full-time work, the horse seemed to have picked up slightly.

Monroe led him quietly through the doors into the dimly lit space with the white walls. Only one light burned in the building and that was inside this room. Monroe had to be ultra careful; if his employers ever found out he was moonlighting he'd be in trouble.

He was talking to Sauceboat now as he turned the horse to face the door he'd just come through. He let go the halter and slid the door closed. Then he took up the rope again and steadily wound it in loops around his left wrist. Talking in low tones, he reassured the big horse that everything was going to be fine. With his right hand he reached slowly behind him without looking and eased his bolt-action rifle off the hooks on the white wall.

Moving his face closer to Sauceboat's head he spoke softly, reaching in his pocket for a Polo mint and holding it at waist level. The trusting horse lowered his head to lick the mint from his palm. With his right hand Monroe swung the rifle dextrously till the muzzle rested in the centre of Sauceboat's forehead.

The horse stood calmly, crunching the mint, looking straight ahead, listening to the soft tones of this man who'd won his trust. Monroe said, 'Bye-bye big fella.' And he squeezed the trigger.

18

Frankie Houlihan got into the red Subaru estate car that had been a present from Kathy just after eleven on Thursday morning and drove down the rutted track away from the cottage. Rain fell softly. Every few seconds the wipers swished. Frankie was going racing for the first time since Kathy's death. Bobby Cranfield had talked him into it by way of several long phone calls.

Kathy had introduced Frankie to Bobby whom she'd met after contacting the Jockey Club to find out what she had to do to be able to ride in a race over jumps. Bobby was PR Director for the Jockey Club, a job he did for love as he had made over thirty million pounds from selling his international PR agency.

Bobby knew of Kathy's reputation as a journalist, knew that if she rode in a race and wrote about it hundreds of thousands of readers would learn a bit more about racing in the UK and might be tempted to get involved, so he sorted everything out for her with just a few phone calls. He had horses of his own with several trainers and the weekend after contacting him Kathy was in Miles Henry's yard, one of the top Lambourn stables, being legged up on to a quiet gelding (Frankie smiled as he recalled Kathy telling the story of Bobby's call to tell her they'd get her down to Lambourn and let her sit on an old schoolmaster to start with).

And that had been it. The beginning. Over two years ago. And six weeks back had been the end. A fall to start it and one to finish it. Frankie's skin prickled coldly at the thought as it always did. There was the sick sinking feeling in his gut too. A parishioner had once told him that if there was really a God he must have a bitch of a sense of humour. Frankie had considered it blasphemous but since Kathy's death he'd recalled it again and again. Six weeks without her. Long days and nights of trying to make sense of everything. Grief hadn't yet hit him, not properly, for there was something in him that refused to accept he'd never see her again.

He was heading for Wincanton in Somerset. Passing Stonehenge, Frankie thought how small it looked although it was a good way from the road. He and Kathy had passed it a few times and always promised to stop off on the next trip but they never had done. It looked ghostly now through the fine, misty rain.

Frankie climbed the grandstand stairs and knocked on the door of box number thirty-two, which had a plaque saying *Mr Bobby Cranfield.* He went in and was surprised to find only Bobby there and the lunch table set for two. The box could hold at least twenty people and there were usually more than that as Bobby loved to entertain. He sat in his wheelchair parallel to the glass front and the track beyond so his left side was towards Frankie. Bobby smiled warmly; 'Come in Frankie. You look wet.'

Frankie shook his hand as he removed his coat, which was covered with moisture as fine as though he'd been walking through thick fog. A waitress appeared, smiling as she took Frankie's coat and offered him a drink. Frankie asked for mineral water.

He sat down in the only empty chair. 'How are you Bobby? It's good to see you.'

'I'm as well as I've ever been, and even better now that I've got some decent company.' Cranfield's eyes shone with genuine pleasure at seeing Frankie.

As Cranfield's useless legs were beneath the white tablecloth, Frankie thought that nobody seeing just his upper half would know he was disabled. He looked fit and tanned and healthy with his thick, lead-grey hair. He was around fifty, Frankie knew, and he had a well-equipped gym and a pool at his big house in Oxfordshire and Frankie had seen him work out in both. His party trick was launching himself into the pool from his chair by arm strength alone; then he'd exercise by keeping himself afloat moving only

107

his upper half as his dead legs dangled below him.

Kathy had always seen Bobby as a living example of how she feared ending up. Every time they met, Frankie had seen a glint of terror in Kathy's eyes and when she'd learned that Bobby had been crippled in a fall from a racehorse yet had still gone ahead with her plan to ride at Cheltenham, Frankie thought it one of the most courageous things he'd ever known.

Frankie settled in the chair and silently counted the cutlery to gauge how long a lunch Bobby had planned. He was also wondering what was on the agenda with just the two of them there. He said to Bobby, 'My Holmesian powers of deduction tell me that the chef, at this moment, is not outside slaughtering a four-hundred-pound pig to make sure nobody goes hungry here.'

Cranfield smiled. 'If you didn't have that accent I'd still know you were Irish. Who else uses ten words when one will do?'

Now Frankie smiled. Cranfield said, 'You're dead right. Nobody else is coming. We have the box to ourselves. Even Caroline,' at which point the waitress stooped and put Frankie's mineral water on the table, 'has agreed to leave us alone once she's served the starter.'

'So the starter's joining us too. Who's gonna get the races off on time?'

'Very funny. I'm glad to see you're in good heart.'

'I'm doing fine,' Frankie said, wondering when Bobby was going to tell him why he'd asked him here.

'Managing to fill your days?'

Frankie nodded. 'I read. And walk a bit.'

There was a longish silence as they looked at each other, Cranfield with his kind smile and Frankie with the pain in his eyes still clear for all to see despite his affected jauntiness.

'Are you sleeping OK?' Cranfield asked.

'Not really, but self-pity never was the best sedative.'

'It's grief, Frankie, not self-pity. Perfectly understandable grieving. Don't give yourself a tough time over it.'

Frankie averted his eyes, sipped his drink. Cranfield said, 'Would it help to talk?'

'If I start I'll never stop.'

'I don't mind. That's what friends are for.'

'I'll take you up on it sometime, Bobby, but not now, if you don't mind.'

Cranfield reached across to grip Frankie's forearm. 'Of course not. Of course not! You know where I am when you do want to talk. Just give me a call.'

Frankie nodded. 'Thanks.'

Cranfield sipped white wine. Caroline brought two smoked salmon terrines then left again. Frankie said, 'I guess this has kinda messed up your timings, me not wanting to talk.' He looked at his watch.

'I mean there's a full afternoon's racing to get through and there's just me and you. And I'm not talking. And me the best talker too, by far, of the two of us. It has the makings of a peaceful afternoon, does it not?'

Cranfield smiled at his friend's sense of

109

humour. 'Oh, you'll talk all right, Frankie boy, maybe not about Kathy but when you hear what I've got to say, you'll talk!'

Frankie boy. It was the first time anyone but Kathy had called him that and he suddenly felt an unexpected and unreasonable stab of antagonism towards Bobby for saying it. But it passed in a moment as his curiosity took over. 'I'm listening,' he said.

Cranfield drank more wine then said, 'I want to ask a favour of you.'

'Uh-huh?' Frankie wondered what this multi-millionaire racehorse owner could want from him.

'I want you to help us out at the Jockey Club.' Frankie's dark eyebrows moved closer together as he frowned quizzically. 'Help you out at what?'

'In the security department.'

'Doing what and for how long?'

'Working as an intelligence officer, an investigator.'

Frankie smiled, a forkful of fish halfway to his mouth. 'You know, you should have waited a few seconds, Bobby. I always wanted to do what they do in the films when somebody's so surprised at something over dinner they splutter food everywhere.'

'See, my timing's good. I'd have been in the line of fire.'

Frankie smiled. 'Stop winding me up.' And he ate.

'I'm not, honestly. There's a long-standing vacancy. They've interviewed for it twice and can't get the right person. You'd be ideal.'

'And how do you figure that out?'

'Well you used to be a police chaplain at one time, didn't you?'

Frankie almost did splutter his food as he laughed. 'You're a case, Bobby. Now stop the kidding.'

'I'm not kidding. I remember Kathy telling me you spent some time as a chaplain to the Royal Ulster Constabulary.'

Frankie, his eyes still creased from his smile, looked at Bobby Cranfield and could tell he was quite serious. 'You're really not kidding, are you?'

'Really not. I think you'd do a great job for us.'

'The RUC chaplaincy was a joke. It was a politically motivated request to the archbishop in Dublin by a friend of his in Belfast who wanted a favour. The RUC has a tiny minority of Catholic members. My appointment was supposed to show that it was a cross-religious group. I ended up about as busy as a cloakroom attendant in a nudist camp.'

Bobby chuckled then said, 'But didn't you have training in police procedure as part of your chaplaincy, or whatever they call it?'

'I did, but only to help me understand the lives of these fellas. It was hardly MI6 school.'

'But you got the same training as a new police recruit would have?'

Frankie shrugged and put down his fork. 'Well, a sort of sawn-off version, I suppose.' Kathy was never far from his mind and she seemed suddenly to move in much closer. And he could hear her laugh and see her shake her head and

111

say to him, 'What a brilliant idea! What a great job! Go on, Frankie, take it, it'll be fun!'

Cranfield saw the change in his features. 'You're sort of warming to this now, ain't you, Frankie?'

Frankie nodded slowly, reluctant to let Kathy go, wishing Bobby would disappear for a few minutes. And Kathy said to him, 'And remember, you're used to getting confessions out of people.' Suddenly he felt a happiness, a peace he'd thought he'd never know again. That gag was typical of Kathy and he knew somehow that it hadn't formed in his own head. He knew she was back with him in everything but body. His eyes filled. He thought quickly of Bobby, not wanting to make him feel uncomfortable, but he found himself quelling the instinct to dab his eyes with his napkin before the tears flowed. They were tears of joy as much as anything and he wanted to feel their warmth on his cheeks.

Frankie drove away from Wincanton before the end of racing with an appointment in his diary to meet the Jockey Club's head of security in London the following evening. He pulled into the first layby, switched the engine off and sat staring at the darkening sky, willing Kathy to come back close to him the way she had done in box thirty-two. Willing it and wanting it almost like a drug. He concentrated, closed his eyes, recreated the conversation with Bobby in his mind, reached the same trigger point which had brought her to him. But she'd slipped back to the perimeter; he could see her there, waving reassuringly and he heard her say, 'Don't worry Frankie, I'll come

112

back when you need me most. I'll always be here with you, watching over you, loving you. But live your life. Live your life!'

'I don't want to,' he said quietly, his face contorted, his throat sore from the constriction of grief, from trying not to cry. And he tried to say 'not without you'. His lips formed the words but his throat choked them to silence. Kathy receded, faded, still waving. She didn't turn away, just faded. 'Come back, Kathy!' he managed to say although he felt his throat closing completely and the pain was intense. Then all the dams burst at once, convulsing his body as though the car had been seized by some earthquake and Frankie's throat finally opened and out came a sound, a cry, so primal, so vital that he would always remember it with wonder. It was a sound he could not have created and it finally uncorked the well. In the deepening rainy gloom Frankie writhed and wept and moaned, his limbs moving, out of control, hands trying to still his rolling head. It felt as though it went on for a long time and towards the end he began to feel himself emptying, draining of all emotion, of all movement and sound till he lay slumped in his seat like a boneless bag of flesh.

The ordeal exhausted him, purged him. Unable to move, he became aware of the deepest peace he had ever known. Peace beyond what he'd believed possible. Peace so complete that it crossed his mind that he might have died or was dying and that this was the out-of-body experience he'd heard tell of. His eyes closed, slowly, in the way of a toddler when sleep overcomes him while he's playing. Frankie was vaguely aware of his breathing, much slower and deeper than he'd ever known it. He slipped into a blessed sleep.

19

'How many criminals do you think are active, full-time, in racing?' asked Robert Archibald, head of the Jockey Club Security Department.

Frankie wondered if a precise figure existed, wondered if his answer would be noted and used against him if wrong. He'd spent half an hour with this fellow in his plush office with its chesterfield sofas and two-hundred-year-old pictures and he still couldn't figure quite where Archibald was coming from. He seemed a very nice man for somebody who headed a security department.

Frankie hadn't exactly expected a member of the SS but Archibald seemed to ask him questions as though he himself did not know the answers; as though Archibald were the applicant. Maybe it was his way of trying to be disarming.

He'd ask these strange questions or, even more disconcertingly for Frankie, he'd just make an odd statement and leave it hanging in the air. Things like 'Jockeys. Show me one and I'll show you a dozen ... fifty.' Then he'd clam up and stare at Frankie with those unusually dark, almost black eyes. Unblinking, concentrating and nodding slightly as though Frankie was already talking and he was trying to encourage him to open up even more. If Archibald's words ran to more than a sentence, Frankie noticed that he seemed to lapse into an almost Dickensian style of speech.

Frankie had been trying to box clever and be as vague as his interviewer in both answer and statement. This time he said, 'Well one's too many, that's what I say.'

'But if you had to put a number on it, what would it be?'

'Well, I think racing's pretty straight so it wouldn't be a big number.'

Archibald stared again, his eyes even wider and he nodded and stayed quiet till Frankie couldn't stand the silence any longer and blurted out, 'Twenty or so, I suppose.'

Archibald stopped nodding but his thin face gave nothing away. 'Would that it were so few,' he said. 'There'd be no need for us to be sitting here as the dusk falls on the streets of London. A vacancy in this department would not exist.'

Frankie endured another twenty minutes of this before stepping out into the twilight rain and heading for Marble Arch tube station. Archibald had left him bewildered. He felt he'd just spent an hour with a drunken *What's My Line* panel and he smiled dazedly and shook his head as he turned to go down Oxford Street.

The security chief hadn't let him know one way or another whether he'd passed. Had it been an interview at all? Bobby Cranfield had led him to believe the job was his. He was annoyed with himself for not taking time to make it clearer exactly what would happen next.

Afraid of getting lost or stuck in jams, Frankie had parked in south-west London and taken the forty-minute tube ride into the city. On the trip back he surveyed the mostly grim faces of his fellow-passengers and speculated on what troubles each had, tried to imagine himself inside the body of each. Wondered, as the train hurtled swaying through these airless tunnels, that if life-swaps were possible, how many of these would throw theirs in the ring and take a chance, unknown, on picking up one less worrisome than their own.

Would Frankie?

He thought not. If giving up the hurt he was feeling, the despair, meant erasing the memory of what he'd had with Kathy then he'd never surrender that at any price. The pain had eased immensely since that cathartic moment in the car, that opening of the floodgates of grief. There was a certainty in him now that Kathy would always be with him in more than just memory. The experience of her coming to him, speaking to him as though alive again had renewed Frankie. There was a bonus too; for all he had preached for so many years about everlasting life in death, he'd had nothing but his own faith to fuel the belief. Now he knew for sure that people lived on in God. In God or in their own loved ones. Not just as wishful figments for the bereaved, but as individual people again, living souls, personalities with warmth and love, real in all but flesh.

As Kathy had always done, he'd left a light on

in the cottage. The yellow glow from it seemed to rise and fall as though it were on a ship as the car bumped over the ruts and potholes in the track encircling the forest. There was an answerphone message from Bobby. 'Well done today, Frankie. Robert Archibald was most impressed. He said you seem the type to go to the very top in the Jockey Club Security Department. Give me a call.'

Frankie said to the empty room, 'The man really is barmy.'

Frankie spent the first two weeks in his new job learning about procedure. They teamed him up with Geoff Stonebanks, who'd been a racing intelligence officer for ten years. Jockey Club Security was responsible for providing stable guards at every racecourse to help prevent un-authorized access to stables. These guards were employed on a part-time basis. The team of intelligence officers, six of them including Frankie, were full-time employees.

Geoff Stonebanks was as competent and cynical as his colleagues. He was an ex-police-man who lived in Lambourn. He'd moved there when he got the Jockey Club job because he thought that living in the racing village, with his ear as close to the ground as it could possibly be, would prove an advantage. But he'd soon learned that the place seethed with rumour and counter-rumour about who was up to what. He'd long ago given up the notion that every stable lad was a potential mole of any real reliability.

The worthwhile informants ran to single

figures only, although Stonebanks had good relationships with all of them. When Stonebanks heard he was going to be 'inducting' Frankie Houlihan, he didn't relish the prospect. He thought even less of it when he heard of Frankie's background. The fact that he'd been a priest didn't trouble him; Stonebanks knew it took all sorts in this business. But when he was told of Kathy's death, he felt awkward about spending a couple of weeks with Frankie.

Stonebanks had a reputation as a good listener. But it was a skill he'd worked hard at and one he preferred to lock up in his briefcase at the end of his working day. He lived quietly with Jean, his wife of twenty years; they seldom socialized, and before he met Frankie, Stonebanks was worried that the ex-priest might want to extend their relationship beyond working hours. The man was due some sympathy, no doubt about that. But Stonebanks wanted to keep the relationship purely professional. So he felt some relief when a smiling Frankie Houlihan, dressed in a black suit and crisp white shirt, was introduced to him by Robert Archibald on the morning of the first Monday in November.

They shook hands and Stonebanks liked Frankie immediately for the openness of his face and the way he held himself when Stonebanks knew he must still be grieving, and nervous about the new job to boot. And he envied Frankie his comparative youth and slim, fit look. Stonebanks had been fighting a battle against overweight for years and found it hard to get clothes to hang properly on his sixteen-stone frame. He smiled and said, 'Welcome to the craziest goldfish bowl in the so-called leisure industry.'

Frankie returned the smile. 'And are we swimming or throwing in the food?'

Stonebanks admired his quick wit. 'Depends how clean the tank is. Mostly, we chase our own tails.'

20

Frankie's induction was to continue by way of his meeting each of the three investigators who were not London-based. He'd spent a day at Plumpton with Gordon Drewery, two days up north at Carlisle and Ayr with Jamie Robson and his final trip was to Warwick to meet Jack Webster who was responsible for the Midlands. On his way to the track on what was the coldest Saturday of the season so far, a coughing and spluttering Webster called him to say he was dying with a cold and was very sorry but he wouldn't be there. Frankie said, 'Don't worry, we can meet some other time. Is there anything I can do at Warwick to help you?'

'You can tell Julie on the bar in members' to bring me a hot toddy after racing.'

Frankie smiled. 'I'll pass on the message.'

Frankie had been racing mad for years and one of his ambitions had been to visit all fifty-nine British racecourses. He chalked up a new one with Warwick. This was his first visit and he thought it an attractive little course with a good atmosphere. As the first race-time came nearer and the crowds built steadily, Frankie wandered around, introduced himself to the stable guards and chatted a while with them, had a cup of tea and a sandwich in the members' bar and wondered which of the four serving girls was Julie if, indeed, she wasn't simply a figment of Jack Webster's imagination.

This was the first time since he started the new job that he'd been to a racecourse unaccompanied. He found himself seeing everything with new eyes compared with when he used to come racing as a spectator. Every huddled group in the bar was now made up of potential conspirators; stable lads leading their charges out of horseboxes all seemed shiftier than he could ever remember. Who was that prosperous-looking man speaking to Crosby Allen, the bookie? They looked up to no good.

Frankie thought about it as he sipped his tea and found himself smiling at his own ridiculous thoughts. Still, he supposed that every new employee in any business was mentally primed like this in the early weeks. He wondered how long it would take him to become as cynical as Stonebanks and the others. For a moment he forgot everything and considered with pleasure how he'd tell Kathy tonight about his silly suspicions. When the sadness hit him he didn't regret having the thought for the momentary comfort it had brought.

Kathy was never far from his mind. When

Frankie looked carefully through the Warwick racecard as he finished chewing his sandwich, his eye stopped at Zuiderzie, the horse Kathy had fallen from at Cheltenham the day he'd met her. The impact of seeing the name stunned him. He stared at it as though it were the only thing that existed. It had been more than two years since he'd seen the horse and many of the things that had happened since suddenly cascaded through his mind.

Miles Henry had called Frankie after Kathy's death and sent flowers and a card. But looking at the racecard Frankie remembered that Miles was no longer training Zuiderzie; nor was the horse owned any more by Bobby Cranfield. After falling with Kathy at Cheltenham, Zuiderzie had lost his confidence over fences and his next few runs had been over hurdles. Frankie noted that today's race was a handicap hurdle and that Zuiderzie was very low in the weights. The race-card form commentary told him that the horse hadn't won for more than three years. He was 33/1 in the betting forecast.

Come race-time, Frankie made his way to the paddock. There was Zuiderzie belying his eleven years and prancing round like a two-year-old constantly working the bit in his mouth and shaking his head till the metal jangled. He looked smart in his apparently new, dazzling scarlet rug with embroidered trainer's initials. Frankie leant over the rail as Zuiderzie danced past tugging at the reins held by a smiling young blonde girl whose scarlet fleece matched her charge's rug. 'Hello, you old rogue,' Frankie said. The horse's ears pricked and he turned his head slightly. Frankie smiled sadly.

As the bell went for the jockeys to mount, Frankie made his way back to the grandstand uncertain whether his heart felt heavy or light. He was glad of this tangible connection with Kathy. So much time since the funeral had been lived in his head; memories, emotions, regrets, fears. Nothing to grasp. Nothing solid to grapple with or embrace. Now here was the horse that had brought him together with this wonderful, beautiful woman. And he felt her near him, sensed her presence. Not as close as the first time but comforting nonetheless. He smiled.

The PA boomed out the message that they were off. Frankie Houlihan raised his binoculars and watched Zuiderzie lead all the way and win by fifteen lengths. When he lowered those binoculars, tears spilled from the small rubber eyecups and left stains on his white shirt.

Belinda Cassell had only been in racing two months and the seventeen-year-old was so thrilled with the victory of 'her' horse Zuiderzie that she'd hadn't shut up about it since rushing out madly to welcome the horse back in.

Belinda was his groom and she just knew that if she looked after another thousand horses in her career she'd never ever forget this beautiful chestnut gelding, her first winner. Willie Creaney, the box-driver, had been charmed by her reaction at first (he fancied her anyway) but her non-stop chirruping on the journey home was wearing him down and he was sympathizing in advance with whoever ended up as her husband.

Some racing people believe that a horse knows when it's won. In the back of the swaying box Zuiderzie didn't feel at all special. He was shivering and sweating heavily.

When they reached the yard and Willie Creaney pulled the ramp down he saw the horse and ran into the house to ring the vet. Peter Culling took the call on his mobile and told him urgently that he'd be there as soon as possible. Culling checked his watch and said to himself, 'Bang on time. Remarkable stuff. Remarkable.'

He smiled and accelerated towards Lambourn longing for a blue flashing light to stick out on his car roof.

For a horse who, like Sauceboat, had supposedly died on Peter Culling's operating table the previous night Zuiderzie was looking remarkably well when Gerry Monroe picked him up on Sunday morning.

The trip to Hewitt's place up the hill was getting so familiar now that Monroe was recognizing individual potholes in the road approaching the house. And there was Hewitt at the end of the drive as ever. Monroe was growing increasingly curious as to what the man was doing with these horses. The temptation to drive the box away after dropping Zuiderzie then creep back to the house on foot was strong. But Hewitt paid well and Monroe needed the money. If he was caught prowling around he might lose the 'contract' or get another visit from Gleeson.

Later, on the journey to the slaughterhouse

with the now drowsy animal, Monroe's mind went back to Hewitt's oft-repeated plea for a quality horse; he was thinking it was about time he did something about it. He didn't know what the quality was of the horses he'd already brought, didn't know their names. He'd just collected them through his normal contacts. Their names and racecourse abilities had been of no interest to him. He assumed that if any famous horse were to be put down it wouldn't be himself who'd be pulling the trigger. Anyway, he'd be sure to read about such casualties in the *Racing Post.*

Four of the horses he'd ferried up to the big house had come from Culling's place. The vet had made a point of not being there when Monroe called (it dawned on him now that it had always been a Sunday morning when he'd picked them up after being contacted by Culling on the previous evening) and the horses, unusually in his trade, had seemed perfectly sound, quite healthy. When he got home, Monroe logged on to the *Racing Post* site on his PC and started doing some research.

21

The bookie, Compton Breslin, was not cut out for rambling or any other country pursuit and the sight of his twenty-stone frame in wax jacket and plus-fours, leather walking boots polished to a shine, made Peter Culling snigger. The vet had insisted he'd only deal with Breslin on his terms and this was one of them; Breslin would never meet him in a public place or telephone him. After a coup they'd meet in these woods halfway between Lambourn and Newbury, walking casually towards each other and passing in silence if anyone else came into view.

The vet would always be there first and try to make his way up an incline to force the fat bookie to climb that final hundred yards. By the time Breslin reached him he'd be panting and sweating heavily. This Sunday afternoon was no different, and Culling hated him for the way he neglected himself, eating and drinking as though heart disease didn't exist. As though he thought you were here for ever and guaranteed good health.

At forty-three, Culling was convinced he himself would die soon. His father had been dead at forty-five, his paternal grandfather at forty-four. His maternal grandfather had died on the eve of his fiftieth birthday. Hearts. All of them from faulty, diseased hearts. The thought of his male ancestors being freely allowed to breed, to pass on these genetic timebombs, would often drive Culling into a terrible rage.

Why couldn't humans be under some control? Why couldn't it be like the world of the thoroughbred, where the constant quest in breeding was to eliminate imperfections? How could his father be so selfish as to sire children knowing his own father had died so young, knowing his own heart was nothing but a clutch of quickly decaying valves?

If Hitler had won the war, he would have weeded out these people and he, Peter Culling, forty-three years old and wifeless and childless because of his own commitment to stop this Culling line of useless men who could not keep their hearts beating past their mid-forties, would never have been born. How, wondered Culling, can God put a child on this earth to grow up relishing each day, loving the sunshine and the women and the good life? How could he give someone such a tremendous appetite and ecstatic enjoyment of the fine things and then make him face the fact that it was all going to be taken away at a ludicrously, ridiculously young age? What kind of God is that?

Well, Culling was going to try and defy God and beat his father and his grandfather and all the other weaklings in the family line. He was going to try to live again through cryogenic refrigeration. Culling's own medical background confronted him with the strong argument against the likely realization of such an ambition but his logic in pursuing it was that if it didn't work he'd be no worse off. On the positive side, he knew of the giant strides medicine had made in his own lifetime. It might take them a hundred years to bring him back but what was a century against eternity?

As soon as he had enough money he was going to America, to die in the hands of the Everlasting Life Company of Michigan whose technicians would take him, within a minute of his heart giving out, and place him in suspended animation; freeze him in a metal cylinder that would be temperature-controlled by computer for as long as it took for medical science to come up with a way to bring him back – and keep him back. Then he would live properly! Then he'd marry and start a new Culling strain, a strong line of sons who'd never have reason to curse their father the way he cursed his.

And here, arriving at the top of the hill, was this despicable animal who obviously did not give a toss about his heart or any other part of him. Especially his pride, if these stupid clothes were anything to go by. He knew Breslin dressed like a vaudeville clown on the racecourse, but he'd thought that part of his brash act to fleece punters. Here he was in civilization proper, dressed worse than that other ninny who was always on TV waving his arms around and yelling like a lunatic.

'Jesus, Peter, can't we meet at the bottom of a hill sometime? This is bloody killing me!'

Culling smiled. 'Better vantage point here, we can see if anyone's watching.'

'We're surrounded by bloody trees! How can anyone be watching?'

'Trees are easy to hide behind.'

Breslin hobbled towards a fallen log and almost collapsed on to it, red-faced and still breathing hard. Despite his constant fears, tests had shown Culling's heart to be perfectly healthy and he was fit and proud of it. He was older than the bookie too and he had to try hard not to show his contempt as he watched sweat drip from the fat man's brow on to the knee of his ridiculous blue tweed plus-fours. Breslin looked close to cardiac arrest and the vet chided himself; he knew he should be protecting this valuable source of income, not putting it at risk.

Culling scanned the trees while he waited for Breslin to recover. The woods seemed silent but for Breslin's breathing. No birds sang. The grey squirrels who sometimes hurtled around were nowhere to be seen, and the air was still and cool.

Breslin seemed better. He leant forward, elbows on his knees. 'That was a nice one yesterday. Extra special because some heavy hitters were in there backing the favourite.'

Culling stuffed his hands in the pockets of his thigh-length brown coat and turned to the bookie. 'So you'll be paying me a bit more?'

'I'll be paying you what we agreed, but I'm thinking hard about your other proposal.'

'Well the price has gone up.'

Breslin, annoyed, sat straighter. 'Since when?'

Culling smiled slyly, his inward-slanted teeth and narrowed eyes making him look wolfish. 'Since I've given you four winners in a row.'

'Well what do you expect? I had to check what you were giving me.'

Still smiling the vet crouched low to Breslin's eye level. 'Well now you know how good it is.'

'So what's the deal?'

'Three grand to tell you the favourite will lose. Ten grand to give you the winner as well.'

Breslin found it hard to control his anger. 'It was five till yesterday!'

'Well it's ten now. Take it or leave it.'

Breslin stared at him for a long time. Culling held his gaze. Breslin said, 'Tell me who's actually doing it?'

'Why?'

'Because if there's a third party involved it's more risky. If someone else is doing the doping then–'

'Who said they're being doped?'

'Oh come on, Peter! For the first time in its life that horse ran yesterday like the Devil was up its arse!'

'And how many positive dope tests have you read about? How many out of the four I've given you?'

'None. Doesn't mean to say they're not being jabbed, it just means you've discovered something the lab boys can't detect yet.'

'You're wrong.'

'How are you doing it then?'

'None of your business, Mr Breslin! All you need to know is that the information is one hundred per cent. There's no third party involved. The next one will be in three weeks' time. Do you want in on it?'

'Will it be on a Saturday again?'

'Why?'

Breslin shrugged. 'The others have been, that's all.'

'And does it matter?'

'It doesn't bother me either way.'

'So do you or don't you want in on it?' Culling's impatience was showing.

'Maybe at the three grand price.'

'Not the ten?'

'Let me think about it.'

'Well before you start taxing your brain maybe you'd like to count out yesterday's payment.'

22

All weekend Frankie Houlihan had found it impossible to get Zuiderzie's victory out of his head. It was almost as though Kathy had steered the horse home from above. Frankie had wanted to go to the winners' enclosure and congratulate the winning connections but he'd been unable to trust his emotions and didn't want to take the chance of embarrassing everyone, himself included and, potentially, his new employers.

So on Sunday evening he sat down and wrote to the winning trainer, Martin Brockbank, a Lambourn resident he'd never met. And he ended up telling this stranger the whole story of the romance from meeting at Cheltenham right up to Zuiderzie winning at Warwick. It was the first time since Kathy had died that he'd written everything down, just let it flow, and it gave him much more comfort than he'd expected from it. Reading over his words again he smiled as he doubted he could send this to a stranger. Then he thought, *Why not? Why not let someone know exactly what she meant to me? Someone who didn't know her, who wouldn't feel awkward about hearing all this.*

So he sealed the envelope and reached for his

new *Directory of the Turf* for the address of Martin Brockbank.

Gerry Monroe lived alone in a two-bedroom council house on the edge of Lambourn village. The second bedroom housed his computer, which sat on a desk he'd made from white pine. Every screw in the wood was flush, its slot at the same horizontal angle as its neighbour. Each surface was smoothly varnished, even the feet.

Monroe used the computer to trawl the internet for crime stories and for playing simulated empire-building games. Since collecting the last horse from Culling's place, he'd spent each evening searching the results pages of the *Racing Post Online*, checking Saturday runners. Using *Timeform* books which gave a written description of the appearance of each horse, he tried to discover the identities of the horses he'd picked up from the vet.

Four nights' work produced a shortlist of nine. Frustrated, Monroe got up and paced the room. There was something lurking in his mind, the solution to this; he just couldn't tempt it to the surface. He checked the time; he believed in being in bed before midnight except at weekends. It was ten to. He went into his bedroom. Twenty minutes later, on the edge of sleep, it came to him.

Hurrying back to his computer he logged on again to the *Racing Post* site and went to the cuttings library. Any racehorse which died or was seriously injured had to be formally scratched from all its race entries. Monroe keyed in 'scratchings' in the search field. Within three minutes, his shortlist was down to four. Monroe returned to bed, smiling. His self-esteem was rising. So was his confidence.

Next evening, Monroe went to Culling's house and rang the bell. He knew the vet lived alone and he was aware Culling had a reputation as a good, reliable, value-for-money operator. Other than this he didn't know anything about the man.

The light came on in the hall.

Monroe was just about to find out a bit more about Culling's character. As the shadowy outline through the glass door drew nearer, the slaughterman took a breath, tensed his shoulders, then tried to relax; this was his own first big test.

Culling looked surprised to see him. His eyes widened slightly but he didn't speak. Monroe, hands in trouser pockets, smiled. 'Hi, Mr Culling, hope you don't mind me dropping by. I wanted to talk to you about those horses I've been picking up ... on Sundays.' It was almost imperceptible but Monroe saw him flinch and said, 'I was hoping we could, eh, renegotiate the deal?'

Culling tried a bluff. 'Have you been drinking or something?'

'I don't drink much, Mr Culling, like to keep my wits about me if you know what I mean.' Monroe's smile had that unmistakable glint of one-upmanship.

They looked at each other for a few moments then Culling stepped back and opened the door wider. 'Come in.'

Culling led him to the conservatory at the rear. The vet didn't like to give anyone access to the rooms he lived in. He'd had the conservatory built especially to accommodate visitors. It was a sort of sterile area; it held none of his belongings, gave no clue to his personality. There was a wicker couch and chair, each plumply cushioned, a smoky-glass-topped table and a single cactus plant in a big brown pot in the corner; no pictures, no reading material, brown floor tiles; one lamp with a weak bulb in the corner.

He indicated that Monroe should sit on the couch. The vet sat in the chair, put his elbows on his parted knees and clasped his hands together. Monroe's triumphant smile hadn't changed. He said, 'No, I won't bother with a cup of tea, thanks.'

Culling stared at him blankly, as though he hadn't heard the remark. Monroe's smile faded slightly. He said, 'I wondered what the names of those horses were, the last four I've collected.'

The vet shrugged. 'Why?'

'Professional curiosity.'

'To what end?'

'I think I can make some money if I know.'

'How?'

This wasn't going to plan for Monroe. He said, 'I came to ask questions Mr Culling, not to answer them.'

The vet sighed tiredly and ran his fingers through his thinning hair. 'I come to bury Caesar not to praise him,' he said, almost to himself.

'No burials here, Mr Culling. I've got some resurrections planned, but no burials.'

'You're talking in riddles, man.'

Monroe, smiling, opened his arms. 'You started it!'

Culling shook his head. Monroe said, 'Zuider-zie, Sauceboat, Kilkenny Lass and Broadford Bay.'

'Uh-uh?'

'Those were the horses.'

'So?'

'They all won the previous day. Unexpectedly. At a big price.'

'And?' Culling's face was losing a bit of colour.

Monroe cranked the smile up a few more watts. 'And you were the vet in attendance at each of the courses. And each horse was dead within forty-eight hours of winning. And I was the man who killed them. And you were the man who took the big profit. And now I want a favour... Enough "ands" for you in there, Mr Culling?'

Culling bowed his head. Monroe realized he did it because he hadn't wanted to let Monroe see him swallow so hard. Monroe said, 'I don't want a cut of your take. I want you to get me access to the passport database for horses.'

Raising his head the vet said, 'Why?'

Monroe got up, feeling properly superior now, not having to wait for permission from his social 'betters', something he'd hated all his life. He said, 'Never mind why, I want a complete copy of the database of passports of all horses in the UK.'

Frowning heavily, Culling watched him but didn't reply. Monroe said, 'Have it for me for Monday and then you can get on with your business and I'll get on with mine.'

Culling nodded slowly. 'OK. OK, I'll get it.'

'Good. I'll call round. Same time.' It was an order. 'Aren't you going to see me out?'

The vet rose wearily and led him to the front door. Out on the step, breath white in the frosty air, Monroe said, 'I'll bet you I make more money than you do.'

Culling looked puzzled, then said, 'I'm sure you will, Mr Monroe. If you say so.'

Monroe's smile disappeared. He looked angry, hard. 'Don't patronize me, Culling,' he said in a low, menacing voice. 'How much do you want to bet that I have more money than you one year from now?'

'Nothing! I don't want any bet with you!'

'Bet me! Bet me ten grand! Come on, you've got a head start. You're a smart man with a degree and letters after your name. I'm a noth-ing, an ex-jockey, a slaughterman with half a brain. You'll win, won't you? Bet me!' His voice was high and tense, ice-blue eyes full of anger.

Culling lowered his voice almost to a whisper. 'All right, I'll bet you. You have a bet.'

'Ten grand. One year from today. Money on the table. Whoever's got the least gives the other ten grand. Right?'

'Right. Right.' The vet sounded suddenly exhausted.

Monroe held out his hand. 'Shake on the bet!'

Culling reached slowly for his hand. They shook. Monroe pulled his hand away, sparks of rage still in his eyes. He raised a finger to face level and jabbed it towards the vet. 'I'll see you on Monday!'

He marched away across the block-paved yard, shoulders swinging, head high, ambition and self-congratulation almost consuming him.

23

On the first Sunday in December, Frankie rose, as he usually did, not long after dawn. His shaving mirror offered him as concise a summary as any doctor could have about his sleeping habits in recent weeks. Pale complexion, dark rings below his red-veined eyes; a generally haunted and hunted look. Frankie paused to stare at himself then looked down, thinking that Kathy would have hated to see him like this.

Bobby had been right, the new job had helped, and being with people was an advantage. Company had forced him to be as normal as possible, to be light-hearted when it was called for, to laugh from time to time, not to visit his troubles on others.

But the demons kept at bay in the daylight hours had swamped him after dark, careered around in his head like malicious burglars returning to a property where they knew access was always available, where they could torment the demented, helpless caretaker all night long with still pictures and film shows of his past.

Twenty minutes after daybreak he was dressed and sipping tea in the kitchen, standing by the window watching the morning take shape. He ate some cereal and a piece of wholemeal bread and banana. He wasn't hungry but felt he should try and look after himself for the sake of appearance. Afterwards he cleaned up, washed the dishes, pulled on a thick fleece and his old brown tweed cap that Kathy always laughed at and went out to welcome the sun as it rose over the frosty fields and woods.

Frankie returned just after nine and saw the message light flashing on his answerphone. It was Geoff Stonebanks, his colleague at the Jockey Club, asking Frankie to call him. They had had their final day together on Friday. Frankie was now formally out on his own. He wondered, as he dialled the number, what the big man could want. It was the first time he'd ever called Frankie at home.

Stonebanks answered on the second ring. 'Frankie, hope I didn't wake you?'

Frankie managed to find a smile for that. 'No, I was out. Sorry.'

'Don't apologize. Listen, we've got a bit of a problem.'

'Uh-uh?'

'You know Ulysses?'

'Uh-uh.' Frankie knew him all right, Ulysses was the ante-post favourite for the Cheltenham Gold Cup.

'He's been kidnapped.'

'When?'

'Last night, from his box at Jack Quigley's. The kidnapper left a note.'

'How much does he want?'

'Quarter of a million.'

Frankie wasn't really sure what questions he should be asking or how he should be reacting. 'Who's the owner?'

'A man called Christopher Benjamin, a real fun guy. About as popular in racing as a sixteen-stone jockey.'

'Have you spoken to him?'

'I have. About ten minutes ago.'

'Is he after paying the ransom?'

'Doesn't look like it, but he's of the definite opinion that as the police have no immediate solution to offer, we should be getting his horse back for him before the cock crows thrice.'

Frankie sighed. 'Sounds like a nice man to work with.'

'You bet. Can you meet me at Quigley's place at noon?'

'Surely. Near Wantage, isn't it?'

'About two miles north. Call me when you're close and I'll talk you in.'

The ransom note for Ulysses had been written with a black indelible marker in block capitals on a plain piece of A4 paper. Stonebanks had already been to see the police, and they'd given him a photocopy of the note. YOU REFUSED AN OFFER OF £500,000 FOR YOUR HORSE THREE MONTHS AGO. IT SHOULD BE EASY FOR YOU TO PAY HALF THAT MUCH TO GET HIM BACK ALIVE. YOU HAVE FORTY-EIGHT HOURS.

Stonebanks had met the owner, Christopher Benjamin, once before. It had been obvious

138

when Benjamin introduced himself that he did not recall that meeting. Stonebanks chose not to remind him. They stood in Ulysses' empty box. Benjamin was impeccable in a light grey suit, white shirt, navy tie, polished shoes, the soles now ridged with a centimetre of reddish mud. In contrast, Ulysses' trainer, Jack Quigley, looked haggard and weary, unshaven. Frankie felt sorry for him.

They'd been over the story already with the police. The kidnapper had come in the night, poisoned the dogs with doctored meat, tied muffles (they reckoned, as no one had heard a sound) to Ulysses' hooves and simply led him out of his box. Frankie had noticed how uneasy Quigley was, constantly trying to avoid catching the obviously angry eye of Christopher Benjamin who'd been sniping indirectly at him almost since they'd arrived.

To no one in particular (though all knew who the target was) Benjamin would say things like, 'The Gold Cup favourite. How can he simply be spirited away in the night? From a modern stable?' and 'How would people in normal business expect a valuable asset to be protected by those in charge of it? Is it right to rely on a few barks from a sleepy, vulnerable animal? Good God, surely not in this day and age.'

And Frankie would cringe a bit for poor Quigley, who was defenceless and knew it. Many top horses would have twenty-four-hour stable guards prior to running in a major race but there wasn't a trainer in the country who'd mount that guard four months before the event. OK, Frankie thought, maybe Quigley should have had some modern alarm equipment fitted but, as ever, hindsight was wonderful.

They went back inside the house. Quigley had builders in and the kitchen was a mess. He led them to a big basement room kitted out with a snooker table and a bar. A coffee machine stood in the corner and Quigley made them all a hot drink. They sat at the bar. Benjamin drew his fingers though his thick, silver-grey hair and looked at Stonebanks. 'Well, what next? Or maybe I should say, what first?'

Stonebanks said, 'We need to talk to all the staff, to the builders, to any suppliers who've been here in the past six months, to–' Benjamin interrupted him. 'Wait a minute, wait a minute! We have forty-eight hours, Mr Stonebanks. Two days!'

'With respect, Mr Benjamin, we need to start somewhere. We can make a couple of assumptions but–'

Benjamin interrupted again. 'Look, the police have given me all this already. They seem to think this is about as serious as some ragamuffin kid stealing a kitten from a litter. I want Ulysses back safe and I want him back quickly.'

Stonebanks looked at him over the rim of his cup. 'Even if it means paying the ransom?'

Benjamin shaped his face in that sneering, half-smiling sort of way that said, is this man some kind of idiot? And Frankie disliked him even more. Benjamin said, 'I'm not paying any ransom, Mr Stonebanks. Don't we pay enough in fees all round to keep our horses in training, and

140

people like you and your silent colleague in jobs?'

Stonebanks had been leaning back against the edge of the snooker table. He straightened. 'OK, Mr Benjamin. We'll do our best. We need to speak to everyone who's been on the premises recently. I'll start with Mr Quigley and my colleague Mr Houlihan will speak to the head lad.'

'Talk fast, then, Stonebanks. I want that horse back! Call me at my office within the hour!' Benjamin said and marched out, throwing the empty plastic cup on the floor to roll and dribble the dregs of its coffee on to the grey carpet.

Stonebanks and Frankie spoke to nine of the staff who were there and took contact numbers for the three who weren't. There were four builders and they seemed quite pleased to be interviewed about this mysterious kidnapping. Eileen Quigley, Jack's wife, was red-eyed and swollen-faced after all the crying she'd done over the two poisoned dogs whose bodies still lay in the yard awaiting the police scene of crime unit. She was upset too at the prospect of Jack losing the horse and, potentially, Benjamin's twelve other horses in the stable if the angry owner decided to move them elsewhere.

Stonebanks and Frankie left a stressed and weary Jack comforting Eileen in the kitchen and went to Stonebanks's car so he could make the call to Benjamin. Sitting in the passenger seat behind the rain-speckled windscreen Frankie winced in mock pain as he could clearly hear Benjamin's raised voice through the earpiece of Stonebanks's phone. Stonebanks was looking at him, shaking his head ruefully as if to say, 'He's lost the plot completely'.

Stonebanks stayed utterly calm throughout which enraged Benjamin to the point where the owner simply hung up on him. Stonebanks held the phone away from his ear and stared at it. Frankie said, 'Gimme that and I'll drop it in a bucket of iced water for an hour.'

Stonebanks replied, 'Drop him in a bucket of iced water.'

'And hold his head under,' Frankie said and they both smiled. 'What next?' asked Frankie.

Slotting the phone back into its cradle Stonebanks said, 'More phone calls. Check with our lads to see if they've heard anything. Speak to the missing staff. Ask the local plods to monitor any calls. Check out the suppliers connected with the stable. Stick brushes up our arses and sweep the yard too.'

Frankie smiled. 'Jack said they've not used anyone new for more than two years.'

'Well, have any of the suppliers taken on new people, even admin staff who might not have been to the yard?'

'Not that he knows of.'

'Worth checking with the suppliers themselves.'

'I will,' Frankie said and made a note in the slim little spiral notebook that he kept in his shirt pocket and was only just becoming less conscious of when he pulled it out, especially in company.

Stonebanks eased himself back in the seat. The windows were misting over. He drummed lightly on the beige steering wheel of the big Rover.

Frankie said, 'What do you think?'

'Mmm, I don't know. I don't know. I almost think, from the way Benjamin's blustering so much, that he's got something to do with it himself.'

'Really?'

Stonebanks turned to him, face still flustered-looking despite his apparent calmness on the phone. 'Well, what do you think? He's raving so much, threatening all sorts. It's almost as though he doesn't want to give us time to think. And he keeps on about the bloody deadline, pressure, pressure, pressure.'

And Frankie learned something about Stonebanks then; the big man *was* rattled, Benjamin had got to him despite his calm exterior throughout the phone conversation. Frankie wondered if he was already clutching at a straw by suggesting that Benjamin might be involved but he kept quiet. Stonebanks had been doing this job for a long time, maybe he'd developed an instinct for this sort of thing. But deep down, Frankie didn't really think so.

The phone rang. Wearily Stonebanks reached for it then sat up straighter when he realized who it was. Frankie could hear some of the words coming through the earpiece; it sounded like their boss, Robert Archibald. Stonebanks's demeanour confirmed that it almost certainly was and when the big man started saying things like, 'Of course I will' and 'Yes, of course, I realize...' Frankie guessed that Benjamin had gone straight on to the Jockey Club security chief after hanging up on Stonebanks.

The upshot was that Stonebanks had to stay at Quigley's yard for the next forty-eight hours, base himself there and help monitor any calls from the kidnapper. Archibald had pulled strings with the police to hurry the installation of recording equipment.

They left the car, Stonebanks cursing and stuffing his phone into his coat pocket as they moved across the yard, dodging puddles and passing the bodies of the dead dogs which had been covered with empty plastic feed bags. 'Bloody phone taps! These people watch too many films! Unless it's your bloody father or your brother who phones demanding a ransom you've about as much chance of catching them with phone taps as I have of riding a Derby winner! So, two completely unproductive days for me when I could have been out there actually trying to do something. What a waste of time!'

But Mrs Quigley didn't think so and she welcomed the news that Stonebanks was staying with a zeal that dismayed him even more. Obviously, thought Frankie, Eileen Quigley was a fan of the very films Stonebanks had been slagging off. He felt sorry for the big man. Behind the orders the boss had given out Frankie was sure there was little hope of a result. But Eileen's expectations were great and the fact that they came from a 'lay' person, as Frankie thought of her, made the burden even heavier. He could see from her face as she sat them down and fussed and made tea that she saw them, or at least Stonebanks, as the saviour. Poor Stone-banks.

It was dusk by the time the phone tap was set up. The dark grey cordless phone had been moved on to the old oak kitchen table. Frankie thought this smooth cold piece of plastic which allowed contact with any other point in the modern world appeared incongruous resting on the gnarled wood that looked a thousand years old.

For the first ten minutes, all four of them watched it. Jack nursed a large Scotch and the only sound in the room came when he raised it to his lips and the ice clinked. They watched as though the phone were a bomb; watched as though they were shackled there. Even their blink rates decreased with the concentration.

Then it rang.

24

As he put down the phone in the darkness of the remote call-box deep in rural Oxfordshire, Gerry Monroe, not for the first time, congratulated himself on his sharp criminal brain. He had upped the stakes with the Ulysses people, told them that he'd torture the horse and leave it in a hell of a mess if they didn't come up with the cash by midnight on Tuesday.

He wasn't expecting them to pay up. Not this time. This first one was experimental. He needed to find out if he could get it all together, pull the whole thing off. The money didn't matter this time. He'd deliberately asked too much because he needed to see the reaction when they got the horse back dead. He needed to see how deeply they'd probe. Not very deeply, he suspected, but he had to see proof of that before taking the plan to the next stage.

Pulling on his helmet he mounted the big black Kawasaki bike and fired up the engine. Under a moonless sky the twin headlights carved a path through the countryside blackness picking out squashed creatures and the faintest of white line markings.

He smiled behind the visor, as he sped through the night, at his brilliant idea. How easy it had been to scare Culling into getting those files. Now he had access to information on all thoroughbreds registered in the UK. He had the markings for every horse in racing from its passport. He knew everything from each animal's overall colour to the pattern of hair growing on its flanks.

And he'd left not a trace behind.

Monroe whiled away the remainder of his journey planning how he'd spend his money once he was a millionaire. An expensive racehorse did not feature in his budget.

On Tuesday evening in the dining area of Jack Quigley's kitchen, Jack, Frankie, Stonebanks and Ulysses' owner, Christopher Benjamin, sat around the old table. The telephone was no longer the centre of attention. The kidnapper had said on Sunday that he would not call again until five to twelve on the Tuesday. If they had the money then he would make arrangements for collection. If they didn't Ulysses would be dead by midnight.

Benjamin had no intention of paying. Nobody at the table doubted that he had the funds to pay, he'd made millions trading in the international money markets. But he simply wasn't going to. He'd been there for most of the past twenty-four hours and had ruled like a prison camp commandant. The tension around the yard had grown almost tangibly as the hours ticked by. In the trainer's house the atmosphere would have frayed the nerves of the calmest man.

Stonebanks and Frankie had spent much of the past two days liaising with the local police, interviewing Quigley's suppliers and ex-employees, talking to colleagues and paid contacts within the industry but they'd come up with nothing. And this laid them open to increasingly frequent thrusts of Benjamin's sarcasm and general rudeness.

Stonebanks and Frankie both thought that someone with a grudge against Benjamin was a much more likely suspect than anyone Jack Quigley might have been involved with but neither wanted to voice the thought.

At seven-thirty Eileen Quigley had offered to cook dinner. 'Nobody's hungry!' Benjamin snapped at her. 'Just make some tea and sandwiches!'

Frankie's eyes went to Jack when this happened and for the first time he saw a spark of real anger in the balding trainer's tense, tired face. But Quigley stayed silent. Frankie looked at Benjamin and just resisted shaking his head slowly.

He was beginning to despise the man and he couldn't remember feeling that way about anyone before.

At nine-forty Benjamin looked at his big shining watch for the hundredth time that day then muttered something incomprehensible and strove to deepen the creases of his frown. Nobody had spoken for a while and Stonebanks said, 'Chances are the guy will give us an extension. He must know that forty-eight hours is a joke.'

All eyes turned to Benjamin. He said, 'And what sort of extension would you like, Mr Stonebanks? Would a year be long enough?' He shook his head slowly as if to say, 'Idiot'. He continued, 'Even if you had a year, there would be as much chance of you people finding him as, as...'

'As you learning some manners,' Frankie said.

Benjamin froze for a few seconds then turned to Frankie. 'What did you say?'

'I think you heard what I said, Mr Benjamin.'

'What I heard was you being insolent and insubordinate. You've said so little in the past two days I was beginning to wonder if you were mentally handicapped in some way. I thought maybe you were on some special help scheme with the Jockey Club.'

'I'm not going to trade insults with you,' Frankie said.

'You're not going to trade anything with anybody, young man, especially with your local shopkeepers as you will have no salary to do any trading with when I speak to your boss.'

148

Frankie smiled.

Benjamin raised his voice. 'Do you hear me?'

'I hear you. I've said my piece. Let's all quieten down a bit. It's been a long day.'

'Don't tell me to quieten down, you little Irish bog man!'

'Talking of bogs,' Frankie said and got up and left the room.

'Come back here!' Benjamin shouted. Frankie kept walking. Quigley and Stonebanks fought hard not to smile. 'Are you his boss?' Benjamin asked Stonebanks.

'Unfortunately not,' Stonebanks said, thinking to himself that if he had been he'd have recommended Frankie for a big salary increase.

'Then tell Robert Archibald I don't expect the insolent idiot to be in a job at the end of this week!'

'I'm afraid you'll have to tell him that yourself, Mr Benjamin.'

'Then you're a witness! I'll be citing you!'

'Fine.'

When Frankie came back five minutes later he resisted a provocative smile or comment and settled back into his chair. It was just after ten o'clock.

Eileen Quigley walked in. Her slumped posture and general demeanour as well as her exhausted-looking, tear-stained face said everything about how the past two days had affected her. She was just the right side of forty but looked years older even though she'd obviously put on make-up recently. She'd changed her clothes too in the past hour and wore loose blue trousers and a black cotton top. In a hollow voice she said, 'Can I get anyone tea or coffee?'

Benjamin turned in his seat. 'No you bloody can't! What you can get is a *Yellow Pages!* Do you have one of those or has somebody stolen that too?'

Frankie looked at Jack. The anger spark was even brighter. Eileen Quigley reached into the cupboard above the TV and took out a *Yellow Pages* directory. Wearily she brought it to the table and laid it as carefully and apprehensively in front of Benjamin as she would have put food before a wild animal.

Benjamin threw it across the table at her husband. 'I suggest you turn to the section marked Transport and find someone who has a couple of horseboxes for hire tomorrow. If Ulysses is killed tonight, you'll be making calls in the morning to arrange for the removal of my other twelve horses.'

Jack looked at him, his eyes showing the first real signs of defiance. But then he slowly picked up the book and started leafing through. His wife let go a sob and sank back to lean on the short L-shape of the breakfast bar. Jack reached the page he wanted, took a pen from his shirt pocket and circled three telephone numbers. He ripped the page out. Then he walked around the table to where Benjamin sat. He put the page on the table in front of his major owner, the man who paid him almost £15,000 a month to train his horses, money which meant the difference between surviving in the life he'd always loved and going out of business. And he said, 'Put this in your pocket and get out of my house. Make the calls yourself. If Ulysses walked back through that door right now I still wouldn't train another horse for you. I'd sooner starve to death.'

Benjamin was speechless. He looked at the torn-out page, then up at Quigley's angry but triumphant face. And what Benjamin really saw was the source of his power evaporating, the loss of his control which was based on fear. He said, 'Sit down man and don't be so bloody stupid!'

'No, you get up. I want you out of my house in the next sixty seconds and your horses out of my yard by noon tomorrow.'

'Listen–'

'No, you listen, you ignorant bastard! Get out before I punch you all the way to the door and through it! Get out!'

Benjamin looked shaken as he got to his feet. Quigley suddenly seemed easily capable of what he threatened. The owner moved slowly towards the door. 'What about the call? What about Ulysses?' he asked in a much weaker voice than he'd been using earlier.

'We'll let you know in the morning when you come for your horses,' Quigley said.

'But I'm entitled to–'

Quigley interrupted. 'You're entitled to the same treatment, the same civility as you've shown us in the past two days so you're entitled to be treated like shit. Keep walking.'

Benjamin stood and looked at his ex-trainer. Quigley moved towards him. Benjamin hurried out.

There was silence for a few seconds, then

Frankie started clapping. Stonebanks joined in as Eileen walked proudly towards her husband of sixteen years and put her arms around him. Jack Quigley smiled peacefully.

25

Things weren't panning out for David Hewitt the way he'd expected them to when he'd agreed to Corell's offer of the house and full lab facilities. Before moving in, he'd been worried about the supply of horses but they'd been plentiful – Hewitt had no complaints on quantity. It was quality he needed. He'd told that to Monroe often enough and now the slaughterman had come to see him with a proposal. Hewitt was nervous about calling Corell. Monroe wanted a lot of money but Hewitt knew it could make a big difference to the project. Trouble was that in nine months he hadn't delivered a single thing although Corell hadn't put him under any pressure.

He sat down on the arm of the chair in the library and watched the CCTV shot from the gate-mounted camera as Monroe's motorbike accelerated out of picture. Through the tall window, its wooden shutters in a tight concertina by the sides, the early-evening moon seemed huge, the richest yellow he could ever recall seeing it, like an enormous burnished coin.

He was missing his girlfriend Marcia, and felt

almost unfaithful when he spoke to her on the phone as he had to lie about where he was. Corell had stressed the importance of nobody knowing what was going on in the big house.

The big house.

He'd walked around it all at the start, grateful for the space and the peace after the chaos of the university lab. Now the silence enveloped him, especially at night, a sinister silence. He played rock music and sometimes watched TV but he'd found that keeping busy was the best way of warding off loneliness. He'd always had the capacity to lose himself in his work, and these past few weeks had shown him how valuable an asset this was. Hard work made the days seem shorter. It would also bring him more quickly to his goal. He'd have the professional satisfaction of leading his own field, not to mention a very big payoff from Corell and a share of future profits.

At the beginning, he'd tried to convince himself that this was a legitimate venture, that Corell was fully above board. But when he'd met him and his driver, Gleeson, and especially Gerry Monroe, he could no longer pretend, not even to himself, that these people were operating within the law. Monroe had just confirmed this with his proposal. Hewitt ran his fingers wearily through his thick fair hair and sighed. If he made this call to Corell, if he engineered the acceptance of Monroe's proposal, he was as good as colluding in whatever they were doing. Monroe had said, 'Don't worry about the names, you don't need to know anything in advance except that I can deliver. I'll tell you the names when I bring you the horses.'

He got up and went to the small table by the door. Kelly Corell's number was on a piece of paper by the telephone. Hewitt dialled.

Brendan Gleeson was in a betting shop in the centre of Dublin when his mobile rang. Impatiently he pulled it from his pocket, about to switch it off so he could watch the end of the two-fifteen from Navan in peace. Then he saw that it was Corell calling. He hurried outside and ran thirty yards down the street making sure the blower commentary was out of earshot before he pressed to accept the call. His boss sounded a bit on edge and that made Gleeson nervy. 'Where are you?' Corell asked sharply.

'I've just come out of the supermarket, Mr Corell. Just getting something in for the tea for me and the boy.'

'Get yourself up here in the next ten minutes.'

'Sure. Sure, Mr Corell.'

Gleeson ran to his car and drove fast to the club Corell owned. Twenty minutes later he was on his way to the docks. Beside him on the passenger seat was a grey canvas holdall with ten thousand pounds in Bank of England notes inside it. Gleeson had raced to the waterfront hoping to catch the three-fifteen ferry, cursing everyone in his way. But when he reached the terminal the ferry was still in port and the long queue of vehicles told him they hadn't even begun loading. The winter weather had done him a favour in delaying the sailing but now that he was here, he wanted them to get on with it.

He watched the yellow-jacketed shore crew begin signalling them on board just after four o'clock. In the dimly lit hold, Gleeson parked and pulled his handbrake on tight, leaving the car in gear. Grabbing the bag he hurried upstairs to quench his thirst.

Ten minutes later he was sitting at a table by the window through which the shore lights twinkled in the gathering dusk on the dark surface of Dublin Bay. In front of him on the pale blue table-top were two pints of Guinness and two large Jameson's whiskeys topped up with lemonade. He finished a glass of the whiskey in one drink then followed it by gulping a half-pint of Guinness. Only then did he relax, easing himself back in the seat, smiling as he waited for that familiar glow to take over and shift his troubles outside the worry zone.

Gleeson had no concerns about carrying the cash. He'd hide it on himself, among his clothes. When they searched at Holyhead it was always the vehicle itself they checked. If he took the bag they'd look inside it but he'd just leave it on board once he'd hidden the money. Easy. He drank half of the other whiskey. He'd need to be careful. He didn't want to fail a breathalyser on the other side, didn't want them to smell the drink off him especially as he'd persuaded Corell to let him bring the car. He'd argued it was just as quick by the time you'd taken into account the drives to the airports at each end and all the ballsing about with check-ins and stuff. There was also a much higher chance of being caught with the cash if he'd flown, with all that bag searching and frisking at the airport.

No, this was best.

An hour later he knew he was drunk. The ship still hadn't left port. The announcements had said that the sailing might have to be postponed until the next day but they'd wait for just thirty minutes more to see if the weather in the Irish Sea improved. Gleeson judged that it was a hopeless case and decided to have a few more drinks. He'd drive confidently here in Dublin, even drunk.

But the ship sailed at five-thirty and a cursing Gleeson eased himself out of the rigid seat and, swinging the grey holdall, walked unsteadily towards the illuminated toilet sign. On the way back from relieving himself Gleeson noticed three men playing cards at a table by a big brown pillar. He walked over. A pile of notes lay on the table. Cigarettes burned in the glass ashtray, glasses with varying levels of Guinness rested on beer mats. Gleeson smiled. 'How'ye doin' lads? Mind if I sit in?'

As the ferry rode the swell past North Stack to cover the last few miles into Holyhead Gleeson was back in his seat by the window. The bag was empty. There was no money in his clothes except sixty-seven pence in change. Corell's money now belonged to the three poker players who'd had almost equal shares in the past three hours. The anaesthetizing effects of the booze were wearing off and Gleeson stared into the night feeling as bad as he could ever remember. His face was desolate as the lights of the port glinted in his cold, resigned eyes. He'd be as well staying aboard and dropping himself quietly over the side halfway across the sea. It would save time and worry and an awful lot of pain. He knew he was a dead man.

26

It had been a mild, wet autumn and winter frosts had not yet been regular enough or sufficiently vicious to kill all the insect life. A swarm of flies fed on the bloodied wounds of the carcass. The horse lay in a shallow stream. Monroe had carried out his promise to mutilate the body and the big bay had been shot twice; once through the forehead, ploughing a hole like a dark sticky-edged pit in the clean white blaze, and again just below the left ear leaving brain matter smeared around the exit wound. The entry hole the bullet made lay submerged in the stream causing water to suck and blow, spouting at the flies, unsettling them for a moment before they crowded back. The horse's neck and flanks carried deep crescent-shaped slash marks. It was a week before they found him. The stream ran through an old abandoned construction site in Northampton-shire, on land that had been mapped out for a bypass until objectors got their way.

In Monroe's last call to Quigley the killer had offered a clue; 'Think of being a bookie at Newbury. What's behind you and what's in front of you?' and he'd laughed and hung up. Nobody had been able to decipher the cryptic message. A man walking his dog found the body. When they went to recover it in a horse ambulance borrowed from Newbury racecourse, the meaning of the clue dawned on Frankie and he said to Stonebanks, 'If you're a bookie at Newbury, behind you is the water jump and in front of you is the new stand they're building. A construction site.'

Stonebanks nodded. 'He must have whiled away a nice evening thinking that up. Bloody lunatic.'

The police were there as Stonebanks backed the trailer as close to the bank of the stream as he dared. Stonebanks and Frankie, wellingtons on, waded into the water hauling the chain and Frankie winced as he lifted the eyeless bloodied head to let Stonebanks ease the heavy links around the horse's neck. A sergeant and a constable with a camera watched from above, a darkening sky behind them, as Stonebanks secured the chain and Frankie went back to start the winch motor. The mechanism ground noisily, gradually taking up the slack in the thick chain until it tightened around the horse's neck, squeezing brown blood from the eyeballs and exit wounds as the big body started moving slowly up the shallow banking.

Stonebanks could see that the underside was almost hairless, the flesh shrivelled from being submerged for so long and he shook his head in disgust. He'd watched this horse racing more than once. It had been one of the most athletic, majestic jumpers of fences he'd ever seen. Those ripped and wasted muscles had propelled the half-ton thoroughbred around miles of track and over hundreds of jumps. And he ended up like this because of some madman.

They drove the carcass south to an abattoir to be kept in cold storage until the forensic people had seen it.

Back in his house in Lambourn, an excited Gerry Monroe had been waiting all week for the news to break in the press.

It was late when Frankie got back home. The cottage seemed even quieter than usual. It was a perfectly still night, barely a leaf rustled.

A letter lay on the mat. Frankie went over by the window where, as ever, he'd left the lamp burning. He switched the kettle on and opened the envelope. It was from Martin Brockbank, the trainer of Zuiderzie, and Frankie coloured a little as he recalled the emotional letter he'd sent pouring out his life story after Zuiderzie's Warwick victory.

It was a kind letter, handwritten and, Frankie thought, striking exactly the right note of sympathy and interest in Kathy's involvement with the horse. But Frankie's brows creased in the lamplight as he read that Zuiderzie had not survived more than a few hours after the race. He'd been struck by some mystery illness and had been put down. Brockbank said he realized that this would come as a blow to Frankie on top of the troubles he already had and that all at the yard missed the horse, who'd been a real character. But, said the trainer, 'That's racing,' a statement Frankie had heard and read hundreds of times over the years he'd followed the sport. That calm acceptance of the drawbacks as well as the triumphs seemed to be typical of most people who were in the game in any professional capacity. Frankie identified with it easily but the news of the horse's death hit him much harder than he'd expected. Zuiderzie had been the only living, breathing thing that he and Kathy still shared, as a memory, a touchstone. Frankie thought of his mother again, and of God and wondered if he had indeed been cursed.

The other dead horse made front-page headlines in next day's *Racing Post*: ULYSSES SLAUGH-ERED. KIDNAPPED GOLD CUP FAVOUR-ITE FOUND DEAD IN STREAM.

There was a picture of Robert Archibald, Jockey Club Security Department Chief on page three. He said he'd be doing everything he could to find the killer of Ulysses and that all trainers should take precautions to protect their charges as another kidnapping could not be ruled out.

'Damn right it can't,' said Gerry Monroe aloud as he read it. 'Damn right.' He folded the paper and pushed it aside then spun on the swivel chair to tap his keyboard and bring the thoroughbred passport database on to the big bright screen.

After days and nights of research, Gerry Monroe decided on his next kidnapping target. He was going to have to travel north for this one if it was to be taken from the stable. He'd need to check the place out first. He knew Lambourn inside out and he'd known how easy it would be to take Ulysses from Jack Quigley's place. But

Graham Cassidy, who trained the very promising stayer, Angel Gabriel, was a stranger to him.

Cassidy's was a small stable up on the Shropshire–Cheshire border. The yard had never hit the headlines; it had never had anything good enough to but Monroe had checked out all the press cuttings and he knew Angel Gabriel had the right mix. The articles told him the horse was a precious family pet who all but lived in the house with the Cassidy family. The fact that the big chaser was also a live Grand National prospect was a bonus; it helped Monroe put a commercial value on the horse as well as a sentimental one. He wouldn't go so high this time because he wanted to have a realistic chance of collecting the ransom. Having said that, within his own mind he had a reputation to protect and he wasn't giving anything away cheap, family pet or not.

The press cuttings also told Monroe that the Cassidy family, with their very generous income from Mrs Cassidy's children's books, had no money worries. In fact they seemed the perfect happy family with their twenty-year marriage and two smart kids, their beautiful cottage home adjoining the yard in the lush countryside away from all the backbiting and jealousy of the big training centres like Lambourn. The perfect happy family. Monroe smiled to himself and said aloud, 'Not for much longer.'

27

The postmark and the typeface of the address showing through the window told Maggie Cassidy that another royalty cheque had arrived. She loved how they tended to come on Monday mornings to make that normally dreariest of days much easier to face.

She kissed the envelope and carried it back to the sunny sitting-room where a half-finished cup of coffee and a just-lit cigarette in an ashtray sat on the polished circular table next to the big floral easy chair. Graham, as ever, was out with the horses. Billy and Jane were at school. A fine frost still blanketed the countryside, working with the sun to cast that wonderful shade of winter light that Maggie loved. She'd had a huge picture window put in, almost half the size of the south-facing wall, so she could watch the weather and the light as the seasons came and went.

Maggie smiled as she luxuriated in opening the envelope, sliding her index finger into the gap at the top and slowly pulling the gummed ridge away from the body of the envelope. She didn't know how much the cheque would be for and she loved not knowing. Since the books had begun to sell really well and had been translated into more than fifteen languages, there was no way of keeping track of royalties. She just had to wait until the statement and the cheque came from her London agent.

This little ritual Maggie was going through showed her how much this money meant to her. All the years of struggling to survive made these moments so, so sweet.

The flap was fully open now. She could see the computer-generated codes on the edge of the cheque. She stopped and smiled, sipped coffee, drew deeply on her cigarette then eased the paperwork out and slowly plucked the cheque from the folds of the statement: £57,648.92.

Her smile widened slowly and she read the figures again and checked the written amount to make sure she hadn't made a mistake. Almost sixty thousand. This was the biggest one she'd ever had. And her agent was working on an auction deal for her next three books which he said might bring in as much as half a million.

She laid her head back on the soft upholstery, closed her eyes and wondered, not for the first time, if this was all really happening. They'd struggled for years as a family, working like slaves, all of them, to try and fulfil the dream that had started off as just Graham's – to win the Grand National. Not just to train the winner of the great race but to breed it, rear it, own it. At the outset, when they'd first met, Graham's dream had been to ride it too. But he'd been just twenty-five then. When he hit forty he'd conceded that part of the dream to encroaching age and expanding waistline. But he still badly wanted the other two legs of what he called his 'dream treble'.

It was an obsession with him, one she'd never

known him not to have. His determination, confidence and enthusiasm for realizing the dream had been a big factor in her falling for him. She loved the passion he showed. At the beginning, she'd have preferred that passion to be for her but she accepted that even if it had been, it would have faded many years ago, tarnished by familiarity, and the ravages of time on her looks and figure. No, Graham's passion was sustainable because it never needed to be focused on just one creature. If a horse was never going to make the grade it was quickly dismissed from her husband's thoughts, relegated to run in small races. A new focus was sought, a new horse, sleek, muscular, with a bold eye, a regal head; 'the Look of Eagles' Graham called it.

She'd decided it was probably best his dream wasn't of what she herself might achieve for him or she would have been traded in and replaced several times over the years. She knew she'd never be Graham's number-one love but he was rock-steady as a man and as a husband and Maggie had come to value that more and more. Some of her friends had much more 'interesting' spouses; life-and-soul types, romancers, off-the-wall men who could shock and surprise. But they could also be unfaithful, drink too much, abuse their wives and display most of the other flaws of unpredictable men. Graham would do fine for Maggie every time.

Staring at the cheque, she was trying to figure out what she'd buy him for Christmas. Her head went back again, her eyes closing slowly. This would be their third Christmas where debts would present no worries. Rather than resent money and what it did, or what lack of it did, as she'd done for most of her Christmases, she'd quickly learned to love it, almost to covet it. That scared her because it was the type of love where there is also always a fear in the background that you'll lose your lover. That he'll up and go one day just when you were getting used to all the pleasure and security he'd brought. Disappear in the night, no forwarding address.

Maggie clutched the cheque tighter and tried to push the fear from her mind. She was almost fifty years old. If her agent could land this big deal, she could kill this terror, this dread of loss, once and for all. It wasn't as though she and Graham had another fifty years to survive. Twenty-five, maybe thirty. Half a million would be enough for that, wouldn't it?

She got up and went out to the yard. In the middle of the quadrangle made by the boxes a chestnut mare called Mrs Molly stood sweating. Hazel, her blonde groom, held the horse's bridle while Graham Cassidy felt the mare's nearside foreleg for signs of heat which would signify a return of the tendon injury Mrs Molly had suffered more than a year ago.

Maggie tiptoed quietly towards them. Around her the pitched roof of the stable boxes still showed a frosty collar just above the guttering where it was in shade. The sun, weak as it was, assisted by the heat rising from the horses within, had helped thaw the rooftops. But it was cold still, enough for the breaths of all four in the yard and the steam rising gently from Mrs Molly to be seen clear and white.

Hazel smiled as Maggie approached holding a finger to her lips, eyebrows raised. Graham was bent double. She stood behind him, waited till he straightened then softly put her hands over his eyes, still cradling the cheque in her palms. 'I smell money,' he said.

'How much do you smell?' asked Maggie, deepening her voice, mock-mysterious.

Her husband took a deep sniff. 'I smell enough to buy me that new suit I want for Christmas.'

Maggie continued in the deep voice, 'Then you're only smelling the second line of the cheque.' She rose on tiptoes to push the cheque a foot away from his face, still holding it with two hands.

He opened his eyes. 'Good God!' he said. 'I should have said I smelt a new horse!'

Maggie laughed loud. 'No chance!'

Hazel smiled but cursed them both silently for not telling how much it was.

When Maggie told her children, at dinner, and showed them the cheque, their reactions reflected their characters and their own desires. Billy, thirteen, his thick light-brown hair, longish face and sharp jaw making him look already much like his father, spent most of his waking hours trying to come up with the 'big idea' that would make him millions. He scanned the internet for stories of young men like himself who'd made their fortunes in the world of e-commerce even though he'd decided that all the seats were taken in that particular millionaires' stadium.

Billy knew he'd have to invent something completely different to make his fortune. But he reckoned he'd a very good chance of doing that because all the entrepreneurs were falling over each other to come up with the next high-tech scheme. This convinced him that if he concentrated on the more practical, solid, day-to-day things people needed then he'd be much more likely to succeed. He'd probably even overtake these guys. The internet bubble had to burst – had to. He was convinced of it.

'Aw Mum! Brilliant!' Billy said as held the cheque. 'All that just for writing silly stuff for kids and drawing a few pictures!'

Smiling and reaching to take the cheque back Maggie said, 'Yes, easy, isn't it? Why don't you try it, Billy boy?'

He shrugged. 'I would but it's too boring. I'd rather use my brain inventing things like what I've just come up with. And it's very lucky for you Mum that you've got that money 'cause now you'll have a chance to take a stake in my invention.'

'Which is what?' Maggie asked, pouring gravy over her beef and glancing at Graham and Jane who were smiling knowingly and shaking their heads.

Billy chewed and smiled too and he was nodding gently as if to say, 'Go on, shake your heads and mock but one day I'll be rich and you won't be shaking your heads then.' He said, 'Mum, you need to promise to stake me for a patent application first.'

'Stake you? Stake you! Have you been watching

those old gangster movies again?'

He coloured slightly. 'Nooo, Mum, that's what we say in the business, stake. It means that you're not just, like, giving me a loan or anything. It's a proper stake in the business. An investment for you.'

Maggie nodded as though sizing up the proposal. She cut a piece of beef. 'And how much do these patent applications cost?'

'Oh, about five grand would do it, I would think.'

'Five grand! To send a letter somewhere telling people what you've thought up?'

'It's not like that Mum, there's lots of paper-work and research and stuff to do. Five grand'd just be for the European rights to the Hot–' he stopped himself.

His sister said, 'To the hot what?'

Billy was annoyed with himself for almost giving it away. He looked across at Maggie. 'Mum, are you in?'

'I might be. Depends what comes after hot.'

There was a big pause now and Billy felt the eyes of his whole family on him. They'd laughed at him before, plenty of times. He knew they didn't really mean to hurt him but they did. He was the only one in the family who wasn't really great at something and he wanted to be, wanted to be the same as them. As good at something as his dad was at training horses; as good at something as his mum was at writing; as good at something as Jane was at being beautiful and having lots of friends and fund-raising and all the other stuff she did.

168

And coming up with ideas was all he could really do. He wasn't very good at school, didn't like it much. Hated being around girls because he felt so embarrassed and awkward at not having anything to say, to talk about, like being a good footballer or runner or PlayStation wizard like the others were. But the power of his mind was promising. He knew that, even if nobody else did.

'Come on Billy,' Jane said, 'The hot what? The hot water bottle? I'm afraid you're too late with that!'

They were waiting. Billy tried to look defiant as he said, 'The Hot Harrow.'

There was silence for a few moments then Graham said, 'The what?'

'The Hot Harrow.' Billy was pleased that he'd stunned them with this one and his enthusiasm returned. 'It's especially important for you, Dad. I thought of it last weekend when we were harrowing the all-weather gallop. I know it's supposed to be all-weather but it isn't really, is it?'

'Not really, I suppose,' his father said.

'Because it gets quite hardpacked if the frost gets into it and you need to harrow it for ages before a horse can even set foot on it.

'Right, fine. But how does the Hot Harrow work?' asked Graham.

'Simple, the tractor's dragging the harrow. You harness the heat from the tractor engine and feed it to the metal on the harrow so it not only breaks up the frost with force, it melts it too and that makes the whole thing much quicker.'

Graham nodded. 'Uh-uh, and how do you harness the heat?'

'Well, that's the bit I'm still working on,' said Billy, less confident now.

'The hardest bit,' Graham said.

'Not that hard, Dad. I just need to think about it a bit more.'

'Good. It's a good idea, Billy. Keep working on it.

Billy smiled at the praise from his father then turned to his mother. 'What do you think, Mum? Are you in?'

'I think it's a good idea too. You solve the heat-harnessing problem and, er, get back to me. Isn't that what they say in the business world?'

Billy nodded, still smiling widely.

His sister Jane sat opposite him at the oval yew table. She could never remember a day when that table had not been there. Jane was certain she had memories of sitting at it in a high chair with a bowl of soggy mush on the plastic tray in front. She sat there now almost fifteen years later, a very pretty girl, small for her age, smaller than any of her friends but with shining auburn hair, blue-green eyes and traces of summer freckles still spread across her delicate, slightly upturned nose on to her cheeks. Unlike most of her friends she wore no make-up or jewellery, had no piercings for studs and no intentions of letting anyone 'punch holes in her'. Her skin was smooth, blemish-free and her family were proud of her prettiness. Jane feigned indifference to her own looks but in her heart she was proud of them too – and proud of being different.

She swallowed some of her pasta and said to Maggie, 'Congratulations, Mum. Were you expecting a cheque for that much?'

'No, God, no! Nothing like that much.'

Jane's eyes showed a tiny spark of triumph. 'Then why don't you give half of it to my Banish Blindness fund?'

Billy pretended he was choking on his food. 'Half of it! You're kidding! That's almost thirty grand!'

Maggie knew she wasn't kidding and she was stunned both by the request and by the deviousness of her daughter's first question. And she was confused. She didn't know what to say in reply and Jane was looking at her, waiting coolly for that reply. Jane's fund-raising activities were something Maggie and Graham had always supported. The girl was tireless, had been since she was twelve and saw a TV programme about famine in Africa. And now she'd just proved she was also wily and a bit ruthless and Maggie was suddenly seeing a new side to the first child she'd borne, and her mind and her emotions weren't quite coping. She looked at her husband. He raised his eyebrows in a way that said, 'I can't help. Over to you.'

She looked at Jane and said, 'Of course I'll make a contribution to your fund.'

'A half?'

Billy spluttered again. Maggie felt anger showing in her eyes and hoped that it would make Jane back off. But Jane stayed cool, waiting. Maggie didn't know if her daughter felt in any way uncomfortable at what was such an obvious confrontation, one that she had cunningly engineered. What she did know was that Jane would be thinking that the end justified the means. Those people in Africa blinded by cataracts could be easily and cheaply treated, and twenty-eight thousand pounds would give an awful lot of people their sight back. If achieving that meant making her mother feel uncomfortable and embarrassed then Maggie knew that Jane would be able to live with that. She made a decision.

'How much have you raised so far?'

'Just over six hundred and sixty-two pounds. Mum, this would make such a difference.' And her face softened and Maggie saw her daughter again, saw that pleading look which told how deeply she really felt about this.

Maggie nodded. 'And when does this particular campaign end?'

'I wanted to send the money off just before Christmas. Just think what a gift it would be for those poor people to know they were going into the new year with the hope of being able to see again. To see their families.'

Maggie had been going to say that she'd match the final total but now that seemed mean and paltry. She said, 'Whatever your final total is, I'll multiply it by ten and write you a cheque.' She suddenly had a quick flashback to Jane's devious set-up question. There was no telling what manipulations her daughter might get into to really jack up the final total so she added, 'Up to a maximum of ten thousand pounds.'

Jane smiled and Maggie was relieved to know

172

she wasn't going to argue with that. Not right away, at least. Billy said, 'Oh, Mum! That's twice the cost of a patent application, that's not fair.'

Jane turned to her brother. 'The Hot Harrow isn't going to make anyone see again, is it?'

Billy was lost for words and blurted out. 'OK, maybe it won't, but it could help the people over there once they can see to grow crops and stuff!'

Jane said, 'And when was the last time there was frost in Africa?'

Billy went redder, mad at his sister, too clever for him yet again. 'Well, just a normal harrow then. I could help pay for those through sales of my Hot Harrow! Couldn't I Dad?'

Graham said, 'You could, I'm sure you could, but I think it's time we all calmed down and finished eating. There's evening stables to be done yet. You'll all need something hot inside you before we go back out in the cold.'

Billy groaned. Jane smiled a small triumphant smile. Maggie found she couldn't finish her meal and got up from the table. 'I'll wash up.'

Jane scooped the last of her pasta into her mouth and through it said, 'I'll dry, Mum!'

Maggie turned to her. 'It's OK. I'll wash and dry.' She took Jane's plate. Their eyes met, and Maggie knew in that moment that her relationship with her daughter would never be quite the same again.

When the family came out into the half-lit yard to complete the ritual of checking the horses and giving them their last feed, Monroe could see their breaths pluming in the night air. He was crouching by the fence in the bare-treed orchard,

173

the darkness offering all the cover he needed. The three square lights on the walls of the stables sent beams through the mist, making the Cassidy family look like ghosts as they separated and drifted away from each other to disappear into the shadowy boxes.

28

When Stonebanks asked Frankie if he'd mind covering Ascot for him on the Saturday before Christmas, Frankie was relieved and glad to accept. It rescued him from the seemingly inescapable assault from all angles of the coming festivities, and also gave him a solid excuse to decline Bobby Cranfield's invitation to have lunch and spend the day in his private box.

He'd thanked Bobby for the invite but had already said that he thought it was now inappropriate to be his guest at racemeetings. Bobby was PR director for the Jockey Club and Frankie was an employee. Nepotism was rife in racing. Without it, the game would probably grind to a halt. But now that he was getting into the job properly, Frankie was keen to prove himself through his own hard work; whatever he was to achieve, he didn't want people thinking it would be on the coat tails of one of the directors. Anyway, Bobby also owned quite a few horses now and Frankie had laughingly said to him, 'What if I end up investigating you or one of your trainers or jockeys sometime? I need to be seen to be acting absolutely independently.'

Bobby had laughed it off too and tried to persuade Frankie to join him for lunch at the very least. But Frankie won the debate and Bobby, good-naturedly as ever, conceded. His parting shot was, 'Well Frankie, you're not allowed to have a bet so you wouldn't have been able to take advantage of my big tip for Saturday. My trainer reckons Arctic Actor is a certainty in the handicap hurdle. When you see me in the winners' enclosure, you can at least shake my hand!'

Frankie promised he would.

Despite his failure to make any headway in the case of the kidnapping and death of Ulysses, Frankie was beginning to sharpen his skills in his job and his confidence was growing steadily. Few people on the racecourse knew who he was. He dressed in a quite casual manner; sometimes he'd wear a tie, sometimes not. He had a variety of sweaters and trousers which he wore in cycles, trying not to dress the same two days running. He had bought two new coats and now had five in all.

He felt it was important that none of the regulars began to notice the same man appearing frequently on the southern racecourses on week-days as well as weekends, drifting around the betting ring, the paddock, the Tote windows, the stables area. Anyone who had noticed him wouldn't have seen him doing much. He never approached a bookmaker or had a bet on the Tote. They wouldn't have known that he had a small but high-quality camera in his coat pocket. Nobody so far, Frankie was certain, had seen him taking pictures of 'interesting' people and who those people were talking to or drinking beside, or betting with. Sooner or later they would twig him and find out exactly who he was but until that time he had an advantage which he intended to keep for as long as possible.

At Ascot Frankie spent the first two races wandering around the betting ring; wherever he was in that noisy gathering he could always hear the braying voice of Compton Breslin, the well-known bookie.

Frankie couldn't pass him without smiling. Like himself, Breslin never wore the same clothes two days running but whereas Frankie dressed for anonymity, Breslin wore the most out-rageously bright and stagey clothes imaginable. Frankie knew that this and his brashness, his sometimes personal and loudmouthed chal-lenges to circling individuals clutching cash, were all a carefully planned part of Breslin's strategy. Bookmakers were already the natural enemies of punters; if one gave cause for personal dislike as well then all the more reason to try and take his money. And Frankie knew, as most did, that Breslin was the only winner in the long run. The fat bookie drove a gold Rolls Royce, of all things. From the moment he parked it and got out he'd be shooting his mouth off at racegoers approach-ing the entrances, handing out gold-edged business cards to them, inviting them to come and take him on.

In the ring before the start of the handicap

176

hurdle, Frankie had to concede that Breslin did at least put his money where his mouth was. Bobby Cranfield's horse Arctic Actor was a hot favourite with most bookies at 6/4. Breslin called 13/8 and 7/4 and was taking all the business on the favourite without reducing his price as most of them did, had to do, to balance their books. But Breslin just kept shouting the odds, coining in more and more cash while his colleagues looked on sour-faced. Frankie knew they'd all love to see the favourite win now so Breslin would be crucified.

Then he stopped and wondered at his use of that word and felt almost as though he should apologize silently to Jesus.

He moved away to watch the race from the stands. If Bobby was right about Arctic Actor being a certainty then Breslin would be taking a very cold bath indeed. Frankie made a mental note to go back into the ring after the race, just to see if Breslin could maintain the same confident demeanour when paying out.

But there was never any danger of the money bet on Arctic Actor going anywhere except into Breslin's bank account. An unconsidered outsider called Colonialize led from the tape, went well clear early and was never caught. Frankie watched him gallop past the post to an almost silent reception from the crowd. One of the things that had attracted him to racing many years ago had been the sheer passion of the spectators as they cheered their horse on; close finishes involving fancied horses were particularly atmospheric. But when 20/1 shots finished well clear of the others, things tended to be more funereal than festival. Frankie smiled wryly; that's racing, he thought. He felt a twinge of sympathy for his friend Bobby Cranfield but he knew there'd be no serious damage to the man's platinum-edged wallet. Still, Bobby would be embarrassed at tipping the horse to his friends. It had finished second but not for a moment had it looked like catching Colonialize.

Dusk was falling when Frankie drove away from the racecourse and by the time he turned along the track towards the cottage there was only a tinge of purple light left in the sky. His mood had darkened too on the way home. This cottage that had been his refuge these past months seemed slowly to be developing a life of its own; a possessive, enclosing, jealous life. Whereas before the silence had been comforting it now seemed moody, as though the cottage resented him for leaving it alone during the day.

When they'd moved to the cottage, Kathy had brought with her a trunk full of decorations and lights and a battered old foldaway tree she'd had for years. She'd adored Christmas and when he went inside Frankie decided to try and make the place look brighter and to do what Kathy would have done, would have wanted. He opened the trunk and started taking out colourful strands of paper.

An hour later he realized it had only made the place look even sadder. The Christmas tree winked forlornly in the corner, ashes lay cold in the grate, wreaths hung on the insides of the doors like tumbleweed in some ghost town. This house was closing in on him, trying to smother him.

Frankie put his head in his hands and decided that he'd better go and see a doctor.

The tall narrow chestnut Colonialize was led shivering into Peter Culling's operating theatre and the lad who looked after him was sent away. Culling injected the horse and stood watching as the shivers visibly slowed as though some internal battery was running down, then eventually stopped. He led the horse to a box and started rubbing him dry with some straw.

Back to the house then for a couple of hours in front of the TV before calling the trainer to report, in a sad voice, that the horse hadn't made it. Next he called Gerry Monroe and asked him to pick the horse up in the morning.

'I'm busy in the morning. I'll do it in the afternoon,' Monroe said.

Culling paused, trying to keep his temper under control. Since giving in to Monroe that night, this whole business had become fraught to the point where he couldn't manage the stress, couldn't keep it in check. And he knew what it must be doing to his heart. He was nailed between the power Monroe now had and the dread of being caught by the authorities, a chance which was increased the longer the horses stayed on his premises. Culling had two assistants. Part of his strategy of doing his doping on Saturdays was that only he was on the premises on Saturday nights and Sunday mornings.

'It has to be the morning, Gerry,' he said nervously.

Monroe's voice hardened. 'It doesn't *have* to be anything other than what I say, Mr Culling!'

'I didn't mean it to sound like that. It's just that, well, if things don't work out as planned, I won't be able to provide any more horses for you.'

'So? I'm sure there are some more bent vets around.'

Culling's face went red. His grip on the receiver tightened and he knew he had to get off the phone before his blood pressure rose any higher. 'Do it when you can make it, then. The horse will be in the usual place. Goodbye.' He hung up and made himself walk slowly to the conservatory to practise deep breathing.

Monroe had planned to spend one final evening up north to do a last recce on the Cassidy place. Still, he already had a pretty good handle on procedure in the yard. On two days that week they'd had runners. Graham Cassidy had driven the box so it was a fair assumption that when they had a runner, the boss would be away leaving just Mrs Cassidy and one groom. There were only eight horses in the yard and that didn't merit a head lad, which made Monroe's task easier.

He'd considered going in on a raceday and simply leading Angel Gabriel across the fields to where he'd park a trailer. Mrs Cassidy seemed to go out very little and Monroe reckoned she locked herself away somewhere to work on her writing. But in the end he'd decided not to take the risk. There appeared to be no form of alarm around the stables. The three security lights came on if anyone approached after dark but he'd noticed them do so when no one was around and suspected that small animals also triggered the beams.

The Cassidys had a couple of dogs who seemed to live inside most of the time. He'd yet to hear them bark. He was pretty sure he could simply sneak in during the early hours of the morning and damp the big horse's feet with rubber boots normally used for horses with foot problems. He had half-considered going in tonight, Saturday, but Culling's call had made his mind up for him. He'd head south again, pick this horse up from the vet's and take it to Hewitt's place.

He decided he'd steal Angel Gabriel in the early hours of Christmas Day and as he made his way back across the fields towards his car he congratulated himself on the irony of his timing. He smiled as he tried to recall the line in his head from his primary school lessons. 'And the angel said to Mary, "You are with child." And Monroe said to the Cassidys, "You are without horse."' And he laughed aloud at his cleverness and said, 'Shit, that's brilliant.'

29

Frankie moved out of the cottage on the Saturday night. His first impulse had been to find a hotel in London and book in for a week. But he knew the intensity of Christmas, or at least the commercial side of it, would be even more acute in the capital. He recalled seeing an ad in the travel pages of Saturday's newspaper and he scanned through till he found the 'hideaway for those who hate Christmas!'. It was a country house hotel in Builth Wells over the Welsh border, remote enough to lose himself for a few days but not that far from civilization. If needed he could be back in London reasonably quickly. He'd worked every weekend since he'd started, already had a day off booked for Monday and racing stopped for three days on the run-up to Christmas. If he could have Tuesday off that would give him a week away from everything; work, the empty cottage, Christmas.

As he drove west he thought about where he'd really like to be going – to a monastery somewhere for a week-long retreat. He felt the need of God, of his comfort, much more at that moment than he ever had in his life. But it was denied him because of what he had done. He'd convinced himself of this. There was no road back, especially for the hypocrite. He had a yearning too for his mother, for her forgiveness, her love. But he knew she despised him, was certain that if he knocked on her door she would spit in his face.

At the hotel, he was relieved at the complete absence of Christmas paraphernalia and also at the calm, professional welcome he received. The hotel was baronial inside and the sound of his footsteps on the marble reminded him of the echo in grand churches. His room was spacious and tastefully decorated, the big bed supremely comfortable. He'd arrived too late for dinner but had no appetite anyway and he hung up his clothes and climbed in between the cool sheets.

He lay a while luxuriating in the softness as the bed seemed to envelop him, hold him tenderly, almost as though it were human and knew of his sorrow. And he slept.

Sixty miles north of Frankie, Maggie Cassidy lay awake beside her sleeping husband. Her mind had been in turmoil since she'd taken a call the previous afternoon from her agent. He told her with delight that the auction for her next three books had brought a winning bid of half a million pounds. The news stunned Maggie to the extent that while she was saying to her agent how wonderful it was, she imagined that it was happening to someone else, that some other woman was speaking.

Maggie agonized for hours, then finally decided she would keep the news secret, deposit the cheque quietly in her bank and get on with life. That would be best for everyone. Definitely.

After less than four hours' sleep, Maggie was awakened by the first phone call congratulating her on her good fortune. The story had made the Sunday papers. Maggie hurried to the bathroom and wept quietly.

After lunch on Sunday Frankie went walking in the countryside around the hotel where lush, sheep-dotted pastureland covered the low swell of the hills. The weather was cold but fine and Frankie thought the sky looked a remarkably rich blue. He'd been out for an hour and his spirits had picked up considerably when he took a call from Bobby Cranfield.

'Frankie, I'm sorry to trouble you on a Sunday.'

'No problem, good to hear from you. Sorry about your horse getting stuffed yesterday.'

'That's why I'm ringing. You were on duty at Ascot yesterday, weren't you?'

'Yes.'

'Did you pick up anything unusual around that race?'

Frankie thought for a few moments. 'Not really ... no. Nothing I can think of. Why?'

'Well something wasn't quite right about the way Colonialize won that race. He's run against mine half a dozen times in the past and never got anywhere near him yet he won yesterday as though he could have gone round again. I've been through the formbooks, it wasn't even his style of running to make all, he's always been held up.'

'Maybe that was the secret then,' Frankie said. 'Maybe the front-running tactics suited him much better.'

'I don't think so.'

Frankie noted the hesitation then the deliberate pause before Bobby said, 'He ran as if he'd been doped.'

Frankie's inexperience made him ponder as he tried to gather his thoughts. He said, 'Wouldn't he have been dope-tested after the race?'

'He was. We won't get the results until next week but I'll be awaiting them, as they say, with interest.'

'And no doubt hoping that you're wrong. The last thing we need's a doping scandal.'

'Dead right. Anyway, I also called to see how you were. I should have asked that first. Very rude of me.'

'Not at all. I'm OK. Felt I had to get away from the cottage for Christmas so I've found myself a nice quiet country hotel. If I can persuade Stonebanks to cover for me on Tuesday then I'm going to stay here for a week and just unwind.'

Bobby Cranfield sounded immediately concerned. 'Frankie, you mustn't spend Christmas on your own. Come and stay with us! We'd be absolutely delighted to have your company over Christmas!'

'No thanks, Bobby. It's very kind of you to offer but I really would rather be on my own.' He could sense the frustration, the exasperation in Bobby but the older man restrained himself. 'Well I understand, but Frankie, if you change your mind, promise you'll call me.'

Frankie smiled. 'I promise.'

'Good. Good. Well, I'll let you get on with your relaxation. Have a very happy Christmas.' It was out before he realized how hollow it must sound

185

but Frankie quickly put him at ease.

'I will, Bobby, and I wish you and your family the same.'

'Take care, Frankie.'

'And you. Bye.'

'Bye bye.'

As he pressed the 'End' button on his phone the thing that had been niggling at his mind these past few minutes came through clearly; Compton Breslin. The bookie had been persistently offering longer odds against Bobby's horse than anyone else. That could mean that he himself simply didn't fancy it or it could mean that someone had told him it was going to lose. And if Colonialize had been doped, not only had Breslin probably been told that the favourite would lose, there was every chance he'd have known that Colonialize would win.

Frankie considered ringing Bobby straight back. Then he thought about how he'd often heard Breslin shouting the odds about a fancied horse although he'd never paid particular attention to whether those odds were longer than those offered by his competitors. Yesterday was probably no more than normal practice for the big bookie. Frankie decided he'd wait until the dope test results were through before deciding what to do about Breslin.

The Welsh sky was still clear but a cold wind had got up. Frankie checked his watch, turned up his collar and headed back towards the hotel.

30

On Monday the *Racing Post* carried the news of Maggie Cassidy's half-million-pound book contract on page three along with a picture of Maggie and Angel Gabriel. Reading it over breakfast Gerry Monroe cackled with glee. 'Christmas has come early.'

Frankie too read the *Racing Post* over breakfast, checking through all the comments from Ascot on Saturday and looking at the betting analysis to see if he could glean anything from the race Colonialize had won. There were no unusually large bets reported on the losing favourite and not a single decent-sized bet reported on the winner.

Scanning through the rest of the paper Frankie noticed the piece on Maggie Cassidy and he found it heart-warming. She was a writer just like Kathy had been, albeit working in a different format. He held the page up better to catch the light from the big window behind his table; there was a resemblance to Kathy too in the woman's looks. She wasn't quite an older version but she had the same-shaped eyes and jawline and the same sort of mischievous look about her. The article went on to discuss Angel Gabriel's prospects in the Grand National and suddenly the image of the dead Ulysses in the stream sprang to Frankie's mind.

He left an almost full cup of tea and went to his room for his diary. In it he found the number of Jamie Robson, his colleague in the north-west. When he rang he heard a message telling him that Jamie was away for Christmas and that all business calls should be directed to the Jockey Club Security Department in London.

Frankie reached back into his briefcase and took out his *Directory of The Turf* telephone book. He found the Cassidy number and dialled; engaged. He tried for more than twenty minutes before getting through and was answered by an exasperated Maggie who by now couldn't help but laugh slightly as she said, 'Hello, the Cassidy madhouse!'

Frankie guessed that every time she'd put the phone down it had rung again. He said, 'Is that Mrs Cassidy?'

'It is she.'

'We haven't met. My name is Frankie Houli-han, I'm a racing intelligence officer with the Jockey Club Security Department.'

'Oh, hello. What can I do for you?'

'I'm sorry to trouble you. Jamie Robson, who I think you probably know, would normally have rung you but he's away on holiday.'

'Lucky him. I could do with one.'

'Would it be possible to speak to your husband? I'm sorry to be so formal but it's probably best if I speak to the actual licence-holder.'

'Is anything wrong?' Frankie could read the tone exactly and knew Maggie suffered from the same brand of fatalism he did; if things were going outrageously well then something bad was sure to come along.

'No,' he said. 'Nothing at all, just a sort of pre-emptive call on my part. Nothing really to worry about.'

She hesitated then said, 'Can you hold on? Graham's out in the yard. I'll just go and get him.'

'Sure, and by the way, congratulations on your good news.'

'Thanks. Thank you.'

He heard the receiver being put down on a hard surface and he waited for what seemed quite a long time before he heard footsteps approach and voices growing louder. A rattle again as the receiver was picked up; 'Graham Cassidy. Can I help?'

Frankie introduced himself and went through the same spiel as he had with Mrs Cassidy. 'I hope you don't mind me calling, Mr Cassidy. I read the piece about your wife's good fortune in the *Racing Post* and thought it was worth mentioning to you that the department believes that the person who kidnapped and killed Ulysses a couple of weeks back may well, eh, strike again, to use a tabloid phrase.'

'Oh, thanks. Thanks. We hadn't thought of that. Good point. I'm glad you rang.'

'That's OK.' Frankie was relieved. He'd been unsure of the reaction he might get and had half-thought that grannies and egg-sucking might have been mentioned.

The trainer said, 'Is there, eh, anything in particular you'd recommend we do? Security-wise, I mean?'

That caught Frankie out. 'Well, it's up to you really. I'm not familiar with the security you have in place at the moment.'

'Not much, really. We've got some lights that come on automatically in the yard at night if anyone approaches. But to be honest, we don't pay much attention when they do. We're usually sound asleep by ten.'

'You've got no form of alarm system?'

'Well, there's one in the house but nothing in the yard. An alarm going off in the middle of the night would probably leave us with a stable full of nervous wrecks anyway.'

'Do you keep the place locked at night?'

'No, we're too afraid to. Had a fire here about ten years ago and three horses were trapped in a locked stable. To be honest, I'd rather they were kidnapped than burned to death if a fire broke out.'

That left Frankie at a loss. 'Well maybe you should contact your local police crime prevention officer and see if he can suggest anything.'

'Good idea! Cassidy sounded pleased. 'I'll do that. I'll give him a call.'

'Fine. Well, I'll let you get on with your celebrations.'

'Indeed, yes. Thanks.'

'Happy Christmas.'

'And to you and yours, Mr Houlihan. Oh, do I need to take your number?'

'You're welcome to.'

'Fine. I have a pen...'

31

In the twilight of Christmas Eve, Jane Cassidy finished laying a bed of fresh straw in the box of the animal she'd known and loved for most of her life. She had clear memories of her four-year-old self clutching her mother's hand as she watched her father help the straining fat mare deliver the slippery sac of dark hair and legs that was to be christened Angel Gabriel and known to the family as Gabby. As mucus from the mouth of the foal dripped from her father's fingers as he cleaned it to open the airways, Jane had said, 'Has he been chewing gum, Dad?' She recalled how her mum and dad had laughed.

And that foal had grown alongside her. Many an hour in summer had been spent just sitting on the paddock fence watching him graze close to his mother, seeing him play on those gangly legs. And there was the first time the electric clippers had been used on his coat and he'd panicked and her dad had said, 'You hold him, Jane. Hold his head. You're the only one that can keep him quiet.' And she'd done it with great pride and great love of both the horse and her father for making her feel so special.

And she'd helped break him too. She'd been riding ponies before Angel Gabriel had been born and by the time they'd come to break him, when she was nine, Jane was an accomplished

191

rider. Like all their horses, he'd been broken gently, with no fear. Most racehorses were broken as yearlings but her dad had been determined to let Angel Gabriel reach full maturity before doing anything with him. This horse was his great hope. He wasn't to see a racecourse until he was six years old, an age when many others were already battle-scarred.

But Jane's father had wanted a mature, strong-boned, clean-winded horse, physically and mentally sound, to work with, to develop and train and hone, to bring home his dream. Jane smiled in the gathering gloom of the box as she thought back to something she'd overheard her mother say on the phone when Angel Gabriel was five. 'He says he wants to wait until the horse is ready but I think he means till *he's* ready. He's got so much hope invested in Gabby that he keeps putting off the first race. He can't bear the thought of having the dream broken.'

She never knew if her mother was right but it hadn't mattered. Gabby had finished third at Haydock in his first race and had now won fourteen races and over one hundred thousand pounds in prize money. It had taken Jane till his third season before she lost her terror of him falling in a race and being killed or badly injured. She'd travel to the races with him, standing by his stall in the swaying horsebox, determined to be beside him on what might be his last trip. During his races, she'd be in the stand watching every stride except the one before and after each jump when she'd close her eyes and pray he landed safely on the other side. She only ever saw him

192

jumping when she watched the video at home afterwards and it was watching these that helped her lose her fear.

It was obvious to her that Gabby was a natural jumper. Almost every National Hunt horse makes a mistake at some point during its races but Gabby was that rare animal who was almost foot-perfect. He was sixteen hands of muscle which was exceptionally well distributed on his skeleton. His excellent symmetry made him look compact and also played a major part in giving him superb balance and agility. Jockeys loved him, not only for the confidence he gave them but for the heart and the grit he had. He hated being beaten and would fight for every inch of ground when something loomed up alongside him and usually he would simply grind his opponents down, force them to give in.

The racing public loved him for his spirit and his wonderful jumping. And Jane Cassidy loved him because he was all the things the public knew and more; gentle, intelligent and loving. When she'd been a child, it wasn't unusual for her mother to find her asleep in his box, curled up in the straw between his metal-shod feet. He was also a constant in her life. He'd always been there, had never scolded her or fallen out with her or teased her. Gabby had always been glad to see her no matter how foul a mood she might be in. He seemed to know her footsteps as she approached and he'd give a small whinny of anticipation then nuzzle her warmly as soon as she reached him.

Jane forked the straw for the hundredth time, trying to make it level. A brand-new bed of this thickness was a rare treat. As with other yards, bedding was usually sifted each day and the droppings and wet straw removed. The remaining straw was simply topped up. But for Christmas, Angel Gabriel had a fresh, sweet-smelling cushion.

She put the fork outside the box and unbuckled Gabby's rug. Taking a stiff-bristled brush she worked on his black tail, cleaning away the wisps of straw and the dust. Then to his mane, singing softly to him now, making his ears prick and swivel. 'Silent night, holy night...' Her voice was pleasant. The horse stood very still, seeming to be listening intently. 'You like that one, do you?' she asked and his ears flicked again. After the carol she took a softer brush and began working on his sleek, muscled shoulder. She spoke to him, 'Remember, I'm going away soon. Going to Ireland to see Poppy. She's hurt herself. I'm going to help her get better. Be away for a while but Dad'll look after you... Doesn't Dad always look after you, eh? Don't worry. Will you miss me? I'll miss you. I'll miss your smell, well not your poo, I won't miss that! And I'll miss the warmth you give off when it's cold like this.' She was crouching beneath him now, doing his underside, knowing he'd be nodding furiously as he always did when she brushed his belly.

When she finished she put his rug back on and filled his haynet and water bucket, then stood back and looked at him. 'You're all done up for the party season,' she said and moved forward again and hugged his neck. 'Happy Christmas, Gabby.'

As the Cassidy family finished eating Christmas Eve dinner strong winds were whipping over the Shropshire fields. Maggie Cassidy washed up, taking pleasure in hearing the gale outside and listening to Graham and the children talking at the table, safe and warm.

The atmosphere was perfect. Everything was set for a proper, traditional Christmas. The tree stood glowing in the corner; logs burned in the big grate, warming the cushions in the inglenook. The dogs lay dozing on the rug and the family were in harmony. Even the horses were well. It was unusual not to have at least one animal down with something or other but all were fit and healthy. December had brought three winners, a good bag for such a small stable. Graham was as happy as she'd ever known him. Above all, there was money in the bank and more on the way.

Maggie stopped for a few seconds, just stood completely still to make sure she took in this moment. She forced her mind to concentrate on the meaning of it, the beauty of it, for she knew she would never get it back again. Tears of joy filled her eyes but never quite spilled over.

Graham Cassidy had intended to keep the fire going until it was time for bed but the wind blew with such force outside that it funnelled gusts down the chimney, making the flames and smoke billow out dangerously over the hearth. Graham damped the fire down and decided to go and check the horses.

Travelling north on the M6, Gerry Monroe was losing time. The high sides of the horsebox caught the crosswinds like sails and anything above forty-five miles an hour saw him wrestling with all his strength to keep the box in the inside lane. Although he cursed constantly, he wasn't too despondent. He knew the weather would be making so much noise around the yard, clattering every loose slate, screaming through each gap, setting every hanging thing swinging, that the trade-off was worth it. Unless Angel Gabriel spooked at it all, it should be an easy task to lead him out of the stable and away.

32

The storm battered Ballard Hall, Frankie Houlihan's hotel hideaway, with all it could muster but the solid oak doors and two-foot-thick walls would not dignify the attack with so much as a rattle or squeak.

Yellow light shone from just one first-floor bedroom where Frankie lay listening to Fauré's Requiem on the bedside radio. He was feeling emotional. Not just because it was Christmas Eve and Kathy wasn't with him. He'd just taken a call on his mobile from his sister, Theresa, who'd got the number from the message on his answerphone at home.

She'd told him that all the family was well, including Mother. It had warmed Frankie to hear her voice, to hear her talk of his brothers and sisters. Theresa had tried to persuade him to call them all, wish them a merry Christmas. 'Maybe next year,' Frankie had said.

When she hung up, Frankie was surprised to find he'd been talking for almost forty-five minutes. He'd been glad to hear from her but her call had left a melancholy on him and he was so, so tired of melancholy. He needed some joy and some laughter, needed it like sometimes you need sleep; he had to have it to function fully again but he did not know where to find it. He could lie down when he needed sleep. There was no practical thing to turn to for joy or spontaneous, happy laughter.

He craved that. And he craved some spiritual sustenance; had done since he'd given up the right to it by walking out on God. He'd been desperate for it since losing Kathy, desperate for the right to pray again. It was a right he denied himself because he thought he must deserve some punishment, some eternal penance.

Easing himself off the bed he began pacing the room, his bare feet sinking deep in the rug that led to the window, his navy towelling dressing-gown swinging gently at the heavy hem. For the first time in his adult life he should have been celebrating a non-religious Christmas, a lovers' Christmas, a commercial Christmas. The first Christmas when what he was celebrating was not the birth of Jesus Christ.

He stopped by the window. The rain rattled angrily on the pane and the heavy clouds, pushed by the wind, moved as if in fast-forward, showing glimpses of a bright and peaceful moon. But no star in the east.

He was up early next morning out running in the wet, shining countryside of the Welsh borders. When he returned to his room he found a message on his mobile phone. It was from a grievously serious Graham Cassidy. 'Mr Houlihan, I'm really very sorry to be ringing you on Christmas Day but I'm afraid the worst has happened, as you warned. I'd very much appreciate a call whenever it's convenient.'

A seventy-five-minute drive on almost-deserted roads took Frankie to the Cassidy place. On the way he called Geoff Stonebanks and told him about the kidnapping. Stonebanks asked Frankie if he could handle it until next day, then he'd try to organize some back-up. Frankie told him not to worry, that he'd already arranged a meeting with the police and would update Stonebanks next day. He could tell that the big man was distressed about this happening on Christmas Day, but not half as distressed, Frankie thought, as the Cassidys would be.

As he turned to go along the final rough road towards the Cassidy place he felt guilty for feeling relieved that this had come up to break the melancholy, the monotony of these days. It was a pity that somebody had to suffer so his mind could be occupied by something other than self-pity.

The door was dark green with a diamond-shaped window so thick that the glass distorted the light and movement inside. Below the window hung a Christmas wreath, its foliage damaged from the battering the wind had given it against the door. As he waited for a response to his brief press on the bell button Frankie could see the scratch marks the holly had made in the door's paintwork.

When Maggie Cassidy opened the door and saw him she knew somehow before he spoke who he was. The man with the nice Irish voice who'd spoken to her the other night. He hadn't said anything yet but she knew it was him. Just over six foot tall, she judged, slim, strong-looking with thick dark hair, and eyes that were a vivid blue as the reflection of the pale sun on the glass caught them.

'Mrs Cassidy?'

She smiled and held out her hand. 'Mr Houlihan. Please come in.'

Frankie walked past her. The door opened into the kitchen. Frankie had seen so many of these kitchens now with their big pine tables and Agas, their tiled walls hung haphazardly with pictures, framed and unframed, the deep windows, the brightness, the colour. Frankie had been at quite a few trainers' houses and all of their kitchens looked pretty much the same, like the Cassidys', although this one was definitely the tidiest he'd seen. It was homely-looking but neat and very tidy. Frankie wondered if the Cassidys had a cleaner although the 'memory' of Mrs Cassidy's handshake a minute ago suggested she'd done plenty of hard work in her own life. When shaking hands with women, Frankie was sometimes aware of, and embarrassed by, how soft his hands were compared to those he was shaking.

Maggie closed the door and moved towards the table. 'Please sit down, Mr Houlihan. The kettle's just boiled if you'd like a cup of tea or coffee.'

'A cup of tea would be nice.'

She smiled. 'Fine. You look like a milk and no sugar man.'

'I am. I am indeed. I didn't know it was so obvious.'

'Ahh, it is. A slight turning down of the right eyelid at the corner. Always gives it away.'

She was smiling warmly and Frankie was beginning to wonder if he'd come to the wrong place. He watched her pour the hot water into a pale blue teapot. He liked her as he had done when he'd seen her picture in the paper and when he'd spoken to her briefly on the phone. She seemed naturally friendly and at ease, confident. He liked confident women. Admired was a better word, Frankie thought, under the circumstances. It wasn't right to like other women, that wasn't the expression he was looking for. You could admire a woman for her achievements, and being confident these days was, he supposed, an achievement in itself.

Maggie Cassidy turned towards him. Her shoulder-length hair was thick, and looked to Frankie as if the grey had been rinsed back to her natural rich brown colour. She said, 'Are you hungry?'

'No, thanks.'

'You had breakfast then before you left home.'

'I haven't been at home but I did have a fine breakfast this morning.'

'And what did you have then?' she asked.

'I had porridge and bacon and eggs, toast and marmalade and two cups of tea,' Frankie said, feeling rather like a child.

Maggie laughed lightly. 'If I'd eaten that at eight o'clock, I'd be a stone heavier by now!'

'Ah well, I went for a run beforehand,' he said lamely.

'Maybe I should take up running?'

Frankie shrugged and smiled then looked away, suddenly feeling awkward. Maggie brought two yellow mugs of tea to the table and sat down opposite Frankie. She pushed his across and he reached to take it. He smiled a thank-you and sipped. He could see the lines now around her eyes and mouth and judged that she was mid-to-late forties. She wore a light covering of make-up; no lipstick but some sort of stuff on her skin and a trace of eye shadow and mascara. She returned his smile and he saw a deep intelligence in her hazel eyes; but there was a vulnerability there too; she was obviously finding it tough to completely mask the stress of what had happened.

'How is your husband?' Frankie asked.

She was silent for a few moments, then said, 'Philosophical, I suppose. That would be the best way to put it. At least that's the face he's putting on to others. I know he'll be churned up inside at the thought of Gabby being away from him, never mind with some kidnapper. Graham's spent his life bouncing back from things, he'll find some way to handle this.'

'Is he around?'

'He's out with the horses. Getting on with things. Making the best of what's left.'

Frankie saw the façade drop away now, the lightness of the last few minutes collapsing as she suddenly looked tired and very strained. He was tempted to say something about there being a chance of getting the horse back, something to offer some comfort but he knew it might just raise false hopes. He said, 'Have the police been?'

'Been and gone. Seemed interested from a novelty viewpoint but I'm afraid I wouldn't hold out much hope of them getting Gabby back.' She stared at the floor, looking almost blank for a few seconds then she looked up. 'Were you involved with the last kidnap?'

'Involved in trying to solve it.'

She smiled wearily. 'Of course. That was what I meant. Did you feel there was ever a chance of getting that horse back, what did you call him?'

'Ulysses.' Frankie felt suddenly put on the spot. 'It was a very very tough situation. We had little contact from the kidnapper, just three calls in all. And the owner was...' Frankie knew he'd need to be particularly careful here. '...extremely upset and emotional about the whole business, perfectly understandably.'

'Did he ever consider paying the ransom?'

Frankie was reluctant to get much deeper in. The racing world was very insular. Nice as she seemed he didn't know Maggie Cassidy or what her capacity for gossip might be and the last thing he needed was Christopher Benjamin, Ulysses' owner, hearing on the grapevine that Frankie had been discussing his private business. He said, 'We would always advise that the ransom shouldn't be paid.' He thought he saw a

202

definite look of relief in her eyes.

'How much did they ask for?'

'Quarter of a million pounds.'

'Did the owner actually want to pay?'

Frankie was growing increasingly uncomfortable but he understood what Maggie was doing. She was simply trying to prepare herself for the unknown. He said, 'Nobody wants to pay out that sort of money, Mrs Cassidy.'

'Please call me Maggie.'

He sipped his tea. 'My name is Frankie.'

She nodded slightly and looked thoughtful. Frankie said, 'Will your husband be out with the horses for a while yet?'

'Had enough of me, Frankie?' she smiled tiredly.

He felt himself blush slightly and raised his mug high to try to cover it. Still half-shielding his warm face he said, 'I just wondered if we shouldn't go through the questions together, all three of us. Just to save repetition.'

'Repetition, hesitation, deviation,' she said, more to herself, it seemed, than to Frankie.

Frankie looked baffled. Maggie said, *Just a Minute*. It's a radio panel game where the players have to speak for a full minute on a nominated subject without repetition, deviation or hesitation.'

'Not easy,' Frankie said and smiled at his thoughts.

'What's so funny?'

'I used to know some old priests who couldn't do five seconds of that, never mind a minute.'

Maggie's eyes twinkled warmly now. 'I used to

know some old women who could do five minutes of it easily.'

They both smiled companionably then Maggie stood up determinedly and said, 'Right, let's go out and see Graham.'

They found him in one of the boxes, grooming a dappled grey gelding, brushing methodically, quietly, unaware of their presence outside the metal bars of the box. Frankie saw a slight change in Maggie's face as she watched him and he couldn't interpret it. There was a steeliness in it. He couldn't pin it down beyond that. Still, he had no way of knowing how this disaster would affect the Cassidys deep down, what damage it might do to them. Crossing the yard to these corner boxes he'd become acutely aware of what this loss must actually mean to such a small set-up. Losing any horse from here would be a major blow, to have the Grand National favourite snatched away, well, he just couldn't imagine how they must be feeling, for all Maggie's smiles and brave face.

He watched her. Her mouth was slightly open as though about to speak but she seemed transfixed by the sight of her husband. He wore tan jodhpurs tucked into ankle-length rubber and canvas boots, and a dark green fleece top with a horse's head and the word Aintree large on the back. He looked very lean and fit to Frankie and still had a full head of hair although the grey showed through clearly even in the gloom of the box. There was no sound except for the brush sweeping a perfect rhythm down the horse's bright flank and Graham Cassidy's equally rhythmical breathing.

Maggie said quietly, 'You'll brush the spots right off him.'

'Bet I don't,' said Graham without looking up.

'How much?'

'Bet you fifty pence.'

'Better make it ten. We're saving up for a ransom.'

The joke seemed to end there for Graham and he stopped brushing and stood completely still as though he'd been knifed. She said, 'Cheer up, Mr Houlihan's here.'

The trainer turned slowly, a light sheen of sweat on his brow. As he came towards the half-door he forced a smile on to a face that looked ingrained with desperation and hopelessness and Frankie admired him hugely for the effort. The smile was fully formed as he reached for Frankie's hand. 'How do you do, Mr Houlihan? I'm so sorry to have called you on Christmas Day. Been bothering me ever since I put the phone down.'

Frankie took his hand, feeling the fine grit that layered his skin from the hard grooming. 'No need to apologize. I was having a very quiet time. It's nice to meet you. I'm just sorry that it's under these circumstances.'

'Yes. Well ... don't worry.'

Frankie could see he was at a loss as the frown returned to his face, the desperate look to his eyes. He reached to touch the trainer's arm. 'I'll help in any way I can. Don't be thinking it's a lost cause, Mr Cassidy.'

'Graham, please,' the trainer said.

'Graham.'

'Frankie.'

'Typical men,' said Maggie, 'only met a minute ago and already into monosyllabic conversation.'

All three smiled. Graham said, 'Shall we go inside and have a cup of tea? I'm sure you'll want to ask some questions then get back to your family and your Christmas celebrations.'

'Don't worry about me. My family are not around this Christmas, so I'm in no hurry at all.'

Maggie touched his arm and said, 'Oh, you'll have Christmas dinner with us then!'

Frankie blushed again. 'I hope you don't think I was angling for an invitation, giving you some sad story!'

Maggie said, 'Of course we do!' as Graham was saying, 'Of course we don't,' and all three ended up chuckling. It lifted Frankie's spirits, cheered him to see the momentary relief of Graham's burden. Laughter had been the last thing he'd expected to find at the Cassidy house. Laughter and friendliness in a troubled place. On Christmas Day. Praise be to God.

33

On the way south with Angel Gabriel in the back, Monroe had decided to stay off the motorways. He couldn't be certain when the alarm would be raised at the Cassidy place. That howling storm had helped him simply walk the horse out of its box. He couldn't believe how easy it had been –

but that also planted a thought that he might be the victim of some set-up.

The eaves had moaned, the windows shook in their frames and the slates had rattled but not a dog had barked. And there hadn't even been a lock on the stable door. He'd simply slid a couple of bolts back and led Angel Gabriel out. The horse had hesitated at the door and spooked slightly a couple of times on the way to the horse-box but otherwise had been a real gentleman. But it had all been just too easy and Monroe wondered if he was being tailed or something.

There was also the factor of having to go even more slowly with the horse in the back and the strong crosswinds. It had been hairy enough at times, he thought, doing some pretty low speeds on the way up with maniac drivers suddenly finding themselves halfway up your arse. The last thing he needed was an accident. Anyway, as he was driving through the night he could stick to the A and B roads, they'd probably be quieter than the motorways too.

He spent some of the journey refining his plan, plotting how best to handle things with Hewitt. If only he knew what the guy was doing at that big house on the hill and how the Irishman, Gleeson, was involved. Was Gleeson just the bagman for a bigger organization or was it some scheme of his own? Nah, couldn't be, thought Monroe, the guy surely didn't have the brains to come up with anything halfway decent. It had to be funded by someone else.

Whatever, there had to be scope in it for him to get a share. He'd proved in these past few weeks he was smarter than many. Much cleverer than some of the big shots who thought they were something in this game. He hated most of the people still involved in racing, despised them just for being at the hub while his fear and his past had condemned him to life on the edges of the racing community. Monroe the nobody – well, that's what they thought. The Cassidys wouldn't be thinking that when he rang them. He wasn't on the edges any more. He had the racing world by the balls. When news of Angel Gabriel broke they'd be shitting themselves from Portman Square to Perth.

Much as Monroe wanted to terrorize the racing world by leaving butchered horses for them to find, Mrs Cassidy was a very rich woman and if he asked for half a million this time there had to be a chance she'd pay it.

If they did decide to pay, how could he make sure he'd get the money without the cops appearing from everywhere? He was smart enough to know that the establishment punished people like him a hell of a lot more severely for extortion than for killing horses. If he got caught trying to haul away a bag with half a million quid in it he knew he was probably looking at fifteen years in jail. There were other ways of making money from this. Long-term payback, maybe, but much, much safer. He'd need to think about it. In the meantime he'd enjoy thinking about the rich Cassidys and how anxious they might be feeling. A bad day to feel anxious, and there was only one person in the whole world who could ease that anxiety for them. And it wasn't Santa Claus.

34

In the Cassidy kitchen they settled down to Christmas dinner just after three o'clock. Maggie and Graham sat on one long side of the big rectangular table. On the opposite side, Frankie sat between Jane and Billy. The tension was almost tangible; it had been building all day and Frankie felt that his presence was a hindrance to the natural expression of the anger and frustration that they must feel. Jane in particular looked very distressed. Her eyes were red and puffy and she seemed constantly close to tears.

He'd left them alone for a couple of hours to go and visit the police. When he'd come back it was obvious that Jane and her mother had been crying. Since then it had been politeness in front of the guest and stiff upper lips all round although Graham seemed to be the one trying hardest while suffering most. The trainer was obviously upset and anxious for the call they all knew had to come but he strove to present an air of steadfastness, a sense that whatever happened they would plough on through life.

Maggie drank a glass of chilled Chablis. The others had soft drinks. Graham carved the turkey methodically while the kids and Maggie made comments about his carving style and Frankie smiled dutifully and even laughed lightly at some of the gentle ribbing. He knew it was mostly for his benefit, to try to make him feel more relaxed and he thought a lot of them for trying so hard, but when all their plates were filled with turkey and stuffing, roast potatoes and mixed vegetables, he felt it was time to say something.

Before he picked up his cutlery he said, 'I'd like to thank you all for making me feel so welcome. Especially on a day when you really should be alone with each other... If you know what I mean! Kind of Irish, I suppose!' And he dropped his eyes as they smiled and laughed and he felt the blood come to his face again.

Maggie said, 'Don't be daft. If you weren't here we'd be fighting already, throwing sprouts at each other and knocking drinks all over the tablecloth.'

Graham nodded, smiling approvingly at his wife.

Frankie said, 'Thanks. What I wanted to say too was that you mustn't feel that you can't let rip because I'm here. I'm sure you're all very frustrated and very angry over Gabby and I know this dinner won't be sitting too well in your stomachs worrying about him. I want you to feel free to say anything you like if it makes you feel better.'

They went quiet. After a few moments Jane said, 'Do you think he'll call today, Frankie, the kidnapper?'

'I hope he does. The longer he leaves it the more on edge we're all going to be.'

'What sort of ransom do you think he'll ask for?' Jane said.

Frankie shrugged and cut a piece of turkey. Mopping gravy with it he said, 'There's no way of knowing.'

There was silence again for a while then Billy, still chewing, spoke. 'I thought you weren't supposed to go to the police if somebody kidnapped you, I mean kidnapped your son or your horse or whatever.'

'I think that's what the kidnappers would certainly prefer,' said Frankie.

Billy said, 'Well Dad called them right away.'

Frankie spotted the potential for conflict but was sure Graham wouldn't take what he'd said the wrong way. 'Your father was absolutely right in calling the police. For a start, the horse has been stolen. It may not even be the kidnapper, we're just, kind of, making that assumption.'

'But it looks favourite that it's the kidnapper, doesn't it?' Billy said.

'Coming so soon after the last one, I suppose it does. You're right,' said Frankie.

Billy warmed to Frankie then. Not many adults had ever told him he was right about something. Maggie had been watching, scanning each of the faces as they spoke. Frankie's sincerity, his mild blushing and lack of worldliness endeared him to her. At times it seemed to her as though three children sat opposite. She said, 'How long have you worked for the Jockey Club?'

'I only started a few weeks ago.'

Billy said, 'Phew, this is a big job for you then, isn't it?'

Frankie chuckled. 'I suppose it is if you look at it that way.'

Graham said, 'Were you in racing before this then?'

'Only as a spectator. Me da ... my father loved

the racing and used to take me to The Curragh and Leopardstown when I was Billy's age. Ever since then I tried to go as often as I could, which wasn't as often as I liked.'

'So what was your job before this?' Jane asked.

Frankie had been trying to prepare for answering this question. When Kathy had been alive, the question hadn't bothered him too much because she was almost always around when it was asked and as far as he was concerned that was testament enough, that people could see her, see how easy she must be to love; so back then he'd answer easily, unfazed. But this was the first time he'd been asked since Kathy died. He had never been among people, socially, who hadn't known. Now they were waiting, these kind people who'd taken him in when they had plenty of troubles of their own. He knew as he opened his mouth to answer that his relationship with all of them was about to start changing because he knew the questions that had to come next.

'I was a Catholic priest.'

Jane and Maggie stopped and looked at him. Graham and Billy carried on eating although Billy, chewing again said, 'I've seen priests at the races quite a few times. I used to plan to follow them to the bookies 'cause I thought they got tips from God.'

They all laughed.

Jane asked, 'How long were you a priest for?'

Maggie tutted. 'Jane! That's none of your business.'

'Oh, Mum! I was only asking!'

The first awkward silence. As the architect of it,

Frankie thought it best that he filled it. 'I was a priest for eight years. I spent a year of that as chaplain to a police force. They gave me some training in police-type stuff and that, believe it or not, was a sound enough background to get me this job.'

'So, did you get made redundant from being a priest?' Billy asked.

'Billy!' Maggie said, although she was more curious than any to hear Frankie's answer and she was relieved (although she tried not to show it) when Frankie gently raised a hand and smiled in a way that said, 'It's OK, don't worry.' He said to Billy, 'I sort of made myself redundant.'

Billy said, 'Oh, I've heard about that too. They do that in factories when they need to cut jobs down. They say there'll be voluntary redundancies. They do it when they've got too many workers. Is it the same? Did they have too many priests?'

Frankie was conscious that only Graham was eating now, showing no particular keenness to hear his answer. Maggie and Jane were riveted. Billy was just curious. Frankie said to him, 'Well, it wasn't quite like that. I sort of failed my own quality control test if you like and decided it would be better for the Church if I found myself another job.'

Billy nodded, still chewing. 'So you found this one? Do you like it better?'

'In many ways I do. It's very interesting. And I get to have dinner with some very nice families.'

Billy said, 'Is it a well-paid job working for the Jockey Club like you do?'

'Billy!' Maggie said. 'It is very bad manners to ask questions like that! Especially of guests!'

Billy looked slightly hurt and embarrassed. He looked down at his plate and said, 'Sorry.'

Frankie said, 'No problem. And to answer your question, it's not that well paid and I'm sure you're bright enough to get a job that will pay an awful lot more. But then again, money's not everything.'

'Well said,' Graham put in.

Billy said, 'It is when you haven't got any.'

Smiles all round again. Frankie noticed that Graham had almost finished his meal and the others were well ahead of Frankie too as he'd been doing most of the talking. Billy had done his fair share but hadn't let it interrupt his chewing and forking rhythm. Jane finished and wiped her mouth with her napkin. Frankie saw her glance slightly nervously at her mother then turn to him and he sensed, he knew, that a particularly awkward question was coming. As he steeled himself, the phone rang.

As Graham spoke to the kidnapper, none of the family, except Graham, could stay seated. They gathered around him, Maggie behind with her hand on his shoulder, Jane and Billy flanking him, their heads forward and tilted trying to hear what was being said by the kidnapper. Frankie stood further away, towards the opposite end of the table.

Graham said, 'That depends.'

'On what? It's a simple enough question,' said the voice on the other end. 'How much is he worth to you?'

'He's worth quite a bit.'

'Put a price on it.'

Graham kept calm. 'If we put him up for sale, we might get as much as two hundred thousand pounds.'

'But you wouldn't put him up for sale, would you?'

'No, we wouldn't.'

'So he's priceless.'

Graham disliked the smugness. He said, 'He is priceless. But we could have lost him in a fall. He could have broken a leg at exercise.

'Are you saying that if you don't get him back, it'll be just one of those things?'

Graham hesitated, uncertain about the psychological game he was getting into. 'I'm saying that we care for that horse more than you could know but things happen in racing. We've got over setbacks before.'

The pause was at the kidnapper's end now. The family knew there was a slight break in proceedings as Graham looked at each of them in turn and smiled reassuringly. Maggie reached for her husband's free hand and squeezed it.

The kidnapper spoke. 'You seem quite a cold person, Mr Cassidy. How does the rest of the family feel? How does Mrs Cassidy feel?'

'They feel the same as I do.'

'Cold? They don't care?'

'I've told you how much we care. Please tell me what the ransom fee is.'

'Straight and to the point, Mr Cassidy, I like that.'

Graham Cassidy didn't answer.

215

The kidnapper said, 'You'll be glad to hear that the ransom fee, as you put it, will not affect your standard of living in any way and that, unlike you, I am a very caring person. I care for how you people live and so I don't want a single penny of what you have now.' He paused. Graham waited, finding himself inadvertently holding his breath. The voice continued, 'I'll settle for the cheque your wife gets for her big book advance. Half a million pounds is the price.

'No,' Graham said immediately, deliberately avoiding the eyes of the family. Jane was looking particularly anxious and frustrated.

'You're a very decisive man for a trainer, Mr Cassidy. Most of them are bullshitters who wouldn't know a straight answer if they fell over one. But I think that either you're in shock or maybe the police are there advising you to play the cool guy. You tell them that I'm the only really cool guy in this set-up because I'm holding all the cards. Ask them how cool I was last time with Ulysses. I don't mess around. I don't get panicked. I just get impatient. And I do what I say I'm going to do, so listen. I'm going to be very, very generous here and give you what is left of this year to think about this and make up your mind. I'm going to call you again on New Year's Eve to tell you where to collect your horse. If you decide to pay the money, I want it on New Year's Day, in cash, used fifty-pound notes. I am not going to be messed around with excuses about raising the cash with banks being closed over the holidays and so on, that's the reason I'm giving you almost a week. Half a million on New Year's

Day and you get your horse back alive. Otherwise, bring the knacker's lorry for the carcass. And to help you make up your mind, ask the police what state Ulysses was in when they found him. I like to kill them nice and slowly.'

The anger rose in Graham's eyes. His face reddened. 'Don't harm the horse,' he said, swallowing the lump in his throat, surprised at his hoarseness. Jane guessed that her father had been listening to threats and she leaned into the mouthpiece and yelled, 'Don't you dare hurt Gabby! Don't you dare! I'll kill you if you hurt him!'

Graham's instinct was to cover the mouthpiece but he overcame it. He was proud of his daughter although her yell caught Billy by surprise and he recoiled, grunting with fright as the tension was broken. The kidnapper said, 'That's what I like to hear, some proper emotion. This is an emotional time, Mr Cassidy, don't be embarrassed about joining in. It is Christmas after all.' The line went dead.

Calmly, Graham held the receiver out towards Frankie who took it and unclipped the small microphone from the earpiece. Unplugging the cable from the grey Dictaphone he rewound the tape. 'Is it OK to play back now?' he asked Graham. The trainer nodded as he hugged his daughter. They all sat down and watched the Dictaphone as it played out the conversation. When the half a million figure was mentioned, everyone except Graham looked at Maggie. Some colour left her cheeks, otherwise she showed no reaction.

When the tape finished Jane, her pretty face still very agitated, looked at her mother. 'Mum?'

It was a challenge. The shortest and mostly clearly expressed question Frankie had ever heard. He was aware of the already tense atmosphere at the table beginning, almost, to crackle. Around the room, lights glowed; two lamps, the concealed bulbs below the rows of kitchen units, the Christmas tree, but as Jane posed the question Frankie felt that everything else around was fading, that the only place that was really lit was this table, the only place that mattered in the world, never mind this house. And the faces; the anxiety, the troubles, the sense that all except Frankie had been involved in a long-running, high-stakes poker game and now just Jane, fourteen going on forty, and Maggie remained in the running for the pot.

Maggie said, 'We need to take advice from the police.' Frankie could hear the tiny breaks in her voice.

Jane said, 'Mum, what can the police do? What can they say? We need to pay the money!'

Maggie looked at her daughter. Frankie could see turmoil behind Maggie's eyes and he felt himself shift uncomfortably, involuntarily. He felt he shouldn't be there. Maggie said to Jane, 'Let's see what the police say. We have a week.'

'But I'm supposed to be going to Ireland tomorrow! I can't go knowing that Gabby might get killed by that man!'

'The police might catch him before a week's up,' Maggie said. 'We've got a recording of his voice.'

Jane stood up suddenly, and crossed her arms. 'They won't catch him! How can they catch him with just a recording of his voice? They don't keep voices like fingerprints or anything, do they Frankie?' She turned to him and for the first time he saw the full power of her personality. It burned in her eyes, pulsed in the clenched jaw muscles, glowed in the reddening cheeks and he saw her mother in her then, very clearly, and he saw something of Kathy. She'd said his name as a woman would, not a child, there was no lack of confidence in the way she'd said it, the opposite in fact. It had been a command to back her up.

He said, 'They may have some voice tapes but not many although that doesn't mean that this won't help them. They have experts who advise on things like accents and sometimes they can pin accents down to almost the street someone lives in, certainly to the village.'

'But how much time does that take?' Jane asked.

'Well, let me go down to the station now with this tape and get an opinion from them. There are other factors too. The way he talked about trainers makes it sound like he may be in the racing industry or possibly worked in it and lost his job or something. This could be a kind of revenge thing and if he was sacked it may have been for some sort of offence. There's every possibility he already has a criminal record. If he has a record, it would greatly increase the chances of the police catching him.'

'In six days?' Jane asked, not at all comforted or convinced.

Frankie said, 'We need to report this anyway so let's see what the police say when we do.'

Jane sucked in a breath and folded her arms firmly again. Her father said, 'Jane, do you really want to see this man getting half a million pounds for walking in here and stealing Gabby? Wouldn't you like to see him caught?'

Billy nodded. 'Yeah, you're the one who's always banging on about fairness and justice and all that stuff for everybody in the world. It's not fair just to hand over loads of money to this bloke for stealing what isn't his, is it?'

Jane said, 'Shut up, you! What do you know about fairness?'

Maggie said, 'Who's not being fair now? It's not fair to take out your frustrations on your brother. Especially when it's me you're upset at.'

'Well, it's just so obvious to me what the right thing to do is! You've got half a million pounds coming in soon and it's money that you weren't really expecting to get so it will make absolutely no difference whatever if you hand it over to pay for Gabby! To get him back!' She put her hands on the table and leaned across, her eyes filling now. 'Mum, I've been with Gabby since I was four years old! I grew up with him!'

Billy said quietly, but in a point-scoring sort of way, 'I've been with him since I was two. I've grown up even more with him.' Jane ignored him and kept her gaze pleadingly on her mother.

Frankie watched as Maggie returned her gaze and he saw a change in Maggie's eyes; it was her turn to challenge. She said, 'So when my cheque comes in, Jane, do I give it all to the kidnapper?

How many cataract operations would half a million pounds buy?'

Frankie glanced at Graham and saw him flinch slightly and he knew Graham thought that Maggie should not have said that. The smile on Billy's face told Frankie that the boy considered it a masterstroke. Jane finally burst into tears. 'Oh Mum, that was a horrible thing to say!' and she turned and ran out of the room.

Maggie looked defiant, defensive, prepared for criticism. Graham smiled at Frankie. 'Sorry, tension's a bit high.'

'Don't apologize. It's understandable.' Frankie got up. 'Probably a good time for me to go and try and get some time with the CID.' He picked up the Dictaphone. 'I'll call back if you like, or I can come in the morning and give you an update.'

Maggie, gathering herself, trying to regain her composure, looked at him. 'Won't you stay with us tonight?'

Frankie smiled. 'It's very kind of you to offer me a bed on Christmas night. More than the innkeeper did for a certain couple two thousand years ago. I think it's time to–'

'To get away from this mad family?' Maggie asked wearily, smiling.

'To let you have some time on your own, maybe.'

Maggie said, 'It's after five. It's Christmas Day. By the time you get away from the police station you're not going to find it easy to get into a hotel.'

'I'll make a few calls on my mobile on the way

to the station and whatever happens I'll call later and tell you what the police have said.'

Graham stood up and said, 'If you don't find anywhere, please come back. You're more than welcome to stay with us as long as you want. We're very, very grateful for your patience and for all your help.'

Frankie put the Dictaphone in his pocket and buttoned his jacket. 'For all my helplessness more like. I wish I could do more.'

Graham said, 'Not at all. We realize it's an almost impossible task.'

'Don't resign yourself to losing him just yet. We've got a week.' Graham nodded, smiling gently. Maggie got up and so did Billy. Frankie said, 'I'll give you a call.'

As Frankie went out the door he heard Billy saying, 'Dad, wasn't it Christmas *Eve* when the innkeeper said no to Mary and Joseph?'

35

Frankie discovered that Maggie had been right, there were no rooms to be had within a fifty-mile radius and he knew he was going to have to stay close by the Cassidys for the next few days. They welcomed him back warmly and he guessed that they had appreciated his effort to try and let them return to some form of private life. The children were in bed when he returned. Maggie showed Frankie to his room and offered supper.

Frankie politely declined. She said, 'Will you have a drink, then and tell us what the police had to say?' Frankie asked for a whisky.

All three sat around the dying embers of the log fire. The Cassidys didn't expect much from the police who had been straight with them from the outset, saying that wire taps and call-tracing equipment and all the other stuff you saw on TV was expensive and time-consuming to set up and very seldom produced results. Off the record they'd said that the only realistic prospect of catching the kidnapper was to agree to pay the ransom then try to arrest him as he came to collect.

Frankie told them that the CID had pretty much confirmed this to him after hearing the tape. 'They said it would be a nice piece of evidence to help with the conviction if they did manage to arrest him at the pick-up point but they stressed that it's against procedure for them to advise anyone to pay a ransom.'

Graham cradled a tiny amount of brandy in a large glass. 'Nothing more?' he asked.

Frankie shook his head. 'Sorry.'

'So the police would have us pay the ransom so they get a crack at this man?' asked Graham.

'Unofficially only. Pay it or arrange to pay it. They're not that concerned about the money. The pick-up is the key for them. If you decide to pay then whatever you agree with the kidnapper needs to be convincing enough for him to believe that when he turns up every penny he asked for is going to be there.'

'Even if the suitcase, or whatever it is he wants

it in, is empty or full of paper or something?'
Graham asked.

'That's right. But if the cash isn't in it and the
police fail to catch him – I mean if he escapes
with an empty suitcase then you're probably not
going to get your horse back.'

Maggie sipped whisky. Frankie watched the
shadows and light cast on her face and glass by
the glowing embers of the fire. She said, 'Or if he
gets away with the full half-million but the police
have chased him halfway across the country first,
do you think we still get Gabby back?'

'I kind of doubt it,' Frankie said.

'So do I,' said Maggie.

They were quiet for a while, then Maggie
finally asked the question they all knew had been
hanging in the air. 'Frankie, what do you advise?
What's the Jockey Club line, should we pay the
ransom?'

'The official line is that paying a ransom only
means misery for someone else in the future. If it
becomes known that people will pay up then it
won't be just this guy who'll be back for more.
There'll be some proper criminals queuing
round the block.'

'So you don't think this creep is a "proper"
criminal?' Maggie asked.

Frankie swilled his drink and the ice tinkled. 'I
think this guy is in the industry somewhere or
has been. He's obviously used to handling
thoroughbreds, familiar with the running of a
racing stable. That reference he made to bull-
shitting trainers – I just think he's been in the
business and somebody has done him down big-

224

time. I get the feeling he's not just doing this for the money. He's got a major chip on his shoulder.'

Graham nodded in agreement. Frankie said, 'I'll start making a few calls tomorrow morning, digging around. Let's see what we come up with.' He sounded positive.

Maggie smiled and swallowed the rest of her drink. 'I suppose six days is quite a long time really.'

Frankie nodded. 'God made the world in six days.'

Maggie's smile widened and she looked warmly at Frankie. 'A final plug for your last employer.'

'Final?' Frankie asked.

'Before bed, I meant,' she said, covering her mouth as she yawned. 'We can always try praying, I suppose.'

Frankie nodded slowly, almost regretfully and Maggie said, 'I'm sorry. That was thoughtless of me.'

Frankie smiled wearily. 'Ahh, forget it. No offence taken.' He stood up. 'If you don't mind, I think I'll go to bed.'

Maggie got up. 'Not at all, it's been a long day.' She walked with him to the door leading into the hall. 'I put some clean towels on your bed.'

Lying in the darkness, Maggie and Graham spoke in low voices about the day's events and about Jane's planned trip to Ireland. It had been hurriedly arranged when they'd learned that Jane's cousin, Poppy, had broken her arm in a fall from her pony a week before Christmas. Jane was going to spend the remainder of the holidays with her to help her, cheer her up, although Maggie doubted she'd be cheering anyone up in her current state of mind. Maggie sensed that Graham had thought she'd been wrong to confront Jane with the theoretical option of what to do with the money. But he'd said nothing. It annoyed her that he would raise it when he thought it apt rather when she was ready to discuss it. In the final few minutes of silence before they drifted off to sleep she thought he might just bring it up and when he said, 'Maggie...' she became alert again.

'Uh-uh,' she said, feigning drowsiness to mask the tension rising once again.

'He's a very nice fellow, isn't he, Frankie Houlihan?'

'Yes. He is. Very helpful.'

'He has plenty of troubles of his own, I think.'

Maggie hesitated as Frankie's face rose sharply in her mind's eye. 'I think you're right.'

There was silence again for a while then Graham said quietly, 'He's very good-looking, isn't he?'

Again she hesitated. 'Mmm, Yes, I suppose he is.' And she blushed in the dark.

36

The vet, Peter Culling, had, as usual, monitored his food and alcohol intake closely over Christmas. Since his late thirties, death had never been far from his mind and the habit had formed in him of counting down the days between Christmas and New Year. The annual achievement of waking up on 1 January brought mixed emotions. He was relieved to have survived into another year, to be able to build up his savings for the crucial 'suspension' of his life but New Year's Day also brought the spectre of death closer, edged him towards his next birthday, dragged him nearer the cliff edge of mid-forties and certain heart failure.

He knew as well as any doctor what physical measures were needed to protect his heart as long as possible; he could have lectured on the subject with the confidence of knowing he practised what he preached. His diet was high in vegetables, omega-3 oils, wholemeal bread. He took little fat and his weakness for alcohol was served by two glasses of red wine each evening – another heart booster and one of the few comforts in his life – and the occasional glass of cognac. He didn't smoke and he took regular exercise, always reaching, but never exceeding, the recommended pulse rate to maintain fitness safely.

What he wasn't so good at handling was the stress side which he knew could be as bad for his heart as twenty cigarettes a day. And he found the stress unmanageable because it emanated from the fear of death that was with him almost constantly. The thought of not having enough money to pay the Everlasting Life Company of Michigan to preserve his body tormented him. The deadline for getting that money shortened every day. Culling's interpretation of 'deadline' was literally a hanging rope and in his mind he saw nature herself hitching the noose that little bit tighter daily. Now there was the added burden of Monroe knowing what he was doing. A ticking bomb, indeed. So with another New Year's Day looming he had decided to take a chance and do one at Kempton on Boxing Day.

This was one of the biggest racemeetings of the year and it took Culling far outside the guidelines he'd set himself at the start. His scheme had been designed to work on smallish racecourses in bread-and-butter races, preferably not televised. He'd taken a slight chance at Ascot with Colonialize but that race hadn't been on TV. This was Kempton's major meeting. They'd have their biggest crowd of the season and the TV cameras would be there. The press room was certain to be full and all eyes would be focused on the racing. When his chosen horse won, at the usual big price, the performance would be dissected much more carefully than if he'd chosen a little race at Huntingdon.

On the positive side, betting would be so heavy that day that he could charge Breslin, the fat

bookie, a considerable premium for the information. Culling reckoned that this, plus maybe just
two more in the next six months, would see him
with enough money to feel safe, secure. Every
time this thought came to his mind he wanted to
put his head in his hands and cry with the relief
of it. He longed for that day when he could
finally stop all this, empty the stress from himself
safe in the knowledge that the future was his.

Culling chose a horse called Gallopagos. As
with the others, it led all the way. The winning
margin was twelve lengths, the price 20/1. After
the race, Culling was approaching the stables
when he heard a stewards' enquiry called over
the PA. He stopped, choosing not to enter the
stables as mild panic hit him. What had the
stewards found out? Had anyone seen him in the
stables earlier? He knew he shouldn't have risked
this one, it was too big a meeting. This was the
one that would finish him. The panic was swamp-
ing him now, affecting his breathing, thumping
his heart against his ribs so he could feel every
beat.

Hurrying to his car he locked himself inside. If
anyone saw him like this, that would only add to
the suspicion. Five minutes later he heard the
announcer say that the stewards had enquired
into the poor performance of the favourite in the
last race and had accepted the trainer's statement
that he had no explanation.

Culling laid his head back on the headrest and
moaned in relief. He simply couldn't put himself
through any more of these.

37

On Boxing Day, Graham Cassidy rose even earlier than usual to feed the horses; Jane's ferry was due to leave Holyhead at ten-thirty and it was a long drive. Just the two of them were in the car and Graham was glad of that. The tension between Jane and Maggie had still been fizzing that morning. Jane hadn't spoken a word at breakfast despite urgings from her parents to talk about her trip. She had been so looking forward to seeing her cousin Poppy again and had been confident she could help Poppy over her injury better than any doctor could. But she'd remained stubbornly silent other than to mutter the odd please and thank you, yes and no. And she'd taken leave of her mother coldly with a brief hug and a turned cheek.

Graham left her to her silence as he drove, knowing that she'd come out of it in her own good time and for her own reasons. It was almost an hour before she did and even then, when she spoke, she sounded very down. 'Dad, do you think we'll get Gabby back?'

'I don't know. I hope so.'

'What if we don't?'

He felt himself shrug involuntarily. 'Then we'll get on with things.'

'With *things?*'

'With our lives. It won't bring the world to an end.'

She turned now and he didn't need to take his eyes off the road to know she was angry. 'How can you say that, Dad? You're the one who dreamed all your life of winning the National. You're the one that said Gabby was a miracle sent to us to help us get your dream, make it come true.'

'That's right. I was. I still have the dream but somebody's put it on hold for us for whatever reason and there's nothing we can do about it.'

'So you just accept it?'

'What else should I do?' Graham had never found it difficult to stay calm and it helped that he could easily anticipate most of his daughter's questions.

'You could tell Mum to pay the ransom.'

'I wouldn't pay it myself if I had the money so why should I tell her? If we pay the ransom, we're just sending the message that it's OK to kidnap someone else's horse and make even more money. Do you think that's right?'

'I think anything that gets Gabby back is right.'

He paused for a few seconds then said quietly, 'You don't really think that. I know you don't.'

'I do! How can it be wrong to do whatever needs to be done to get him back?'

'Well where do you draw the line? Would you kill this man who has him to get the horse back?'

'Yes, I would!'

'Oh, come on, Jane. Nobody loves the horse more than I do but he's a horse, that's all. Even if he hadn't been taken, he could have walked out this morning and put his foot in a hole. Then we'd just need to get used to the thought of him

231

not being there.'

'But Dad, that's not the way to look at things! You can't go through your life just accepting everything bad that happens to you! You'll just get dumped on all the time! What would you do if it had been me that had been kidnapped? Would you kill the kidnapper to get me back if you had to?'

'Oh stop being so melodramatic!'

'I'm not! I want to know! I want to know if there is at least something in your life that will make you angry and make you stop being walked all over!'

'The best I can offer you, Jane, is that I'd gladly give up my own life for you and for Billy or your mother. Gladly.'

She folded her arms, lowered her head and stared to the front again and Graham felt the tension increase one more notch. He drove on in silence, angry with himself for having to play the dutiful father, having to try and give his daughter, his children a sense of perspective on life that would help them handle all their own disappointments. Inside he raged over the loss of this wonderful horse, cursed himself for not taking more precautions, hated the kidnapper with an intensity that made him feel that he too could easily kill the man. Above all he wished he had the money to pay the ransom.

38

Delayed half an hour by the weather, the Dun Laoghaire ferry finally left Holyhead and ploughed its way out into the choppy Irish Sea. On deck only three people braved the late December weather. One of them was Jane Cassidy who sat on a wet bench, her bright blue Gore-Tex jacket pulled close around her, watching the Welsh coast fade into the gloom of spray and lowering cloud. The hood of her jacket covered her head and most of her face and the wind howled around her so wildly that she spoke aloud, almost shouted, just to find out if she could hear her own voice. The words sounded inside her skull but the wind whipped them violently away from her before they could echo in her ears.

She could have flown over. Her mother had offered that when the idea first came up for her to go. But Jane had persuaded her mother to pay her ferry fare instead and donate the balance to her blindness charity. Another reminder of how cruel her mother had been last night; Jane folded her arms.

How could she not see the difference between something Jane was involved in as a 'mission' and something so close to her like the prospect of losing Gabby? How could she stoop so low as to use that against her? She couldn't wait to tell

233

Poppy just what her mother had turned into. She'd say, 'Well, if that's what success does to a person then I don't ever want to be successful. When you can't see the difference between your family, between something you love and care for and, and business ... money, well, what's the point?'

If Gabby was killed by this man, if he never came back again because her mother wouldn't pay the money then Jane had decided that she wouldn't go back either. Let her mother try and live without her like she would have to live without Gabby – see if she could learn her lesson that way. Jane could stay with Poppy, she was sure that would be possible. She could finish her schooling in Ireland and go to university in Dublin; she'd heard it was cool there and even if they did get Gabby back she'd probably go to Trinity College anyway in three years or so. She'd have a place of her own then and wouldn't have to be ruled by her mother. Dad was OK. She could live with Dad.

Sean Gleeson was worried. It had been almost three weeks since he'd seen his father. The word on the street was that he'd ripped Kelly Corell off for ten grand. Pat Pusey had already been at the flat three times looking for him. Sean had opened the door the first time and Pusey had told him to tell his 'oul' fella' that if he didn't get the money back to Corell before Christmas then he wouldn't be seeing in the New Year. The next twice Pusey had come along, Sean had locked the door and pretended there was no one home. Pusey had been roaring through the letterbox so hard his spit had run down the inside of the door.

Sean was scared of him. He used the flat now only to sleep in, spending the day wandering the streets with Pegasus, riding him down by the canal and around Fairview Park. Sean had some money left, saved from his winnings over the summer on the ponies and from the hundred pounds Cosgrave had given him for riding at Laytown. Even if his father never came back, he'd survive. It wasn't as if he ever gave Sean any money anyway. He just drank it and punted it.

Life hadn't been too bad since his mother had left but sometimes he missed her. He didn't want to lose his father too. Sean knew that at fourteen he could still be taken into care and he couldn't face disappearing into the system to end up in some Jesuit-run place where he'd need to rise at five every morning and wear his knees out with the praying.

There was just Sean and Kevin's family left now in the Mansions and the Corporation had boarded Sean's place up once already. But his mates had helped him rip the boards off and they'd burned them and roasted potatoes in the embers. Anyway, plenty of people just squatted in empty flats and houses and if he eventually had to become one of those for a while he'd cope, so long as he had somewhere to keep Pegasus. He'd handle it because it was what he was used to, and it would make his dream all the sweeter when he became a top jockey and bought a big house where you could stay in all day if you wanted without having to worry about the Corporation or the likes of Pat Pusey.

Sean untied Pegasus from the railings and scrambled on to his bare back. A tiny spur of rubber, a design flaw rather than a feature, protruded from the heel of each of his black wellies and Sean prodded Pegasus in the ribs with them. The grey pony moved forward in a steady walk through the archway out on to Killarney Street. Sean looked to his right, to the twinkling Christmas tree that bore the names of all those from St Joseph's Mansions who'd died from drugs. Dozens of names. He knew them all, there was no need to read the list which grew longer every Christmas. But he knew that no more names would be added after this year. He might not be here much longer, especially if his father never came back. And that only left Kevin and his parents. Rochelle, his ma, was the best fighter against the dealers the Mansions ever had. There'd be none of her family's names on any Christmas tree.

Sean turned left and headed on to Portland Row, wondering where best to look for his father today. There was a rumour that he was back in Dublin and Sean supposed it could be true. The last place he'd have come was the flat because he'd have known Corell's men would come there looking for him. But it would have been a brave or very stupid thing to come back at all unless he had Corell's cash. Sean knew what the gangster was capable of.

There were lots of stories about Corell. He was supposed to have killed his own girlfriend, cut her throat and left her on the stairs in St Mary's

Mansions. The word was that two of his men had held Lampy McGurk off the top of the roof of one of the blocks by his shoes while Corell made poor Lampy watch him untie the laces. And what about the fella he'd nailed to the snooker table? Sean hoped his father wouldn't come back till Corell was dead although Corell had a fear of nothing, they said, and he had a few of the Garda in his pocket so he could live a long time.

The pony's spine felt sharper than usual beneath him and Sean shifted to try and ease the discomfort. He'd noticed lately that his ankles touched Pegasus' sides a bit lower than they used to and he hoped he wasn't about to start sprouting. Jockeys needed to be small.

It was teatime and the streets were quiet. The pony's hooves echoed on the road. Sean thought of his father again. All he knew was that he'd left on the boat to Holyhead three weeks ago on a job for Corell and hadn't been seen since. Something in Sean hoped that he'd stolen the money to use it trying to find his mother who, Sean knew from his Auntie Phoebe, was in London somewhere. But he guessed the bookies would have given big odds on that one. He had probably drunk half of it and lost the other half on the horses.

He'd gone away on a boat – if he ever came back it would probably be by boat too. For want of anything better to do, Sean turned the pony south and headed for the ferry terminal at Dun Laoghaire.

It was dark when he arrived there and raining steadily. He sat on Pegasus close to the bus stop and when everyone got on the first bus that came he urged the pony beneath the green plastic canopy, taking up all the shelter and ignoring the mumbled complaints of the first three people, all women, who came to wait for the next bus. They moaned among themselves about it and Sean sat smiling, watching the comings and goings through the terminal doors, trying to recall what his father was wearing when last he'd seen him.

Four more people came towards the bus shelter. Steam was rising from the wet pony, filling the shelter. The queue frowned and held their noses and all joined in the grumbling. 'What the feck's goin' on here?' 'Bloody stinkin' horse!' 'Is that fella mad or somethin'? Waitin to ride a pony on to a bus?' 'Hey, get that stinkin' gipsy horse outta here! This is for folk that can pay their fares!'

Sean turned to them, a glint in his eye. 'Ahh, sure we'd love to move but hasn't the pony got well and truly stuck to the pavement here? The blacksmith was testin' out a new kinda glue so he was when he put shoes on him yesterday, and the stuff's gone and mixed very badly with the rainwater and stuck us to the tarmac as tight as yer own hair is stuck to yer head!'

The people looked at each other in puzzled silence. A woman said, 'Ahh, away wi ye! Yer havin' us on so ye are!'

Sean raised a finger to his breast. 'Cross me heart and hope to die! It's the truth. The guards have gone to find the blacksmith and bring him to set us free.'

'And how's he gonna do that if the horse can't

pick his feet up?'

Sean said, 'D'ye see that manhole back there?'

They all turned.

'He's goin' down there with the fire brigade, so he is and they're gonna bore up with a special tool and operate on his hooves from underneath.'

Some of them now looked as though they thought there might be something in this. Some said 'Now yer takin' the piss' and other such comments. At this Pegasus raised a hind leg in the way ponies do when they want to rest their weight for a while, so that the toe of his hoof was barely touching the ground. The queue moved forward as one, with a mixture of shouts and laughter and pushes and urgings to 'get out and give us peace'.

Laughing lightly, Sean nudged Pegasus in the ribs. As the pony ambled out into the rain, some people across the street stopped to see what the commotion was. One of them walked briskly across the road and was almost next to Sean before the boy noticed that it was Pat Pusey, Corell's hired thug. The plunging weight of fear in Sean's stomach dragged the laughter back into his throat, silencing him.

Pusey gripped Sean's left calf as he walked beside him. Looking up he said, 'Here to meet yer da, Sean?' There was a triumphant note in Pusey's voice, otherwise it was cold and hard.

'No, I'm not. I don't know where he is! Honest!'

'Don't lie to me, son! What boat's he on?'

'Honest, Pat, I don't know. I mean I don't know where he is. He's not on any boat, I don't think!'

'So what are ye doin' here, entertainin' the feckin crowds?'

They'd walked half the length of the terminal building on the opposite side of the road. Plenty of people were still around. Pusey reached for the reins and tugged viciously on them. Sean pulled Pegasus to a halt. Pusey looked up. 'Where is he, now?'

'I don't know, Pat! If I knew I'd tell ye, sure I would! I haven't a bleedin' clue. I just came down here to give the pony a bit of a walk out!'

'Walk out my arse!' And he reached and grabbed Sean by the front of his denim shirt and yanked him off to land sprawling in a puddle. Pegasus trotted quickly away, ears pricked, tail up. Pusey hauled Sean to his knees and started dragging him across the road towards the terminal entrance. 'Come on, I'm gonna be with ye when ye meet yer da in here!'

Sean stumbled after him shouting, 'Get off me! Leave me alone!' Pusey forced him through the doors into the main terminal. People turned to watch and to tut disapprovingly at this angry-looking man dragging a boy who looked very scared, but nobody tried to help. Pusey went along the wall where the luggage trolleys were then stopped and spun Sean, forcing him against the hard tiles. 'Where is he? He owes us ten grand!'

Pusey was really hurting him. Sean's jacket wasn't that thick and the way Pusey was gripping him made his shoulder-blades protrude and rub against the wall. Tears came to his eyes though he tried to stop them and he answered as he had all the times before, 'Pat, I don't know where he is! Honest!'

'You're a liar!'

Suddenly there was female voice, angry, shrill, young, and a hand on Pusey's arm. 'Hey, leave him alone! He's just a child! Stop hurting him!'

Pusey, surprised, stopped shaking Sean. He relaxed his grip although he still held the shirt front. Sean eased forward off the wall and stood balanced again, relieved, curious yet worried still. He saw the very angry, very pretty face of Jane Cassidy. Her eyes looked a sort of blueish-green and Sean saw a fearlessness in them. He wished she'd look at him but she just stared at Pusey, her hand still on his arm.

Pusey glanced around him and saw some people nearby look away and shuffle off to distance themselves from this embarrassing scene. He glared at Jane and in almost a whisper said, 'Piss off, you little nuisance.'

'No I will not piss off!' she said very loudly and Pusey reddened. 'Take your hands off his shirt. You've no right to be assaulting him! I'll call the police!'

Pusey tried again, voice still low but more menace in it now. 'If you don't bugger off and mind your own little Miss English business, you'll be next.'

'What was that, you're going to assault me next?' She was shouting. 'You're planning to assault a young girl when you've finished with this boy!'

Pusey began to look panicky now as two men moved towards him from the terminal entrance.

Jane saw them too and began screaming, 'Help! Help!' still holding on to the arm of Pusey's jacket but trying to make it look like he was holding her. The two men started running towards Pusey who immediately let go of Sean and wrestled himself free of Jane's grip. He turned and ran leaving Sean looking after him, dazed and confused at the speed of things. The two men stopped beside them and the taller asked, 'Are yous all right, now?'

'We're OK,' said Jane confidently. 'Thanks for coming to help.'

'Who was the fella that was botherin' ye?'

'He was tryin' to rob me,' Sean said. 'I think he was drunk or somethin'.'

The tall man said, 'Give us a shout if you need us. We'll be in the bar over there.'

'Thanks, mister,' said Sean.

Sean and Jane stood looking at each other, he in his crumpled charity shop clothes, she in her sky-blue Gore-Tex jacket that had cost almost one hundred and fifty pounds. 'Are you all right?' Jane asked and Sean could see that there was a bit of an actress in her, as there was in most girls. The question was asked with wide eyes and a sort of 'Uh, I don't believe what I just saw' expression.

He nodded. 'I'll be fine. Thanks.'

Jane stared, still frowning. 'Was he really trying to rob you?'

Sean straightened, adjusted his jacket and adopted an offended look. 'What are ye tryin' to say? Don't I look as though I'm worth robbin' then?'

She looked apologetic. 'No, of course not. I'm not saying that at all, it's just–'

'Just what? My clothes are needin' a bit of a wash from bein' dragged through puddles by that madman...' Sean paused and quickly looked behind him to make sure Pusey really had gone. 'And there's a few horsehairs stuck to me here and there and,' he looked down, 'I've got wellies over me Nike trainers to keep them dry and...' His expression changed from one of mock hurt to one of wide-eyed realization. 'Shit! Pegasus!' He hurried towards the exit. Jane followed him looking worried. 'Pegasus?'

'My pony. Champion pony. Fastest in Dublin. That bastard Pusey scared him off.'

They went through the open door together into the rain. Jane said, 'Scared him off? When? You know that man? Who is he? Why was he trying to beat you up?'

Sean was looking in both directions. 'Ahh, yer a one for the questions, right enough, miss.'

'My name's Jane. And I think you could be a bit more grateful for my help, to be honest.'

Sean turned to her. 'Is that a fact, now? And what would you like me to do, kiss your feet? Be your butler for a year?'

They looked at each other in silence for a few seconds. 'It would be a start. Being my butler, I mean. I wouldn't let you near my feet.'

'Yer just scared I'd convert ye to wearin' wellies like mine, aren't ye?' They both smiled, at ease with each other now. 'There's Pegasus,' said Sean. 'See ya.' He started along the road. The pony was grazing on a grass strip near the railway line.

Jane walked after him. 'Where do you keep him?'

Sean picked up the rein and zipped his clenched fingers along it, scooting off the water it had picked up dangling in the grass. 'Where do I keep him? In the paddock, of course, by the orchard.'

'Where do you live?' she asked, stroking Pegasus.

'In a mansion.'

She looked at him, a mixture of wariness and anticipated laughter in her eyes. He said, 'You're judging the book by its cover again, Jane. Just because of the way I'm dressed you think I can't live in a mansion?'

She smiled slowly. He said, 'Look, I'll prove it. Hold this.' He handed the rein over and dug in the inside pocket of his jacket till he pulled out a library card. He held it close to her face, obscuring his name on the top line, showing the address. 'See, Joseph's Mansions.'

'And you're Joseph?'

'I'm Sean.'

'Who's Joseph?'

'Me da.'

Your father owns a mansion with a paddock and an orchard?'

'You got it.'

'And you've got raggedy clothes, a pony with no saddle and you get your books from the library?'

'I like plain living. I'm easy pleased.'

'And you know something that that man in there wanted to get from you.'

That brought Sean back to reality and the smile that had been dancing in his eyes faded at the thought that Pusey would return – could easily be watching him now. As soon as Jane had gone he'd be back at him.

She read his thoughts, his hunted glance over her shoulder towards the terminal entrance. She said, 'I'll wait with you, if you like. My uncle should be here any time. Should have been here by now.' She turned around to look at the pick-up point outside the terminal. 'There he is, look, just getting out of the Mercedes. Come on, we'll give you a lift.'

'Err, aren't ye forgettin' somethin'? Where's Pegasus gonna travel, on the roof-rack?'

She smiled. 'Don't worry. Uncle Fergus will go back for the trailer.'

'The trailer?'

'Wait here!'

She ran towards the big white-haired man who was looking anxiously around. Sean saw her throw her arms around him, watched her rucksack bobbing on her back as her uncle swung her gently. Then they were coming back towards him. The big man looked familiar. Could that be...? Jeez, it was, Fergus Gollogly, the racehorse trainer!

39

At the Cassidy place that evening, after dinner, Frankie sat at the table with Graham and Maggie Cassidy trying to use logic and what little evidence they had to fashion some sort of plan. For all Graham's apparently philosophical outlook about the possible loss of Angel Gabriel, they'd decided they couldn't simply sit and tick off the hours and days until the kidnapper called back.

The subject of paying the ransom had not been discussed again after Jane had stormed out twenty-four hours previously. Maggie had been relieved to hear her daughter sounding much more friendly, much better when she'd rung to say she'd arrived safely at Uncle Fergus's and her cousin Poppy had been in good spirits.

Billy was upstairs doing homework. Frankie sat at the table doodling on an A4 pad. Maggie and Graham sat side by side, faces lined with concentration. All three had mugs of coffee from which the steam rose towards the overhead light. The rest of the room was in shadow. Maggie wore a bit more make-up than usual and the smell of her perfume was in the air. Graham's heavy growth darkened his jaw considerably, working with the light to make his face look gaunt and tired. His shirt was badly worn at the collar. Frankie had favoured dark clothes lately, unsure himself whether he was hankering after his priest's garb or simply continuing to mourn Kathy. He wore an open-necked black polo shirt.

'Right,' said Frankie, 'what do we know?'

'He's familiar with horses,' Graham said.

'Very familiar,' added Maggie.

Frankie wrote it down. 'And we know he has access to a horsebox.'

'And that he can drive it,' said Maggie.

'Unless he had an accomplice,' said Graham.

Frankie said, 'Supposing he didn't have an accomplice. He'd need to have an HGV licence if it was a big box.'

'If he was law-abiding he would,' said Maggie and they all smiled.

'Or maybe he just towed a trailer,' Graham suggested.

Frankie pursued it. 'Let's suppose he does have an HGV licence, I wonder if we can access the police lists of licence-holders?'

'Good idea,' said Maggie. 'Though with all the bloody lorries on the roads these days there's probably millions of the buggers.'

Graham was nodding. 'Worth a try, Frankie. Definitely.'

Frankie wrote it down then sipped some coffee. 'What else? We know his accent is from the south and that he's probably spent a lot of time in the south-west, even though he might not have been born there. You're both pretty certain of that, and so are the police. Let's just assume, for the sake of it, that he lives there now.'

They both nodded agreement. Maggie topped up the mugs from a tall cafetière then lit a cigarette.

'And we think,' said Frankie, 'that he may have been in racing at some time?'

'Or maybe still is,' said Graham.

'OK. And that he may well be holding some kind of general grudge against trainers or owners or racing folk in general?'

Nods again. Frankie wrote something then looked up. 'Right, we're working purely on assumptions here, agreed? We have someone who may be involved in racing, possibly living in the south-west, with access to a horsebox. If you had to bet on where he was based, what would you say?'

'Lambourn.' They both said it at once.

Frankie smiled and said, 'I agree. So supposing we get the HGV licence-holders from the police, but only those living within the Newbury postcode which, I think, covers Lambourn.'

'There are still going to be a hell of a lot from that neck of the woods,' said Maggie.

'You're right,' said Frankie, 'but we'll be talking hundreds at most, not thousands.'

'And supposing you get the list, what will you do then?' asked Maggie.

'I'll call Stonebanks – Geoff Stonebanks, a colleague of mine. He lives in Lambourn and knows who's doing what down there. We'll take whatever time it needs to run through the list and see what we come up with.'

Graham nodded, looking suddenly less haggard, more positive. Maggie said, 'So you may be leaving us then for Lambourn?'

Frankie shrugged and laid his pen on the pad. 'Depends on what comes out of this. Let me call

248

my contact now at the police station and see if he's still around. Can I use your phone?'

'Of course you can!' said Maggie and Frankie got up and went to the windowsill where the phone lay. Graham sipped coffee. Maggie watched Frankie's reflection in the big mirror on the opposite wall. She blew a plume of smoke towards the light as she listened to him ask for his CID contact. She watched every small move of his hands and head and shoulders as he turned slightly, seldom still. She'd noticed that about him; he was never at rest.

It took the police until late afternoon on 28 December to produce a list of HGV licence-holders living in the Newbury area; there were one hundred and thirty-four. Frankie worked through them, highlighting the seventy-three Lambourn addresses, then he rang Stonebanks and asked him to call back to save the Cassidy phone bill. Stonebanks sighed when Frankie told him that this was going to take at least an hour. Stonebanks asked for half an hour to clear some things and Frankie took a walk in the quickly falling dusk and tried to figure out what to do if Stonebanks didn't come up with a lead from the list. Even if he did, when you wrote today off, there were only seventy-two hours left, maximum, until the kidnapper's deadline.

Frankie heard Stonebanks grunt a bit as he settled for a long session on the phone. 'Sorry about this, Geoff, but it was the only thing I could think of. Otherwise I'd just be sitting here waiting with the Cassidys and I feel bad enough already that I can't do something for them, that the department can't do something.'

'OK, Frankie, no worries. I know what you mean. I just think it's a dodgy premise to be going on but in your place I'd be doing exactly the same. Trouble is that a big part of your assumption is that this guy is someone with a grudge in racing. If you lined him up along with all the others with grudges the ID parade would take a year. Don't hold your breath as far as drawing up a shortlist is concerned.'

'I'm not – but if anyone can help on this, it's you.'

'As the bankrupt Chinese stamp collector said, philately will get you nowhere.'

'Very funny.'

'Learned it from an old friend of mine.'

'Can we start?'

'Shoot.'

Almost two hours later Frankie had crossed through fifty-three of the Lambourn names. Of the twenty left on the list, Stonebanks reckoned that each was at least capable of kidnapping a horse and just under half of them willing to slaughter it. That gave Frankie eight people to concentrate on. He asked Stonebanks then to listen to the copy of the tape of the kidnapper's voice that he'd sent by courier. Stonebanks listened and said, 'I don't recognize it, Frankie. But I can't say I've heard all your suspects speak, certainly not recently and I don't know any well enough to remember their voices. It takes a while for a voice to register in your brain, doesn't it?'

'It does. Don't worry, it was worth a chance.

How would you feel about rigging the equipment up to your phone and calling each of these guys? We could get some sort of voiceprint comparison then.'

'We could. You get also get yourself a dead horse if one of them is the kidnapper. What's he going to do if he suddenly gets a call out of the blue from the Jockey Club Security Department?'

'I hadn't thought of that.'

'Never mind. Why don't you get yourself down to London tomorrow and we'll work on this shortlist and see what we can come up with?'

'I will, Geoff. I appreciate your help.'

'No problem. You can buy me a drink and a fillet steak.'

'It's a deal.'

40

Packed and ready to leave in the morning, Frankie sat by the log fire sipping whisky with the Cassidys. 'I'm going to miss this little ritual before bed,' he said.

'We will too,' said Maggie. She was sitting on the thick rug. Graham sat, fairly upright, in the long-backed chair. They'd given Frankie the soft easy chair and he loved the way it enveloped him, made him feel secure, especially with the logs burning in the big fireplace.

'And I'm mad because I'll miss morning

stables,' said Frankie. 'I've loved helping out with the feeding and grooming and stuff.'

Graham smiled. 'It's been good to have you. You'd make an excellent stable lad!'

Frankie grinned and raised his glass towards Graham. 'There are worse occupations,' he said.

'Well,' Maggie said, 'the pay's not brilliant but we could probably afford a bit extra for you.'

'I'd do it for nothing. The company alone is worth it. I've really enjoyed my time here. It's been great being back in a family atmosphere again.' And he realized with that little statement that he'd opened up a part of his past that he hadn't meant to. He hoped neither Maggie nor Graham would follow it up.

Maggie said, 'We've enjoyed your company too and we can't say how grateful we are that you gave up Christmas to try and help us.'

'No sacrifice, honestly. I just hope I can do something in the next forty-eight hours.'

Graham said, 'Even if you hit brick walls with your investigations over the next couple of days, will you come back and be with us for the call on New Year's Eve?'

'Of course I will. Of course.'

41

Frankie and Stonebanks spent the whole of the next day in the office. They were still in there at ten that night. Frankie had learned that it was one thing having a shortlist of suspects and something else completely trying to get anything useful from it. He guessed that Stonebanks, with his experience, could have told him this first thing that morning and his respect and liking for the big man had grown because he'd said nothing, just beavered away all day at this lost cause. Frankie knew Stonebanks just wouldn't have wanted to discourage him at the outset on this, his first real case.

It had been a long slog of ringing people, reading files, seeking further possible contacts, trying to discover the whereabouts of everyone on the list on the nights in question and having to do it without being able to speak to the people themselves. Tough and tiring as it had been, there had been comic moments, especially the frequent times when Stonebanks was ready to swear with frustration and had glanced at Frankie, unsure how offensive it would be for an ex-priest to hear such language. Frankie had played on it by frowning seriously when Stonebanks glanced at him and the big man had taken it at face value and stayed silent or substituted softer curses.

At ten-past-ten Frankie said, 'Let's call it quits,

Geoff, and I'll buy you that steak.'

Stonebanks, tie hanging loosely below his stubbled double chin, wearily closed the folder in front of him. 'And a large gin?'

'Two large gins, if you like, and I'll drive you home.'

'Ooh, chauffeur too!'

'Least I can do. This has been an awful trying day. We've got nowhere and you probably knew from the start that we wouldn't. It makes me much more grateful that you stuck with it anyway.'

'You're not giving up, Frankie boy?'

'I ain't. If you'll put me up for the night, I'll prowl around Lambourn for the next two days in the hope of finding something.'

Stonebanks looked at him for a few moments and Frankie knew that he was deciding whether it was best to say what was on his mind. He said it; 'You know you're a million to one against here, don't you?'

Frankie smiled wearily and stretched and ran his fingers through his hair. 'I know, but I'm as well trying to do something as sitting around up in Shropshire waiting for this ... this fella to call.'

A smile spread slowly on Stonebanks's face and he raised a finger to point at Frankie. 'You almost said a bad word then, didn't you?'

Frankie laughed. 'I did. You're right. I almost did. And earlier I almost said "a bitch of a day". My soul will surely be lost after another year or two in the company of people like yourself! Come on, let's go and get a drink.'

'Tell me what you were going to say first!'

Frankie got up, still laughing. 'Don't be daft! Come on.'

Stonebanks folded his arms on the table. 'Nope. I'm not moving till you tell me.'

Frankie put his hands on the table and leant forward. 'It started with "b" and ended with "d".'

Stonebanks got up and came towards him, put his arm around Frankie's shoulder and said, 'That's my boy! I knew you had it in you.'

Frankie straightened, laughing again. 'Come on, Crazy Horse, let's eat.' They walked to the door still linked by Stonebanks's arm. Frankie felt that the day had been more than worthwhile for they'd got to know each other better in this twelve hours than they'd done in all the odd days they'd spent together back when Frankie had just started. He was pleased too that for the second time in the past few days he felt some real warmth towards a human being. Maybe his feelings were coming out of the deep freeze. Perhaps life wasn't going to be so terrible after all.

Stonebanks knew a little restaurant where they'd get a table and when the big man went to the toilet, Frankie sipped his beer and called Maggie Cassidy for the second time that night. They'd spoken at around eight when Frankie had told her that they'd made virtually no headway. He'd promised her a call when they'd finished just to make a final report. Stonebanks had returned and finished his gin by the time he hung up.

'Sorry about that. Just giving Mrs Cassidy an update.'

255

'How did she take it?'

'Well. They've all been brilliant, the whole family. I'm amazed by them.'

'Sounds as if they made you welcome up there.'

'Very welcome. Very warm people. The classic happy family.'

'Not too many of those around, outside storybooks and Hollywood,' Stonebanks said.

'You're right. There aren't.'

'So how big a blow is this going to be if they don't get their horse back?'

Frankie shrugged. 'They'll take it on the chin and move on.'

'Even the kids?'

'Eventually. Jane might be upset longer than the others but they'll pull her through it.'

Stonebanks looked beyond Frankie and smiled and rubbed his hands. 'Here comes the grub!'

42

Maggie and Graham Cassidy sat in their kitchen opposite Frankie and the man from the local CID who was called John Burnham. Burnham was the only one who'd said much in the hours they'd been waiting for the call. He was near retirement age and had done little but talk about all the things he planned to do, from fishing to making videos of his grandchildren. Frankie was annoyed. Apart from a few conciliatory mumbles when he'd first introduced himself to the Cassidys, Burnham had shown no regard for the nerves and tension so obviously present.

Graham Cassidy, who Frankie thought the mildest of men, was growing frustrated with the policeman and started making excuses about having to check the horses. The third time he did this Frankie signalled to Maggie to follow him. When he was alone with Burnham Frankie asked him politely to just sit quietly until the kidnapper called. He explained that the Cassidys were particularly tense and needed to be able to think, to consider their options. Frankie was sufficiently tactful for Burnham to interpret it as being asked for a favour and he said he'd be happy to try and ease the burden for them.

When the Cassidys returned, Burnham had moved to a chair by the window and he sat looking out, leaving just the three of them at the table. The phone lay in the centre, Frankie's small microphone attached to the earpiece. A thick pad of writing paper and two pens were beside the phone although the pens had seldom been out of the anxious fingers of one or other of the party. Frankie had got back about noon and had told them over lunch of his frustrations during the past couple of days. He and Stonebanks had done what they could using the list of HGV licensees but had turned up nothing.

They'd only managed to completely eliminate three people on their shortlist of the eight Stonebanks thought capable of doing this and had simply been unable to gather enough information about the others to make a judgement. Maggie had told him not to worry and

257

both had thanked him for at least trying. And since then, all they had done was wait by this phone, sitting and staring. Twice Maggie had picked it up and checked that there actually was a dial tone; that had made Graham smile nervously. They'd discussed what they were going to do; the money wouldn't be paid and there would be no bargaining.

The police had decided against setting up call-tracing equipment as they were convinced the kidnapper would use a public call-box and would be long gone by the time they got a car there. The Cassidys accepted this and they conceded too that they weren't going to see their horse again unless the kidnapper had a change of heart.

They'd been waiting for eight hours, the last of them in almost complete silence as Burnham had fallen asleep in the chair. Maggie thought Graham had looked increasingly sad as time went on; the stress of it all seemed to be ageing him as she watched. She said quietly, 'I can't wait for this to be over.'

Graham looked at her sombrely and slowly stood. 'I'm going to check the horses,' he said quietly, defeatedly, and went out.

'Are you all right, darling?' Maggie called after him. There was no answer. 'Excuse me,' she said to Frankie and followed her husband.

She stood at the open door and watched him cross the yard in the glare of the security lights, his feet dragging, shoulders slumped, head down. He slid the big barn door aside and went in, seeing her as he turned to close it and waiting, watching her. She went across the yard, stopping in front of him. He looked completely dejected and very close to tears. Maggie had never known him like this. All she had ever seen in him was determination, hard work, obsession with his horses, a dedication to raising his children properly. Now here he was, a man almost broken.

And here she was, so protective of this money, of their 'security', she'd blinded herself to what was really important. She thought of everything they'd been through together, all the tough times when he'd always picked himself up, picked all of them up too and soldiered on. She loved him. She needed to show it, needed to practise it. Needed, somehow, to survive all this.

She put her hand out for his and he lifted his right arm towards her and placed his hand in hers and she felt it as heavy as though he'd been dead. 'Come into the tack room,' she said softly, 'it's too cold in those boxes.

The tack room had a small old-fashioned gas stove. Maggie lit it and switched on the single striplight. There was a long bench Graham had bought from a school that had closed; it was heavy and shiny with dark brown varnish and had been in the school's gym for generations. Graham liked things that had a bit of history about them. She sat beside him on the bench in front of the stove and beneath the racks of saddles and bridles and pictures of their horses and a couple of sponsors' horse blankets for races they'd won. Maggie took one of these off the wall; it was red with big silver lettering. She sat down and laid it across their knees and put her arm around her husband.

He hung his head and they sat in silence for a minute. He said dejectedly, 'We'd best go in. He might call.'

'Let him call,' she said, moving her hand to stroke his neck. 'We've waited long enough for him. He can wait for us.'

He was silent again for a while then said quietly, not looking at her, 'I want you to know and I want the kids to know how sad I'll be to lose Gabby.'

He sounded close to tears and it caught Maggie out. She'd thought he'd keep all this inside himself. 'I know,' she said, still stroking him gently. 'And for all Jane's histrionics the other night, she'll know too how much Gabby means to you. Billy does too. They've both grown up feeding on your dreams, for goodness sake. They'll know.'

'I just don't want them to think that because I try and take what life deals out, try to just get on with it, that I don't care and that I wouldn't fight if I could.'

She sensed there was more to come and stayed silent.

'If there was some way of getting to this guy, some way of meeting him face to face…'

'There is,' she said. 'We could pay the ransom.'

He looked at her. 'No. We've been through all that.'

'You're right, we have been through it but it's always been from my point of view and that's been ultra-selfish of me.'

And she saw the look in his eyes change and she

knew he agreed with at least some of what she'd said.

But he said, 'Nonsense. You did what you thought was best, was reasonable. And you were right. Or should I say *we* were right.'

'Should you say we?'

She saw that look in his eyes again. He said, 'All things considered, yes.'

'All things considered meaning that you thought you didn't really have any say because the money was coming to me and not you or to us?'

'Maggie, I was the one who said no to him on the phone last week, wasn't I?'

'You said no because you thought you had no right to bargain with money, with a cheque that had my name on it rather than yours, or ours. Isn't that right?'

He wouldn't answer, looked away again at the stove. Maggie said, 'Answer me one question, honestly. Just one and I won't ask any more. OK?' Staring at the floor now, he nodded. 'If you had a half a million in the bank, your own money with no call on it for anything else, would you pay the ransom?' He kept staring at the floor. 'Would you?' she repeated.

'Yes.'

She lifted her arm from his shoulder, pushed the blanket aside and moved to the floor in front of him on one knee then on to both knees. She was smiling warmly and she put her arms around his neck and kissed him. 'Come on. We've got a kidnapper to make pick-up arrangements with.'

'You can't, Maggie, not just because of me.'

'Who else matters?'

He shook his head slowly. She touched his chin, pushed his head up. 'Who else matters?' she asked again, very softly, tenderly. And he put his arms around her and kissed her and pulled her close, holding her there for what seemed a long time. She shifted on her knees on the wooden floorboards and said, 'Graham, we need to go and we need to go now!'

He pulled her closer. 'Why now?' he whispered.

'Because my bum is burning!'

As far as Monroe was concerned, the phone call was to be a formality. There was no way the Cassidys were going to pay and when they said they would he had laughed. When he found out they were serious he told them he'd call back to make arrangements for the pick-up and the delivery of the horse. And now, as he straddled his bike by the call-box in the Berkshire countryside, he knew he was facing the true test of his criminal brain. He prided himself on being a sharp thinker and now he had to prove it. If he did he'd be half a million pounds richer. If he failed, he'd be spending a long time inside.

He sped back to Lambourn, to the abattoir he worked in. His own little house in the village held no appeal for him now. It just reminded him he had never made it as a jockey, never got to the top in racing and as he rode along the wet roads in his leathers he wondered exactly what sort of house half a million pounds would buy. He knew that property up north was much cheaper and also was aware that if he suddenly bought a big place down here questions would be asked.

Yet he wanted to stay close to Lambourn, wanted the bastards to see that he had made it. Trouble was that half a million wasn't enough to prove anything these days and that was why he had the back-up, the main plan. Once he had some serious money, he'd make sure nobody could touch him. They could ask all the questions they liked but he'd have answers. Answers for everything; for the big house and the Merc and the maid and the swimming pool and the tennis court and the long, long holidays. Barbados was the place, he thought. That was where all these rich racing bastards went to be with their own kind. Sunny Barbados where pond life like him couldn't afford to go. Barbados, the Newmarket of the Caribbean. Well, he'd be there and he'd outbuy them all. He'd let them see what it was to be able to spend!

And why not take this half a million to get him off to a decent start? He'd figure something out to make the pick-up safe. It couldn't be that hard, could it? It wasn't as though he had to bring the bloody horse along! He'd call them next day and tonight he'd decide exactly how he was going to do this. To hell with the abattoir, he spent enough time there as it was. Anyway, the pubs would be buzzing in the village with New Year's Eve parties. He'd go there, have a few beers, make his plans for collecting the dosh then find some bird to bring in the New Year with, a new bird, none of the old slappers he normally ended up with. A new one for the new year.

43

When the police heard that the Cassidys intended to pay the ransom they pulled Burnham off the case and sent two new officers to speak to them. They went through all the warnings – by paying up they'd simply be encouraging the kidnapper to choose another victim, and handing over the ransom did not guarantee the safe return of their horse. But Maggie and Graham stuck to their guns and were pleased that Frankie stood by them. He knew he should have taken the professional stance and sided with the police but he preferred to support his friends.

The CID brought with them a much more sophisticated monitoring kit to record the phone call. When it finally came, the recorder silently switched itself on automatically.

'Still want your horse back?' Monroe asked.

'Yes,' said Graham.

'And you're still willing to pay?'

'That's right.'

'Well the price has just gone up. A million.'

Graham clenched his jaw and looked suddenly very angry.

Monroe laughed. 'Only kidding! I'm a man of my word, Mr Cassidy. Got a pen?'

'Yes.'

'Got the money?'

'We'll have it for when you want it.'

'You've got forty-eight hours.'

'Fine. We can do that.'

'Good. Listen. Half a million pounds in used notes. I want you to go to Charnock Richard services on the M6 at six p.m. on Thursday. You should park in the last row of bays before the final exit for the petrol station. In that row you will see a black Volvo 740 with a French registration plate. It is a left-hand-drive car. Take the money and put it on the back seat of the car. The door will be open. Then get in the driver's seat; the keys will be underneath it. The car has a satellite navigation system and your destination will be pre-programmed. You'll hear audio directions as well as see them on the screen on the dashboard. The car also has special electronic equipment which detects mobile phone, police radio and radar output. I will be monitoring every sound. If you make any calls to the police or anyone else you'll be collecting a dead horse. Tell the police that if they track you in any way, by road or helicopter or by fixing a bug any-where, tell them you'll be suing them for half a million. If you do everything right and reach the satnav destination without anything going wrong, you'll get your next set of instructions. Got all that?

Graham was still scribbling. 'Yes.'

'Call it back to me. I don't want you blaming me if anything goes wrong.'

Graham read it back.

'Right. Good. One final thing; you need to remember this codeword ... Barbados. It's the one you will recognize me by. When you hear it, you'll hand over the money. What is it?'

'Barbados.'

'Good, now say hello to the nice policemen for me and to the Jockey Club guys.'

Graham said, 'When do we get the horse back?'

'As soon as I've counted that half a million. So make sure you don't get it all in fivers, won't you?' He hung up.

The younger of the CID men moved towards the tape recorder and started rewinding it. 'Right,' he said, 'let's start making plans.'

The abattoir wasn't due to reopen until 6 January and Monroe knew he could safely take the rifle he always used as long as he returned it before then. He bound the weapon in thick black bin bags and strapped it to his bike using leather from an old bridle, although he had to reposition it a few times to make it fit comfortably under his right leg.

He'd been nervous making that phone call but everything now looked fine and his confidence was high; the plan was a brilliant one and it bolstered his belief that he was set for the big time. He was sure it would work, certain he'd now get the money with the absolute minimum of danger to himself. What he did realize, as he put the final touches to the rifle strapping, was that with this 303 weapon that could kill a man at a mile, he was raising the stakes beyond the point of return. It was a calculated gamble; he reckoned that if they caught him he'd get ten years for the kidnappings alone and ten years was as good as a lifetime for him. He'd be over forty when he got out, well past the age when he could hope to make his mark.

Carrying a gun would get him another five years at least but for what he planned to do he decided it was easily worth the risk. Research on the internet into past kidnap cases told him that a high percentage of people were caught at the pick-up point. He'd studied the various ways kidnappers had used to try and get clean away and some of them had seemed quite ingenious. Everything he'd picked up in those hours trawling through news archives had, he thought, served him well. He'd soon find out if he was right. Then they'd add his story to the archives – only he'd be one of the rare few who got away.

When Maggie Cassidy had made the bold decision to pay the money she hadn't reckoned with the practicalities of getting the cash in forty-eight hours. The police had been unable and unwilling to help, and after much racking of brains, Frankie had volunteered to call his millionaire friend, Bobby Cranfield. Maggie had thanked him but said she may as well try her agent first. He was going to have to give a letter of guarantee anyway that the half a million was coming her way. Maggie knew he had some very influential friends in the City and thought she should ask him if he could actually help get the cash.

The money was delivered next day by a security courier. It was in a much smaller package than Maggie had imagined but it was all in fifty-pound notes so she supposed it would be right. She spent an hour with Graham and Frankie counting it in the kitchen. After two attempts they got it right and laughed nervously as the tension continued to build.

After dinner Frankie called the CID. He returned to the table as Maggie lit a cigarette. 'Any news?' she asked.

Frankie said, 'They're still trying to get a result from the French police on Volvo 740s but they reckon they have things pretty much as they want them at the service station.'

'And there's no black Volvo in place at Charnock Richard right now?'

'Not as far as they can see.'

Graham shook his head. 'How the hell is this guy planning to do this?'

Frankie shrugged. Maggie drew on her cigarette and shook her head slowly. Graham said, 'He sounded so confident, didn't he? Surely he can be the only one who's dropping this car off? If this navigation programme is set from the service station then who else could set it? Who else could take the car there?'

'He could get somebody to do it for him,' Maggie suggested, 'somebody who wouldn't necessarily be involved. He could simply pay an accomplice to do it, tell him what to put on the system when he leaves it and that's it. If the police picked the guy up we'd be no further forward and we'd have lost the horse.'

Frankie said, 'Don't worry. Whoever drops the car off won't even know the police are there. They've got all sorts of thermal-imaging equipment and infra-red cameras. They'll make sure

268

they get some good video of him and if it's safe to track him, they'll try and do it.'

'What if it's not safe?' asked Graham. Frankie could see that now the commitment to pay had been made, Graham had grown much more animated, much edgier.

'They've promised not to do anything to jeopardize the horse's life,' Frankie said.

Graham said nothing for a few moments, then, 'Do you trust them, Frankie?' It was a plea for reassurance.

Frankie said, 'It's the first time I've worked with them. If we were stuck with Burnham I'd be worried but these other two seem pretty slick. They have a final briefing meeting in half an hour and they've asked me along so, if you don't mind, I'll leave you for a while.'

'Not at all,' Graham said. 'You'll be back for your usual nightcap, I hope?'

'Wouldn't miss it.' Frankie smiled.

Maggie and Graham sat together by the fire and talked of their plans if things went well next day, never entertaining the thought that they might not. Just before ten Graham got up. 'Frankie's getting dangerously close to missing his nightcap. I'll just go and have a last look at the horses.'

'Fine. I'll pour us a drink.'

In the barn, Graham was glad to see that all was well. He spoke quietly to the horses as he stepped into each box to run his hand down a neck or a flank. He loved the warmth of them at night, the smell of them. When he'd seen them all he went to the door; as he closed it he said to them, 'Your old mate Gabby will be back tomorrow, God willing.'

Then he sensed someone behind him. At the same time he felt cold metal digging into the back of his head. He froze, hand still on the half-shut door. Out of the side of his right eye he could see the shadow of the gunman cast by the security lights. It was a rifle he held. He recognized the voice too when he heard him say, 'Barbados.'

44

They told Billy about the theft of the money. Maggie decided they had no choice, with the place swarming with police and the endless interviews with them. But they thought it best not to tell Jane. They'd just agreed a one-week extension to her holiday in Ireland as Poppy was doing so well with her company, although Maggie was convinced that this lame duck she'd picked up, this Sean Gleeson, was more likely to be the reason Jane wanted to stay. Anyway, if she'd told her about the hold-up, about her father having a gun shoved in his face and the money gone, she'd have been rushing home to take over and comfort everybody. So they told her they were in negotiations with the kidnapper and that they were hopeful.

By mid-afternoon Maggie was alone in the house although two policemen were stationed outside, the condition Graham insisted on before agreeing to go to the station and look through some mug shots – a pointless bloody exercise as he'd told the CID man. The thief, the kidnapper had been wearing a black mask covering everything but his eyes which had been a quite vivid blue. That was all he could tell them but the straw-clutchers had insisted that the mug shots might trigger something in his mind.

CID – Maggie shook her head slowly in disgust as she sipped coffee and lit her tenth cigarette of the day. At least they'd had the grace to be embarrassed at being so deeply taken in by all that French Volvo satellite navigation stuff. It proved to her that most policemen were no more well versed in handling kidnappings than she herself was. Apparently Stonebanks, Frankie's colleague, had told him the Met would never have believed all that stuff. It was these 'country boys', as he called them.

And now Frankie was gone too, back to London to make his report.

She thought of last night when the man came in with the gun to Graham's head (her stomach lurched sickeningly as she recalled it). Her first thought had been how glad she was that she had shown him some love these past couple of days, happy she'd agreed to pay the ransom even though that was what had brought the trauma about.

Poor Graham. He'd been devastated by what had happened. She knew it was worse for men. She was supposed to be the weak one. In Graham's mind he should have been able to offer protection but he'd been as dumbstruck and afraid as she had been. And she knew what it had done to his dignity. Part of the reason, she thought, was that this whole thing had been panning out like some movie or novel and everybody knew what to do in movies.

The baddie came in with the gun. The goodie overpowered him or outsmarted him, maybe killed him but at least locked him up until the cops arrived. But when the scene came to be played, the cold reality was that the instinct to stay alive favoured inaction, compliance, surrender. And that's what they'd done, almost without a murmur. She realized it had affected Graham badly, that her presence had made his self-loathing more acute. She knew that worse was to come for Graham because of the weight of guilt he felt now about losing the money. If he hadn't agreed to let her pay, last night would never have happened. Now, not only had they been terrorized, all the money had gone and they held out little hope of ever seeing the horse alive again. Everything lost in a few minutes.

The tears rose again.

Frankie and Stonebanks were in a basement bar off Oxford Street in London. Frankie had formally debriefed his own boss, Robert Archibald, and had his reassurance that there was nothing more he could have done. 'You went beyond the call of duty,' Archibald had said. 'There can be no criticism of you or of the department.'

Frankie was telling Stonebanks how guilty he

felt at not being there when the gunman had come in.

Stonebanks said, 'Why? What do you think you could have done?'

'I don't know. What would you have done?'

'With a hunting rifle in my face? Probably started crying for my mummy.'

'You're just trying to make me feel better.'

'I'm trying to make you wake up and smell the coffee! This guy knew what risks he was running. He's just added armed robbery to kidnap and the killing of at least one horse. Do you seriously think he wouldn't have used that gun if you'd been there and tried to stop him? He'll get twenty years if they catch him and he knows that. Does he seem the type that would have just handed over the gun if you'd asked him? Or maybe you felt you could have rushed him or something daft like that? How quickly can you cross a room? Faster than a bullet? And if he shot you, do you think he'd have left the Cassidys alive? Come on, Frankie, there was nothing you could have done, even if you'd been there.'

Frankie drank some beer and stared at the door. He knew Stonebanks was right, he'd just needed to hear it, needed to know that it was nothing to do with incompetence or lack of will, lack of courage. And he realized how petulant and self-pitying he must have sounded. What had Maggie thought? He felt he'd run off with his tail between his legs. Was that how she had seen it? And what about Kathy, watching from above, how had it looked to her?

'Look at the upside,' Stonebanks said, 'you'll

have the whole department behind you now.'

Frankie frowned quizzically. 'That's an upside?'

Stonebanks laughed. 'That's my boy!' He raised his glass in mock salute and Frankie did the same. 'At least the Cassidys have had a look at this guy now, heard him speak, seen him move. What has it added to the picture?'

Frankie sat back, legs stretched, hands in his lap, eyes to the ceiling. 'I don't know. Graham said he had the build of a jockey. He compared him to Derry Callaghan, remember him?'

'I remember him well.'

'Graham said that was who he reminded him of. Short and stocky, looked like he'd run to fat eventually but very fit-looking, strong...'

'He was right, Derry did run to fat. He's about fifteen stone now.'

'Do you keep any sort of picture file of past jockeys?' Frankie asked.

Stonebanks shook his head. 'We issue them with licences, keep files on their medical histories and disciplinary records but no pictures as far as I know. Anyway, I thought he had a motorcycle mask on?'

'He did but Maggie said his eyes were very blue. Sky-blue. Very striking.'

'Lenses.'

'Pardon?'

'He was probably wearing coloured lenses. He's been pretty smart so far. If all he was showing were his eyes you can bet he wouldn't be doing it knowing they were such a distinctive feature.'

'Maybe, but I wouldn't mind trying. What about the Racing Post? They'd have pictures of

274

jockeys going back years. We could go and have a look there.'

'We could, if you've got a few years to spare. I think they file all their pictures by name rather than profession.'

'But surely their pictures will be on computer? They must have some sort of subheading for files?'

'Maybe. We'll check in the morning.' Stone-banks stretched wearily.

'That's twice you've said "in the morning" and now you're yawning. Are you dropping some class of a hint here?'

Stonebanks smiled. 'You're a fine detective, Frankie. With those powers of observation, you're sure to catch this guy.'

'Come on, Geoff, it's only half-ten!'

'Come on yourself! I've got to drive to Lam-bourn.'

Frankie smiled. 'I know you have. I'm only kidding. Thanks for your help and for your company.'

'Thanks for the beer. You staying much longer?' Frankie sighed. 'Nah. Guess I'd better go home too.' A slight tension filled the pause that followed, then Stonebanks said, 'You're welcome to come back with me.'

'Thanks. I'll be fine. I need to face the hoover-ing and washing and cooking at some point. It might as well be tonight.'

'Sure?'

'Positive.'

Stonebanks smiled. 'See you tomorrow.'

'You will. Drive carefully.'

As soon as Stonebanks left, Frankie got up, for he knew if he sat there he would find another excuse not to go back to the cottage that night. He hadn't set foot in it for more than a week and the longer he'd stayed away the less inclined he was to go back and this brought more guilt flooding in. Why didn't he want to go back to the home he'd shared with Kathy? Until he'd got this job it had been his refuge. He'd never wanted to leave. The cottage and its memories, its photos of her, of them, wardrobes full of her clothes, shelves of magazines with her writing in, her pictures; it had been a haven, a cocoon. Why did he see it now as a prison?

He went out into the night and geed himself up. Maybe he just needed to get used to it again. Perhaps this bleak winter was affecting him. His best memories of the cottage had been summer memories. Now the woods were dark and bare, the fields wet and dreary, colourless. The cottage, silent and mournful, almost dead itself. And as he set off driving through London's bright lights and busy streets he realized that the main reason the cottage had lost its attraction was that his grief was beginning to ease. It pained him that thoughts of Kathy had not been so frequent of late but it was a fact nonetheless. And he'd even been laughing.

Last night had been dejection and misery but even those had been new experiences for him on the scale on which they'd happened, new because of what had caused them. And now he was in the middle of a very important investigation where, by the way this criminal had behaved, people's

276

lives could eventually be at stake. He felt a sudden nervous thrill in his gut and he knew in the same second that Kathy would sympathize. Kathy, of all people, would understand the thrill of danger, the magic of exploring new experiences, discovering new depths within yourself. That was what her whole life had been about and now, through her death, Frankie was beginning to appreciate this. Kathy would have no trouble understanding and that made Frankie feel a lot better. It sowed the seed in his mind that come next New Year, if God spared him, he might be living somewhere else. He'd wait and see what the spring would bring in the cottage, the summer maybe. Wait and see how much more he would learn about himself. And he knew he couldn't learn if he returned to the level of grieving he'd been indulging in; he had to start consciously opening himself up.

His term as a priest had been closed emotionally. His time as a husband had been intensely devoted to one thing only. All his adult life had been spent sealed off from the world out there. He'd had insights into the characters of many people but was now realizing that he knew little about his own.

45

Apart from when they were asleep, Sean Gleeson and Jane Cassidy spent almost all of their time together. When Uncle Fergus had seen how good a rider Sean was he'd let him ride some work and Sean found that sitting on a racehorse was everything he'd imagined it to be and more. It had made him rue his youthfulness and wish for the next five years to pass in a night.

They'd ride out in the mornings and again in the afternoon, no matter what the weather. In between they'd sit with Poppy, and Sean would tell tales of what the children in Dublin got up to and how the pony races were organized. They'd groom and feed the horses and Sean would talk about the races he'd win when he became a jockey but as much as he tried to shut out the other world, Sean was growing increasingly anxious to find out what had happened to his father. But any time he said that, Jane would go mental, demanding to know how he could possibly care what happened to such a horrible man, and Sean would regret then having told her of some of the bad things his father had done.

The schools were due to re-open in a few days. Uncle Fergus had already been dropping hints to that effect. Nobody would care if Sean never turned up at school but he'd been away from it too long. He knew that jockeys didn't have to be particularly smart but wanted to have the education for after his riding career. He was aware that most jump jockeys didn't last much past their mid-thirties and although he hoped to have enough money to retire by then he just wanted to be sure he could do something else.

But returning to school meant returning to St Joseph's Mansions. Jane had argued that it didn't. They'd been sitting in the hay barn, in a huge chair they'd made of bales. First she said that he could go to Poppy's school. But Poppy attended a private school – that cost money. 'Well,' she'd said with her usual confidence, 'we can find another school near here.'

'That's a long way from Dublin city,' Sean said.

'You can move in here, with Uncle Fergus. Pay for your keep by working with the horses.'

'That would be just grand,' Sean said. 'But how would Uncle Fergus feel about it and what would we tell the school people? There's all that stuff about legal guardians and everything and I don't want that.'

'Why?'

'Well, I want it, I want to be here. This has been the best week of my life and I'd love to stay here but you'll have to go home soon yerself.'

'I can sort that. I can move here. You know I don't get on with my mum any more.'

'Maybe. But I still have things to do, Jane.'

'What things?'

'Find out where me da is. And me ma, too.'

And Jane crossed her arms and furrowed her brow in the way Sean had come to know so well. He wasn't looking forward to saying goodbye.

279

Frankie took the call on his mobile just after eight in the morning. It was Stonebanks. 'Sorry Frankie, but it looks like they found the Cassidys' horse. He's dead.'

'Where? When?

'Outside the main entrance to Cheltenham racecourse, would you believe. The head groundsman found him when he arrived about half an hour ago.'

Shocked, Frankie sat in the car, shaking his head slowly.

'Shot and mutilated,' Stonebanks said. 'Very similar to Ulysses, so I hear.'

'Bastard,' Frankie said.

'Indeed,' said Stonebanks, surprised.

'Has anyone told the Cassidys?'

'Not as far as I know.'

'I'll call them.'

'Sure?'

'Positive. I'll call now. If I wasn't so far south I'd go and tell them personally.'

'Drive up. Call them, then drive up. I know how close you are with them.'

'What good would it do? I'd be better off here now, trying to catch this this...'

'Bastard?'

'Yes.'

'There are other things. You can check in with the police there. Maybe you'll pick something up from them. Get yourself on the move, go on. Let me know if there's anything I can do.'

'OK. Thanks, Geoff.'

'No problem.'

He pulled the car over, parked by the edge of the wood and sat looking down at the small screen on his mobile. The Cassidy number was programmed in. He scrolled to it and pressed 'send'. Maggie answered.

'Maggie, it's Frankie Houlihan.'

'Hello Frankie. How are you this morning?'

'I'm well. How are you?'

'I'm fine. Coping.'

He wished she hadn't said that.

'Is there something wrong?' she asked.

'More bad news, I'm afraid. They think they've found Gabby. He's dead.'

'Ohh.'

'I'm so sorry, Maggie.'

'It's OK. It's all right.' He could hear the shock in her voice.

'I'm heading up to you now, if that's OK?'

'Yes. Of course.'

'I should be there by noon.'

'Good. Good. I'll tell Graham.'

'See you later then.'

'Yes. Bye.'

He cursed silently as he put the phone into its cradle – then it rang again. It was Maggie. 'Frankie, how did he die?'

He drew a breath. 'He was shot, I think.'

'So he wouldn't have suffered?'

'I don't think so, Maggie, no,' he lied. The horse had been mutilated. It was highly likely that had happened after death, Frankie thought, there was no way this guy would have wanted to try and keep a pain-enraged horse still enough to shoot it through the head. But Frankie couldn't be cer-

281

tain that there had been no suffering at the hands of this lunatic.

'Good,' she said. 'That's not so bad then, is it?' She sounded completely stunned.

'No, it's not.'

'OK. Take care on your journey.'

'I will.'

As he drove north he thought about the way people's lives worked out. There they'd been on the run-up to Christmas, the happiest of families. The Grand National favourite was safe in his box and in the post was a cheque that would make them secure for life then, bang, all gone, in tatters. He thought of his own misfortune and that of many of the parishioners he had served over the years. And he thought about justice and about God and could make no real sense of either.

Maggie and Graham decided to try and keep the news from the children until Jane returned the following week. It would mean asking Fergus to try to make sure Jane didn't see any newspapers or TV news for a couple of days. They'd need to do the same with Billy but that wouldn't be so hard as he spent most of his time in his room trying to think up new inventions or playing computer strategy games. Luckily he was still off school so none of his mates would alert him, although she'd need to screen his calls. Maggie rang Fergus who seemed devastated by the news, and agreed to try his best to keep it from Jane.

46

The *Racing Post* editor told Frankie Houlihan he'd be happy to help with the picture library but that it was probably going to take a week to get it in the shape he needed it. Frankie thanked him and booked a day to go and scan through all the pictures with Maggie. He was still with the Cassidys. He'd travelled to Cheltenham with Graham who formally identified Angel Gabriel; Frankie had found it a harrowing experience.

The horse had been so badly mutilated that Graham broke down in tears in front of Frankie and the Clerk of the Course. Frankie had seen many people cry before and recognized the racking sobs of true shock and grief as he tried to comfort the trainer. The Clerk made mildly embarrassed comments about how terrible the whole thing was and Frankie helped Graham back to the car before returning for an official interview with the man who had found the dead horse.

On the way back north, Graham, red-eyed, turned to Frankie. 'Frankie, let's not tell Maggie what he did to him.' Graham barely recognized the sound of his own voice, this croak through the tightness in his throat.

'Of course not. No, it's best we keep it between us.'

'Yes. Definitely.'

They travelled in silence for a while, Graham staring glassy-eyed at the road and seeing nothing. 'What about the press?' he asked. 'Will there be pictures in the papers?'

'Don't worry. I asked the Clerk of the Course to make sure nobody took any press pictures. The police will want to take some for their files, that's all.'

'Good.' Graham bowed his head and said quietly, 'We can't even bring him home... They'd see what a mess he's in...'

'Don't be worrying about that. I'll make sure he's taken care of.'

'Thanks, Frankie. You've been a tower of strength. I don't know what the family would have done without you, I really don't.'

'Ahh come on now, you're a great family. This has been a terrible, terrible thing but you all have the strength to get over it, to help each other.'

Graham shook his head and let out a long sigh. 'Jane is going to be inconsolable. My God, she's going to be completely devastated. She'll insist on having him home. She'll want him buried in the paddock. Oh Jesus!' Graham covered his face with his hands and started weeping again.

Frankie took a hand from the wheel and reached across to touch Graham's shoulder, to squeeze it softly. 'I'll sort something out, Graham, I promise. I know some good vets. I'm sure I can get one to work on Gabby, to get him cleaned up and his wounds fixed so you'll be able to bring him home.'

Graham nodded, face still covered, sobbing. 'If you, if you could ... that would be great.'

284

They drove on and after five minutes Graham had recovered and composed himself. He apologized for breaking down.

'Don't be daft. It's perfectly natural, so it is. The grief's better out.'

'I just couldn't believe it,' Graham said. 'After he'd taken the money I honestly thought we'd get him back. What on earth is the point of killing him? I thought he just came to the house to get the money to reduce the chances of the police catching him at the supposed pick-up point. What in the name of God did he stand to gain by killing Gabby afterwards?'

'I don't know, Graham. I really don't. It just makes me glad that you didn't try to tackle him the other night because it's obvious now, if it wasn't before, that you'd have been tackling a madman.'

They talked about the police and their effectiveness, about the mug shots Graham had sat through for hours with nothing to show for it. Then they travelled in silence for a while until Frankie, driving, was aware of Graham turning purposefully towards him as he spoke; 'I want to do everything I can to help you catch this man. Apart from what he's done to Gabby, which I think I could kill him for, I want Maggie to get her money back. I want that more than anything else.'

Frankie considered saying that he was sure Maggie wasn't that worried about the money but he knew that wouldn't make Graham feel better so he just nodded. 'I'll put everything I can into catching him, Graham. My boss has already told me we have the backing of the full Jockey Club Security Department.'

'So what are the chances?'

'Depends on how solid our suspicion is that he might be an ex-jockey. If he is, and he doesn't wear contact lenses, our chances might be very good indeed.'

When Frankie brought Graham back home, Maggie asked no immediate questions. The shock and misery were etched in her husband's lined, grey face. Maggie realized that this man she'd known and seen almost every day for over twenty years was old now – old and tired and defeated. Alongside him, sympathetic and patient as ever, stood Frankie Houlihan, young still, and strong, with most of his tribulations to come, she thought. She went to her husband and hugged him. His head rested heavily on her shoulder and his hands barely linked at the small of her back. He started sobbing quietly. She looked at Frankie and knew he could see the pain in her eyes as he slowly raised a hand to chest height and backed away to slip quietly outside.

Frankie hated this feeling of helplessness. This was the second time he'd experienced it – the thug taking the money from under their noses had been bad but this was somehow worse. He'd taken much more than money from Graham Cassidy. He'd taken his vitality and his dignity, his hopes and his dreams and there had to be something Frankie could do about it; had to be.

He walked towards the bottom of the drive. It was a gloomy day and away across the patchwork of fields, Frankie could see dark swathes of rain sweeping over the countryside. Turning up the collar of his coat he went left at the end of the drive and walked along the hedge-lined road. He concentrated on emptying the emotion from his mind, tried to think logically and make some sense of what had happened.

The kidnapper was no fool, the way he'd conned the police over the pick-up proved that. It was almost certain that there was a reason behind everything he'd done. So why kill a horse after he'd been paid, a horse that was of no use to him? In killing it he was killing his own chances of ever being paid a ransom again. And why the mutilation? It was senseless and this man didn't seem the type to do senseless things. Whether or not he was an ex-jockey whose picture was on file, there had to be something in his behaviour to work on. Rather than assuming, as they'd done in the last twenty-four hours, that the man was simply a violent lunatic, maybe the assumption should be that everything he did made sense to him.

Frankie walked on, vaguely aware of the sound of his feet on the fine gravel and the wind in the bare branches of the trees. He decided to start with the biggest puzzle of all: why kill Angel Gabriel? The killing of Ulysses was slightly more understandable as no ransom had been paid but, having said that, the deadline the killer had given for the money was ridiculously short, almost as though he hadn't wanted it to be paid, as though he actually wanted to kill the horse.

Now if he was depraved in some way, he could

simply kidnap horses and kill them without running the risk of telephone calls and police involvement. Then there was the dumping of Ulysses in a stream – why? It must have been a hell of a lot of trouble to get that horsebox or trailer into position to place the body. The drag marks on the ground showed that he'd had to use some form of winch to get the horse properly into the water; why hadn't he just winched it out and dumped it in a field?

And why hadn't he left it in a public place, as he'd done with Gabby? It was as if he hadn't wanted Ulysses found for a long time yet he'd taken the opposite tack with Gabby. Frankie couldn't figure it out. He walked for twenty minutes then turned back as the rain shadows moved nearer and the wind rose. Weather approaching. Kathy's face loomed in his mind. She'd so loved the weather, especially dramatic weather. He looked to the sky and spoke to her; 'Kath, if either of those horses arrives in heaven, ask them what happened.'

In the kitchen, Maggie Cassidy sat alone, smoking, sipping cooling coffee, trying to block everything out. She'd had to lead Graham to bed like a child and tuck him in. She had never known anyone cry the way he had, the sobs coming from so deep in him she could almost physically feel them force themselves up, dredging his emotions at their very core. His weight on her had increased as he seemed to lose the power of his muscles until he hung, exhausted, as she tried to hold him up. And when she'd got him to bed and pulled the covers up to his neck and stroked his clammy forehead he had dropped quickly into the soundest sleep, his breathing long and deep and even, his body limp as a rag doll, unmoving. She returned heavy-footed to the kitchen, wondering if he would ever again be the man she knew.

Graham hadn't spoken a word to her. She knew nothing of how Gabby had looked when they saw him. She didn't know if she wanted to know anything now. If this was what it had done to her husband, the strongest of men emotionally, what would it do to her? How would she tell the children? What would she tell them?

A knock at the door made her jump. She put down her cigarette and opened the door. Frankie stood there, dark hair and pale face framed against the gathering stormclouds. She said, 'Come in. No need for you to knock.'

Frankie took the step up into the kitchen and she closed the door quietly. She saw him look around the empty room. 'Graham's gone to bed. I think it's all finally hit him.'

Frankie unbuttoned his coat. 'Poor fella. The strain's been terrible on all of you this past week.'

Maggie clicked the kettle switch. 'Take your coat off, I'll make some tea.'

They sat in silence for a while, cradling the hot mugs. Then Maggie said, 'Will you stay a few more days, Frankie?' She hoped it hadn't sounded like a plea. She couldn't gauge what he was thinking as he looked at her but she knew he was going to decline.

He said, 'I want to get back, Maggie, and get working on this. I want to find this man. And ...

289

and I think you should have time on your own with the family to come to terms with all this, if you don't mind me saying.'

She reached for another cigarette. 'I'm not sure I want to try and come to terms with it now. After he took the money, I was confident we'd get Gabby back.' She lit the cigarette, drew hard on it and rested her head on her right hand as she exhaled. She looked suddenly tired. 'I never thought what we'd do if we didn't get him back. Didn't prepare for it. And now it's happened so suddenly, I don't know what to do. It's sort of the end of everything. I just wondered if you could stay with us for a while.'

'To save you from facing up to things?'

She looked at him. It was the first time he had ever been blunt with her and she couldn't decide if he'd done it deliberately or had just put it awkwardly. 'Yes, I suppose that's part of it.'

'Maggie, I feel useless here. I feel I've been useless to you all throughout this and I want not to be useless.'

'You're not, don't be silly. You've been a great friend and a great help.'

'But I didn't stop him stealing your money or your horse. I didn't do my job properly and I want a chance to try and make amends because I think we can catch this fella.'

'It wasn't your responsibility. You did all you could. You even phoned to warn us to be careful. It was our own stupidity that cost us Gabby.'

'And half a million pounds.'

She nodded.

'Well I'd like to try and help get it back,'

Frankie said. 'I've arranged a meeting soon for you to look at some pictures and they might just throw up a good clue. And if I can get my brain working properly I think there's some sense to be made out of all the mad stuff that's gone on.'

'So you're going back to London?'

He nodded. 'London, Lambourn, wherever I need to go to feel I'm actually doing something, to feel I'm working.'

She looked at him. 'I'd like to feel I was doing something too. I'd like to help.'

'Fine. I think it'll do you good. Maybe you could start by doing what I'm doing and concentrate on trying to think like this fella. Try to put yourself in his shoes and come up with a good reason for what he's done. Assume he's smart and emotionally stable. Have you a pen and paper?'

She went to a small plastic pot that stood on the windowsill and picked out a pen. Then she opened two drawers before pulling out a dog-eared writing pad. Bringing it to the table she scribbled lightly to get the ink running. Frankie said, 'Right, let's go back to the very start.'

47

On 6 January the abattoir Monroe worked in was due to re-open after the Christmas break. He had twenty-four hours left to carry out the next stage of his plan. He regretted his haste now in dumping the carcass so publicly at Cheltenham. His motive had been to have the horse found quickly, to confuse the police if possible, making them wonder whether it was a kidnapper or a psycho of some kind they were dealing with. And he had to admit to himself that he'd done it to illustrate his power too, to have owners and trainers all over the country wondering if they were going to be next.

But he'd forgotten to check Cheltenham for CCTV. Although he'd arrived there at three o'clock in the morning, there was a chance that the system, if they had one at the gates, had been switched on. It was a remote possibility and the fact that it had been so dark made it even more unlikely that he'd have anything to worry about. But if the horsebox had been filmed, Monroe reckoned he could turn it to his advantage.

He booked the horsebox on the last ferry to Dublin on 4 January. Once on board, he hid in the cab until the hold had been secured then settled himself on the padded bench seat to wait out the journey. The silver-coloured suitcase containing the half-million pounds was beside him. He stroked the surface, liking its dimpled, steely feel and he was glad he'd bought the best to hold the money, his money now, money that was just the beginning. He passed the time by counting the bundles then secured them again as the ship slowed and turned to enter the harbour. He shut the case away in the overhead locker.

It was dark when he drove off the ferry. The route he'd planned was on tape and the cassette was in the player. He switched it on and listened to his own voice guide him across to Mullingar and his final destination, Lough Ennell. The road ran nearest the lough at its northernmost tip. Monroe drove the section three times. It was eleven o'clock. He passed only one car during the twenty minutes driving the lough road but after his error at Cheltenham he wanted to take no more chances. He drove away from the lough and parked in a layby where he waited until one o'clock in the morning.

Returning to the shores of the lough he backed the box into a field entrance, took a heavy flashlight from the overhead locker and climbed out. Cloud obscured the moon and he could see little outside the flashlight beam which he trained on the grassy slopes leading from the road to the water's edge. He walked about two hundred yards from where he'd parked the box. He'd learned on the internet that Lough Ennell was deep close to the edge on this northern side. Once in the water, there was supposed to be eight to ten feet of gradual slope before the sides fell steeply away to a shelf thirty feet below the surface. He only had to make that shelf. If he got lucky and the box dropped beyond it, all the better, the final depth was more than a hundred and twenty feet. The rocky ground running down to it was steep enough to give the horsebox the necessary momentum but the road was narrower than he'd hoped. The real risk was going to be in getting the box nose on to the drop-off point, then inching it past its centre of gravity. Once it started toppling, a quick jump clear and he was away.

Monroe set two rocks at the road edge to guide him then he returned to the box, unloaded his Kawasaki from the back, took the suitcase from the overhead locker and left it beside the bike which he'd fitted with false number plates. He got back in, started the engine and sat for a few seconds. Did he really want to risk someone happening by, catching the silver suitcase in his headlights and stopping to investigate? He jumped down again and brought the suitcase back into the cab.

He reached the marker rocks. The road seemed even narrower from his seat well above it. He checked his mirrors, then got out on to the road to make doubly sure no other traffic was in the vicinity. He could see no trace of light from either direction. Jumping quickly back in he started his manoeuvres, driving a couple of feet forward then back, turning just a little each time to try and get the box facing the edge. By the time he was happy with the positioning, he was sweating heavily with effort and tension. He'd been here now for more than half an hour without seeing another vehicle and he knew he was stretching his luck.

Still, just the final few inches forward now. Holding the clutch to the floor, he shoved the stick into first, gripped the suitcase handle with his left hand and opened the door with his right. It swung closed again. Once more he tried. It closed again. He let go the case, changed into neutral and put the handbrake on. Then he pushed the door open wide till it fixed on its struts and held. Now he chose first gear again, took the suitcase handle and eased his foot off the clutch. The box crept forward and lurched over the edge. Monroe turned quickly, pulling the suitcase after him, but as the left front wheel dropped over the edge the door swung violently inwards as Monroe was halfway out; the metal frame hit the crown of his head, fracturing his skull and knocking his unconscious body back into the cab.

The heavy box quickly gathered speed, grinding noisily in low gear towards the lough's edge. The front bumper broke the cold, dark waters at forty-three minutes past one. Two minutes later the moon found a gap in the clouds and glinted on a patch of oil on the surface of Lough Ennell. It was the only sign that anything had happened, and the small slick was already being dispersed by the wind and the choppy waves.

48

After leaving the Cassidys, Frankie spent the next couple of days travelling between Lambourn and London, having brain-storming sessions with Stonebanks and other colleagues. The racing intelligence officers based around the country promised him they'd mine all their possible contacts to try and find the smallest lead. He rang Joe Ansell, the vet who was trying to repair Angel Gabriel's mutilated body. His assistant asked if Joe could call back in a while. Frankie knew Joe had been working hard since the carcass had been delivered. The wounds would hasten decomposition and Joe was restricted to doing his cutting and stitching in what amounted to a makeshift cold storage unit at the Horse-racing Forensic Laboratory in Newmarket. Joe had promised the horse would be ready to go back to the Cassidys by the end of the week.

Frankie called Maggie to find out how they planned to handle the burial. He asked first about Graham and the children.

'Graham hasn't left his bed since he came back from Cheltenham,' Maggie told him. 'All he does is sleep. The doctor says it's a combination of shock and depression and that the medication will steadily bring him out of it.'

'Poor fella. You should have Gabby home by the weekend, that might help him, eh? I'm just waiting for Joe Ansell to call me back with confirmation. Will Jane be back by the weekend?'

Maggie sighed. 'If I can get her away from Sean.'

'First boyfriend?'

'First proper one. Seems a real character. Fergus likes him too.' She told Frankie what she knew about Sean.

'Sounds an interesting kid.'

'To say the least!'

'What about Billy, how's he been?'

'Oh, Billy won't change! Spends most of his time in his room on the computer. Still trying to dream up get-rich-quick schemes.'

'Like the Hot Harrow?'

'He told you about that?'

'He did. Among others. He's a good boy. Be a millionaire one day.'

'Huh!'

'Don't knock it. They say an ounce of perseverance is worth a pound of talent.'

'Who says? I've never heard anyone say that.'

'You just heard me.'

'And I think you made it up!'

'I probably did. It's good to hear you sounding a bit brighter.'

'Oh, *nil desperandum* and all that.'

'Give Graham and Billy my best. I'll see you at the weekend.'

'Look forward to it.'

The cottage in the woods felt somehow as though it had been deserted for ages, much longer than the time Frankie had actually been away. He laid his bag on the bedroom floor and began to unpack slowly, stopping to open the windows, then reaching round to the outside of the pane to scrape off the wet leaves stuck to the glass. The place smelt damp and stale, felt cold and unwelcoming. He hadn't the will to set about it the way he knew he should to try and put some warmth and life back into it and as he stared through the open window to the trees beyond, he realized that the wish to keep this as a proper home had died with Kathy.

But he had nowhere else to go and he needed a base. He knew that he also needed to discipline himself, push himself to do the chores that had to be done. So he changed into his old jeans and the red sweater Kathy had liked and he set about cleaning and tidying, airing and washing and he found that the busier he became, the more his spirits lifted.

The worktop area in the kitchen closest to the door was where he tended to dump things; letters, bills, the contents of his pockets, his watch, and as he sorted through the collection he found the letter he had meant to answer, the one from Zuiderzie's trainer, Martin Brockbank. As he picked the letter up, his mobile rang.

'Frankie, it's Joe Ansell.'

'Hello, Joe! Thanks for calling me back.'

'No problem. I wasn't far from the phone when you rang but I was just trying to be absolutely certain about something I'd found before I spoke to you. Just left the horse a minute ago.'

'Angel Gabriel?'

'Well, yes, the one who's supposed to be Angel Gabriel.'

'Supposed to be?'

'I've just spent over two hours removing dye from his head. Underneath the dye this horse has a lovely white star.'

'White? White hair?'

'What do you think, white corduroy?'

'Angel Gabriel had no white on him.'

'That's why this horse ain't Angel Gabriel.'

When Frankie finished the call he stood staring out of the window, trying to gather his thoughts. What the hell was this guy up to? Was Angel Gabriel still alive? If so, what did this madman plan to do with him? He already had the ransom money. Brockbank's letter caught his eye and he picked it up again. The picture of Zuiderzie in the paddock at Stratford came back to him, followed immediately by the picture of the corpse of Ulysses. He recalled thinking how alike both horses were.

Running back upstairs, Frankie grabbed his diary and skipped back through, checking the date he'd gone to Warwick against the date of the first kidnap – close, very close. He ran back downstairs and took his *Directory of the Turf* from the shelf to find Martin Brockbank's number. Halfway through dialling the Lambourn number Frankie stopped. Was his inexperience and over-excitement making him act stupidly? Maybe something was going on but he shouldn't discount the fact that Brockbank himself might be involved. A call to Stonebanks would be much more sensible.

On the way to Stonebanks's place, Frankie considered ringing Maggie Cassidy and decided against it. The last thing they needed, especially Graham, was to have their hopes dashed a second time. Best to wait till he had something more solid. Then he remembered he'd have to ring, have to tell them something. They were expecting the corpse for burial within the next couple of days. He'd told Joe Ansell he'd come back to him. It was almost certain they'd need to preserve the corpse now pending a criminal investigation. He'd sound out Stonebanks.

Stonebanks was working from home as he tried to do a couple of days a week. He wore a pair of black chinos and a grey polo shirt; it was the first time Frankie had seen him without a collar and tie. Stonebanks nursed his coffee, needing both hands to hold the barrel of a mug with his initials on. He said, 'You think both horses are still alive?'

'I think they could be,' Frankie said, trying to contain his excitement, to appear calm and professional.

'And the horse we dragged out of the water was Zuiderzie?'

'That's right. I think he put him in the stream as part of the mutilation process. Remember how decayed his skin was where he'd been lying in the water?'

Stonebanks nodded. 'And the horse Joe Ansell's got isn't Angel Gabriel?'

Frankie nodded, finding it hard now to mask an almost childish triumphalism; it was shining in his face and he could feel it and knew he could do nothing about it. Stonebanks obviously noticed it and a smile spread on his face too. 'If you're right here, Frankie boy, you've made a major name for yourself! Now talk me through it and I'll try to pick some friendly holes in it.

Frankie put down his cup and settled forward, elbows on knees. 'If I'm right and yer man has just found lookalikes for these horses, what's to stop him finding a couple more that are alive and racing and putting these top horses in as ringers in their place? What a killing he'd make on the betting side!'

Stonebanks said, 'It'd be a damn sight harder to find lookalikes that good when the horse had to be left alive, if you see what I mean? I accept that a distraught owner, expecting to see his horse dead, wouldn't look that closely at a mutilated body but it would be different on the racecourse, be much tougher.'

'Fine, but let's assume, for the moment, that the connections are in on the scam too.'

Stonebanks shrugged. 'Fair enough.'

'Ulysses and Angel Gabriel are both young enough for him to be able to wait a year or so to get things dead right and if he does, he'd make an awful lot more out of the bookies than he'd have made from ransom payments.

'And who'd be training these horses in the meantime, keeping them reasonably fit and happy?'

'Not a big problem, is it? If I'm right and he's got hold of the carcass of Zuiderzie, then there's every chance that he's in the business just now. He might even be a trainer rather than an ex-jockey.'

'God forbid,' said Stonebanks, shaking his head. 'So finding out what happened to Zuiderzie after he was put down is a key factor, you're right.'

'So what about Martin Brockbank. Do you think it would be safe to talk to him upfront?' Frankie asked.

'Straight as a die, Brockbank. No problem there at all. You'd just need to be careful not to make too big a thing of it or word will get out that something is cooking. Just take it easy with him, tell him it's just a routine check on horses that, eh, what can we say...? Did you mention that Zuiderzie won on the day he was put down?'

'That's right. I was there. He absolutely hacked

up after leading all the way. Won at a big price.'

Stonebanks stared at him for what seemed a long time then put down his coffee mug and started massaging his jaws. 'Won easily and very unexpectedly at a big price and next day he's dead?'

Frankie nodded slowly. Stonebanks said, 'Have you checked his dope test?'

Frankie shrugged, open-handed. 'No. Should I have?'

'I don't know. It just seems odd.'

'Now you mention it, I remember noticing how on his toes Zuiderzie was in the paddock that day, which was very unlike him. Kathy used to always say how docile he was, how laid-back. I just put it down to some class of rejuvenation or something since he'd left Miles Henry and joined Brockbank's yard. If it had been a positive dope test, we'd have heard about it by now, surely?'

Stonebanks got up and went to the phone. 'Somebody might have heard about it but it wouldn't necessarily have made its way back to us. Let me call the lab boys.'

Fifteen minutes later he got a call back from Newmarket with the result of Zuiderzie's Stratford dope test. 'Thanks,' he said and hung up, then turned to Frankie. 'Negative. I suppose that makes it easier to go and talk to Brockbank. We don't have to worry about him being involved in anything.'

'Are you coming along?' Frankie asked.

'No, it would seem over the top then. He might get suspicious. Why don't you just make it look like a social visit? You've exchanged letters, no reason for you not to drop by and introduce yourself, reminisce about old times, get him talking about the horse.'

'Good idea, Geoff. Good idea.'

Frankie couldn't contact Brockbank till he returned from racing in mid-evening but the trainer seemed happy to hear from him and invited him for breakfast and to watch some schooling next morning.

Frankie and Martin Brockbank got on well and chatted about racing in general and their respective careers. It was after breakfast as Brockbank showed him round the yard that Frankie brought the subject back to Zuiderzie, saying, 'It must have been a real shock to you to lose him after he'd won his first race for so long.'

'We couldn't believe it, Frankie. It happened so soon after it too. He'd just got home and we had to call the vet out. It must have started on the journey back. The poor bugger was standing there shaking like he was made of metal and somebody had hit him with a hammer. Shaking like a bloody tuning fork, he was. Culling operated on him that night, within an hour, in fact, but just couldn't save him.'

'Culling's your vet?'

'That's right. Good man. Good vet. If Peter Culling couldn't save him, nobody could.'

'And what was Mr Culling's verdict? What killed him?'

'Aggravated colic, I think he called it. The non-aggravated version is bad enough, I can tell you. I don't want to see this other type again.'

'Pity the owner.

'Yes, and his lass. Zuiderzie was Belinda's first winner. She's still not over it. Still keeps a lock of his mane in a locket she wears.'

'Poor girl. So did the owner take him home, have him buried?'

'Nothing so romantic, I'm afraid, Frankie. There ain't too many can afford to do that these days. We let the vet dispose of him through the local knacker's man, helps pay a bit off the final bill.'

'Yeah, I suppose.'

Brockbank smiled as they stopped by the box in the corner of the yard and a big brown intelligent head appeared over the top of the door. The horse sniffed at his trainer's shoulder and began nuzzling him. 'Never mind,' Brockbank said, 'here's the next serving of hope, the thing that keeps us all going. Frankie Houlihan, meet this year's Triumph Hurdle winner, Barabas. Barabas, meet a man with very good connections!' Frankie smiled and reached to stroke the big nose.

49

Employing the same caution he'd used with Brockbank, Frankie returned to discuss things with Stonebanks before ringing Culling to arrange an appointment. Stonebanks said he'd known the vet for years and although he seemed quite a reclusive individual personally, he had no reason to believe he was anything other than a hard-working vet. He was properly licensed, long-serving and he covered a number of race-courses in an official capacity as well as running his own business in Lambourn.

When Frankie rang and introduced himself, he felt that Culling had been thrown and that the vet had been shocked too when he'd mentioned that he wanted to come and speak to him about Zuiderzie. Culling had tried to cover his reaction by claiming he was on his mobile giving emergency advice and could he call Frankie back in a few minutes? So Frankie gave him his mobile number and sat in Stonebanks's kitchen waiting for the call. He and Stonebanks probed and twisted what they had so far to see if they could squeeze anything more from it.

Then Frankie remembered what he had to do. 'Geoff, we've got to find some way of keeping that horse at Joe Ansell's above the ground and in decent shape.'

Stonebanks looked puzzled for a minute then said, 'Ahh, you're right.'

'Not exactly the easiest thing to store, is it?'

Stonebanks shook his head. 'You can say that again. He'll need to be frozen or he'll be stinking in a week. What's happening with him where he is?'

'Joe Ansell's put him in a cold room he uses but that was just to allow him to be able to work with the cuts and stuff. I don't think he's got anywhere he can actually freeze the body and keep it.'

Stonebanks looked thoughtful, then said, 'I know a guy, Maurice Sinclair, who has a big meat

305

processing plant. He might have some sizeable units there. I'll give him a call.'

Culling couldn't stop sweating. It was chilly in the conservatory where he paced the tiled floor, wide-eyed, unable to calm himself or control his thoughts. They were on to him. Everything was crumbling, about to collapse, all that he'd worked so hard for this past year. He was so, so close to finalizing everything, to getting to America, to his own promised land and now this. The Jockey Club Security Department. Jesus, what had tipped them off? Why Zuiderzie? Oh, but that was the way they worked, wasn't it? They'd have the evidence for all of them but they'd just pursue one case, the one they were surest of, one was all they needed.

He loosened his tie. Suddenly the image of the fat, sweating bookie, Compton Breslin, came to his mind and he hated to think of himself in the same state as that slug used to get into when he'd made him climb the hill. What about Breslin? Had the security people approached him? Had he given them some sort of tip-off? Or had Monroe finally opened his mouth? There was no reason why he should. Come to think of it, there was no reason in Breslin's case either. He'd had a call from the bookie just the other day to see when the next one was planned for.

Well there'd be no next one now. God, he'd promise there'd never be a next one if only he could get away with this. A conviction would see him turned back at the barrier at any US airport, deported as a criminal. Culling made himself stop and sit down in the wicker chair. He held his head in his hands, gripped his cheeks in clawed fingers that pressed white islands into his sweaty, flushed face. He had to stop panicking and make himself think rationally.

OK, worst-case scenario. They know I've put all the horses down. They know all have won at a big price the same day. They know the dope tests came up negative. The horses can't be tested again. But let's say Breslin *has* opened his fat mouth and said he's paid me money.

But why? Why kill the golden goose and all that? No reason unless Jockey Club Security have nailed him for something else and he's offered me as a sacrificial lamb.

I could leave now, head for the States, sell the house to get the last bit of money I need. But they have an extradition treaty, I'd just be brought back, humiliated... Unless I could manufacture an early death. Something acceptable to the Everlasting Life Company. Something that wouldn't poison my system, jeopardize my chances of being revived...

Culling got up and hurried to his library.

After half an hour waiting for the vet to return his call, Frankie said to Stonebanks, 'How far is Culling's place?'

'A couple of minutes' drive.'

'Will you take me there now?'

'Think that's wise?'

'He sounded awful flustered by my call, promised to call back in a few minutes.' Frankie looked at his watch. 'That was half an hour ago.'

Stonebanks hauled himself out of his chair. 'OK, let's go.'

They drove past the vet's place, and through the gates Frankie could see a green estate car on the gravel in front of the bungalow. 'Is that his car?' he asked.

'Yes.'

'So he's still at home. Park up somewhere, Geoff, would you? And wait for me.'

'No problem.' Stonebanks pulled over.

'Thanks.'

The big man switched off the engine, unclipped his seatbelt and turned to smile at Frankie and give a small salute. 'Good luck!'

'If I'm not back in quarter of an hour come in with all guns blazing.'

'Yes sir!'

As Frankie got out and walked the short stretch of pavement to the gates he smiled and shook his head. He realized Stonebanks's tone of voice and knowing smiles meant that he thought Frankie was going off the deep end and that he was willing to let him make his own mistakes.

He rang the bell beside the brass plaque that said Peter H. Culling MRCVS. He heard Culling's footsteps coming down the hall and saw the rippled outline through the bubbled glass door. He was slightly smaller than Frankie but looked fit; mid-forties, maybe, thinning sandy hair and a quizzical look in his hazel eyes. He had a book in his right hand, hanging by his side, and he wore brown corduroy trousers and an open-necked white shirt. 'Can I help?' he asked.

Frankie smiled and held out his hand. 'Frankie

Houlihan, Jockey Club Security Department. Thought I'd save you a call as you were so busy.' Frankie could almost see the vet's brain whirring as he tried to force a smile and decide what to say. He masked things by raising the hand with the book in it then apologizing and turning back inside to put the book on a table in the hall. When he came back to shake Frankie's hand he looked a little more composed but the wideness in his eyes was still there.

'How do you do?' he asked. 'I'm so sorry I didn't get back to you. Had a problem with one of the private, non-racing clients I handle. Got his horse away in Ireland with him hunting and wanted some advice on the phone so I've had my head buried in some reference books since you called. I do apologize. Please come in.'

Frankie followed him down the hall. 'No problem, I thought something must have cropped up and I didn't want to go ringing you again if you were still on the mobile.'

They went into the conservatory. Frankie said, 'I don't mind waiting, you know. Please finish what you're doing and I'll sit here a while and enjoy the peace and quiet.'

'Not at all. Crisis over. I was just double-checking something. Please sit down. Can I get you a drink?'

'No, thanks. I really don't want to keep you. It's no big deal. I just wanted to try and find out a few things about a horse I believe you treated.' Frankie sat in a deep, wicker-framed, well padded floral chair.

Culling stayed on his feet, pacing slowly. 'Ah

309

yes, you mentioned on the phone, it was Zuiderzie, wasn't it? Poor bugger. I always feel worse for the lad, you know, when we lose a horse. They're closer to them than anyone.'

'Indeed. It's a hard business.' Frankie was learning quickly that with nervy people like Culling it often paid to ask no questions and let them babble on trying to fill the silence. He sat smiling at the vet.

Culling kept pacing. He said, 'I remember Martin's box-driver calling me. The horse was in a really bad state when I got there, shaking and shivering. Shocking sight. I got him here as soon as I could and opened him up. Thought it was a twisted gut. If you catch them quick enough, sometimes you can save them but I'm afraid it wasn't to be. Died on the table, poor bugger.'

Frankie nodded, looked like he shared the vet's care and concern. 'He'd won that day at Stratford, as I remember.'

Culling looked straight ahead now and quickened his pacing. When he spoke, Frankie noticed the pitch of his voice had increased slightly. 'Yes, that's right, he did. Even more unfortunate.'

'What do you mean?'

'I mean for the connections. Just back to winning form, you know, then that had to happen. Most unlucky.'

'Would you have taken a blood sample before operating?'

'No. No time for that, I'm afraid.'

Frankie said nothing. The silence was broken only by Culling's footsteps on the stone floor.

Frankie said, 'So what happened next?'

'What do you mean?' He stopped now and looked at Frankie.

Frankie shrugged slightly. 'Did you call the knacker's man in?'

'Yes, of course. Of course.'

'And who do you use?'

'Forgive me, but may I ask what exactly it is that you're trying to establish?'

'I'm afraid I can't go into too much detail just now. It's to do with something completely separate that the department is working on. We thought there may just be a link somewhere.' Frankie sat forward, elbows on knees and lowered his voice slightly. 'To be perfectly honest, it's not a racing problem as such, it's to do with the illegal exporting of horsemeat to Europe. Our friends in Whitehall have asked us if we could help out. As if we didn't have enough to do!'

Culling seemed to relax slightly and returned Frankie's smile. Frankie said, 'So who's your knacker's man?'

Culling suddenly looked troubled again. He backed slowly towards the chair opposite Frankie's and sat down. It was his turn now to lean forward, elbows on knees, expression pained as he shook his head. 'Look, this is really embarrassing for me. I'm, eh, I'm in a bit of a spot.'

Frankie nodded encouragingly, still smiling. 'If I can help you out I will.'

'Well, you see, I don't call the knacker's man direct, I use one of his employees who'll turn out any time, day or night and, well, to be honest, he pays me a bit better than his boss does.'

'So he's moonlighting?'

'I suppose he is. Ask no questions, hear no lies.' He opened his hands in explanation or apology, Frankie wasn't sure which.

'So can you give me a name?'

The vet massaged his freckled cheeks with his hands. Frankie said, 'I'll make sure your name's kept out of it if anything comes of this.'

Culling, head still bowed, raised his eyes towards Frankie. 'Can you guarantee that?'

'Yes, I can.'

'His name's Gerry Monroe.'

50

It was almost midnight when Frankie left Canary Wharf and the office of the *Racing Post* newspaper. He drove north much faster than he'd normally have done, unable to keep the adrenaline coursing through his body away from his accelerator foot. He'd had a good day. A bloody good day, even if he said so himself. He'd learned a lot about his job and about people and how to handle them and it excited him. He felt more powerful than he'd ever done as a priest. Much more.

Back then people had believed he could grant them eternity in heaven through absolving sins. That suddenly seemed like nothing compared to what he, as a person, felt he could now do. He'd been dead right about Culling; spot on. He knew the man was involved in something. OK, the vet wouldn't have made the best poker player in the world but Frankie had got him on the hook and played him like an expert. Back in the car with Stonebanks a triumphant Frankie had drummed on the dashboard and said with considerable delight to the big man, 'Know when I knew I had him? When he didn't ask why *I* had asked about taking a blood test before the operation! Why on earth would I have asked that? Why didn't he question it?'

And Stonebanks had agreed and congratulated him and asked where they went next. Well here was where they went next, corroboration. He'd called Maggie Cassidy and she'd promised to wait up although Graham was still bed bound and suffering from depression.

It was two-thirty in the morning and pitch-black on the final run to the Cassidy place. Through the trees and gaps in the hedges he saw, as he drove, the light coming from the kitchen windows and the sight warmed him. Turning into the drive he thought he caught Maggie in his headlights as she stood at the window, arms folded, watching, waiting. Excited as he was at the news he had to give her, he decided it was best, at this stage, not to mention that he thought the horses might still be alive. Monroe was almost certainly the kidnapper, he had picked up Zuiderzie; Zuiderzie looked very like Ulysses, but it wasn't certain yet that his theory was correct. And if Zuiderzie was a fake Ulysses then which horse had Monroe used to stand in for the corpse of Angel Gabriel?

He cut the engine in the hundred yards or so

before the door and coasted up, the steering wheel suddenly heavy in his hands as the power steering was lost. He didn't want to wake Graham or young Billy. As he got out of the car, Maggie was already in the open doorway of the house. She smiled as he closed the car door softly and put his finger to his lips as he mock-tiptoed across the drive to the house. She laughed quietly. 'You look like a drunk trying to creep in and not wake his wife.'

'I feel drunk, with power!' he said and Maggie was surprised when he hugged her warmly. They went inside. Embers in the grate still gave off a good heat and Maggie took his leather jacket and hung it up as he sat by the fire.

'Whisky?' she asked.

Checking his watch, he said, 'Don't know whether to say too late or too early.'

'Must be neither, then, which makes it just the right time.' She poured him a large whisky with ice in a heavy cut-crystal glass. She already had a drink sitting on the hearth and she settled on the rug as Frankie had seen her do so many times before. She raised her glass. He moved out of the seat towards her and they touched glasses gently. 'Here's to getting your money back.'

She smiled. 'Come on, then, don't keep me in suspense!'

He drank some whisky then went to where his jacket hung and took an envelope from the inside pocket. He took out two pictures and showed her one. She made a face which said, 'Maybe, maybe not.' He handed her the other print, which was of a man in a mask with just his vivid blue eyes

314

showing. 'That's him,' she said immediately.

'That's what I told Stonebanks. That's corroboration. That's Gerry Monroe. And this is now a legitimate job for our friends in the police! I'll call them first thing in the morning.'

She looked straight at him, smiling admiringly. 'You're brilliant Frankie, well done!'

'All in a day's work!'

'Oh, I can't wait to tell Graham.' She hurried along the hall towards the bedroom but was back within a minute.

Frankie said, 'That was quick.'

'He's sound. I'll leave it. I'm dying to wake him but the medication makes him so groggy. It'll be such brilliant news to give him in the morning, at the start of a brand-new day!'

'Should make a different man of him!' Frankie said and gulped down the last of his drink. 'Although we still need to catch Monroe.'

'Surely that shouldn't be too difficult, even for the police. They know who he is now, for God's sake. It should just be a matter of picking him up.'

'I hope so. Depends where he is.

She moved to pick up his glass. 'One more?'

'Sure! Sure, if you're having one?'

'Why not? We're celebrating aren't we?'

'We are, we are.'

An hour later Frankie was on his fourth large whisky. Maggie had already had two drinks before he arrived. She was on her sixth. Frankie too was on the rug now, sitting, legs outstretched, warming in front of the fresh logs which crackled quietly. They'd talked about all that had happened since they'd first spoken on the phone, agreed that they now felt they'd known each other for years. They discussed plans for getting Gabby back and maybe the money although Maggie said that if this whole thing had taught her anything it was the value of love and family and normality, lack of upset, the beauty of a quiet life.

They'd been silent for a while, sitting companionably, stockinged feet almost touching, staring into the fire, listening to the tick of the clock and the occasional hollow howl of the wind in the chimney. Maggie said, 'Tell me about your troubles.'

Slowly he turned his head away from the fire, smiling as he looked at her.

'You've helped so much with ours, with mine. I know you have some of your own.'

'Ahh, perceptive, you women!' He lowered his eyes but raised his eyebrows.

'Tell me, Frankie.'

He stared at the floor then into the fire again and he seemed to gaze way beyond it, into the distance. The yellow embers reflected in his eyes and Maggie couldn't be sure if tears were there. He said, 'I'll tell you about a girl called Kathy who was all the stuff in all the love poems and all the romantic books and movies and every pop-song lyric and, and ... sentiment that was ever written all rolled into one ... to me, she was. She was as much a part of me as the leg you see before you on the floor. When we were apart, her face was never out of my mind for a second. Not just her face but, her person, her being. 'Twas with me in me mind as solid as though she herself was me mind. She wasn't just a part of me, Kathy, she was a part that made me so much better than I was, so much more than I was, for she added all the things that I didn't have. She was beautiful and intelligent and brave, very brave ... and honest and fair. She loved adventure and she loved coming home and she loved the weather and being outdoors, in the woods, in the rain, on horseback, on foot, with me, holding hands, feeding her life into me as surely as if she were giving me a transfusion. And I know that there are many who'll say this but I know without even having to think about it or analyse it or anything deep, any stuff like that, that there never was a couple anywhere that loved each other more than we did. There was no possibility that there could be. You'd be as well saying there were degrees of the speed of light as saying any couple loved like we did...' He drank.

'...anyway, couple's a poor expression for us, for the way we were. We were one, one person. Neither of us realized until we met that we'd each been only half a person. Then we clamped together ... couldn't even see the join.' He smiled sadly.

Maggie watched him. 'How did she die?'

'She was thrown from her horse at Stratford after she won a race... She never regained consciousness.'

Shocked, Maggie put her drink down and got on to her knees, resting her bottom on her heels. 'My God, was that your wife? Frankie, that was only a few weeks ago!'

'October twelfth. Eleven weeks and six days ago.'

Tears came to her eyes as she watched him. The ironic smile, supported by alcohol, that had shown on his face from time to time had slipped slowly like a tired mask to leave him staring blankly into the fire, eyes cold and forlorn now. Maggie moved slowly towards him. She took his hand in both of hers. 'Frankie, I am so, so sorry. Here we are worrying about a horse and you've lost your wife. She was the one you left the priesthood for?'

He nodded but didn't look at her, eyes still blank. She said, 'If I could take her place and send her back to you, I would.'

He turned slowly towards her now and looked into her eyes. 'Would you?'

'I would. Without a second thought.'

His eyes slowly filled and the tears spilled over. She leant forward and put her left hand behind his neck, pulling his head down to cradle it on her bosom.

51

Hewitt left the big house once a week and travelled to Swindon to buy groceries. He had never gone into Lambourn since he'd arrived in the area, agreeing with Kelly Corell that it was best to keep away from the village, to protect his

318

anonymity. He avoided Newbury for the same reason. Swindon was much less focused on racing and he could shop there without too much fear of someone saying, 'Hey, aren't you the guy that moved into Kennedy's old place?'

Wheeling his supermarket trolley past the news-stand, Hewitt stopped dead. The face of Gerry Monroe stared at him from the front page of the *Racing Post*. The headline was, EX-JOCKEY WANTED FOR KIDNAPPING: £50,000 REWARD. Hewitt bought a copy and pushed it into one of the shopping bags. He was nervous about being seen reading it. He now knew Monroe hadn't been kidding and the two horses he'd been looking after for the slaughter-man were probably exactly the ones he'd said they were when he'd called the other day, Ulysses and Angel Gabriel.

Hewitt found himself by his car without realizing he'd walked there. He got in and opened the newspaper. The owners of Angel Gabriel were offering the reward for the capture of the kidnapper and the return of the stolen ransom money.

Hewitt's mind spun. He was in deep now. He was harbouring two kidnapped horses, two very popular horses. And he was holding ten thousand pounds in cash for Monroe in payment, waiting for the slaughterman to come and collect it. The only people likely to be coming now were the police. His hands shook as he loaded the shopping bags.

Back in the house, he called Corell and told him.

'And you still have the ten grand Pusey brought you?'

'It's still here. It's in a cupboard in the lab. I don't want to be found with it, Mr Corell. And the horses, what will I do about them?'

'Don't be worryin', now, everythin'll be fine. Wasn't that exactly what we wanted, a couple of good horses to help you on a bit?'

'Mr Corell, I thought everything was going to be above board when I took this on. I was never willing to take any risks.'

'Shhh now, will ye? There's no risk here. I'll sort any problems out. That's my side of the deal. Haven't I always got you just what you wanted when you wanted it?'

'Well, you have and I'm grateful but I just feel this is getting out of control and I hate being involved in something that's out of control, I really do, Mr Corell. I can't stress that enough to you!'

'David, listen to me ... you're not involved in anything, d'ye hear me? You're a good straight fella doin' a good straight job. Now if you have no more need for those horses, tell Monroe to get them to hell out of the place.'

'I don't know when he's coming back! I can't tell him anything!' Corell thought the scientist close to breaking-point. He said quietly, 'Would you give me Mr Monroe's number and I'll contact him and ask him to get the horses out of there?'

'Hold on. Hold on a minute. I'll get it.'

While he was waiting for Hewitt to come back, Corell's desktop phone rang. He told the caller to hold. He took Monroe's number and promised Hewitt he'd call back soon. Pat Pusey was on the other phone sounding pleased with himself. He told Corell, 'Yer man's in jail in Limerick.'

'Who?'

'Brendan Gleeson.'

'Sure, that's sharp work by the guards in catching him for stealing my ten grand, and me not even reported it yet.'

Pusey laughed dutifully then said, 'I wish it was for that, boss, but it was drunk and disorderly. Want me to go and get him?'

'Get it done in twenty-four hours. I've another job for you after that.'

52

Frankie and Stonebanks had spent forty-eight hours in Lambourn trying to trace Monroe. The man had had few friends but Frankie had spoken to his former girlfriend who claimed she hadn't seen him for over a year. Stonebanks had spoken to his employer, the owner of the abattoir, who'd said it didn't surprise him to find that Monroe was a criminal, that he'd always seemed a bit shifty, a bit of a loner who'd been resentful of most things, especially his fellow-workers. He also asked Stonebanks to add his missing horse-box to the list of lost property. Stonebanks took the registration.

The January night was cold and Frankie and

Stonebanks stood by the gas fire in Stonebanks's house drinking tea and eating lemon sponge cake. Stonebanks's police contact called. Frankie watched him smile for the first time in days as he made positive noises and jotted down notes. He hung up and turned to Frankie, still smiling. 'The horsebox left Holyhead on the Stena Line ferry for Dun Laoghaire on January fourth. It hasn't come back.'

Frankie smiled now. 'He's in Ireland with them.'

'That's a fair conclusion, I think, Mr Houlihan.'

Sean and Jane hadn't missed a single evening doing the final rounds at Uncle Fergus's place. They'd help feed the horses and check them over then bid them good night with a final pat on the shoulder or stroke of the nose. Afterwards they'd usually go back inside and tell Poppy how all the horses were and watch TV with her for a while or sit talking, sometimes long into the night. But Jane had sensed something different today with Sean and it didn't really surprise her when he asked her to come into the barn after evening stables.

She followed him as he climbed high on the hay up to the chair they'd made, just room enough between the sweet-smelling bales for them to sit comfortably side by side. This was the first time they'd been here after dark and although there was sufficient light from the dusty neon strips in the centre of the barn, it was colder than ever and Jane shivered and moved closer to Sean as they settled down. He wouldn't look at her.

'What's wrong?' she asked.

Sean stared at his feet. 'I don't know how to tell you...'

Jane swallowed a lump but tried to make a joke. 'You're not pregnant, are you?'

He barely smiled. She knew it must be bad. 'You're leaving,' she said quietly.

He nodded.

Now she stared at her feet, crossed her ankles and swung them slightly, linked her hands in her lap for a few seconds then crossed her arms and put her chin on her chest. The silence lasted a minute or more then Sean said, 'I'll come back.'

'You'll never come back if you leave. It'll never be the same.' There was anger in her voice. 'Stay!' It was a command.

He shook his head slowly. 'It's just for a few days. I'll be back.'

She jumped off the hay bale and stood, arms crossed defiantly. 'Right, I'm coming with you!'

'Yer kidding!'

'I'm not.'

'Uncle Fergus won't let you. Shit, it's worse than Chicago where I live! They have girls like you for breakfast. No – nobody eats breakfast where I come from. They'd have you for a late snack.'

'Oh, is that so, Sean Gleeson? Is that so? We'll see!'

Rather than meet, as usual, at Stonebanks's house, Frankie had asked that Stonebanks meet him in the George pub in Lambourn, the one most popular with the racing fraternity. Stonebanks had taken a bit of persuading that it would be a good idea for them to be seen to be concentrating on this case in public but Frankie had made all the right decisions so far. Frankie was convinced that the reward would play a big part in someone in Lambourn coming forward with information and he wanted them to have the visual 'prompt' of seeing him and Stonebanks around as much as possible.

They sat drinking beer. It had been two days since they'd last met face to face. Stonebanks had been to Ireland with a CID officer to seek the help of the Irish police in tracing the horsebox. Frankie had been back to visit the vet, Peter Culling, to try and find out how much he knew about the private life of Gerry Monroe.

'How was good old Dublin?' Frankie asked.

'I didn't see that much of it – busy, I'd say. Your old home town, wasn't it?'

''Twas. Many years ago.'

'Do you miss it?'

'Sometimes I do. But it's changed now. Everywhere changes and it's kind of upsettin' when you've got such good memories of some of the places you knew as a kid, if you know what I mean.'

Stonebanks smiled. 'There are still plenty of criminals there according to your Garda man.'

'No doubt. No doubt,' Frankie said, smiling too.

Stonebanks explained that the Garda had been very helpful and promised to do what they could, although they'd warned that Monroe might have disappeared 'into the west' where there were still

324

some very remote places. Frankie said, 'Let's give them a chance for a week or so then maybe we'll go over ourselves and have a look around.'

Stonebanks nodded slightly and half-raised his eyebrows in a way Frankie had come to know as being non-committal. Stonebanks was a tough man to move from his home comforts for too long. He drank some beer and asked Frankie how he'd got on with Culling.

Frankie grinned. 'He's a strange character and I'd bet he knows a lot more than he's telling. I deliberately mentioned, again, the fact that Zuiderzie had won unexpectedly the day he died and yer man seemed to get extra nervous. He was working at Warwick that day which is where Zuiderzie won. I think there might be some connection between him and the horse winning.'

'Like what?'

Although he felt like he was acting in some corny movie, Frankie had a good look around him to see if anyone might be able to hear before saying, 'Take me through the dope-testing procedure again.'

'You think he might have doped the horse? The sample was clean. You know that.'

'Take me through it anyway.'

Stonebanks put down his glass and started talking, using his hands a lot as Frankie had learned he was sometimes inclined to do. 'After every race the stewards will nominate horses to be routinely dope-tested; the winner is almost always one of them. They're taken to a special box where a vet will take a sample of urine, split it into two smaller samples and label each. One is

325

sent to the lab at Newmarket for analysis, the other is offered to the trainer to keep for reference, just in case.'

'In case a test proves positive and he wants to have it double-checked?'

'That's right, but nobody takes that sample. They know that whatever comes back from the lab will be spot-on and as no trainer in his right mind would dope his horse anyway, it's looked on as a pointless exercise.'

'Culling was the senior vet there that day,' Frankie said. 'Would it have been possible for him to insist on taking the urine sample from Zuiderzie himself?'

'Possible but highly improbable. It's the job generally given to the most junior vet, as I'm sure you can imagine. In fact even he, although he shouldn't, sometimes gets the stable manager to do it for him.'

'The stable manager?' Frankie sounded incredulous.

'Come on Frankie, do you know how long you can wait around after a race for a horse to start pissing? Do you think these guys are going to be doing this six, eight, ten times a day?'

'Fair enough,' Frankie said. 'But Culling would have had access to the dope box at any time?'

'That's right.'

'So he would have had access to the samples?'

'Yes.'

'So he could have switched the one for Zuiderzie?'

'Yes, I suppose he could have.'

Frankie sat smiling, trying not to look too

326

triumphant. He picked up his glass and drank, still looking at Stonebanks over the rim.

'Come on, Frankie! Speculation, pure and simple! What motive could he have had?'

'Making money, by any chance?'

'Betting?'

'How else?'

'It would be much, much easier to dope the favourite to lose than an outsider to win.'

'Granted, but if you've got the knowledge and the opportunity and a good chance of getting away with it, how much better is it to dope an outsider to win? You're nobbling the favourite just as effectively and you can bet the winner too at a big price.'

Stonebanks shook his head slowly. Frankie sat forward across the low table, elbows on knees, hands clasped gently, head tilted, almost priestly again. 'Geoff, I was there that day. The horse looked very geed-up in the paddock, which was unlike him, he led from start to finish and was never in danger; his usual style was to be held up. He got back to the yard in a muck-sweat the likes of which the trainer had never seen before. Culling's called out and two hours later the horse is dead on his operating table, then on its way to the dogmeat factory in Monroe's knacker's van. No chance of any further dope tests then, is there? The evidence has been destroyed. And if it has gone for dogmeat still full of dope there's going to be a few surprised dog walkers out there when their little Scottie whizzes past a couple of greyhounds after eating his dinner!'

Stonebanks smiled, shaking his head again.

'You and your blarney make a good-sounding case of it, Frankie, but in the end it really is nothing but speculation. You've had a couple of results and you think you can suss everything now. No offence!' Stonebanks held out his hand, open, at arm's length in a conciliatory gesture. 'I'm not having a go, Frankie, it's just that the confidence you get from being right once or twice can make you think you've got the whole world worked out. Believe me, I've done it.'

Frankie wasn't upset. 'OK, Geoff, fair comment but just keep an open mind yourself.'

Stonebanks held up his glass in a toast, smiling. 'Always do, Frankie boy. Always do!'

53

Frankie had been staying in a guest house in Lambourn for a few days, politely refusing Stonebanks's repeated offers to stay with him and Jean. He found he needed the time on his own, especially in the evenings when Kathy filled his thoughts. As he lay awake on Saturday night he decided he'd go home next day, back to the cottage just to see how things were. He'd also take a trip up to the old churchyard to see Kathy. He hadn't been there for weeks and that added another layer of guilt on top of his already heavy burden.

Not for the first time he lay in the darkness bargaining with himself on how much he'd pay, what he'd give for a peaceful night's sleep, a natural rest, unaided by sleeping pills. Things had been steadily improving. He could now sleep for much of the night but there was never a feeling of being properly rested when he woke, even when he could recall no dreams. He thought back with deep longing to the nights he had spent sleeping with Kathy, waking up rested and nourished and relaxed and peaceful. Oh, what he'd give now for one of those.

And he hadn't felt her around him for a while; more guilt. Was it so wrong to wrap himself up in this work of his? Was it unreasonable of him to try and use this job in exactly the way Bobby Cranfield had urged him to, to help him get over the grief? It was helping, he knew that.

Awake again in the early hours he rose and left payment for his room. He drove to the church-yard, reaching it as the sun rose in a cloudless sky. His boots cracked the thick ice on the puddled path to Kathy's grave and the stone itself was frost-topped in the brightness of the morn-ing. The flowers he'd brought on his last visit lay withered and dead in the vase but in their rime coating they glittered like jewels.

The flower-seller had not been at the gate and Frankie came empty-handed. He promised Kathy two bouquets next time as he spoke aloud to her, his hand on the stone, melting the frost till water trickled in tiny paths down the front and into the lettering. He told her all that had been happening and said it was probably worthwhile repeating it all for he felt she had maybe not been so inclined lately to be watching over him.

He squatted, elbows on his knees, coat tails trailing in the whitened grass. He touched her name on the stone and said, 'I'll always love you, Kath.' He reached for the dead flowers and carried them from the grave.

It was almost noon as he approached the cottage. The sky was still clear and the woods looked stark against the blue. The cold had stiffened the muddy ruts on the track and they tested his suspension to the full. As he pulled up outside his mobile rang; the screen told him it was Bobby Cranfield. 'Bobby, how are you?'

'I'm in great form, Frankie. Good to hear you sounding so well.'

'And you.'

'I just wanted to say how delighted I am personally at the progress you're making in this kidnapping case. You've been a bloody revelation!'

'Team effort, Bobby, team effort.'

'Ah, modesty forbids, as ever!'

They talked for a while about the case, then Bobby invited Frankie to his box at Ascot the following Saturday. 'You must join me in the box, you cried off last time when that horse of·mine got stuffed, remember, Arctic Actor?'

'I do remember. You fancied him strongly that day.'

'Thought he couldn't get beat – but never mind, he runs again on Saturday and we're even more confident. You must come along, Frankie, have a day off, you bloody-well deserve one!'

'Bobby, it's very kind of you to ask. Can you

just let me see how this week pans out? Can I give you a call maybe Wednesday?'

'Sure, of course you can. You know where I am.'

'Good... Good.' Something was niggling at Frankie's mind, causing him to lose concentration.

'Fine, then,' Cranfield said, 'I'll let you get on.'

'Yes ... Bobby ... what was the name of the horse that won the race yours got beat in, can you remember?'

He laughed. 'It's burned in my brain, old boy! Cost me a fortune that day. He was called Colonialize.'

'That's right, I remember now. Do you still think he was doped to win that race?'

'Why do you ask?'

'Something I'm working on. Could turn out to be nothing, but you just reminded me of that day you called me.'

Cranfield hesitated. 'I know it might have seemed a bit over the top at the time, Frankie, a bit sour grapes maybe, but I did do a lot of thinking before making that call. I know the dope test turned out negative and that sort of finished it in my mind, but if you're asking if it was a calm assessment at the time then the answer is yes.'

'OK. Thanks.'

'Can you say any more at the moment?'

'Not really. I'll call you when I can.'

'Well tell me about it when I see you on Saturday.'

'I'll do my best to make it, Bobby, thanks.'

'See you then.'

'Bye.'

Frankie sat staring through the windscreen. Colonialize had won that race in exactly the same manner Zuiderzie had won his, bolting off from the start, leading all the way and coming home unchallenged at a big price to upset a hot favourite. Frankie remembered walking though the ring that day and marvelling at the fat bookie Compton Breslin laying over the odds on Arctic Actor, taking fistfuls of money without flinching or shortening the price. Excitement grew in Frankie as he called Stonebanks's number.

'Geoff, get hold of one of your books and tell me who trains Colonialize.'

'What the hell are you up to now, Frankie?'

'Just tell me, Geoff!'

'I don't need a book, Tony Moffat trains him not three hundred yards away from where I'm standing.'

'Have you got Tony's number?'

'Hold on.'

Stonebanks came back with the number.

'Thanks. Call you back in a minute.'

Moffat's wife answered and it took a couple of minutes before the trainer came to the phone. Frankie introduced himself. Moffat said he'd heard about him. Frankie said, 'Sorry to be making a business call on Sunday but I wanted to ask you about that horse that won at Ascot for you, Colonialize. Have you anything else planned for him soon?'

'I'm afraid not, Mr Houlihan. The horse died on the operating table the night he won at Ascot.'

The elation made it difficult for Frankie to find a tone of commiseration. 'Oh, I'm really sorry, what happened?'

'Horse arrived home shaking like he was sitting on a pneumatic drill and sweating so bad there was a pool of water under him. I called the vet out right away and he did his best. Some form of aggravated colic apparently.'

'That's a real shame, I'm sorry. Who did the operation to try and save him?'

'Peter Culling.'

'Oh yes, I know him. Well I'm sorry, real bad luck.'

'Was it something in particular about the horse, Mr Houlihan?'

'No, not really. One of the bigwigs has some harebrained notion about establishing patterns for horses who win at grade one courses, load of nonsense. You know what they're like.'

'I do, er, yes, I know what you mean.'

'Anyway, I hope you have better luck for the rest of the season.'

'Me too. Thanks.'

When Frankie rang him back, Stonebanks wasn't that impressed. 'Frankie, who else would the guy call but his vet? The fact that it happens to be Culling could be purely coincidental.'

'How coincidental, Geoff, come on! The guy's a one-man practice, he works for the Jockey Club on course a hell of a lot. How many trainers can he realistically have on his books? A handful at most and now two of those, that we know of, maybe even more, have lost horses where he's been officiating at the course and also carried out the operations. Isn't there some rule that they must register dead horses?'

'They only need to let Weatherbys know for administration purposes so the horses can be scratched from future engagements.'

'Where can I get a list of those scratchings?'

'Call Charlie Cooke at Weatherbys tomorrow, he'll sort you out with those.'

'Only one problem; as I recall, Colonialize was too thin to be passed off as Angel Gabriel. Still, it doesn't blow any holes in my theory. Monroe would have had lots of horses through his hands, not just the ones he got from Culling.'

'True, but you're going to need some sort of solid evidence apart from the resemblance between Zuiderzie and Ulysses.'

'I know, I know, I'm working on it. Once I get this list of scratchings and make a few more calls, I'll go and see Culling again. Hey, you know the dope test sample from Zuiderzie, would that carry any sort of chemical ID for the horse himself?'

'Like a blood sample does? I don't know. It must have some sort of DNA imprint, I suppose. Even if it did, you'd need something to compare it with either from Ulysses or Zuiderzie and neither's around.'

'I was thinking that we might ask the forensic boys at Newmarket to go back to where we found the horse's body. Remember we had to drag him up the bank of that stream? There's bound to be pieces of loose flesh still around that these guys could find to analyse.'

'Could be. Could be, Frankie. It's been a few weeks but with the type of equipment they have, they may well be able to get something.'

'Will you ask them?'

'Sure, but you're still going to need something else if the urine sample's no good. That sample might not even be around any more.'

'Geoff, will you stop saying *you* all the time? It's us, remember. We're in as a team here. I'm not trying to win any prizes on my own.'

The pause was at Stonebanks's end this time. 'You're right. Or should that be we're right? I'll get on with my end of things, O Master.'

Frankie chuckled. 'Do that. I'll speak to you soon.'

54

Uncle Fergus dropped Jane and Sean off on Grafton Street in Dublin at ten in the morning promising to return and pick them up at five that afternoon. Jane had persuaded him to let them have the day out together so Sean could show her the city's sights. She'd argued Sean into agreeing to go back with her after they'd spent the day trying to find news of his father. It was cold and clear and as they made their way through the streets Jane wished that it was sight-seeing they had come for. She wanted to spend time with Sean away from the farm. Being in the big city together made her feel they were a proper couple in a proper relationship.

She knew Sean hadn't been himself since last night. He was edgy and had gone quiet. Normally she couldn't shut him up. As they crossed the Liffey on O'Connell Bridge she said, 'How far is it, Sean?'

'Not far.'

'How far's not far?'

'Fifteen minutes maybe.'

She took his hand and stretched her legs a bit to match his pace. She noticed a wariness in Sean that hadn't been there since the night they'd met. He was constantly looking around, scanning the faces of the people, especially those coming towards them. 'What's wrong?' she asked.

'I'm lookin' out for Pat Pusey and I don't want to see him.'

'The man at Dun Laoghaire?'

'The same.' Suddenly he turned left into Abbey Street Lower. 'Come on!' He pulled her along.

'What's up? Did you see him?'

'No. But there's more chance of it if we go all the way up O'Connell Street. We'll go the back way.' They turned left into Gardner Street which was busy but didn't seem, to Jane, as prosperous as O'Connell Street. She was nervous. After the tales of home Sean had told her, she expected the streets to be derelict with hollow-eyed men peering at them from doorways. She decided he must have exaggerated everything. They were so close to the centre of the city.

Sean hurried her across the road into Railway Street. The further along that street they went, the fewer people they saw. Graffiti marked the walls and pavement. Halfway along, Sean nodded towards a block of flats on the left, St Mary's Mansions. 'That's where Corell left his

336

girlfriend after he cut her up.' Jane gripped his hand more tightly.

The flats on their right looked grim. Some houses were boarded up. Scruffy, snotty-nosed, coatless children played in the cold gutters. The day itself seemed to Jane to lose its sharpness, its brightness. She thought of home and how lucky she was. She was missing her family, even Billy. She'd rung home most days, lifting the phone each time with hope, desperate for good news about Angel Gabriel. There had been none.

She knew that Sean, too, travelled in hope. She wished she hadn't said those nasty things about his father. Nobody could help what their parents were, and for all he'd been bad to Sean and his mother, Jane could understand how Sean still felt something for him and worried about him. She looked across at him and saw how tense he looked. He let go her hand, apparently to button his jacket, but Jane noted that he conveniently forgot to take it again.

At the junction of Railway Street and Buckingham Street they stopped. Sean pointed at the flats across the road in Killarney Street. 'Joseph's Mansions,' he said. She stared. It looked to her like some sort of prison building; metal sheets covered all the windows, graffiti was everywhere. The railings surrounding the block were rusted and dirty, and the strip of grass behind them was overgrown. In the bare branches of a tree was the twisted frame of an old bicycle.

Sean looked quickly around him then said, 'Come on!' He ran across the road. Jane followed. They hurried towards the arched entrance and went in. But Sean put a hand out to stop her before they left the cover of the arch and entered the quadrangle. He peeked out to the left; he didn't know who might be at the flat. It would be dead unlucky to find Pat Pusey or another one of Corell's men there at this time of day, but it was best not to just run right in.

The place was silent. He stepped cautiously into the quadrangle. Jane followed. She stood and looked around, feeling she was in a deserted prison yard or one of those terrible concentration camps when the war had ended. Almost every door and window was blocked with thick metal sheeting. A huge puddle of dirty brown water held the wreck of a child's tricycle, a burst football and a flotilla of papers and polystyrene packaging. The only sign of human life was a string of washing running diagonally between the corners of the flats across to her left. To her right, a few pigeons paced the dirty tarmac. Four huge rusty bins like vats stood in a row below the overhanging first-floor balcony. Signs fixed to the walls by Dublin Corporation disclaimed all responsibility for injury to any person venturing further.

Sean said, 'I think we're OK. Come on.' They moved towards a doorway in the centre of the row to their left and started up the stairs, the urine stench as offensive as Sean remembered it. Jane said, 'Uggh, that's horrible.' Turning the corner to go to his door, Sean met Kevin, the only other boy still living there.

'Shoggy! Where've you been?' Kevin said.

'On my holidays in Switzerland.'

'Have ye just come back 'cos yer da's dead or are ye stayin'?'

What was left of Sean's father lay on a slab in the morgue. His body, stretched out, took up just a few inches of vertical space. The bones and vital organs had been almost pulped. After throwing him screaming off the roof of a twenty-storey block of flats, Corell's men had gone back down for the body and had done the same thing twice more. The mashed corpse had lain there in full view for hours – the people knew better than to report anything. The man who stole from Kelly Corell had to be left on display till the police happened by.

55

Frankie and Stonebanks stood together in Stonebanks's study at home. They watched in silence as the fax machine slowly rolled out the list from Weatherbys of all horses which had been scratched from races in the past six months because they were dead. The machine beeped and stopped; Frankie carefully tore the sheet of paper and brought it to the table. He sat down and scanned it. There were fifty-seven horses on it. Frankie could have had the list an hour previously but he'd asked Charlie at Weatherbys to place a tick beside each horse that had died after a victory last time out. Apart from the two they knew of there were four more. The name of one of them stopped Frankie's breathing. He froze completely, the paper in front of him at arm's length. Stonebanks watched him then reached for the list, taking it from Frankie's fingers. He looked at the six ticked horses, then, puzzled, at Frankie. 'What's wrong, Frankie?'

Frankie stared at him. Stonebanks said, 'Jesus, you look like somebody just hit you with a hammer. What's up?'

'He killed Kathy,' Frankie said. 'Sauceboat. That was the horse she rode.' Shock had anaesthetized him. He spoke in a monotone. Stonebanks looked again at the list. He reached for his form book, skipping quickly through the pages to check the other horses that had been ticked. All had won at a big price after leading all the way, exactly the same as Zuiderzie and Colonialize had done, and like those two were trained in Lambourn. Stonebanks looked across at Frankie. 'I know the trainers and I know the vet...'

Frankie waited.

Stonebanks said, 'Culling.'

Frankie linked his fingers, elbows askew on the table, and looked down. At least there was some reason to it now. His mother had been wrong, there'd been no punishment from God for what he'd done, no deliberate punishment at least, no grabbing back of a life in return for his desertion. Somebody had killed her. A man. Not God. Not his mother. Not Frankie. An evil, greedy man had killed his wife.

Frankie stood up. 'Let's go and see Culling now.' He spoke evenly although some emotion was back in his voice.

Stonebanks watched him. 'Not a good time, Frankie. We need to look at all the angles.'

Frankie pulled his jacket on. 'Won't take us that long to get there.'

'Frankie, sit down and think for a minute. Supposing Culling did operate on these two, supposing it was on the same day they won, supposing Monroe picked up both corpses, it doesn't incriminate Culling. He could claim it was all simply coincidence.'

'Geoff, come on! This fella killed my wife and you're telling me to sit down and think! Get real! What is there to think about?' Frankie leant forward holding out his open hand as though trying to make Stonebanks understand how simple it was.

'Frankie, whoah, slow down! You've just had a shock that would stop a bloody train and you want to go haring off after this guy. What kind of a state is your mind in? Try and take a step back for a minute and look at the situation, will you. I'm sorry for you, I really am, but I can't just let you go after Culling right now. You've got a pretty personal interest now for a start, don't you think? Uh?'

Frankie stared at him silently.

Stonebanks continued, 'Do you seriously think you're fit to do your job objectively right now? Because that's what you need to do. We've probably got enough to call the police in. Why don't we do that?'

'A minute ago you were saying it could all be a coincidence, Geoff – make up your mind.'

Stonebanks looked flustered at that. 'If it is, let the police dig deeper.

'If it is, or appears to be, the police won't bother digging deeper or they'll botch it the way they did with the kidnap! I'm not saying *I*, Geoff, not I, I, I! Don't you think I know inside myself how I'm reacting to this? I know when I'm calm and I know when I'm able to do my job. I'm saying *us*, let's you and me go to Culling's place. The betting is that these horses were doped to win, the dope sample switched by Culling on course, then the horses killed by him so they couldn't be tested again if anyone became suspicious in the few days after each race. For goodness sake, I told you that Bobby Cranfield called me the day after Colonialize beat his horse at Ascot, the *day after*, before all these suspicions blew up! He said then he thought the winner had been doped!'

Stonebanks looked up at him. 'Frankie, I'm not saying you're wrong. Not in the least. I'm saying we can't prove it. It's a sound theory but we simply can't back it up.'

'Maybe Culling will confess!'

'Why should he? Why on earth should he? He's been a respected Jockey Club vet for years. His character is totally unblemished. There'll be bloody ructions if we go steaming in like the Sweeney trying to get a confession out of him. Can you imagine what they'd be saying about us? About the Jockey Club Security Department? About you, on your first assignment?'

The passion and impatience slowly drained from Frankie's face as he realized the logic of what Stonebanks was saying. He sat down again, slowly shaking his head. Looking at Stonebanks he said quietly, 'He could be involved in the kidnappings too, you know. There's no telling how close his relationship with Monroe is.'

'Can't have been that close or he wouldn't have named him so quickly to you, would he?'

Frankie shrugged. 'Maybe.'

Stonebanks sighed. 'You could easily be right about Culling, Frankie, but there's nothing to really suggest he's tied in with the kidnappings. At best we've got two different cases here and we need to make up our minds which one we're going to try and crack first.'

Frankie nodded.

'Now is it going to be Monroe or Culling? If we go for Culling with absolutely no solid evidence, we could lose him completely. He could up stakes and disappear. If we can get Monroe and tell him Culling dropped him in it originally, there's every chance Monroe will tell you all you want to know about Culling. At least than you have some evidence.'

Frankie knew he was right. He couldn't risk confronting Culling and losing him, couldn't have lived with that afterwards. 'You're right Geoff, I'm sorry.'

'Nothing to be sorry about, Frankie, nothing whatsoever. If it's Culling, we'll get him. I promise you.' He leant across the table and clasped Frankie's arm. Frankie smiled wearily.

Stonebanks said, 'Right, let's get to work. Let's

try and nail this horse-switching theory of yours. I'll call the lab about the urine sample and speak to the forensic boys about a visit to the stream where we found the corpse.'

Frankie watched him, all businesslike and confident, pick up the phone.

56

Maggie had expected the news about Monroe to pick Graham up, get him back close to his old self. It had had little effect and she was becoming seriously worried about his health. She sat in his bedroom waiting for the doctor to arrive.

It had been a morning of tears. Frankie's outpourings to her about Kathy had affected her deeply. And Jane had called with the dreadful news that Sean's father had been killed in an accident; that she was going to the funeral next day, and that Sean might come home with her for a while to help him get over it. She had agreed, very reluctantly. There'd be enough for her to handle when Jane found out about Gabby. Maggie would have to tell Billy too and she'd need to try and stop all the upset affecting Graham any further, need to cope with the whole thing on her own – and nurse him. God, she wondered, was there to be no end? Sitting in her favourite chair staring out of the big picture window as the rain moved across the fields, Maggie buried her head in her hands.

'Are you OK, Mum?'

She massaged her eyes, her face, pushing a tired smile on to it before turning to see her son, Billy. He'd become almost a recluse in his own room since all this trouble had blown up and now she cursed herself for neglecting him too. Billy stood, hands by his side, almost as though he was at school in front of the teacher. He looked concerned. 'I'm fine,' Maggie said. 'Just a bit tired. What about you, what have you been up to?'

Billy shrugged and pushed his hands into his pockets. 'Nothing much.'

'Why don't you go out on your bike, get a bit of fresh air?'

'Nah, don't feel like it.' He looked at her, face still serious, concern in his eyes. She smiled back. He said, 'Is Dad going to be all right?'

Maggie got up and went to him, ruffled his hair. 'Your dad will be fine. The doctor's on his way to see him, just to check him over and probably give him some more pills.'

'Is he really sick, Mum, or just depressed?'

Maggie considered telling him how much of an illness depression could be but thought better of it. 'Just a bit depressed and very, very tired. He'll be over it in a few days. Don't worry. OK?'

Billy nodded slowly. Maggie ruffled his hair again and went to switch the kettle on. She said. 'Your sister rang this morning.'

'Is she all right?'

'She's fine, but a bit weepy. Her boyfriend's dad died suddenly.' Billy's shoulders seemed to rise slightly as he tensed. 'I miss her, Mum.'

Maggie turned towards him. 'Ooohh, I wish I had a tape recording of that! Wait till she hears.' She was smiling as she teased him but he stood stiffly and she saw his eyes fill up. She went over and as she reached him he threw his arms around her waist. 'My dad won't die suddenly, Mum, will he?'

She clutched him to her. 'No, no, of course he won't! Get that right out of your head! He'll be absolutely fine!' She eased him away from her and squatted down till they were face to face. She reached to wipe his tears with her little finger.

'I just want us all to be together again, Mum. It doesn't really matter that much about Gabby.'

'Shhh, shhh! I know you do. We all do. Everything will be fine, I promise you.' She pulled his head gently on to her shoulder and he clung to her again. 'There, there,' she said, caressing the back of his neck. 'Everything will work out, Billy. Honest.'

At the cemetery, Jane walked with Sean ahead of his mother and Aunt Phoebe who had lent her sister the money to pay for this funeral. There was no one else except the priest. The undertaker's men, helped by the gravediggers, carried the coffin with little effort. Only Aunt Phoebe had seen what was left of Brendan Gleeson; she had formally identified the body to save Sean further distress. The Garda had found no evidence of crime. They had heard, as everyone else in the streets had, what had happened but they knew from experience that there was no chance of convicting Corell or anyone else. The officer in charge had put it down as a suicide. Sean had been too shocked by the death and too afraid of the police to argue that it was murder. Jane had complained strongly on his behalf, marching into the police station and demanding to see the superintendent, but it had done no good. A cold-eyed man in plain clothes saw her and told her they had plenty to do without chasing their tails for years on this and anyway, nobody would be rushing to commemorate the life of Mr Brendan Gleeson.

Except for Brendan's son, he was right. Nobody but Sean mourned the death. As Bridget Gleeson watched the coffin being lowered to the solemn prayers of the priest, she felt only relief that she was finally free, that she didn't need to leave Ireland again if she didn't want to, that she could have her son back. The trouble was that Bridget wasn't sure now that she wanted him back. She'd had three relationships while she'd been away. All but the first man had treated her well. She was enjoying the freedom, having a good time. Watching Jane put her arm around Sean at the graveside she thought that in little Miss Pretty Face, he had quite enough. And he'd lived without his mother all this time. He had already mentioned going back to England with Jane for a while. Well, that would suit Bridget Gleeson just fine.

The priest finished as the rain started, heavy drops falling in dark spots on the mound of earth by the grave. Aunt Phoebe stepped forward and picked up a handful of the earth and threw it in on top of the coffin. Bridget did the same then bent and picked up some more. She turned and offered it to Sean. He looked up at her and shook his head. 'I'll not help bury me da,' he said with determination as the tears squeezed through again, stinging his eyes and the flesh just below, which was raw from rubbing. Jane squeezed his hand tighter then put her other arm around his shoulder and led him away towards the car as the dark clouds finally burst and the freezing rain cascaded down.

57

Two researchers from the horseracing forensic laboratory in Newmarket found shreds of skin and hair at the site where the horse said to be Ulysses had been dumped. But no comparable samples were available from any lab or from his ex-trainer, who had, as part of his training regime, had his horses blood-tested regularly but retained none of the samples. The same applied to Zuiderzie, whose urine sample had also been disposed of by the lab after proving negative for dope.

Frankie needed a break. For all Stonebanks had said that potential doping of these horses and the kidnappings were two separate cases, proof that Ulysses' carcass had actually been that of Zuiderzie would at least have told him that Ulysses and Angel Gabriel were probably still alive or, at least, had not been killed by Monroe at the time he claimed. As far as Ulysses was concerned, although he hoped for the horse's sake that it hadn't been slaughtered, making his arrogant, spiteful owner feel better didn't matter to him. But it would mean an awful lot to Frankie to be able to return Gabby to the Cassidys – which reminded him again, he really should call Maggie.

He'd been avoiding it since that night when he'd told her all about Kathy, that drunken night when he'd been so hyped up with the good news about Monroe that he'd let himself go too far. He had never drunk that much before in his life, never talked like that to anyone about Kathy. He blushed as he recalled it. He had always wanted to tell Maggie about Kathy but not in that way. It made him feel somehow that he'd given away some of their secrets. And when Maggie had said she wished she could take Kathy's place, bring her back to him, well, he thought that was so like Kathy herself to have offered that. Kathy would have done the same.

Kathy. Kathy. Kathy. What a burden had been lifted since finding out about Sauceboat. It was a feeling he couldn't understand; if he was right about the horse having been doped by Culling, surely it was a terrible thing? It might not have been murder but it was manslaughter. An awful crime. And yet, his heart was lighter. A large part of the guilt he'd felt at her death had gone. There was an earthly reason for that death. And now, probably above all this, he had something to hang it all on, someone to blame, a way of finalizing this wretchedness he had thought was going to be with him all his days.

Frankie wanted to spend some more time sitting in the George in Lambourn, jogging memories, reminding people that there was a fifty-thousand-pound reward waiting for the person who nailed Gerry Monroe. He was due to meet Stonebanks in the pub and as he pulled up in the car park Maggie Cassidy called him. He saw her name on-screen and immediately felt guilty for not ringing her.

She seemed nervous when she heard his voice, almost upset. She said, 'Frankie, I'm really sorry to bother you.'

'Don't be daft, it's me who should be sorry. I've been meaning to call.'

'No, no, you've got a million things to do. Look, it's just that Jane's coming home tomorrow. I want to try and plan how best to tell her about Gabby and I just wondered if there was any news about him coming home.'

Frankie closed his eyes and reproached himself. 'Maggie, I'm sorry, I've just been trying to sort things out with Joe Ansell. Joe thinks he might need another week or so.'

There was silence for a few seconds then she said, 'Will he, you know, keep that long?'

'Yes, Joe's confident he'll be OK. You'll have him home in a week. That gives you a bit of leeway to let Jane settle back in. You can delay telling her for a week if you want to.' Frankie wanted so much to tell her what had happened, the temptation was almost irresistible.

'I could do with a week's grace,' Maggie said. 'She's upset enough. Her boyfriend's father was killed in an accident. Sean's coming back with her.'

'Oh that's terrible news, Maggie, I'm sorry. You must be at the end of your tether. Is Graham any better?'

She hesitated. 'I'm afraid not. He's still in bed, still very, very down.'

He was surprised. 'I thought the news about Monroe would have helped.'

'Me too. He barely registered it. It's not the loss of the money, Frankie, I don't think it was even the kidnapping. It was seeing what that bastard had done to Gabby.'

Frankie knew Graham had been keen to keep the details from her. He must have told her.

Maggie went on, 'It's the thought of what the horse suffered that's got to him. I don't think he'll ever completely recover.'

Frankie drew a long breath and sighed. What to do? He believed completely in his theory that Ulysses and Gabby had not been killed by Monroe and he knew that telling Maggie about it so she could tell Graham would give him so much hope ... but if he turned out to be wrong and Graham was plunged back again into thoughts of the savaging his horse had under-gone, it might well be worse in the long run.

She said, 'Are *you* OK?'

He knew she meant was he all right after all the emotions of the other night but he let it pass. 'I'm fine, Maggie. I'm fine. I just wish everything would come together so you can all get your own lives back to normal. I'm just about to go into the busiest pub in Lambourn. I'm meeting Stone-

351

banks here. We're really hopeful of picking up something on Monroe very soon.'

'I'll say a prayer.'

'It's a deal. I'd better get in here. I'll call you as soon as I have something.'

It was Friday evening. The pub was busy, smoky, noisy with music and chatter. The talk was as it had been in this pub on Friday nights since it had opened in the thirties, of hopes for tomorrow, the big racing day of the week. Half-drunk lads boasted of how far their horse would win next day, placed side bets with doubters, mocked others making similar claims. At the bar and in corners, tips were whispered and gossip was exchanged. Frankie and Stonebanks moved around chatting to lads, to the girls (who were also referred to as lads), trying to pick up any scrap that might lead them to Monroe's whereabouts.

The pub grew warmer as it became busier and a young blonde girl playing pool hauled off the heavy yellow sweater she wore, pulling up the skimpy blue T-shirt underneath to reveal her black bra. The lads around the pool table made various noises and one of the girls shouted loudly, 'Ooohh, Belinda!'

Frankie was close by and he smiled with the others as Belinda pulled her T-shirt down again and leant forward to make a shot. Frankie noticed a heavy locket dangling from her throat. He moved closer. The locket was swinging slightly. It was a gold case with a clear front. Inside it was a lock of dark hair. Belinda played her shot. Frankie went up to her and nodded towards the locket. 'You looked after Zuiderzie?'

She smiled widely at being recognized. 'That's right.'

'If you'll let me borrow what's in your locket for twenty-four hours I think I'll be able to tell you exactly how he died.'

Late afternoon, next day, the call came which told them that the DNA analysis on the horsehair from Belinda's locket matched that taken from the flesh and hair found at the place where the supposed Ulysses' body had been left. Stonebanks smiled at Frankie. 'Well done! You were absolutely right!' Frankie shook the outstretched hand, smiling widely and feeling a strange satisfaction, a contentment he'd never experienced.

'It was Zuiderzie, not Ulysses,' he said to no one in particular.

Stonebanks pumped his hand. 'Ulysses may well still be on his travels, my friend!'

Frankie picked up his jacket. 'And I'm on mine. The Cassidys deserve to get this news face to face.'

'You just want to see them smile. And take the plaudits!' Stonebanks said.

'You'll get you share of credit, don't worry!' Frankie laughed.

Stonebanks put an arm on his shoulder. 'Only kidding, Frankie. You deserve it all.'

Frankie was halfway out of the door when he turned. 'You sure you don't mind me heading up there? Don't mind carrying on ferreting around down here for some news on Monroe?'

'I don't mind at all. Stay a few days if you want. We can keep in touch by phone.'

'No. I mean, thanks Geoff, but no. There's too much to be done down here. Somebody must know something about Monroe's whereabouts. If the horses are still alive, somebody must know where they are. They need looking after, vets, shoes and all the other stuff. Somebody must know something. I'll be back tomorrow.'

Stonebanks held his hands up. 'Fine, fine. It's your call, Frankie boy. If you change your mind just let me know.'

58

On the drive north Frankie decided to call Maggie and give her advance warning of the news he was bringing. The decision on telling Graham that the Cheltenham body was not Gabby was one she'd have to make. If Frankie arrived unannounced it might be much more difficult to pull Maggie aside and tell her. It would be easier to do it this way.

When she put the phone down Maggie was elated but she had already decided not to tell Graham about Ulysses. Although it was certain that the carcass Graham had seen at Cheltenham had not been that of Gabby, Frankie had told her to think long and hard before telling him right now. Both horses could have been killed by Monroe since then if he had panicked, and

Maggie was terribly afraid that Graham wouldn't be able to withstand another let-down if she built up his hopes now. She'd asked Frankie if he'd have dinner with them and went to the kitchen now with a spring in her step but trying not to raise her hopes for Gabby too high.

Jane and Sean had arrived home that afternoon. She'd told them that the police and Frankie and his colleagues were doing everything they could to find Gabby but she was sure that Sean had other things on his mind. She'd taken to him immediately and told him he could stay as long as he wanted. She went now to tell them that Frankie was on his way and would be having dinner with them.

On her way back from Jane's room she stopped outside the room Graham had confined himself to since taking to bed. Not their marital bed. He'd told Maggie he'd never had an unhappy moment in the bed they'd shared and he wouldn't defile it now. She'd almost grown used to having the bed, and the room, to herself but she missed him. His presence had always been calm, solid and reassuring. That's what had made the whole thing worse. He'd gone from a man who could bounce back from the worst setback to one who'd had enough, who'd given everything and had nothing left in reserve, no fight.

As ever, the heavy curtains were closed. A lamp burned on the bedside table, the paleness of its light making him look sicker than he was. As she closed the door quietly he opened his eyes and his closed mouth moved very slightly. 'Is this a smile I see before me?' she said as she sat softly on the bed and took his hand.

'Just for you.' She could almost feel the effort it had taken, that tiny smile and the attempt at a note of optimism in his voice, a voice that had been dull and flat since he'd become ill.

She squeezed his hand, stroked the back of it gently. 'Guess who's coming to dinner?' she said. Graham raised his eyebrows slightly in response. 'Frankie.' Graham tried hard again for that smile. 'He says they're optimistic. They're hoping for a breakthrough soon.' Graham nodded slightly and squeezed her hand. 'Fancy getting up for dinner?'

'I'd be no good. Not just now.'

'He'd understand, Graham, I know he'd love to see you. You're the first person he asks about when he calls.'

He stared at the ceiling a while, then said, 'Maybe next time.'

'Should I ask him to pop in here then, for a bit of boys' talk?'

He turned his head to her and she could see the pain back in his eyes. He said, 'I don't want Frankie to see me like this, Maggie.'

She squeezed his hand again, held his forearm with her left hand. 'I'm sorry, darling. I was being thoughtless. I'm sorry.'

'It's OK. You go. Have a nice dinner.'

She leant and kissed him. 'I'll bring yours in.'

Jane led Sean around the yard, conscious that this was their first real experience together which wasn't new for her. All the places she showed Sean, the part of the barn where Gabby had been born, his empty box, the paddock he'd grazed in as a foal, the surrounding fields, the gallops, the other horses, Jane knew every inch of while Sean was seeing it for the first time. They finished the tour back in the barn, settled on a chair made from straw bales. 'What do you think?' she asked him.

'Grand. It's a grand place.'

Jane smiled. 'Wish I could've got a bet on that.'

'What?'

'You saying grand!'

He smiled too and pushed her away in mock disapproval. She said, 'It's good to see you smile again.' He nodded, lowering his head. She took his hand.

'He wasn't all bad, ye know, me da. He used to be good to me and me ma. 'Twas the drink that messed his head up.'

'I know.' Jane had learned in the past few days that searing honesty wasn't always the best thing for getting through life, for cementing relationships.

'He used to be a good laugh, too. We had a swing in the playground and he'd push me high then walk round the front of me and bend down like he was picking something up and he'd be making sure he was just within kicking distance when I came back down and I'd kick him on the arse and he'd go falling, shouting and waving his arms.'

Jane was smiling and nodding.

'I know it's not very funny now but I used to laugh so much I'd nearly fall off the swing.'

'I'd like to have been there.'

357

He nodded, a faraway look in his eyes. The door latch clicked. They both turned. Billy came into the barn and wandered towards them in the aimless way that usually annoyed Jane, but today she found it endearing and realized how much she'd missed her brother. 'Hi, Billy!' she said.

'Hiya,' he said quietly as he reached them, reddening slightly as he glanced at Sean.

'This is Sean,' Jane said. 'Sean, Billy, my little brother.' She said little in the wind-him-up fashion she usually used, quickly dropping back into big-sister character.

'Hello,' Billy said shyly.

'Hello to you,' Sean said.

'What's the latest on the invention front?' she asked teasingly.

Billy shrugged. 'Nothing much.'

'Oh come on, you've always got something on the go up in that room!'

'Mum says you've to come in and meet Frankie. Dinner's nearly ready.'

'Tell us your invention first.'

'I can't.'

'Why? I'm your sister. You can trust me.'

Billy, hands in pockets, looked around then said, 'Promise not to tell.'

Jane giggled and put an arm around Sean's shoulders. 'We do, don't we?'

'We do,' said Sean.

'Say "Promise".'

'Promise. We promise!'

Billy raised his eyebrows and indicated towards Sean without looking at him. Sean said, 'Cross my heart and hope to die!'

Jane stared wide-eyed in mock anticipation. Billy said, 'It's known as the S.E.M.'

'Uh-uh,' said Jane, 'sounds impressive when things have initials. What does it do?'

'It gets rid of all your troubles in life.'

'*All* your troubles? How does it work?' Jane asked.

Billy shrugged. 'You just press a button and they disappear.'

'Sounds a grand thing,' said Sean. 'What does S.E.M. stand for.'

'Sister Eliminating Machine.' Billy smiled mischievously. 'I'm working on a girlfriend version if you're interested.'

'Put me down for one,' Sean said, laughing, and Jane turned to punch him, then ran after the retreating Billy.

59

Frankie was talking to Maggie as she filled the dinner plates with roast pork, potatoes and vegetables. Billy came running in giggling with a smiling Jane hot on his heels and Sean just behind them. 'Settle down, please!' Maggie ordered, carrying the plates to the table.

'I'll get you later!' Jane promised Billy who pulled a face. 'Hi Frankie.'

'Hello. Did you have a good break in Ireland?'

'Yes, thanks.'

'I see you captured one of the natives,' Frankie

said, nodding towards Sean who stood awkwardly in the middle of the kitchen.

'That's Sean. He's my boyfriend.'

Frankie walked over to Sean and held out his hand. 'Pleased to meet you, Sean.'

Uncertainly, Sean shook Frankie's hand. 'Hello, Father.'

Everyone looked at Sean. Jane said, 'He's not a priest any more, Sean.'

Sean blushed pink. 'Sorry.'

Frankie chuckled. 'Nothing to be sorry about, Sean. Call me Frankie.'

Sean nodded. Maggie said, 'Shall we sit down?'

Billy watched where Frankie made for and quickly moved to be alongside him. Jane, Sean and Maggie sat opposite. Frankie spent time gently coaxing Sean into conversation, talking about Dublin and the parts of it they knew. But Frankie made sure he included Billy in the chat. He liked Billy and knew the boy looked up to him for some reason. Maggie had told Frankie how worried Billy was about his father.

'How's the inventing going?' Frankie asked. Jane immediately told the story of what had just happened in the barn, her mother looking at her with obvious approval as she told the story against herself. Everyone laughed.

''Twould be a very useful piece of kit, that, eh Sean?' Frankie said. He turned to Billy. 'You could make yourself a fortune with a machine like that, Billy.'

Billy nodded, smiling. 'I'm working on, well, trying to think up, really, a device for protecting horses from getting kidnapped.'

Maggie and Frankie glanced at each other. Maggie had told Frankie she'd been hoping they could avoid talking too much about the kidnap. Sean had done a lot to take Jane's mind off it but Billy seemed, understandably, obsessed by it. Maggie knew that Billy's motives were centred on his father, not the horse. Getting the horse back, for Billy, was just the means to getting his father back.

Now Sean joined in. 'Maybe they could put those microchips into horses. That's what they've started doing with the ponies in Dublin. Then you'd know where they were all the time.'

Billy nodded. 'That's a good idea, but I thought that any criminals might just cut the horse open and take it out. They put the chips just under the skin so they'd probably be easy to cut out. But it is a good idea.'

Maggie looked at her son with the same approving smile and admiration she'd shown earlier to Jane. She thought it very kind of him to handle the rejection of Sean's idea so well.

'Maybe they could bury them deeper in horses,' Jane said protectively.

Billy nodded. 'Maybe.'

Jane looked at Frankie. 'Mum said you're making progress, Frankie. Do you really think we'll get Gabby back?'

Frankie looked at Maggie who shrugged slightly and half-smiled as though to say, 'We're into it now, might as well go with the flow.' Frankie said, 'We've a very strong suspect, a man called Gerry Monroe. Your mum and dad have identified him as the man who stole the money

361

and we're almost certain he has Gabby and at least one other horse. The police are looking for him here and in Ireland.'

'In Ireland?' Jane asked.

'We know he took a horsebox there, one he stole from his employers. He went there not long after kidnapping Gabby.'

'So Gabby might be in Ireland and we've just left there,' Jane said.

'All we know for sure is that the horsebox went there. We're kind of assuming Monroe was driving it and that the horses were inside. There's a big reward for anyone who can tell us where Monroe is. Your mum put up the money.'

Jane turned to her mother. 'How much, Mum?'

'Fifty thousand pounds. But only if Monroe's caught and the money he stole is returned.'

Jane nodded. 'That's good.'

'Mum,' Billy said, 'couldn't we have another reward for just getting the horse back? That's what Dad needs. It doesn't really matter about this Monroe guy.'

Maggie looked at him tenderly as she realized how thoughtless she'd been. 'Yes, Billy, we could. And we should. Shouldn't we, Frankie?'

'Sure. Of course. I'll talk to the police about it.' He glanced at Maggie and she suddenly realized the spot she'd put him in. Only a few people knew that the dead horses were not Ulysses and Angel Gabriel. The press certainly didn't know.

Jane said, 'But we want to catch this man, too, Monroe, don't we?'

'Without a doubt,' Frankie said.

There were a few seconds of silence then Sean said, 'I have a piece of paper that says Gerry Monroe on it with a phone number ... and some directions to a house ... near Lambourn.'

Everyone looked at Sean and his brow furrowed in a frown and he sat quite still. Frankie said, 'Can I ask where you got it, this paper?'

Sean looked at him silently for a moment then said, 'I took it out of me da's pocket when he was drunk one night. I ... I thought it might be money. He never ever gave me any money and I needed to buy things for the house.'

'It's OK, Sean. You've done nothing wrong. When was this that you took the paper?'

''Twould be a while back, a long while. 'Twas after me da had been to England on a message for Kelly Corell.'

Frankie opened his mouth to speak then stopped, as though pondering, seeking the best words. 'Kelly Corell from Dublin?'

'That's right. The gangster fella. 'Twas...' He stopped as Jane jabbed his thigh with the butt of her fork.

'Your da worked for Mr Corell?' Frankie asked.

'He did. He's his chauffeur mostly but he does a lot of things for him.' Sean didn't seem to realize he'd lapsed into the present tense. Jane sat staring straight ahead as though conscious of her mother's ever-widening eyes on her as Sean's background began taking shape.

Frankie said, 'And you say you still have this paper, Sean?'

''Tis in me room at home. On top o' the chest

363

o' drawers. At least it was when I was last in there for I threw it there and haven't tidied up since.'

Frankie and Maggie smiled at his honesty. Sean said, 'D'ye think it might be the same fella, the one yer after?'

'It might and it might not, but I wouldn't mind seeing the paper. How would you feel about flying over with me tomorrow?'

Sean looked at Jane. She nodded vigorously. Sean said, 'Will it be OK to come back with you too?'

Frankie laughed. 'Of course it will!'

In a corner of the departure lounge at Dublin Airport Frankie waited while Stonebanks ran through in his mind the directions Frankie had just read to him from the paper. 'I think it might be Kennedy's old place. I'd heard someone had bought it last year.'

'Do you know who?' Frankie asked.

'I don't, but I could try and find out.'

'My car's at Liverpool Airport but I'm going to fly back to London and come straight to your place if that's OK?'

'Of course. I'll see what I can dig up by the time you get here.'

Frankie put his phone in his jacket pocket and turned to Sean. 'Hungry?'

'I'm fine, thanks.'

'Want a drink, then?'

Sean nodded. 'Yes, please.'

They sat at the table, Frankie with a mug of cappuccino and Sean with a glass of Coke. Frankie said, 'Are you sure you don't mind going back via London?'

Sean shook his head. 'I don't mind.'

'I can put you on a train to Crewe. Jane and her ma will come and pick you up there.'

Sean nodded. Frankie smiled and said, 'You'll not be away from her too long then. I'm sure you'd rather have Jane's company than mine.'

Sean shrugged and drank some Coke. Frankie wondered what was going through his mind. The kid must be totally bewildered by all that had happened in the past few days. 'I was sorry to hear about your da,' Frankie said. 'It couldn't have been easy for you going back there today.'

'D'ye think Kelly Corell is involved with kidnapping the horses?'

'I don't know. I hope in a way he isn't for I hear he's not a very nice man at all.'

'He killed me da.'

Frankie stared at him. 'He killed your da?'

Sean, grim-faced, nodded and sucked Coke through his straw. 'Jane said I wasn't to tell her ma right away till she gets to know me better so would you please not tell her?'

'I won't tell her without your permission.'

Sean nodded again and said, 'Me da's supposed to have stole ten grand off him but I don't believe he did.'

Frankie, taken aback at the cool way Sean was talking about the murder of his father, said, 'Have you been to the police?'

'They said it was suicide and that they wouldn't want to be wasting time on it but everybody knows it wasn't suicide for Pat Pusey and the rest of Corell's men had been lookin' for me da for a while. That's how me and Jane met, Pat Pusey had me by the throat down at the ferry terminal tryin' to get out of me where me da was and me not havin' seen him for ages. I couldn't tell him and wouldn't't've even if I knew.'

'I'm sure you wouldn't. Did you tell the police this?'

'Jane told them but they paid no heed.'

Frankie shook his head. 'Let's see what comes out of all this kidnapping business. See if Corell is involved and then we'll go back to the police. I have some friends in England who know some people pretty high up in the Garda.'

'They'll not do anything about Kelly Corell for he has the guards in his pocket, so he has. He pays them bribes and has stuff to blackmail a few of them.'

'Well, let's just see.'

'So d'ye think me da might have had somethin' to do with the kidnappin' with him havin' that paper with Monroe's name on?'

'I don't know, Sean. Maybe not. I think Mr Monroe was into more than just kidnapping. It could have been something else completely. The ten grand your da's supposed to have stolen, what was the story behind that, do you know?'

'He was supposed to take the money to a man in England and he never turned up is what they say, but I don't know for I hadn't seen him for a while and he never said much to me anyway.'

Frankie nodded, watching Sean's face, trying to imagine the life he'd had, the relationship with his father. 'Do ye think those directions mean somethin'?'

'Might do. Might be something, might be nothing.'

'What will you do when ye get back, will ye be goin' to that place?'

'I think we probably will.'

'Can I come?'

Frankie hesitated. Sean said, 'Me da must have been there or he wouldn't have had those in his pocket. I'd like to come with you and see where he'd been when he was over in England.'

'Can we wait and see how the land lies when we get to London?'

'OK. It's just that if all this has anythin' to do with why me da was killed, I'd like to try and help.'

Their flight was announced on the PA system. Frankie stood and smiled at Sean. 'That's fair enough. We just need to see how best you can do that. Ready to go?'

Sean got up. As they walked towards the departure gate Sean looked up at Frankie and said, 'Was it hard bein' a priest? Is that why ye left?'

Frankie smiled and put his hand on Sean's shoulder. 'I'll tell you about it on the flight.'

60

It was late evening when they got to Stonebanks's house. Frankie had spoken to Maggie, and Sean to Jane; he was staying with Frankie at least until tomorrow. Sean watched Stonebanks and Frankie sitting side by side at the kitchen table. The piece of paper with the directions and phone number lay in front of them. He'd liked Stonebanks when Frankie introduced him and he liked Frankie too and wondered why couldn't he have had one of them for his da? He felt guilty for thinking that and apologized silently to his father.

Stonebanks tapped at the paper with a pen and said, 'The number is definitely Monroe's mobile, I checked it with his ex-employer.'

'What about the house?' Frankie asked. 'The man who owns it, did you manage to find anything on him?'

'It was bought almost a year ago by a company called In4tel Communications based in Jersey. I'm trying to find out more about the directors and stuff but it's hard work. Anyway, the word is that somebody is definitely living there.'

Frankie nodded. 'Want to go and have a look?'

Stonebanks grimaced. 'We just need to be careful here, Frankie. It's not a licensed premises. We've got no jurisdiction.'

'So we're out driving, we take a wrong turn and

stop at a house for directions.'

Sean was all for this idea but he saw Stonebanks shake his head. 'It's not that kind of place, Frankie. It's remote. Sits in the middle of the woods at the end of an old track. Anyone taking a wrong turn off that road, anyone with any sense, would turn back round again before he got anywhere near the house.'

'It's dark, Geoff,' Frankie pointed out. 'We can drive so far and walk the rest.'

'And how are we supposed to see where we're going?'

'Take a torch,' Sean suggested.

Frankie smiled. 'There y'are. That's the answer.'

Sean said, 'If anybody comes youse can say I got lost and youse were out lookin' for me.'

Frankie said, 'That's a good idea Geoff; at least, if we do meet anyone and Sean's with us it'll make it look less suspicious on our side. It's not as if you'd take a boy with you if you were up to anything, is it? No offence to you, Sean.'

Stonebanks sighed and stood up. 'I'll get the torch.'

The torch stayed unlit as they walked down the track towards the house. The full moon gave sufficient light through the leafless trees, bright enough, at times, to cast shadows. The sound of their shoes on the gritty track seemed loud to a nervous Stonebanks. He said quietly, 'I think the house is just around this bend.'

The house was in view from around the bend but still two hundred yards away. Lights showed through three ground-floor windows. They moved forward cautiously and were still a hundred yards away when Sean whispered, 'I think there's a camera on top of the gate.'

They stopped. Frankie and Stonebanks tried to focus on the gates. Frankie said, 'I think you're right, Sean.'

'We'd best go back,' Stonebanks decided. 'We can get the police here in the morning.'

'Geoff,' Frankie objected, 'whoever's in there could be gone in the morning.'

Stonebanks turned to face him. 'Frankie, this is getting a bit out of our league now. We should go back.' Frankie stood silent. Stonebanks said, 'Can you picture the tape off that camera getting played in court or on TV or something with us creeping around a private citizen's house, two Jockey Club Security Department officials with a teenage kid? No offence, Sean.'

Sean said, 'I could climb up there and cover up the camera.'

'You could Sean,' Frankie agreed, 'but I think we can maybe find another way in.'

'Frankie, come on, for God's sake!' Stonebanks said in frustration.

'No, Geoff, I don't want to let this go. You've got to admit I've been patient. I took your advice in not going straight for Culling, in trying to get Monroe first. As soon as we get Monroe I can get the man who was responsible for killing my wife. Monroe might be in that house now. I can't just turn around now and go and sleep easily tonight. Do you think you could if you were me?'

'I don't know, Frankie. I just don't know!' He seemed rattled.

370

Frankie reached to grasp his arm. 'Why don't you go back to the car and wait?'

'What are you actually going to do?' Stonebanks asked.

'Just have a little wander around the back. There must be another way in.'

'Then what?'

'I'm going to try and look through those windows. If I see Monroe, you can call the police then. I won't go any further than that.'

Stonebanks rubbed his face with both hands. 'Promise?'

'Promise.'

They stepped off the track into the woods and continued towards the house. Twenty minutes later, after skirting the perimeter, they stood touching the eight-foot-high railings which they now knew surrounded the whole property. Stonebanks said, 'This must have cost a fortune.'

'Whatever they're doing in there,' Frankie said, 'they're not taking many chances, are they?'

'I could climb that easy,' Sean offered.

'No!' Stonebanks said.

Frankie said, 'I could climb it pretty easily myself, I reckon.'

Stonebanks sighed heavily and said resignedly, 'I'll wait here.'

'Give us a boost then!' Sean said. Frankie helped Sean over and Stonebanks helped Frankie. Where Sean had scrambled easily down the other side, Frankie jumped, landing awkwardly and rolling in the wet grass. 'Ye all right?' Sean whispered.

'I am.'

They moved towards the windows, picking their way very slowly across a gravel driveway. Frankie was aware of the sudden heightening of his senses as the adrenaline kicked in. He thought of Kathy. The fact that she would have loved this and that he was doing it for her helped him feel so close to her again. He glanced across at Sean, light from the windows on his face now. He looked alert but very calm and Frankie recalled the scrapes he used to get into as a boy and realized that Sean would probably see this as tame compared to some of the things he got up to.

They reached the first window, Frankie at one side, Sean at the other. Frankie moved just enough to squint through the glass with one eye, none of his body exposed. Sean, watching, copied him. They saw no one inside. Frankie crouched and crept towards Sean, straightening as he reached him. Sean followed him around the corner to the next window. The pane was frosted. They stood listening. The clink of glass on glass could be heard from inside.

The final rectangle of light was cast on dark, soft earth. Frankie reckoned it was a flowerbed. Their feet sank almost to the ankles as they crossed it and came alongside the window. Sean ducked this time and went to the other side. Carefully, Frankie moved his head till he could look inside. A man sat in an easy chair, his right profile clearly visible. Beside him on a small circular table was a can of Guinness. He was smoking a cigarette and laughing. The sounds of a TV quiz show were audible. Frankie didn't recognize him.

Sean was looking in too. Then Frankie became aware of Sean turning to stare at him. He glanced across and realized from his face that the boy knew something. Frankie quickly put his finger to his lips and signalled Sean to crouch again and come towards him. When he was by his side Frankie took his arm and pulled him a few yards further away from the window. 'Do you know him?' he whispered.

'It's Pat Pusey. I think he might be the one who killed me da.'

Frankie leant forward till his face was close to Sean's. 'Are you OK?' he asked.

Sean nodded. Frankie thought he looked shocked. 'Are you sure?'

He nodded again. Frankie took his hand and led him away, crouching past the first two windows they'd looked in. Staying close to the walls they made their way round to the front of the house. Frankie wanted to stop there and take stock but the moon shone directly on them and he kept moving till they'd rounded the corner back into deep shadow. He stopped and turned, squatted and pulled Sean to hunker down too. 'Are you all right? Did that spook you, seeing Pusey?'

'A bit, but I'm grand now.'

Frankie smiled and patted his shoulder. 'Good man! Are you fit to have a look round the back of the house with me before we leave?'

'Sure.'

Frankie led again. This side of the house was in darkness. He stopped at the corner and peered

373

round it. He saw some faint lights on a square building, above what looked like stable doors. Shoulder still touching the wall he crept towards the building, stopping opposite it, about twenty feet away. Stables. Both half-doors closed. Frankie and Sean stood silent for a few moments. There was the sound of a shod hoof on concrete. Frankie looked down at Sean. The boy's eyes were wide again, as they'd been when he'd seen Pusey through the window. 'Let's go,' Frankie whispered and they went across to the box doors. There were five of them, all with the bolt across but none padlocked.

Frankie gently took hold of the galvanized steel bolt and worked it to the left. It squeaked. He stopped. He leant on the upper door to take the pressure off the hasp. The bolt slid smoothly all the way across and the door opened with just the slightest of noises. He heard movement inside the box then a head loomed out of the darkness towards him and he stepped back in fright. The head came across the door and the big horse looked at him inquisitively, ears pricked. Frankie had seen many pictures of Angel Gabriel in the Cassidy house; quite a few were head and neck shots as the horse had that distinctive 'Look of Eagles' about him, as Graham Cassidy had said. He reached to stroke the long nose. He couldn't be dead certain but he'd have had a decent wager that this was the horse. There was a strong temptation to use the torch, just for a few seconds, to shine it inside and see if the rest of him looked like Angel Gabriel.

He decided not to. Instead he whispered,

'Gabby!' The horse's ears flicked towards him but he couldn't be sure if it was a reaction to the name or just the sound. But it made him smile. He looked at Sean and he smiled too, slowly, in a way that endeared him to Frankie.

Frankie loosed the bolt on the door to the horse's left; the box was empty. He looked in the one in the right, had to lean over and it took a while for his eyes to adjust to the almost complete darkness. There was a horse there, against the back wall. He opened the two remaining boxes. Empty. He shut them all again, having to push gently at the big horse's nose to move his head back into the box.

They went behind the boxes, kept walking till they reached the perimeter fence then followed it round to where Stonebanks waited. He was holding on to the railings. 'Where've you been?' He demanded. 'I thought you'd gone in for tea or something!'

'We took the scenic route, didn't we Sean?'

'We did.'

'Any the wiser?' Stonebanks asked.

Frankie said, 'One of Corell's men is in there with, we think, at least one other person. There are two horses in a stable block at the back. One of them, or should I say the head of one of them, looks very like Angel Gabriel.'

Stonebanks nodded, seemingly summing up the situation, still holding on to the railings. 'Did you see the other person?'

Frankie shook his head. 'Heard glasses clink in a room. Couldn't see through the window.'

'It could be Monroe,' Stonebanks suggested.

375

'I think that's not unlikely.'

Frowning, Stonebanks stared at the moon. 'We need a reason to get the police in.'

'How about a positive identification of Angel Gabriel?'

'That would help. How are you going to do it?'

'I'll call Maggie, ask her to drive down now.'

'And shin over the fence?'

'She could bring Jane,' Sean said. 'Jane can climb.'

'Good thinking.' Frankie reached for his mobile.

61

Maggie drove faster than she could ever remember doing before as she headed south. It wasn't a good time to be speeding; she couldn't concentrate for long on the road, on the traffic around her. Too many thoughts and hopes were fighting for room in her head. Jane was beside her, equally wound-up, one minute unable to stop talking, the next silent, biting her nails, which she hadn't done since she'd turned seven. Maggie reflected on her decision not to tell Graham. She realized she'd never know how she resisted the temptation to do so. She felt guilty too for giving him another of those pills upon which he'd become so reliant. But she'd had to ensure he'd sleep soundly until she returned, which might not be until the early hours.

Stonebanks met them as agreed outside the George in Lambourn. He introduced himself and they got into his car. The moon was high in the sky as they trekked through the woods, all three in dark clothing. Stonebanks lost his bearings, but Jane put them back on track when she saw the faint light from the house. Frankie and Sean had been back to the house twice. Little had changed. Pusey was still in his chair although he was asleep. Vague sounds came from the room behind the frosted glass but no one had emerged.

Frankie smiled at Maggie through the railings and Sean did the same at Jane. They received two very strained smiles in return.

Stonebanks helped Jane up on his side and Frankie let her put her feet on his shoulders on the other. When she was safely on the ground, Sean reached to touch her arm, then her hair. Her gaze fixed on Frankie as her hand searched for Sean's hand. He took it. Frankie said, 'You'll be in no danger, Jane. I won't let anything happen to you.'

She nodded. 'You'll be fine, Jane,' Sean said.

Frankie led them along the fence to the back of the house. When the stables came in view he stopped and turned to the teenagers. 'Just a thought – if it is Gabby, is he likely to make much noise when he sees you?'

Jane shrugged. 'He could. He might,' she whispered nervously.

Frankie thought about it. 'If you stayed ten yards away to the side and I got him to stick his neck out of the box, would that be enough for you to tell?'

'Definitely.'

'Good. Let's do that.'

Two minutes later Frankie was again easing back the bolt on the middle door. The horse was waiting this time and his head came out as Frankie opened it, going all the way so Jane could see him against the weak lights and get what help she could from the moon overhead. She squinted through the darkness then turned to Sean. 'I need to get a bit closer.'

'Get behind me then, crouch down so he doesn't see you,' he whispered.

Jane crouched behind his shoulder, peeking over when she was five yards away. Frankie watched her; he could see only her right eye and forehead in the moonshine, and he saw a tear rise as she nodded her head. Gabby seemed to sense her, to smell her; he turned and whickered softly. Frankie stroked his nose then pushed slowly, Gabby's hooves scraping the floor as he reluctantly backed away.

Frankie had to get in front again to keep them from running back to where Maggie and Stone-banks stood. Jane reached for her mother through the fence and Maggie pushed her hands through as far as she could. 'It's him, Mum! Gabby's OK!' Whispers, but tense, sharp ones. 'Thank God!' Maggie said. 'Thank God.'

Frankie stayed on the inside of the fence, Stonebanks's coat over his own jacket. He was alone. Stonebanks had taken Sean and the Cassidys back to his house for warmth and safety. Frankie had told his colleague to try to get a couple of hours' sleep before meeting the police and returning before dawn. In the early hours of the morning the lights in the house were finally switched off. Frankie walked the perimeter of the fence then, his feet all but silent on the short grass.

He hadn't walked like this, at this steady pace, since back at the church with Kathy when they'd strolled round the paths, circuit after circuit, or walked in the park, each listening to every word the other said – 'walks 'n' talks'. Frankie smiled at the memory, though a sudden vision of their framed shoes, Kathy's wedding present to him, brought a stab to his heart.

It would have been a year ago when they were still doing their walks, both knowing Frankie was serving out the final weeks of his ministry. Walking in love with Kathy a year ago, patrolling the lair of the people who may have been involved in her death now, this midwinter night. Frankie shook his head slowly, unable to understand how quickly and terribly everything had changed.

In the hours before Stonebanks came with the police, Frankie found some peace in his vigil. The old familiar rhythm of the constant walking, the comforting thought of Kathy being near again, the prospect of maybe making some sense of all this by moving his attention now to Peter Culling. The light at the end of what had been a long, long tunnel.

By six o'clock there were six men inside the grounds; four were armed police, one was a

special negotiator, the other was Frankie Houlihan. Hiding in the woods nearby were another
dozen armed police. Frankie concluded that if
Monroe was still carrying the rifle he'd used to
threaten the Cassidys, he was going to be heavily
outgunned.

The plan was to try and do it peacefully, to wait
until someone came out to feed the horses. If
they were being properly looked after, this should
happen quite early in the morning, probably
while it was still dark.

62

David Hewitt rose within minutes of his alarm
clock bleeping at six-thirty. He switched on the
bedroom light and went to the toilet, then the
bathroom. Under the shower, he was planning
the day with some excitement. He'd been working twelve to fourteen hours a day this past week
and was close to a breakthrough in the project. It
had taken a while for him to adjust to the
presence of the Irishman in the house but Pusey
had treated it as a holiday, boozing and watching
TV. Hewitt admitted to himself that Pusey's
overall laid-back approach had helped him calm
down and refocus on the project. The threat of
Monroe's return, the demands he might make
about the two horses, the possibility of the police
suddenly turning up – these no longer dominated
Hewitt's thinking.

He'd still have preferred not to have the horses there. Apart from the risk of sheltering kidnapped animals, they were too much trouble to look after. He knew Pusey had been told by his boss to make sure the horses stayed there. Hewitt concluded they had their own plans for making money out of them. But Pusey hadn't laid a brush on either of them nor filled a water bucket.

Dressed now, he hurried downstairs. Still, he thought, there was a good chance he was going to make a breakthrough in the next forty-eight hours. Then he could get away from them, away from this house, these woods, back to Marcia, to civilization.

He went outside, pulling on a thick fleece jacket, leaving the door open behind him. The gravel rattled under his boots as he hurried towards the back of the house and the feed room. He stopped, remembering it was always best to get the empty water buckets out of their boxes first. As he reached for the bolt on Ulysses' door he heard someone speak behind him and his mind registered the slight tension in the voice. 'This is the police. We are armed. Stand completely still.'

Hewitt had a sensation of this not happening, of watching a movie. He didn't stand still, he turned around with a silly smile on his face. Two policemen in flak jackets and helmets had rifles pointed at his face. The taller one, his voice a note higher now, said, 'Stand still! Don't move!'

A look of horror quickly replaced the smile on Hewitt's face. His legs gave way gradually and he slumped softly to the ground.

381

Frankie came out from behind the stable block and hurried across to Hewitt. He said to the police, 'It's not Monroe.' Both officers moved closer, their weapons still pointing at the unconscious Hewitt. From his position on one knee, Frankie raised a hand. 'I think you better ease up, fellas. If he opens his eyes now he might die of shock.'

'He might be faking,' the taller one said.

Frankie looked up at him. The big cop crouched quickly and frisked Hewitt, turning him roughly on his stomach to complete the job. Hewitt stirred at this and Frankie signalled the police to back off a bit. 'You OK?' he asked Hewitt, making sure he filled the man's vision as he turned again on his back and opened his eyes. Hewitt looked bemused. 'I think you just fainted,' Frankie told him. Hewitt blinked and sat up, his face level now with Frankie's. 'I'm a Jockey Club Security Department intelligence officer. Do you feel like talking?'

Hewitt looked stunned but blurted out, 'I didn't steal the horses or the money!'

'I know you didn't. Do you know who did?'

'Monroe.'

'Where is he?'

'I don't know. He brought the horses here on Christmas Day. I haven't seen him since.

'Has he contacted you in any way?'

'No. Not at all. Honestly.'

'Who else is here with you?'

'A man called Pat Pusey.'

'What's your relationship with him?'

Hewitt rubbed his eyes, tried to gather his

thoughts. 'None ... none really. He's here to ... to sort of help his boss.'

'To help him do what?'

'To look after me, I suppose. I'm doing some work for Mr Corell, that's his boss, some important research work. I was getting worried about the behaviour of Gerry Monroe and Mr Corell sent Pusey to, well, guard me, I suppose.'

Frankie looked round then turned again to Hewitt. 'Where is Pusey now?'

'In bed, I think.'

'What time does he normally get up?'

'Between nine and ten, depending on how he's feeling.'

Frankie smiled warmly at Hewitt. 'You look very uncomfortable there and I need to ask you more questions. Is there somewhere we can go where Pusey won't hear us?'

Hewitt thought for a few moments. 'We could go into the cellar. It's just a few yards that way.' Hewitt pointed to the centre of the house wall.

'OK. Would you mind just staying sitting for a minute or two more while I brief my colleagues?' Hewitt nodded. Frankie clasped his arm and smiled again. 'Good man!' Frankie straightened and walked back towards the house wall, motioning the tall cop to follow him. Frankie spoke quietly to him then went across to the perimeter fence.

Ten minutes later he was inside the damp cellar with Hewitt. Frankie sat on the corner of a heavy table littered with various pieces of rusting metal and old tools. A vice was fixed to the end opposite Frankie, cobwebs laced between its open

383

jaws. Hewitt stood a few feet in front of him, shivering every few seconds. A striplight cast a greenish glow on them. The tall cop stood by the inside of the door cradling his weapon.

Frankie wasn't making the headway he'd hoped to. After almost five minutes of questioning, Hewitt too was becoming frustrated. He said, 'Look, Mr Houlihan, I cannot tell you what the project is! It's a professional matter. I'm a scientist. I'm retained by Mr Corell to see the project through and confidentiality is a pre-requisite to the success of it. I'm doing nothing illegal.'

'You're harbouring two horses that were kidnapped and a man who is a known criminal in Dublin. The man you admit is your paymaster is one of Europe's biggest gangsters. You admit you've been paying money regularly to Monroe to bring live animals here for research purposes. Mr Hewitt, even if your project isn't criminal in itself, all the other stuff is making you look very unlikely to be awarded the Upstanding Citizen of the Year medal. You may well find that the Crown Prosecution Service takes a more serious view of your behaviour than you seem to.'

'But–'

'And, even if the police don't prosecute you, Mr Corell is not going to be at all pleased with you when all this gets out. You may have seen the indulgent side of him so far. I know a child who can tell you of Mr Corell's other projects, like the reaction of the sphincter when its owner is fixed to a snooker table with a hammer and six-inch nails. The project to test the elasticity of the human body when dropped from two hundred feet on to concrete.'

Hewitt stared at him, unblinking, as though in a trance. Frankie said, 'I'm not kidding you, Mr Hewitt.' Hewitt slowly shook his head. Frankie sighed and continued, 'Look, I'm not too troubled about your project. And I believe you when you say you don't know where Monroe is. But we really need your help in getting evidence on Corell. You tell me you've met him, that he's happy to come here and talk to you. All you need to do is wear a tiny little bug and ask him the right questions.'

Hewitt buried his face in his hands and seemed to sag again. Frankie moved forward in support and helped him across to sit on an old wooden chest with steel bands on its lid and rope handles. 'Are you all right?' Frankie asked, softening his voice now. Hewitt hung his head, elbows on knees, hands still hiding his face.

'Jesus God in heaven, what have I got myself into?' he groaned.

'You can get yourself out of it,' Frankie said.

Hewitt looked up. 'I'm a scientist, man! And I'm a coward. I've never been in a fight in my life. Jesus, you saw me faint out there at the sight of a couple of guns. I thought Corell was a straight-forward businessman. I thought I was being head-hunted from the place I used to work. Do you think I'd be sitting here if I'd known how all this would turn out? My God, I won't even be able to talk if I ever see Mr Corell again, won't even be able to bloody breathe without shitting myself. You might as well ask me to fly in the air as try and deceive this man. Can't you see that? Can't you understand it?' His arms were open in a pleading gesture, his expression was one of despair, of desperation.

Frankie nodded. 'I do see. I'm sorry.' Frankie walked back and leant against the table again, rubbed his tired, gritty eyes and stood thinking for a while. He looked across at Hewitt and asked, 'Has Pat Pusey ever met Gerry Monroe?'

Hewitt shook his head wearily. 'No.'

'Are you sure?'

'He asked me a lot of questions about Monroe, what he was like, what his background was, did I think he was dangerous. He's never met him.'

Frankie was silent again for a few moments, then said, 'What do you want to do?'

Hewitt looked up and Frankie saw hope mixed with fear. 'I want to go home. I want to get my project stuff from the lab and go home.' His voice was weak, like a child's.

Frankie stood up straight. 'Come on then. Your project stuff will have to wait. You can come back for it but if you want out of here now, I can fix that.'

'Home?'

'Police interview first, I think, but I can see no real reason, if you've been telling me the truth and I think you have, that you won't be home soon. Where is home?'

'Norwich.'

'Not that far.' He reached for Hewitt's arm and helped him up.

'Seems a million miles. A lifetime away.'

Frankie led him out of the cellar. The police-

386

man followed, closing the door gently behind him. The first tinge of daybreak showed through. Frankie walked Hewitt towards the fence. 'How are you at climbing railings?' he asked.

63

Back at Stonebanks's house Frankie relished the mug of tea and bacon roll the big man put in front of him. The two other men in the kitchen were police officers; Trevor Prentice, who was in charge of the squad that had moved in to Hewitt's place, and Kevin Wildman, the negotiator.

Frankie had been impressed by Wildman when he'd been introduced in the early hours of the morning. The man had an air of quiet capability about him, confidence untainted by cockiness. In his mid-thirties, he was compact and fit-looking. During the briefing that morning in Stonebanks's house, Frankie grew more certain that they could pull off what they hoped. He knew that to do his job properly, Wildman would need to be cool, unflappable, a good actor. He seemed intelligent. He listened to the brief, asked only pertinent questions, made some notes.

By the time Wildman climbed into the horsebox Stonebanks had arranged, Frankie told his two remaining companions that all they needed was a bit of luck.

Wildman pulled up at the gates, lowered his

window, stared aggressively up at the lens of the CCTV camera and leant heavily on his horn. Within two minutes he saw Pat Pusey walking purposefully towards the gates. When he reached them, Wildman glared at him through the windscreen and stayed on the horn a few seconds longer before jumping to the ground and walking cockily forward to face Pusey through the bars.

'You Pusey?' Wildman asked.

'Who are you?' Pusey was staring just as aggressively as Wildman. They were like boxers in a nose-to-nose. Wildman said, 'I'm Gerry Monroe and you've got ten grand of mine and two horses.'

Pusey seemed confused for a moment then hardened his eyes again. 'Piss off, Monroe. You're a day late and a dollar short.'

'Open the gates, bog man, or your boss doesn't get his project finished.'

'Says who?'

'Says me. I've got Hewitt in the back. You ought to tell him not to go shopping so early in the mornings before his bodyguard's up and about. Or maybe you should get your arse out of bed a bit quicker. Cut down on the old Guinness at night.'

The slightly dazed look was back on Pusey's face as he tried to figure out how to handle this. He said, 'Let me see Hewitt.'

'Let me see my ten grand. And let me in so I can pick up my horses.'

'Your horses, is it? My arse! The horses you stole, you mean! The horses you will not now be gettin' back!'

388

'Oh, I'll be getting them back or you can explain to Corell how you managed to bugger up a year's worth of work and an awful lot of investment.'

Wildman saw the uncertainty begin to deepen in the Irishman. Pusey said, 'Is Hewitt in the back of that horsebox?'

'How do you think I knew you were here? Does anybody else know apart from Hewitt and Corell? D'you think Corell told me? Who else but Hewitt would know you fill yourself with Guinness every night and that you're never out of bed before nine in the morning? Hewitt's in the back with this week's shopping including your two dozen cans of beer. Maybe that'll make you open the gates.'

Pusey looked suddenly angry. He moved closer to the gates and said, 'Listen you cocky bastard, 'cos you nicked a couple of horses from some dopey trainer, don't think you're anywhere near my league. I've put bullet holes in fellas ten times tougher than you.'

Wildman mimicked his accent. 'Ahh now, don't be givin' me all that old bollox your mate Gleeson did. Sure he was full of threats too. But at least he looked the part.' He sneered as he spoke the last sentence.

Pusey reddened quickly. 'Ye think so? Well where d'ye think Brendan Gleeson is now? Gleeson did your ten grand in at cards on the boat – correction, Mr Corell's ten grand. What d'ye think happened to him?'

'What, he had to wash Corell's dishes three nights running?'

'He's dead! I threw him off a twenty-storey block of flats! Three times!'

Wildman sneered again. 'Why? Did you miss the ground the first twice?'

Pusey took a step back, put his hands on his hips and stood shaking his head. 'You have got to have a death wish, Monroe.'

'I've got a wish for my money and my horses, Mr Pusey. Now open the gates and go get the cash and I'll give you back your scientist and ride into the sunset.'

'No, I'll tell you what we'll do. You'll let Hewitt out of the van in the next two minutes then you'll piss off and not come back. Have you got any idea in yer stupid head about how dangerous a man Kelly Corell is? This is a man who doesn't really need people like me to handle people like you. Mr Corell will take great pleasure in doing it himself. He specializes in nailing men to snooker tables and I mean proper men, not boys like you. He cut open his own girlfriend from neck to crotch ... these were people who just said something wrong to him. Can you imagine what you're going to get for fecking up this project of his?'

Wildman put up his hands in mock horror then slowly held them out so Pusey could see them. They were still and steady. 'See how much I'm shaking? Listen to me, Pusey. I'm going to get back into that cab and start the engine. I'm going to reverse a hundred yards then come back as fast as I can. If you want to have gates that actually work you better make sure they're open. And if I hit them, you can take responsibility for what happens to Hewitt as he bounces around in the back.' Wildman looked coldly through the gates then strode towards the cab and climbed in.

He reversed quickly and changed gear. Pusey moved to the side and punched a code into the control panel. The gates swung silently open as Wildman accelerated. He went through and carried on to the stable block. Pusey followed, reaching in his jacket as he went and producing a pistol. Wildman jumped from the cab and went quickly towards the stable doors. 'Hey, Monroe!' Pusey called. Wildman turned to see Pusey pointing the pistol at his head. He stopped and slowly raised his arms.

'That's more like it, Mr Monroe. That's more respectful. Actions speak louder than words sure enough.' Smiling, he walked towards Wildman, stopping six feet in front of him. 'I'm not hearing so much of yer lip now, big man?' Pusey said.

'I don't talk so well with guns pointing at me. You should have let me see it back there and saved us a lot of time.'

'Yer right, I should have. Now you are goin' to open the back of that van and let Hewitt out.'

'Or?'

'Or I'm going to blow your bollocks off.'

Wildman shrugged. Pusey signalled him round, turning with him. 'Open it.'

He walked wide of Wildman to the rear of the box and watched him reach to undo a mechanism of the doors. They swung open. Wildman hit the button to start the ramp lowering then moved to the side. Pusey half-turned away to keep the

391

gun trained on Wildman. As the ramp edge reached the gravel Pusey glanced into the back of the box to see four police marksmen with rifles aimed at him. On the floor was a monitoring and recording machine.

64

Stonebanks had the pleasure of ringing the obnoxious Christopher Benjamin to tell him that Ulysses wasn't dead after all and that the Jockey Club Security Department had retrieved his horse. When the owner recovered from the surprise he told Stonebanks that his department had failed in its duty by not finding the horse within twenty-four hours of it being stolen, and he warned that Ulysses better be unharmed.

Frankie set off north in the horsebox Wildman had been driving to deliver Angel Gabriel to the Cassidys. They knew he was on his way. Graham Cassidy, out of bed, shaved and fully dressed for the first time in weeks, stood at the window watching the road. After a short time, he had to ask Maggie to bring a stool from the breakfast bar. He eased himself on to it. 'I can't believe how weak my legs are,' he said.

'You haven't used those muscles for a long time.'

He went back to his vigil and his thoughts. He knew that Maggie sensed his wish to sit quietly, his need to try and find his way back into normal life. The news that Angel Gabriel was alive, that he was all right, that the Grand National dream was back on the tracks, hadn't lifted him immediately. He knew that what he'd been through, what he'd succumbed to, had much deeper implications for him as a man.

He'd always coped, had handled almost fifty years of life and always found a way through problems. There had never been even a hairline crack in his character, in his mental and emotional make-up, that would have suggested he'd completely cave in one day, as he had done. He'd gone from a hardened veteran of dealing expertly with many crises – maybe not back-breakers for those that made their living in other ways, but very important to him as a trainer – to three cubic feet of bone and blood and meat lying in a darkened room, unable even to get out of bed.

Reflecting on this he knew the experience would change him for ever. He managed a wry internal smile as he thought that Superman must have felt how he now felt the day he discovered Kryptonite.

And when the depression lifted he knew the guilt would try hard to bring it back. He had to confront the fact that he'd failed Maggie, failed the family, the horses, the business just when he was needed most. He knew nothing of this would ever be cast in his face but it didn't ease the ache. Then there was the debt, the huge debt he owed Frankie Houlihan, a man with enough pain of his own, real pain and no family to support him, to see him through it. Frankie had not only held his own life together but Graham's too, the whole family's. There was a proper man. And here was he, a mental wreck, waiting for the real man to bring home his horse. His dream. His life.

The children were outside scanning the road, listening for the horsebox. It was their shouts and screams that brought him off the stool. With Maggie at his side he went out. Maggie told the children to come away from the entrance so the box could turn in. Jane, Sean and Billy all moved reluctantly, each walking backwards as the roof of the box came along the hedge tops.

It turned in. Frankie straightened the wheel and smiled and waved. When he stopped the children ran to the back of the box. Graham and Maggie stayed to greet Frankie as he jumped down from the cab and came towards them. Maggie stepped back and Frankie realized she was putting her husband first. To Frankie, Graham's face looked sad although he was working hard at a smile. He looked gaunt, pale, old. But he managed to open his arms as Frankie reached him and they embraced warmly, Frankie turning him as though in a dance. Neither spoke. Maggie watched as Frankie patted Graham's shoulder gently.

After a minute, Frankie stepped back, holding Graham by the arms. His eyes shone with happiness as he said, 'Let's get him out.' Graham nodded. 'Will you do it?' Frankie said. 'I'll get the ramp down. You go up and lead your horse out, back where he belongs.'

Maggie moved forward and hugged Frankie, briefly but warmly. 'Thank you,' she said quietly.

Frankie squeezed her then broke away. 'Let's get Gabby.'

The children helped with the doors and the ramp. Maggie stopped them from rushing up it. Graham stood at the bottom. Angel Gabriel's head protruded from a stall set at right angles to the rear. The big horse glanced at his trainer then turned his head away as though he'd fallen out with him. Graham smiled properly for the first time since Christmas Eve. He walked up the ramp. 'Come on, you old bugger,' he said, 'we've got work to do.'

65

Two Garda officers flew over to interview Pat Pusey. They asked him if he would testify against Kelly Corell if they arrested him for the murder of his girlfriend. Pusey refused. They told him if he didn't they'd make sure Corell got a copy of the tape of his conversation with Wildman. They added a plea-bargain offer in his own prosecution for the murder of Brendan Gleeson. Pusey accepted. Corell was arrested that night and charged with the murder of Mary Heaps.

Twenty-three tissue samples from racehorses were found in Hewitt's freezer. Each was labelled with the horse's name and the date the sample had been taken. The six winners that Culling had pronounced dead on his operating table were tested and showed significant amounts of a 'go-faster' drug. After being charged with unauthorized experimentation on animals, and being shown a newspaper report on the arrest for murder of Kelly Corell, Hewitt gave the police details of his project.

He'd been trying to become the first scientist to successfully clone a racehorse. Corell had agreed to fund the research in the belief that clones of top-class horses would allow him to make a fortune in betting and that their subsequent careers at stud would bring in millions of pounds.

Under the most severe pressure, Hewitt continued to insist that he had no knowledge of the whereabouts of Gerry Monroe.

Frankie needed Monroe to get Culling fully on the hook. But despite national publicity about the return of Ulysses and Angel Gabriel, with frequent mentions of the reward and publication of Monroe's picture, no one had come forward. Frankie had delivered what everyone else wanted out of this mess. He knew he was in serious danger of running out of time in getting what *he* wanted. All he had to go on was Hewitt's evidence and the doped samples from horses Culling had treated.

Stonebanks stuck to the cautious line he'd taken all along. 'Frankie, what we know is that these horses were doped by someone when they won. They then took seriously ill back at the stables and Culling operated on them. They died on the operating table.'

'Wrong, Geoff,' countered Frankie. 'Hewitt

said they were alive when Monroe brought them in. He delivered them and took them away again the same day. So that's one thing we do have Culling on.'

'What we have is his word against Hewitt's. Whose would you take?'

'I'd take Hewitt's.'

'Would a jury?'

'I don't know.'

'Even if they were alive when they left Culling's place, I'm not quite sure what he could be charged with. What you really need to prove is that he doped them and I think that is going to be very, very difficult!'

'OK, OK! If he doped them, where does he keep the stuff? If it's at home then let's try and get the police in with a warrant.'

'I used up all my favours getting them to turn out at Hewitt's place in the middle of the night armed to the teeth. We're going to need a lot more evidence to get a warrant authorized for Culling's place.'

Frankie shook his head and thought for a while. An idea came to him and he was about to blurt it out then thought better of it. He said, 'Look, why don't I just pay Culling another visit on my own and see what he says. He's a pretty nervous fella and he might just own up to it.'

'Yes, or he might inject you with some of that stuff he gave the horses!'

'I'll take my chances, Geoff.'

'You've taken too many of those already. You're due a bad break, Frankie boy.'

They staked out the entrance to Culling's

place. The vet had been on duty at Wincanton. Stonebanks spent the time trying to talk Frankie out of going in on his own. They reached a compromise – to allow Frankie an agreed amount of time in the house. After that Stonebanks would be coming in to find him. It was dark when Culling's car nosed through the pillars and along the short drive. 'Give me twenty minutes maximum, then come to the door,' Frankie said. Stonebanks nodded agreement. Frankie checked the micro-recorder in his inside jacket pocket was switched on.

Culling was undoing his tie when he opened the door, the light shining from behind him on Frankie's smiling face. The vet was in silhouette and Frankie couldn't be sure if he looked shocked. 'Sorry to call unannounced, Mr Culling. My boss and I have been waiting for you to come home.'

Culling looked back out towards the road. Frankie said, 'He stayed in the car. I'll tell you why if you can spare me five minutes.'

The vet stared at him, cold-eyed, apprehensive. 'I'm tired, Mr Houlihan. It's been a long day.'

'Been a long season. For everybody.' Frankie returned his cold stare.

'What do you want?' Culling asked.

'I've got a proposal for you.'

'On what?'

'On keeping you out of prison.'

Culling started closing the door. 'Goodnight, Mr Houlihan.'

Frankie shrugged. 'Goodnight. I was told to try the easy way and I did. I'll go and get my boss

398

now and the police. See you again shortly.' Frankie turned and started back across the gravel drive.

'OK,' Culling said. 'Come in.'

Frankie turned. 'No thanks. It wasn't me who wanted to give you the chance. My boss told me to do it and I did. You didn't take it.' Frankie started towards the gate again. He heard the vet hurrying after him, felt a hand on his arm. He stopped. Culling stepped in front of him, barring his way. Lights from the porch let Frankie see the film of sweat on the vet's brow. He looked worried.

'I'm sorry,' Culling said. 'Please come in and tell me what your proposal is.'

Frankie stared at him, pursed his lips, looked towards the gate again then turned slowly to walk back to the house.

Culling led him into the conservatory. 'Would you like a drink?' His voice was shaky.

'No, thanks. I just want to pitch this then I'll have done what I've been told to do and I can get out of here.'

Culling's worried look deepened. He joined his fingers, steepled them in front of his still-buttoned jacket. 'Please go on.'

Keeping a note of distaste in his voice, Frankie said, 'Sauceboat. Zuiderzie. Colonialize. Gallopagos. Kilkenny Lass. Broadford Bay.'

Frankie watched Culling's face grow paler. He continued, 'You doped all of them to win. The drug you gave them had side-effects which suited you fine because you knew you'd be the very man the trainer would call. You brought them back here, pretended to operate then told the trainers they'd died on the table. Monroe picked them up next day, still alive. Unfortunately for you, he didn't kill them right away. He traded them on to a scientist for experimental purposes. We have the tissue samples the scientist took. They're pumped with dope.'

The vet was pacing, his chin raised as though he was studying the glass roof. Frankie was becoming convinced now that he was confronting Kathy's killer. He paused, knew he needed to concentrate on seeing this through before his emotions overcame him. He focused on keeping his voice cold, that note of distaste in it that was important to the plan. 'Why aren't you looking at me? Because you don't need to, do you? You know the story, Mr Culling. You're just waiting to see the order I'm going to tell it in.' The vet didn't reply. He kept walking. Frankie said, 'Now we come to the bit that really makes me sick. I want you to know that before I tell you it. Despite what you've read about Monroe still being missing, we know where he is. Gerry Monroe's holed up in a little village in the west of Ireland. Somebody higher up than me decided to do a deal with him. That's how we got the two horses back. He's repaid most of the money he stole too and he's put you in the frame. That was the deal.'

'Why would you let him go?' Culling asked.

Frankie stared at him, battling hard with his emotions now, trying to maintain an air of detachment. 'I wouldn't knock it until you've heard the proposal for you.'

Culling cleared his throat and kept walking.

Frankie said, 'It wasn't my decision to let Monroe go. He's a thief and a bringer of misery. I can tell you the thinking behind it from higher up... Monroe stole a couple of horses and some money. He's given them back. No big damage done to racing. But we know we have a vet out there doping horses. Major damage to racing if he carries on and gets caught. Damage can be minimized by Jockey Club Security catching him, keeping it in-house, saving the reputation of racing and therefore the industry. All very gallant, Mr Culling, don't you think?'

Culling looked more thoughtful now. Frankie went on. 'All just absolutely hunkydory so long as the poor punters out there never find out what's really been going on. If they did they'd lose all faith in the product they spend five billion pounds a year on. No betting revenue, no levy payment to racecourses. No racecourses, no industry. So what do we do, Mr Culling? What do we defenders of justice at the Jockey Club do?' He paused. Culling waited. Frankie went on. 'We let criminals walk. Criminals like Monroe. Like you, Mr Culling.'

Culling paced another two lengths of the floor then stopped. He turned to Frankie. 'I think I grasp your proposal, Mr Houlihan, but please dot the i's and cross the t's.'

Frankie didn't find it difficult to put the necessary edge of anger in his voice. 'Not *my* proposal, I want you to remember that!' Culling nodded. 'You write and sign a confession and a resignation letter. You serve out a month's notice during which you will be watched at all times on a racecourse by one of my colleagues. At the end of that month you disappear from racing for ever. If you try to come back at any point, the confession will be used against you.'

Culling sat down in the chair opposite Frankie. 'If all these things had happened and I signed a confession, how do I know you won't take it straight to the police?'

'For the reasons I've just told you. A call to the police from my boss and they'd be in this room now with me ready to charge you formally. We have a tape Monroe made of a conversation with you. We have his written evidence. The bottom line is, we don't *need* your confession. And I personally, as you might have picked up, do not give a toss if you don't sign the confession. I'm all for doing it the hard way.'

Culling joined his hands under his chin. He took a long unblinking look at Frankie, then said, 'How much time do I have to decide?'

Frankie looked at his watch. 'Three minutes. No – how long would it take you to write your confession, maybe two minutes? That means you have one minute to decide, two to write.'

Culling slowly bowed his head, rubbed his face. He stayed that way for a while then said, 'If you knew why I did it, Mr Houlihan...'

There it was. Here he sat. The man who had taken away the most precious thing Frankie had ever had, would ever have in a hundred lifetimes. And he was offering to explain why he did it. Again, Frankie forced himself to concentrate. He needed a signed confession. 'I know why you did it – for money. Same as the rest of them.'

Culling bowed his head again. 'No, it wasn't like that! I'm dying, Mr Houlihan! I have a year or two to live, at most...' He went on to tell Frankie of his terror of dying, of suffering the same fate as the last three generations of his family. He told him about the Everlasting Life Company, about the plans he'd had. Told him about 'a bookmaker' (not naming Breslin) and his payments. And Frankie's anger grew. He thought it was all some intricately planned lie that Culling had concocted in advance in case he was ever found out.

The vet looked at him pleadingly. Frankie shook his head slowly. Culling got up. 'Look, look, I'll let you see you something...' He went out and came back quickly with a briefcase. He opened it and showed Frankie all the literature from the Everlasting Life Company, gave him the letter accepting him, the certificate guaranteeing a place in their cryogenics capsule. 'Why do you think I live alone?' Culling asked. 'Do you think I don't want a wife and family like any other man? But why should I indulge myself? How selfish would it have been to marry, to leave a grieving wife behind? How selfish to have children? To afflict another generation? All I ever wanted to do was to have another chance. I haven't spent a penny of that money on myself, on material things. I just wanted a chance to live again, to live like you live Mr Houlihan! I did what I did so I can live again after death, to bring children into the world who have the same chance as you of seeing seventy or eighty years of life!'

Frankie looked into his eyes, convinced now that Culling hadn't made this up but unsure whether he was seeing madness at work or desperation. He said, 'And you believe these ... these charlatans can give you this?'

'The principle is sound, Mr Houlihan. Look at the progress there has been in medicine in the past fifty years. It is virtually certain that some day, disease will be completely eliminated. It might be a hundred or two hundred years but it will happen!'

'And you think they can bring you back to life too, to benefit from it?'

'Yes, I think they'll have advanced that far.'

'To be able to play God?'

Culling nodded vigorously and Frankie saw that he truly believed this, and the rage that had been building in him began to fade. He lowered his head, shaking it slowly in disbelief that Kathy had died not because someone had wanted a yacht or a New York penthouse, she'd been taken away from him because this poor, deluded man wanted to live for ever.

Raising his head, he looked at the pathetic, wild-eyed, sweating figure sitting opposite and all he felt was a welling sadness at the pointlessness of it all, at the terrible waste. He needed to leave, to get away from this man. Slowly he rose to his feet. 'Are you going to write the confession or not?'

Culling stood up. 'I'm going to write it. I just wanted you to know why I did it. You seem to despise me. You obviously disagree one hundred per cent with what your bosses have asked you to

404

do. Not your idea, you said, you needed me to know that. Well I need you to know that I didn't do it out of greed or for personal gain.'

'Sure, sure.' Frankie was wearily dismissive. He looked at his watch and said. 'I'm leaving in exactly two minutes.' The vet sighed and left the room. Frankie heard a door bang down the hall. A few minutes later Culling returned and handed him a folded piece of headed paper. Frankie opened and read it.

'Satisfied?' Culling asked.

Frankie looked into his eyes for a long moment then said, 'Bad question to ask, Mr Culling. Bad question.' And he turned away down the hall and out through the door.

Culling sank into the soft chair in the conservatory, put his head in his hands and wept with relief. Less than an hour later he heard another knock on the door and recognized Frankie's outline through the glass. When he opened it he saw two uniformed policemen flanking Frankie and he recognized Stonebanks but not the other man in the long dark coat. Frankie said, 'Mr Culling. This is Detective Sergeant Saunders of Newbury CID. He has your confession and the tape I made.' Frankie sounded exhausted. There was no note of triumph in his voice.

Culling looked terrified. 'You lied!' he said.

'I did.' Frankie took two steps forward and looked straight into Culling's eyes from a couple of feet away. 'Remember the girl who died on Sauceboat? I was married to her. You killed my wife. Your foolish, crazy scheme killed my wife.'

405

Culling looked horrified. He held his breath as Frankie stared at him for what seemed a long time. Then Frankie turned, head low, shoulders sagging, and walked away, back through the gate and down the road.

66

Throughout February and March, Frankie spent every weekend with the Cassidys. They made sure he was involved as closely as possible with the training of Gabby for the Grand National. And he relished it, loved it. Fridays couldn't come soon enough so that he could travel north. He'd traded off all these winter Saturdays with his colleagues, promising to cover for them in the summer. He just didn't want to miss a minute more than necessary of the big horse's preparation for the great race.

His relationship with the whole family developed, bonds strengthened, especially between him and Graham. Maggie said she'd never known her husband talk so much as he talked to Frankie. And Graham steadily began finding himself again, gradually winning back his mental strength in tiny victories. Frankie helped nurture this. He'd seen the damage that had been done to Graham, recognized it, had wanted to help repair it.

Sean benefited too from Frankie's company, as did Billy, who blossomed and grew in confidence with the praise Frankie gave him, the respect he showed. Jane and Maggie, still strong and whole, watched it all from the sidelines and marvelled at how sensitive and soft and insecure men could be. They saw Frankie begin to heal his own wounds through the way he was ministering again, helping others. Frankie too realized this and found that the steady fading of grief brought no weakening of his relationship with Kathy. It improved it. He thought about her just as often but the thoughts were bringing more and more smiles and fewer tears.

As they moved into Grand National week and Angel Gabriel was flying on the gallops, at his best ever, Graham said, Frankie found the anticipation around the yard almost unbearably intense and finally he truly understood the seduction of the training life – the powerful addiction to hope. Three days before the race he hit the downward slope on the racing roller coaster; Angel Gabriel stood on a stone, bruised his foot and was declared by Graham to be unfit to run.

The adrenaline they'd all been buzzing on for weeks evaporated in a minute and plunged everyone but Graham into despair. As he led the badly lame Gabby into his box, he stopped to comfort a distraught Frankie with a smile and a slap on the back. 'That's racing. There's always next year.' And they all knew that Graham was hurting even more than the rest of them but they took strength from it for they realized he was back to his old self.

In early April, after talking with Sean, Maggie

wrote to Sean's mother in London offering her a job and a small cottage. It took Bridget Gleeson three weeks to write back and say no, she was happy in London but would maybe try and see Sean every Christmas if she could afford the fare.

Culling went for trial in April as did Corell in Dublin. Culling got five years for the manslaughter of Kathy Houlihan and three years for defrauding punters by doping racehorses. His lawyer managed to get the sentences to run concurrently. Culling named Breslin and the bookie was charged with conspiracy to defraud and jailed for two years.

After the first day of Corell's trial, somebody with a high-powered rifle shot Pat Pusey dead as he left the courthouse. He had never taken the witness stand. Corell's defence team successfully argued that the tapes of Pusey's conversation with Wildman were inadmissible, that they were the rantings of a small-time crook trying to make himself look bigger by concocting tales of violence and murder. Corell walked free.

On the last day of April a heatwave drifted slowly across Europe and settled over the British Isles. It was to be the longest since UK weather records began. Maggie and Graham watched their daughter and Sean build their loving relationship in the heat of the summer. After a family discussion, including Sean, they wrote to Bridget Gleeson asking if they could become Sean's legal guardians. She replied quickly this time, saying she'd be more than happy to agree.

Frankie spent much of the summer house-hunting. By mid-August he'd chosen a modern flat in an exclusive complex on the outskirts of Newbury, close enough to Lambourn to keep his eye on the hub and far enough away to avoid the back-stabbing and politics.

By early September, the experts were forecasting the end of the heat wave. There had been little more than a few millimetres of rain since June. Hosepipe bans had long been in force across all populated areas of the country, forest and moorland fires had taken animal and human lives.

At Mullingar in Ireland, the water level at Lough Ennell was lower than even the oldest fisherman could remember. Late one Saturday afternoon, Mullingar police took a call from a walker saying he thought that a vehicle was in the lough, a big lorry probably, he could just see the roof. An hour later divers recovered the bloated, fish-bitten remains of Gerry Monroe. Identification proved difficult but the registration plate on the horsebox matched the kidnap and cash theft report they'd had on file since the beginning of the year. It was also a possible link to the abandoned Kawasaki motorcycle with the false number plates which lay rusting behind the police station.

The divers brought out the expensive suitcase Monroe had stored the money in. The quality of the seals had kept the half-million pounds completely dry.

The Cassidys took Frankie's advice and managed to gain the agreement of the Mullingar police not to make public the recovery of the cash until a date to be mutually agreed. It was

November when all the papers for their adoption of Sean Gleeson were finally signed and sealed. The Mullingar police had not contacted them again so they decided to say nothing publicly about getting their money back. In keeping with their promise of a reward they deposited fifty thousand pounds in an account for Sean to which he'd be given access on his eighteenth birthday.

By Christmas, Sean still hadn't got over the shock of it. Often his mind would go back to the night he'd rifled his father's pockets in the hope of finding a flyer. Instead he'd cursed when he'd pulled out that 'oul' piece of paper', the paper that had lain for months in his bedroom because he'd been too lazy to tidy up.

Sometimes he'd wander out at night to talk to Pegasus who had a warm box now and was properly groomed and fed but no better behaved. 'Fifty grand, Peg, for an oul' piece of paper! Would ye credit it?' And he'd move in close to stroke the grey nose and the pony, disdainful as ever, would nudge him hard back the way he came. 'Oi! Don't push yer luck! There's some real horses here, ye know! Any more of that and ye'll be back tied to yer clothes pole in Joseph's Mansions!'

The publishers hope that this book has given you enjoyable reading. Large Print Books are especially designed to be as easy to see and hold as possible. If you wish a complete list of our books please ask at your local library or write directly to:

Magna Large Print Books
Magna House, Long Preston,
Skipton, North Yorkshire.
BD23 4ND

This Large Print Book for the partially sighted, who cannot read normal print, is published under the auspices of

THE ULVERSCROFT FOUNDATION

Other MAGNA Titles In Large Print

ANNE BAKER
Merseyside Girls

JESSICA BLAIR
The Long Way Home

W. J. BURLEY
The House Of Care

MEG HUTCHINSON
No Place For A Woman

JOAN JONKER
Many A Tear Has To Fall

LYNDA PAGE
All Or Nothing

NICHOLAS RHEA
Constable Over The Bridge

MARGARET THORNTON
Beyond The Sunset